The
FIRST
WIFE

has been richly praised

'Clear your schedule and dive into Muna Shehadi's latest triumph, *The First Wife*! Her vivid characters walk right off the page and into your heart . . . I love this book!'
VICKI LEWIS THOMPSON, *New York Times* bestselling author

'I absolutely ADORED this beautiful book. Profoundly moving and very wise, this stunningly original and touching tale is one to savour and re-read. Although at its heart a love story with a twist, it is so much more, layered with wisdom and a woman's brave struggle to carry on going after a life changing event. So very beautiful and thought provoking on so many levels, this is a must read for everyone, a wonderfully absorbing tale that I guarantee will make you think, question and change . . . An immersive delight of a book'
RENITA D'SILVA

'Very compelling . . . a wonderfully heartfelt, multi-layered story of greed and grief, love and loss. The unravelling plotline tantalises the reader with its clever twists and turns – impossible to put down!'
SARAH STEELE

'Captivating right out of the gate. This unique and beautifully told tale, laced with mystery and secrets, will keep readers hooked and rooting for Holly all the way. A deeply moving and insightful story that will stay with me for a long time'
ALISON RAGSDALE

'I loved the combination of mystery and love story – every time I put it down, I couldn't wait to get back to it. I really enjoyed Muna's writing style, too. A compelling mystery, wrapped up in a beautiful romance!'
EMMA ROBINSON

'From the very first page *The First Wife* seduced me with its promise of revelations to come; part mystery, part romance but above all the story of one woman's lifelong mission to be true to herself. I was charmed by its feisty heroine who faces physical, intellectual and emotional challenges with such grace and fortitude. And the sensual descriptions of food were an extra treat!'
JULIE BROOKS

Muna Shehadi's lifelong love of reading inspired her to become a writer. Muna grew up in Princeton, New Jersey, lives in Wisconsin, and has a much-loved summer place on the beautiful coast of Maine, all of which she couldn't resist featuring in her Fortune's Daughters trilogy.

For more information, visit her website: **munashehadi.com**.

By Muna Shehadi

The First Wife

Fortune's Daughters trilogy
The Summer Sister (*previously published as* Private Lies)
The Winter Sister (*previously published as* Hidden Truths)
The Spring Sister (*previously published as* Honest Secrets)

MUNA SHEHADI

The

FIRST

WIFE

REVIEW

First published in 2022
by HEADLINE REVIEW
An imprint of HEADLINE PUBLISHING GROUP

1

Cataloguing in Publication Data is available from the British Library

ISBN 978 1 4722 8649 9

Typeset in Sabon by Avon DataSet Ltd, Arden Court, Alcester, Warwickshire

Printed and bound in Great Britain by Clays Ltd, Elcograf S.p.A.

HEADLINE PUBLISHING GROUP
An Hachette UK Company
Carmelite House
50 Victoria Embankment
London EC4Y 0DZ

www.headline.co.uk
www.hachette.co.uk

To my mother, Alison Shehadi,
into whose life much rain fell, yet who saw only sunshine.

I'd like to acknowledge as always, my wonderful editor Kate Byrne for her faith in me, her wise guidance and her boundless enthusiasm.

I'd also like to extend gratitude for assistance from Jason Steigman for actuary questions; Jessica Litt for help in wills and estate taxes; and Nikita, who answered the phone at Town Line Auto in Machias Maine and has no idea I was planning to thank her publicly.

Warm thanks also go to my west coast crew, Heather Trim and Mary Stodder for earthquake help; to Larry Glusman, Deb Schermer and Stefanie Jacob for sharing thoughts about Judaism; to my brothers-in-law, John, Matt and Seth Stodder for tips on Los Angeles, and above all to my adored husband, Mark Stodder, for sharing memories of his days at UC Santa Cruz, for reading every book I write, and for always getting teary at the sad bits.

The
FIRST
WIFE

Chapter 1

Subject: re: Lyle
Date: July 15, 2017
From: Caleb@FrederickIndustries.com
To: Holly_Penny@Qmail.com

Dear Holly,

Sorry I haven't been in better touch over the past weeks. Or has it been longer since we spoke? Feels like I've lost track of everything since Lyle disappeared. Whenever it was, it was great to hear your voice again, and to catch up, even under such horrible circumstances. I don't think we've been in touch since our dinner together in 2009. Understandable, but I've missed you. Let's make sure a gap like that doesn't happen again.

As for my brother, I don't have good news. We've exhausted every avenue, pulled every string, called in every favor. The US State Department and local authorities in Thailand, where Lyle was last seen, have been unable to locate him and have called off the search. Even though nothing has really changed, it feels as if we've lost him all over again.

Because there was no body, Wisconsin law dictates we have to wait five years to pronounce him dead. So we sit in this ghastly limbo and wait.

I wish I had better news, Holly. We're all still in shock, as I'm sure you are. Lyle must have become seriously ill, or he was caught in the wrong place at the wrong time by the wrong people, or . . . You and I talked about this, I know, a useless circle of questions that refuses to stop spinning.

I'm sorry to drop this on you by email instead of calling, but I'm grabbing a rare minute on a business trip in China and it's the middle of the night where you are. Selfish, maybe, but I needed to share this with someone who loved Lyle as I did. I hope you are reading this on a beautiful day, and that you can do something fun for yourself.

I'll call when I'm back in the States. I'd like to stay in touch. You were the only one of Lyle's wives I truly loved.

All best,

Caleb

Caleb Frederick
President and CEO, Frederick Industries
Milwaukee, WI

May 15, 2022
Via US Mail

> *Please join us as our guest(s)*
> *July 20–24, 2022*
> *to celebrate the life of*
> *Lyle Anthony Frederick*
> *at*
> *Senneck Lodge Resort*
> *Askatste, New York*
> *RSVP*

When Holly Penny was a girl, before her father did time in jail and bankrupted the family, she and her parents would spend summer vacations in the forested hills north of her future college town of Santa Cruz. From their spacious beachside home in Santa Monica, Mom, Dad, Holly and their dog Muffin would drive up the starkly beautiful California coast. Muffin would sit or lie in the backseat, weathering the trip calmly until Dad turned off Highway 9 on to the series of roads that led to Robin Hood Lane, near whose end sat the house they rented every year. Two yards down that turnoff, even after miles of the same forest, Muffin's head would come up, her nose would twitch, her furry body quiver. Then she'd repeatedly trample Holly's lap running window to window to taste the air she knew so well, a special part of her present and her past.

Today, four decades later, turning on to the elegant sweep of Senneck Resort's long-ago-familiar driveway through a piece of the Adirondack woods, Holly knew exactly how Muffin felt, down to the craning neck and trembling body. One big difference: since her backseat view was from a Mercedes chauffeured by a member of the resort's staff who'd met her at the Albany airport, Holly skipped the panting and sniffing.

She and Lyle had stayed at Senneck many times during their courtship and twelve-year marriage for cost-be-damned getaways of varying lengths. On each visit, the staff would welcome the couple as if their return was the most anticipated event of the day. Holly would straighten her back, raise her chin and widen her smile to queenly proportions, smirking inside at the knowledge that the royal welcome was deliberately designed to make her – and every other arriving guest – feel exactly as pampered and important as it did.

Leisurely self-indulgent days, long passionate nights – she and Lyle had spent appalling amounts of money here. But beautiful times, part of a completely different life, so far away for so many years, now being brought closer again in leather-upholstered comfort.

The Mercedes drew up to the familiar stone and wood lodge, its entrance still flanked by urns with stone rims that embraced flowers they could barely contain, today purple and cream blooms over trailing ivy.

Almost before the car had come to a stop, its trunk was being unloaded. Holly's suitcase would be whisked off to her suite, where her clothes would be unpacked, ironed if necessary, and hung in the wardrobe or folded perfectly into antique dresser drawers. In the large private bathroom, her meager collection of drugstore toiletries would be neatly arranged on vanities, marble counters or brass and glass shelving, within easy reach of wherever the staff thought she might need them. Laid across the bed would be a hotel-monogrammed silk robe and matching slippers, both of which would fit perfectly, ideal for breakfast on her private balcony, watching the surrounding mountains change color with the morning light. On the room's flawlessly varnished table, a welcome basket of top-quality seasonal fruit and house-made delicacies tailored to her taste would be waiting next to a bouquet of her favorite flowers.

Not your average in-and-out motel.

For one last time in Holly's life, Frederick money would make this kind of luxury possible, luxury Holly had never been able to take for granted or comfortably immerse herself in in the way Lyle could, having been born to it. However, since very little of her life over the past twenty-plus years since The Change – not menopause, the other one – had allowed for self-indulgence, she'd promised herself that during this stay at Senneck, she was going to wallow in everything the resort offered, guilt-free, like a hippo in mud.

A slender, attractive hippo, with good taste and manners.

As she fumbled for the handle, the car door opened for her – of course it did – letting in a swish of fresh late-afternoon mountain air, a welcome change from the smoggy heat of the Los Angeles summer she'd woken up to that morning.

'Welcome to Senneck, Ms Penny.' The handsome blond kid assigned to greet her wore khaki pants, a blue shirt and a delighted smile. 'I'm Tom. We're glad to have you back.'

'Thank you so much.' Tom looked all of fifteen to her, but was probably in his twenties, probably not even *born* the first time she came here. 'It's wonderful to be back. Hard to believe it's been so long. It feels like forever.'

It would be a lot longer than forever before Holly returned, since on her budget she could afford about a five-minute stay.

One foot out of the car, she swung the other leg parallel and, in a series of walrus-on-land bounces, moved forward until the other foot touched pavement, as she'd been taught decades earlier by the eternally patient staff at the rehab facility.

'Your room is in the lodge, second floor. Mr Frederick is here already.'

Holly started, jolted by hearing 'Mr Frederick', before realizing they didn't mean Lyle. To her, Lyle's younger brother was just 'Caleb'.

'Thanks, Tom. Are the others here yet?' By others, she meant Lyle's next two wives, who'd also been invited to arrive Wednesday. Other family and friends would be joining later, for Saturday's memorial service.

'Not yet.' Tom extended a hesitant hand, probably afraid that if he didn't offer to help, Holly would sit in the car for the rest of the afternoon.

Not out of the realm of possibilities.

Taking that kind hand, Holly hauled herself up and out with

a decent amount of fluidity, in spite of fatigue from the long travel day. Giving her legs time to adjust, and also because simultaneous walking and looking were no longer part of her skill set, she paused to reconnect with Senneck, head full of memories, heart full of bittersweet. Nearby trees had grown impressively in her twenty-year absence, but the impeccably groomed greenery of the grounds still looked as if an invisible army of ants worked continuously to straighten each blade of grass and arrange each flower's petals for maximum perfection. The surrounding mountains still played with shadows and sun on their evergreen-frosted sides, making her want to stretch her arms wide and sprint through the gardens, over the meadows beyond, and up the side of the nearest slope.

Not gonna happen.

Having looked her blissful fill, Holly sallied forth to start her luxury adventure, then stopped at the curb, back to ugly reality. 'Sorry, Tom, I must have left my cane in the car. After sitting on a plane all day, my legs aren't sure what to do about a step up.'

'No worries.' He offered a bronzed arm. 'I'll help you in. Someone will bring your cane along in a minute.'

'Thank you.' For the next five days the staff would fix every one of her blunders, scratch each of her itches, feed all her hungers, a remarkable condition experienced only by the very rich, the very sick and the very young. Holly smiled at Tom, thinking how nice it was to see a kid without tattoos or piercings. That thought was followed by the unsettling realization that she sounded like her mother, complaining about Holly and her friends' fashions in the seventies. And that was followed by the awful thought – happening more and more frequently around young adults – that Holly was old enough to be Tom's mother.

Given that every person, plant and animal on earth aged

naturally and predictably at the same time and at the same rate, why did it come as a total surprise every time she noticed?

She let Tom lead her on toward the lodge's grand front entrance, passing under the grape arbor, immature fruit hanging in tiny ineffectual-looking bunches, leaves tangling and weaving through the supporting white lattice. A picture hopped into her mind, of walking beside Lyle, still a whole, strong young woman, body muscled and slender, that of the dancer she'd worked so hard to become, before she found out life didn't particularly care what you intended to accomplish. Lyle would be gesturing broadly as he laid down possible plans for the next several days, activities that might or might not happen, because that wasn't the point. Planning was half the fun for him, the way he intensified his happiness and anticipation, the way he tackled all the myriad trips they took together, whether around the block or around the world.

'Would you like afternoon tea in your room, Ms Penny? Or out on the terrace?'

Afternoon tea! The Senneck staff must have dug up preferences for Mrs Frederick the First, probably typed on paper for her and Lyle's earliest visits in the 1980s. Someone would have been assigned to excavate Holly from an archived cardboard box. She liked thinking her old life still existed somewhere in a sturdy, reliable manila folder.

Her mind was wandering again. Hadn't Tom asked her a question?

Yes. Tea in her room or on the terrace? Probably one of the hardest decisions she'd have to make over this long weekend. 'Is the terrace crowded? I'm not ready to be in my room, but I'd rather not be around a lot of hubbub.'

Hubbub. A great word, retrieved from the murky depths of her brain, one that deserved to be used more often.

'Definitely not a lot of . . . hubbub.' Tom's lips curved wryly. 'Maybe one or two tables occupied.'

'Then the terrace sounds perfect. Bring on the terrace.'

The spacious, quiet lobby had been redecorated since she'd last been there; shades of blue, green and gold had replaced the yellow and peach tones, an improvement, though it had all been Terribly Tasteful even when it looked like sherbet. As Holly stepped forward, another good-looking employee caught up to them with her cane, which Holly accepted with thanks and relief.

'I'll have your tea brought right out. Milk and shortbread alongside, yes?'

Holly pretended surprise. 'It's like you *know* me.'

Tom's laughter was genuine and easy, as if he hadn't heard that joke probably every day he'd worked there. 'Would you like me to show you to the terrace?'

'No, no, I remember the way. Thank you.' Trying to move with her old energetic grace, she followed the carpeted corridor toward the terrace doors, anticipating its peaceful tile-floored beauty, creamy lemon-colored walls accented by watercolor landscapes and potted plants, huge windows wide open in summertime to let in fragrant breezes. With every step her happiness rose. For a few days she could reabsorb this guiltiest of pleasures, feeling like an elegant duchess from a time long . . .

'Ma'am?' Tom had been following her.

Holly turned too quickly. Her feet tangled. Unbalanced, she pitched forward, yelping in panic. *No, no, no.*

Tom grabbed her, stopping her fall. Holly clung gratefully to his supporting arm, adrenaline pushing her breaths too fast, humiliation heating her cheeks.

'You're okay. I've got you.' His eyes were wide with alarm. Poor kid.

'Yes. Thank you.' She tried to step back and stand on her own, to recover at least some of her duchess dignity, but wobbled dangerously and had to grab for his arm again. 'Thank you so much.'

'No problem. Do you want to sit down? Rest a little?' He gestured behind him toward blue upholstered chairs in the lobby. So polite. Handling her mess like a champ.

'No, no, I'm fine. Fine. I'll make it to the terrace.'

'Yes. But . . . the terrace is actually in the other direction.' He spoke very, very kindly. 'The other side of the building.'

The onslaught of dismay was so strong, Holly's smile sank, unable to muster an appropriate defense. Her sense of direction, gone. Grace, energy, her ability to manipulate numbers, gone. Her thriving actuary career, her marriage, gone. Twenty-three years of being this other person.

'Of course. I remember now.' She didn't remember. She was still certain she was going the right way. 'I don't suppose they moved it?'

Tom smiled the perfect smile, not pitying, gently amused. 'I'm afraid not.'

'Well then, I'll go that way. Thanks again for the rescue.' Holly retraced her steps, cane in one hand, Tom's strong arm in the other, abandoning her attempt to walk like a normal person in favor of her defeated old-lady shuffle.

She should have had tea in her room. She was not her old self coming to Senneck ready to take it on full speed. She was her new self, and her new self needed rest at regular intervals. Her new self couldn't do things like turn on a dime when she was this tired. Not even on a quarter.

Quite frankly, even after all these years, her new self still sucked.

On the terrace, as lovely as she remembered, Tom guided her

to a corner table with the best view of the bloom-filled garden and mountains beyond. Holly nodded to a middle-aged couple, the only other terrace-people, who appeared to have nothing better to do than watch her unsteady progress toward her seat, into which she dropped gratefully, treating herself to a few deep breaths. The couple returned to staring glumly – he at his phone, she at the tablecloth.

During their twelve-year marriage, Holly and Lyle had never run out of talk. They used to pity couples like this one, a self-congratulatory smug pity that any of the silent couples would probably have liked to smack off their faces. Not surprising so many memories were resurfacing after so long without them. Doubtless they'd continue to bob up while she was here.

Tom saw her settled and handed over her room key, one of the long, ornate metal ones that Holly was tickled to see they still used. He left, brushing off her next round of thanks, casually mentioning that the lobby elevator opened on to the second floor not far from her room.

Translation: *Stay away from the stairs, old woman.*

Not old, not old, only fifty-five, which sounded so much older than Holly felt, though she'd aged most of it all at once after The Change. At least during the year or two of slow recovery she'd been able to regain more and more function, in a perverse way growing younger.

As Tom walked out of the terrace, her tea arrived on a silver tray in the hands of another attractive Senneck staff member – ugly dour people need not apply? – a friendly-looking blond woman. On the tray, a teapot kept warm under a rose-embroidered cozy; a silver strainer resting in its cut-crystal stand to catch drips after each use; a tiny pitcher of heated milk – they knew not to bother with sugar or lemon – a green and white china plate offering two sand-colored wedges of what she knew would be crumbly all-butter shortbread made on the premises in kitchens open 24/7, ready to whip up whatever any guest decided he or she wanted at a moment's notice. Beside those, a teacup, a silver spoon and a small bowl of hulled strawberries looking so perfectly red and ripe, Holly's mouth started watering.

Two cups of excellent tea later, all the strawberries and both cookies, even though she'd told herself to stop after one, Holly was fully recovered, optimism restored, ready to explore her room.

She did take the elevator. No more disasters today, thank you, even near ones. Outside her door, *204* set dead center in gleaming brass, Holly paused, smiling already, savoring the anticipation. She and Lyle had always booked one of the two-floor private cottages on the grounds, so she'd never seen one of the lodge rooms, but even before she pushed open the door, she knew she wouldn't be disappointed.

The suite was cheerful and bright, full-length windows facing the mountains – not an ounce of pesky civilization in sight. Holly adored California; California ran through her blood. But in the LA basin, if you wanted acres of private space, you'd have to visit a virtual reality studio or swim really, really far out into the ocean. Like miles.

Comfortable-looking chairs in subtle shades of green and tan sat in front of a fireplace that would be fantastically cozy in winter months; against a wall, a slant-top writing desk whose inside would be stocked with paper, stationery, stamps and postcards for the one in a hundred who still communicated via pen and paper; next to it a bookcase contained a variety of novels, non-fiction works, games and puzzles.

No, she was not disappointed.

In the bedroom, the king-sized bed was made up in muted

blues and yellows that complemented the sunny colors in the wallpaper and rug, and yes, the ivory floral silk robe lay picturesquely draped across the duvet, waiting for some prolonged and exquisite lounging. On the table by the window, the goody basket and a vase of flowers: faintly peach and cream roses, calla lilies and freesias.

Holly caught her breath. Her wedding bouquet. What was it doing here? The original was still in a box somewhere at home, faded brown and fragile.

No. Not at home. Home since her divorce from Lyle had been the Santa Monica guest house of Melinda, her best friend from childhood. That tiny cottage had no room for ancient memories.

Mom and Dad must still have it, then.

She wrinkled her nose. Her parents would have tossed it, either when she and Lyle split up or when they moved. They'd have gleefully picked off the crunchy dried petals one by one and set fire to the whole mess, wishing they could toss Lyle out of her life retroactively with exactly that much fun and ease.

Now here it was, bizarrely, as fresh and lovely as the one she'd held in her hands so many times. What made anyone think Holly would want this reminder of her and Lyle's special day? Lyle had gone on to marry two other women, both of whom would be showing up later tonight, according to Caleb. Eliana and Megan also had Special Lyle Days. Did they have wedding bouquets in their rooms too? She'd like to know who thought that was a good idea. During the triple-groom's funeral weekend no less.

Holly crossed over to the blooms and inhaled. The scent took her back to the island of Hawaii, which as far as Holly was concerned was paradise. Literally. She fully intended to find herself back there after she died.

Until The Change, every year on June 30, her and Lyle's wedding anniversary, they would return to Carlsmith Beach Park in Hilo, where they'd eloped in 1990 during a six-month trip to celebrate their marriage and her graduation from UC Santa Cruz. Every year, clasping this same bouquet – typical Lyle, he never forgot to arrange for it to be ready – she'd stood facing him on that stunning beach as the sun was setting, and the two of them had repeated their wedding vows, giggling on years when it felt silly – like when other people on the beach were partying raucously, or the year it poured. But when the pieces fell perfectly into place, their gazes had been full of the same awe and love they'd felt the first time. *For better or for worse, until death* . . .

No one who took that vow could really understand how bad 'worse' could be, or how he or she, adoring husband, loving wife, would react when that beast entered their marriage.

Holly gently touched the baby-lips texture of a rose. They were just flowers, a beautiful arrangement.

She turned away, then back, frowning at the blooms, something niggling at her slowed brain. How had the hotel known what flowers were in her wedding bouquet?

Caleb must have . . .

No, Caleb wouldn't know either. Would he? Holly put a hand to her forehead, struggling to keep her thoughts from jumbling. This would take some pondering, and like Dr Seuss's Grinch, who puzzled his way to a sore puzzler, the longer and harder Holly pondered, the less effective her ponderer became.

Caleb hadn't been at the wedding or any of the anniversaries. How would he know what flowers to choose? Had he seen a picture?

Holly and Lyle hadn't bothered with wedding photographers. If they'd hired one for an anniversary, she didn't remember, couldn't always trust her memory, though long-ago had stayed more intact than recently.

Caleb must have seen a picture. Or Lyle had described the bouquet to him at some point. The brothers had kept up a correspondence, communicating more often through the written word than on the phone, though they'd talked sometimes too. Lyle believed in paper trails. Even with no illusions that history would want to remember him or explore his thoughts, his love of pen and paper and his eventual grudging use of emails – printed out and saved – reflected his belief that it was important to leave behind more of yourself than bills and a pile of ashes.

He'd also been extremely observant, noticing details most men wouldn't. She could imagine him describing to his brother what flowers had been in his bride's bouquet. Couldn't she?

Maybe.

All water under the dam . . . or no, under the bridge. The flowers were beautiful, and Holly would only confuse herself if she kept wondering how they got here. She'd ask Caleb later.

It would be so good to see him.

Yawning, she crossed to the bed and ran her hand over the soft comforter, tired, but still keyed up from excitement, caffeine and, mixed in there somewhere, a little dread. You couldn't come to the funeral of your ex-husband, the love of your life, and be all skip-around-the-room fluttery, not that Holly could skip worth a damn anymore. There would be complicated, emotional days ahead that neither Holly's parents nor Melinda had wanted her to go through. But Holly had been adamant that she come here, her first trip alone since The Change. Lyle had been her husband. She needed to be here, to tell people what she knew to be true.

And to be pampered within an inch of her life.

She took off her shoes and painstakingly unzipped the plain, slightly worn, probably unfashionable navy A-line skirt she'd worn for years. Mom had insisted on sending Holly new clothes for her stay 'among the elite'. Holly had let her, not caring one way or the other how she looked. She only hoped she could get all of the unfamiliar pieces on the right way.

Sometimes the least consequential life changes from her near-death experience were the funniest, or most humiliating, depending on her mood. Lots of adults might have a poor sense of direction and go searching for terraces in the wrong place, but very few had trouble getting a skirt or shirt on both the right way around and right side out. Nothing made Holly feel like an idiot faster than laying out a favorite dress and having to stand there trying to remember how to start getting it on, as if she were still two years old.

She pulled her strappy purse off over her head – keeping it attached to her body meant she wouldn't put it down and forget where – dug out her phone and texted her mother and Melinda that she'd arrived safely, including a couple of pictures of her fit-for-a-duchess room. They'd be relieved she'd made it in one piece. Another consequence of The Change – people who loved her had a lot more worrying to do.

She moved aside the ivory silk robe, its slippery, lustrous material stuttering over her unlotioned hands, and relocated the embroidered linen bag into which the staff had folded her nightwear, which she'd chosen with a deliberate wink at her surroundings: hot-pink polka-dot shorty pajamas with cartoon monkeys clambering over coconut palms. With a deep sigh of appreciation, Holly climbed on to the so-comfortable bed and lay back on her elbows, drinking in the freeing space of this lovely room after so many years living in Melinda's 'cozy' quarters.

Adding to her Cheshire Cat grin, the knowledge that if Holly suddenly felt like having a glass of Burgundy accompanied by snails swimming in butter, garlic and parsley, or a cup of sake alongside yellowtail sushi, or a flute of champagne with iced Osetra caviar and blinis, she could pick up the phone and speak the words. In an impossibly short time, those words would materialize in concrete form wherever on the property she wanted them served, no charges, no tipping – as if she were a guest in the house of her friend the trillionaire.

Crazy.

Silencing her cell, she pushed it carefully on to the two-drawer oak nightstand, on which sat a box of tissues in a blue lacquered holder, a tumbler and a small crystal pitcher that would be filled with chilled spring water by the turndown crew in the evening. Then, suddenly remembering, she cautiously pulled open the shallow top drawer of the stand. Her grin stretched about as wide as it could.

Alongside a pen, notepad, bookmarks and hand lotion, there was a pack of Life Savers. Unlike the bouquet, Senneck staff would certainly have documented her passion for those. A roll had been in their bedroom every time she and Lyle had visited, a little winking gift. The original five flavors – cherry, orange, lemon, pineapple, lime. None of this newfangled raspberry or watermelon stuff.

Since childhood, the treats had been her favorite candy, a pop of sweet that wouldn't add to her calorie intake when ballet required her to be rail thin. A comfort-food addiction when Dad took the rap for his company's financial misdeeds and imploded the family's life. A tiny burst of energy when she'd been exhausting herself studying for actuary exams. The two-pack-a-week habit amused Lyle, who took to calling her his Life Saver and would periodically surprise her with a roll tucked

16

into her briefcase or bathroom medicine cabinet, or under her pillow.

On one of her birthdays, some February not long before The Change, Lyle had assembled one complete roll of orange, her favorite flavor. He'd repackaged the candies so convincingly that until she saw his face, brimming with adoring mischief, Holly had assumed the prank to be a remarkable factory error.

Holly closed the drawer. So many happy times. So many more that she and Lyle were unfairly cheated out of.

She let herself fall back on the mattress, closing her eyes, willing her muscles to loosen and her brain to slow its firing. But it was hard to relax being back in this memory-charged place. She'd be seeing Caleb again, and meeting Lyle's other two wives, then later in the week more people who'd loved him. Holly would have to find a way to tell them that her ex-husband wasn't dead. That he was out there somewhere, maybe not intending to return any time soon, if ever, but definitely still alive.

Chapter 2

Rest, Holly.

Her body refused. At times she could hardly get her brain going. At others, like now, even after getting up so early that morning and having to manage two long flights, she couldn't turn it off. It was chattering like teeth in the Arctic, and no amount of meditation or progressive relaxation seemed to work. After half an hour, she gave up and retrieved her phone from the night table. Adrenaline would have to carry her through the evening. She'd sleep tonight.

Mom and Melinda were happy she'd arrived safely and oohed and aahed appropriately over the room pictures. There was also a text from Caleb:

Meet me in the gazebo for a glass of bubbly?

The invitation reinstated Holly's smile and an extra zing of adrenaline. Not only had it been too many years since they'd spoken face to face, but it had also been too many years since she'd been able to enjoy champagne in a perfect atmosphere, something she and Lyle had indulged in at the slightest excuse.

What had saved Lyle from being a cliché of an outrageously wealthy person was first, that he was interested in everyone and everything, no matter its pedigree. And second, that he could be equally happy sipping the best of the best in a world-renowned restaurant as taking a supermarket bottle to the least-populated beach in LA for a sunset picnic. Bubbly was delicious anywhere, but its crisp chill always seemed to reach new levels of deliciousness in an idyllic setting, particularly drinking it with a person you adored. And throughout their decade-plus of marriage, she had truly adored Lyle.

Can't wait to see you, Caleb! Be there in ten.

Pushing herself eagerly off the bed, Holly considered changing, but doubted she could pick out a new outfit and get into it in time. Her old navy skirt would be fine for the rest of the day. Caleb wouldn't care if she wasn't a fashion plate, the staff wouldn't care, and Holly certainly didn't.

Seven minutes later, she'd nailed the skirt first try, and was tucking her cane under her arm, grateful for the security it provided, even if falling and dying meant waking up to her Hawaiian afterlife.

A long-ish walk from the lodge down a wide, sloping stone path, the gazebo was a double-roofed circular building with decorative white latticework and a white cupola perched on top like a squat steeple. Screens protected those sitting inside from bugs, but still allowed for mountain breezes and an idyllic view of the property's rippling blue lake, currently being enjoyed by a couple of leisurely kayakers.

The second he spotted her, Caleb leapt from his chair. Tall and athletic, slightly broader through the chest than Lyle had been, otherwise his shape, movement and wide welcoming grin were so like Lyle's that Holly's throat tightened.

'Holly! There you are!' And then it was just him, Caleb, and she was so grateful he was here, an anchor of familiar friendship and kindness for the strange weekend ahead. He'd continued to visit for several years after the divorce, when business brought him to LA. Then for various reasons they'd lost touch, until he called her six years ago with the horrifying news that Lyle had disappeared somewhere in Southeast Asia. In that same devastating call, he'd also told her about the car wreck that had killed his wife, Clarissa, and stepson, Ryan, six years earlier.

For weeks, Holly hadn't been able to answer the phone without a deep sense of dread.

'Caleb. It is so wonderful to see you.' Thankful for her cane, since being this moved and flustered rarely helped her balance, she headed for him, noticing a limp as he came to greet her. Knee injury? Sprained ankle?

'Holly.' His arms came around her; he held on tightly. Holly melted against him, immersing herself in their past, their shared years of grief and, guiltily, the rare pleasure of physical contact with a solidly built male. 'You're about the only person I've been looking forward to seeing this weekend.'

'Same here.' She couldn't say more. It was achingly good to be with him again.

He pulled back, and from his expression, she knew the feeling was mutual. 'You look fabulous. More beautiful than ever.'

'And you . . . really great.' Her brain couldn't produce better, slowed by an emotional traffic jam. Caleb did look wonderful. His dark hair was still thick, though graying like hers. The grooves between his eyebrows and around his mouth had deepened, but his eyes, several shades darker brown than Lyle's, were still young and vivid with intelligence.

'Come, have a seat.' He gestured toward the bald, mustachioed bartender standing behind a highly polished oak bar at the edge of the gazebo. 'I ordered for us already, champagne and a little food so we don't have trouble walking to dinner.'

'I have trouble walking anywhere. Why are you limping?'

His grin faltered. 'It's been a long day. It still happens sometimes when I'm tired.'

20

Holly lowered herself into the metal chair softened with patterned cushions. Still happens? What had she forgotten? 'I'm sorry, I should know this. Did you . . . hurt yourself?'

Caleb looked startled, then smoothed his features, a polite sequence Holly was annoyingly used to when people came up against her misfires. 'In the accident I lost my leg below the knee.'

Holly gasped. How had she not heard? The man had been through so much.

'I didn't know. I'm sure I would have remembered, even with what's left of my brain. I'm so sorry, Caleb.'

'Ah.' He grimaced apologetically. 'I think last time we spoke I told you about Clarissa and Ryan's deaths. It seemed plenty for one call. It's not something I enjoy talking about.'

'No, don't even think about being sorry.' She waved away his regret. 'You were dealing with plenty.'

'I'm doing fine, really. Prosthetics are a miracle.' His handsome face brightened as the bartender approached their table. 'Here we go . . .'

'Your champagne.'

Yes, indeed their champagne. Even her distress over Caleb's painful loss couldn't overcome the pleasure of this beverage of kings, emperors and a temporary duchess. Two flutes of the golden fizzy miracle sat on the bartender's tray next to a small platter blanketed with deeply ruddy slices of what Holly recognized from her travels with Lyle as Spanish jamón, plus a wedge of some soft-rind cheese and two sliced French rolls probably baked that morning. A ramekin of mixed olives came with a matching floral porcelain dish for their pits. 'Anything else?'

'What else could we want?' Holly beamed at the bartender. She didn't make a habit of mourning the Frederick Lifestyle, but it was a treat to play rich again. 'This is perfect.'

'Thank you, Ms Penny.'

'Thank *you*, George.' Caleb waited for George's swift withdrawal, then lifted his glass to Holly, eyes warm. 'Here's to us, survivors both. Not the way we imagined, but here we still are.'

'And grateful to be.' She lifted her glass and drank, savoring the clean flavor and the prickly roll of bubbles across her tongue.

'Tell you one thing.' Caleb gazed pointedly around them. 'Being back at the Garden of Eden sure doesn't hurt.'

'The Garden of Eden wouldn't charge so much.'

'Probably not.' Caleb put his glass back on the table. 'Tell me how your life is going. Job still good? Mom and Dad? Are you dating anyone?'

Holly put down her champagne before she was seduced into gulping the rest – though at this anything-goes place, she could just ask the buff bartender to carry her back to her room. 'Mom and Dad moved to Arizona a few months ago. California was too expensive to retire in. I still have my same job at McKinley Elementary – the kids keep me hopping. I have a decent social life, book groups, nice friends. Not dating, for now anyway.'

Forever anyway. There was only so much she could do to make a brain injury seem like someone's perfect match. 'How about you? Still in the same house? Are you dating anyone?'

'No, not dating either. I tried for a while. Good times, good company, nothing serious. I did move, not far, but there were too many memories in the old place. Clarissa and I bought it together.' He dropped his gaze, then continued briskly. 'I'm in a smaller house now, on Lake Michigan.'

'Oh, nice.' Holly had been to Lyle's hometown of Milwaukee several reluctant times. Being around his parents had been a trial for both her and Lyle. Mr and Mrs Tyler Lyle Frederick could never get over their Midwestern Catholic son rejecting his rightful place in the family business and marrying a Californian atheist whose father was an ex-con.

'I'm glad we're having this time together before the hordes invade. Here's to Lyle . . .' Caleb raised his glass, chin lifted, jaw tight with what must be grief but looked like defiance. 'From the two people who understood him best.'

'To our time together, and to Lyle.' Holly's voice cracked. Grief was a hard bugger to eradicate. Even now, so many years later, after so much therapy and so much determined grit, bits still clung, like miniature orbs of Styrofoam, impossible to brush cleanly away. 'Yet another goodbye.'

Goodbye when they separated and Lyle moved home to Milwaukee, though they'd stayed friends. Goodbye again when a year later, just as Holly was thinking their separation had been a mistake, Lyle announced his engagement to Eliana. Holly had been so devastated she told him not to contact her again and started sending back his support checks. Goodbye a third time when Lyle showed up in Los Angeles a few months before he left the country and several months before he disappeared. Maybe there would be more someday.

'Yes.' Caleb's expression was grim. 'This really is the last one.'

The perfect opening, the one Holly had so carefully hoped and prepared for. She cleared her throat . . . then hunched her shoulders and pushed them back down in frustration. Predictably, she couldn't remember the words she'd chosen to begin with. Or continue. Or end.

She'd have to wing it. 'Have you ever thought maybe Lyle wanted to take time off? From humanity? From civilization? And that he grew to like being disconnected, and is still out there somewhere?'

Caleb's face smoothed into stony blankness. 'Maybe at first. It's a nice fantasy.'

'It seems like something he might do if he'd been through too many . . . tough spots.' Holly wasn't supposed to know that Lyle's third wife had cheated on him, a fact Lyle told her during that last secret visit. 'For all we know, he'll show up Saturday and crash his own funeral.'

Caleb recoiled. 'That'd be a pretty sick joke.'

'Yes, sorry. Too dark.' Holly stretched her legs impatiently, annoyed that her well-planned speech had deserted her. This one wasn't going the way she wanted.

She and Lyle had been eerily, impossibly linked. After the 1989 Loma Prieta earthquake in Santa Cruz, the city was in total chaos, but Lyle had found her unerringly on a side street not far from the severely damaged center of the city, both of them shaken up but neither afraid for the other's safety. During their early years living in LA, when Holly had been home studying for her fourth actuary exam, she was seized with sudden anxiety, and showed up at the Cedars Sinai ER just after Lyle was brought in, bruised and bloodied with a broken wrist from a Jeep hitting his bike.

'Why wouldn't he contact us? Why would he put us through this? He'd have to be some kind of sadistic bastard.' Caleb spoke bitterly, as if he'd always known Lyle was exactly that, when the truth was the opposite. Lyle had been generous and thoughtful to a fault.

'I don't know. But I don't believe he's dead. Somehow I would know.'

'Holly . . .' Caleb laid a palm-up hand on the little table. 'I know this is hard. But you have to believe he's gone.'

'Why?'

'Because he is.'

'I'm just saying it's possible that—'

'It's not possible.'

'Okay. It's not possible.' Holly shrugged. His vehemence surprised and disappointed her. She and Caleb had always communicated well. 'Nice fantasy, though.'

Caleb turned to look toward the lake, hair ruffling, jaw set, then abruptly turned back and speared some jamón. 'So . . . how's your room?'

The subject was closed. So be it. She'd come here for Lyle and to share what she knew; what people did with the information was up to them.

'The room, well . . .' Holly affected a duchess's ennui, eager to smooth over the awkwardness. 'I'll manage, but between you and me, I'm used to a whole lot better.'

He let out the hearty laugh she hadn't heard in many years and missed retroactively, a rare treat. Lyle would weep, rant, celebrate and holler unashamed. Caleb kept his emotions close.

'The room is fantastic, thank you. And I meant to ask, how did the hotel know what my wedding bouquet looked like? Did you tell them? How did you know?'

'I didn't.' He held out a folded piece of jamón on a silver serving fork. 'Have some?'

'Yes, thanks.' She reached for it, remembering the slices she and Lyle had gobbled by the dozen in tapas bars around Spain.

'Lyle wanted you to have it. He planned this whole weekend.' He gestured around them. 'Years ago, before he left the country.'

'He planned his own *funeral*?' She couldn't imagine. 'That's not like him. He was so focused on living. I'm not even sure he knew he was mortal.'

Caleb laughed drily. 'Actually, I made him do it. After Clarissa died, it felt so important to have the ceremony she'd want. But what I was sure she'd want wasn't what her parents

25

or brothers were sure she'd want, which added a lot of nightmare to the nightmare. I told Lyle I was writing down the funeral I had in mind for myself, and pretty much ordered him to do the same.'

'Ah.' Holly bit into the jamón, trying to cover her confusion over what that had to do with her wedding flowers, then rolled her eyes in ecstasy over the taste: deeper than prosciutto, nutty almost herby, intensely satisfying. 'Oh, that is good.'

Caleb helped himself and took a bite, registering the same bliss she was sure had been on her face. 'Mm-hmm.'

'What does Lyle's funeral have to do with my bouquet?' She washed down the jamón with more champagne; she was drinking too quickly, but it was heavenly having the good stuff again.

'You know what he was like.' Caleb relaxed back in his chair. 'I wanted a paragraph. He gave me a three-page document. Down to the last detail.'

'I can totally picture that.' Lyle, throwing himself into creating the perfect, beautiful event. But why would he want Holly to find their wedding bouquet many decades and two wives after it was first hers?

She didn't know how to feel about that, or how to go about working through it, especially with her head pleasantly buzzy. So she focused back on Caleb. 'This weekend must have been a lot to take care of.'

'Are you kidding?' He pointed to his empty glass, then hers, a silent question she answered with a quick shake, no. 'In this place, all I had to do was send in Lyle's instructions and take a nap. Everything's been done for us. I deserve no credit at all.'

He caught George's eye and held up his empty. Holly absently watched the pair of kayakers head for shore. 'And the others? Eliana and Megan?'

26

When she didn't continue, Caleb tilted his head expectantly. 'Eliana and Megan what?'

'Sorry.' Holly's cheeks heated. She'd popped out an isolated sentence fragment and expected him to mind-read the rest of her question. 'Did Lyle want them to have their wedding bouquets too?'

'. . . No.'

'That's weird.'

'It's all weird, Holly.' He folded his arms tightly across his chest. 'All of it.'

'Well.' Something was going on with him, more than just grief over his brother. In the old days Holly would have felt comfortable asking point blank. 'Maybe I will have another glass. I'm not driving tonight. Or for the past twenty years.'

'Sure.' He gave George another signal.

Holly leaned forward and cut a wedge of the ripe, fragrant cheese, rested it on a piece of bread and held it out to Caleb. 'Have some?'

'Thanks.' One bite curved his lips into a smile. 'That's amazing. Your turn.'

'You've convinced me.'

'Are you still living in Melinda's guest house?'

'Not for much longer.' She arranged more gorgeously oozy cheese on another slice of bread. 'With the kids gone, Melinda and Matthew are divorcing. Finally.'

'I assume that's good? She seemed miserable even ten years ago.'

Holly nodded. 'Long overdue. They're selling the house.'

'Where will you go?'

'Not sure yet.' She shrugged, as if the question of whether she'd have a bed to sleep in after August or a roof over her head were pesky details. As if she wasn't putting off finding a place because she dreaded the idea of being jolted out of her hard-won routines. As if it didn't overwhelm her even thinking about trying. California was home and home was California, but California was also bloody expensive. Holly wouldn't be able to stay in Santa Monica, where she was born and raised, unless she did like Harry Potter and rented out someone's cupboard under the stairs. Having to adapt to a new town, a new neighborhood, a new job – even the idea started her panicking.

George appeared with two more fizzing flutes and cleared the old ones in a practiced instant.

Holly took a bite of the cheese she forgot she was holding. Mmm.

Creamy, mushroomy, with a faintly grassy finish, it reminded her of the raw-milk cheeses she and Lyle had eaten in France, some from the finest shops, some from farmhouses they stopped at while touring the countryside.

What fabulous trips they'd had. Holly missed traveling more than any of the many other things her present life lacked. Maybe she'd first win the lottery, then find a companion, like old ladies did in English novels. Someone who could pack without forgetting underpants, who could get Holly from place A to destination B without freak-outs over directions and details she'd mislaid. Time had stopped behaving since The Change, speeding up, then slowing down, years and events rearranging themselves without her permission.

The kayakers were landing; a staff member waited to help them disembark, and to haul up their boats. A puff of wind traveled up from the lake, shivering the purple sweet alyssum in a tiny pot on Holly and Caleb's table.

'I wanted to see you before everyone else got here.' Caleb leaned forward, looking serious again. 'Mostly selfishly, but there's something I wanted to tell you.'

'Oh?' Holly brought her second flute up for another cold, crisp sip, a perfect foil for the rich meat and cheese. She shouldn't finish this second glass, but one more sip couldn't hurt. Maybe two . . .

'I think you should know, in case things get awkward.'

'Between us?'

'No, of course not.' He flashed his admittedly sexy grin, so like Lyle's. 'Never between us.'

'Here's to never between us.' She beamed, attraction re-awakening as her tipsiness intensified and the evening light flattered Caleb's handsome face more and more. 'As for things getting awkward, let me try to guess how. Three wives of the same guy are going to be hanging out together at his funeral for the next four days and . . . Nope, I got nothing.'

She put the glass down, gratified that she'd made Caleb laugh again. If Eliana and Megan were what worried Caleb, he could stop worrying. Holly had come here clear-eyed, with all her feelings healthy, out in the open and understood.

'I found out only a couple of days ago that Eliana and Megan . . .' Caleb exhaled and shook his head, looking both rueful and exasperated. 'I still can't believe I'm having to say this.'

'What? They're planning to give me atomic wedgies?'

'Weirder than that.'

'Come on. There is nothing weirder than that.'

'You're not making this easier.'

Holly scoffed, refusing to get nervous. Lyle had been out of her life for over twenty years, and every painful detail of their past had been examined and worked through in therapy and with her parents and friends.

'Apparently Lyle never told them about you.'

'He—' Holly broke off because she was going to repeat him,

idiotically. *Lyle never told them about me?* Just in time, she realized what he meant. 'You mean he never told them what happened to me?'

'No, that's not it.' He looked as irritable and confused as he sounded, breeze ruffling his dark hair, kind of adorable. 'Until I told them you were coming this weekend, neither Eliana nor Megan had any idea you existed.'

Chapter 3

Another breeze made the alyssum bouquet on Holly and Caleb's table shudder. Holly shuddered along with it. 'Neither Megan nor Eliana had ever *heard* of me? Are you sure?'

'I'm sure. When I mentioned you'd be at Senneck this weekend, each of them said, "Who?" And when I said you were his first wife, they were both shocked Lyle had been married before Eliana.'

'But . . .' Holly struggled to follow the logic. '*Why* would he keep me secret?'

'Because he couldn't stand thinking about you?' Caleb flinched. 'Wait, that came out wrong.'

'Uh . . . I hope so.' She assumed he meant that Lyle had dealt with the pain and guilt of their marriage's failure the way he dealt with all ugliness. Suppress. Refuse to let hideousness infiltrate your thoughts or your world. Poof! It ceased to exist, and so had she. 'What did you tell the other wives about me?'

'Nothing much.' Caleb folded his arms across his chest. 'I told them Lyle married you after college, that I had no idea why he'd kept you from them, and that if they wanted to know more they could ask you this weekend.'

'So . . . you didn't tell them how the marriage ended?' She pointed to her forehead, grimacing. 'Or that I'm . . . ?'

Caleb was already shaking his head. 'Not my story to tell.

Muna Shehadi

You were married to Lyle, then you weren't. Whatever else you want them to know is up to you.'

'Thank you. That was thoughtful.' Except it would be easier if the other wives arrived at Senneck already knowing about Holly's near-death from choking. She hated telling people, but if she didn't, at some point in the conversation they'd give her that look she hated a lot more. That 'Hey, wait a second, is something *wrong* with her?' expression. Half frozen, slightly startled. Like Caleb's when he thought Holly forgot he'd lost a body part.

'Oh boy.' Caleb was gazing down the hill toward the lake, groove deepening between his brows.

'What is it?' She peered in the same direction. The two kayakers were striding up the hill, a tall, dark, laughing young woman and a guy who clearly spent half his life, if not more, at the gym. He walked with that peculiar swagger, arms slightly away from his sides as if he was afraid of touching himself, when the truth was that his lats bulged so dramatically, they forced his arms out of the way.

'Here we go.' Caleb put his hands on the chair, leaning forward as if ready to flee. 'That's Megan. The *grieving* widow.'

Megan. The cheater.

Knowing she'd be encountering wives number two and three this weekend, Holly had thought about how to react, deciding to take the high road, throw away whatever she'd been told by Caleb or Lyle and form her own impressions. If Lyle had loved these women, they'd have to be thoughtful, intelligent, world-curious and polite. A lot to enjoy.

However. Deciding how to react was different than actually reacting.

She watched Megan climb, younger than Holly had imagined, much younger, in her thirties still, long tan muscled legs striding

32

effortlessly up the hill the way Holly's no longer could. Lyle's 'foolish mistake', his 'middle-aged crisis cliché' – those had been his words, delivered in person the last time they spoke, fourteen years after their separation. He'd just found out Megan had been cheating on him throughout their marriage with a guy she'd been dating since college. The discovery had driven him first to despair, then to Los Angeles to see Holly, where he'd told her he was planning a life change. He'd begged her to tell no one about the visit or his plans. Holly had promised. The only promise to Lyle she hadn't kept was the most important one, made at the altar: *till death do us part.*

A few months after that visit, Lyle had flown to Cambodia. A few months after that, he'd disappeared. Wherever he was now, Holly hoped he was happy.

She took a convulsive gulp of water. She wasn't ready for this confrontation, not now, after such a long, difficult day and memories that had shaken her more than she'd like to admit. She was foggy from fatigue and alcohol, and had not been able to process fully the news that Lyle's other wives knew nothing about her.

'Get ready.' Caleb made himself relax back in the chair. 'She can be a little . . . herself.'

He was not helping. 'Can't we all.'

Megan stepped into the gazebo, leaving Side-o-Beef to catch the door behind her. She pulled the elastic out of her wavy chestnut hair and shook it around while doing a quick who's-here sweep of the room. Her liner-enhanced gaze landed on Caleb for a blank second before recognition raised her eyebrows.

'Hey, Caleb!' She strode over to their table with energy that made Holly feel like bracing herself for impact. 'Nice to see ya.'

'Megan.' Caleb rose for a mutually unenthusiastic air kiss

before he sat again and gestured across the table. 'This is Holly Penny.'

'Ah, Holly. The *mystery* woman.' Megan scrutinized her with brown eyes so pale they were nearly golden. Holly sat, twenty years Megan's senior, fighting off panic in her ancient navy skirt and pilled cream sweater, cane at her side, long unstyled hair with myriad shooting-star streaks of gray, face free of makeup except for mascara and blush she'd put on that morning, a thousand hours ago, when she'd hauled herself out of bed in Los Angeles in what felt like the middle of the night.

Megan's pink sandals matched her pink blouse, pink nail polish, pink earrings and pink lipstick. Her white and pink plaid shorts showed not a single spot of dirt or damp, even after kayaking. For the first time since Mom had insisted, Holly was fiercely grateful for the new wardrobe waiting in her room, then just as quickly ashamed of herself. This was not a competition. They were gathering this weekend to honor Lyle. Holly had promised herself to be gracious.

'Hello, Megan.' Quick calming breath to settle her voice. 'It's nice to meet you.'

'Same here.' Megan stared, curious, assessing. 'So you were Lyle's starter marriage, huh? *That* was news.'

Holly didn't know if humans had hackles, but if they did, hers were rising. 'We were college sweethearts, married for twelve years.'

'*Twelve years?*' Megan's astonishment turned petulant as she turned to her brother-in-law. 'Caleb, you didn't tell me that.'

'No?' He sipped champagne with forced nonchalance, sitting ramrod straight. 'Sin of omission. I wasn't keeping it secret.'

'Well it certainly seems that way. You and Lyle both.' She resumed staring at Holly, suspiciously this time. Holly

34

made herself stare back, feeling the strain of the day, praying she didn't get so flustered she'd start stammering nonsense. 'I'd assumed you were a quicky screw-up he didn't bother mentioning.'

'She was *not* that.' Caleb, not even trying to be polite.

'I said I *assumed*. I had no information to the contrary. And it was weird that Lyle told me nothing about her.' She pouted again, at Holly this time. 'Did you ask him not to?'

'No, no, absolutely not.' Holly gave Side-O-Beef a welcoming smile. 'Hello. I'm Holly.'

'Oh, sorry, this is Bodie Bauer-Baker. Bodie, this is Caleb, and this is Lyle's surprise first wife, Holly . . . Pinny, was it?'

'Penny.' Caleb, all but grinding his teeth.

'Nice to meet you, Bodie.' Holly made her smile keep going, wanting to chant his name like a tongue-twister. Bodie Bauer-Baker baked a batch of—

'We'll join you.' Megan pulled out a chair at their table.

Holly's stomach sank. She was fine with a quick hello, but not a long conversation. At the first polite opportunity, she'd have to make a break for it.

'George, hi!' Megan threw the approaching bartender a razzle-dazzle cheerleader smile. 'It's *great* to see you, how have you been?'

'Just fine, thank you.' George glanced at Bodie, did a double-take, then forced his features back to welcome. 'Good to see you again, Mrs Frederick.'

Holly flinched. Mrs Frederick had been *her* name, for longer than either of the others.

Not a competition.

'I'll have the usual.' Megan turned to her bulky companion. 'Bodie?'

'I'll have the usual too.' He gave a nervous laugh. 'Uh . . . not her usual, though. My usual. Which you don't know what it is. I'll have a beer. Budweiser, or . . . I don't know. Whatever you have.'

'Surprise him.' Megan sat and crossed her smooth, endless legs. 'He'll drink whatever.'

George gave the official server nod. 'Anything to eat?'

'No thanks. We'll wait for dinner.'

'I'm actually . . . kinda hungry. Actually.' Bodie sat stiffly, looking incredibly uncomfortable. He put his enormous forearms on the table, then jerked them back as if the surface was scalding and folded them across his pecs-forward chest. 'Didn't have much lunch.'

Holly couldn't imagine how much it would take to fuel that body. Or what it would feel like to touch him. She imagined her fingertip flattening to the bone with the slightest pressure.

'What can I get you, sir?'

'Uh . . .' Bodie looked around helplessly, rubbing his thighs. 'Menu?'

'I told you, sweetie, they don't have them here.'

'Right.' Bodie swallowed, face growing red. 'Okay . . . uh . . .'

Holly's heart melted. Poor kid. 'I'm pretty sure George makes an awesome ham and grilled cheese on sourdough.'

'Yeah?' His face brightened. 'That sounds great. I'll have that.'

'Right away.' George went back to his bar, where Holly knew there was – no, used to be, years ago . . . well, obviously there still was – a grill machine thing, so simple food could be served faster than an order to the main kitchen.

'It is so great to be back here. I *love* this place!' Megan extended her trim arms, then fell back against the seat and tipped her head just so, one of those women who turned every movement into 'you-want-me-and-I-don't-blame-you'.

Lyle would have seen through that in about three seconds, no matter how middle-aged he was. Under all that pink sensuality and money-worship, Megan must have substance and depth.

'It's so intense.' Bodie shook his head, covered with strawberry-blond hair so short it showed patterns of dark and light, like freshly cut grass. Handsome guy. Appealing hazel eyes. Too bad he wasn't made from the same parts that produced normal humans. 'I don't know.'

'What do you mean, you don't know?' Megan turned on him, but her expression was soft. 'What's not to love about it?'

'No, sure, sure, it's incredible. Just . . .' He shook his head again. 'Not my thing, I guess.'

'I don't think it's anyone's thing really.' Holly decided Bodie was okay. 'It's like Fantasy Island. Fun for a vacation, but no one could do this forever.'

'Omigod, I totally could. Thanks, George.' Megan accepted a glass of a deep orange liquid over ice. 'I could live like this every day for the rest of my life.'

Caleb snorted; Megan didn't seem to notice, or maybe she didn't want to. Bodie, however, gave Caleb a dark look.

'I don't know much about you either, Megan.' Holly spoke quickly in case Bodie had a temper. 'What do you do?'

'Since Lyle left or before?' Megan sipped her orange drink. 'Damn, George is good.'

'What is that?' Bodie asked.

'Aperol spritz, but he puts in something extra. Vodka, I think, maybe some lemon juice . . . definitely something else, but I can't tell what. So fabulous. Want to try, babe?'

'Not me.' Bodie held up his beer. 'I don't drink anything that looks like Kool-Aid. Or Windex – what's that blue one you like?'

'Curaçao!' Megan laughed, a nasal cascade that was more funny than irritating. At the same time, she gave her boyfriend a look that clearly said in her eyes Bodie Bauer-Baker walked on water.

That was nice. Heart-warming. If Holly could forget what Lyle had looked like describing his pain. Haggard. Frail. Not the indomitable personality she'd loved so much.

The thought weighed on her, threatening to drag down her mood and drain her resolve to be pleasant.

Her mother spoke in her head, saying she *knew* Holly wasn't up to the emotional overload of this weekend. Melinda showed up and agreed, though she was more worried that Holly's grief over Lyle would reawaken and have to be put to a gruesome death yet again.

Holly was determined to prove them both wrong. She'd be able to leave this tense scene soon. Five, ten minutes tops. In the meantime she'd have to focus, resist the urge to retreat into her head. 'You were going to tell me . . . what you do, Megan.'

'Mm, yes. Sorry.' She was a quarter of the way through the drink already. 'When Lyle and I were married, he—'

'Technically you are still married.'

'Always helpful, Caleb, thank you.' Megan gave him the sharp look he deserved, though it had been a pretty good shot. Lyle had once told Holly, decades ago now, that Caleb could be ruthless. Holly had never seen him behave that way, but most CEOs didn't get to the top and stay there by being doormats, even in a family business. 'When Lyle was *around*, I worked in an art gallery part-time, did a lot of volunteering for the symphony, the opera, the museum. We were members of the University Club, the Yacht Club, the Tripoli Country Club, there was always something going on. And of course we traveled all over.'

Ah. There it was, what Lyle had seen in her, what they shared. Her love of culture, the arts, travel – what Lyle called the only parts of mankind worth celebrating.

A glance at Bodie found him looking queasy, and Holly felt for him again, distantly this time, as if her emotions were moving out of reach.

'And after . . . Lyle left?' Hard work getting those words out, a bad sign.

Megan rolled her eyes. 'Well. Everything changed after that. You know his assets were frozen until he could be declared dead? I'm his *wife*, and I had only our checking account and one little savings account. The rest he'd never gotten around to putting my name on.'

'Can't imagine.' Caleb was smirking.

'Up yours, brother dear.' She glared at him, but not with any real malice. 'So Bodie came to my rescue and hired me to manage his gym.'

Holly closed her eyes for a few seconds, annoyed by Megan's lack of grief over Lyle's supposed death. He deserved to be mourned by his wife, especially this weekend. 'You . . . own a gym, Bodie?'

Bodie looked surprised, as if he'd forgotten, or assumed Holly would know such a globally important fact. 'Yeah. I own an Anytime Fitness in Milwaukee.'

'The place was a mess! His old manager was useless. I came in and cleaned up.' Megan glowed over her accomplishment. 'Runs like a Lexus now.'

'Saved my ass a buncha times.'

'How about you, Holly?' Megan gulped at her spritzer. 'Is that your real name by the way or short for something?'

'Not short for anything.' Holly was regretting the second glass of champagne, eyelids getting heavy, thoughts sluggish.

She wanted to be back in her room. 'I work as a . . . teaching assistant. For kindergarten.'

Megan gave the exact expression Holly expected, surprise then smug satisfaction that she hadn't been outdone. 'That's *great*. I love kids. Never wanted any, but . . . wow, good for you. So important.'

Holly nodded, wondering what Megan would think if she knew that twenty-three years ago Holly had been earning a solid six-figure salary as an actuary, managing over a dozen people in one of the largest, most successful insurance companies in the world.

Sometimes that person seemed so distant and foreign that Holly wasn't sure it really had been her. Twenty-three years since she'd been with Lyle in the kind of marriage every newlywed dreams about. Twenty-three years since she'd lived so effortlessly and so well, not as the dancer she'd always dreamed of becoming, but in a career she enjoyed, one which gave her the financial independence she'd sworn to achieve after her family's bankruptcy, even though as Lyle's wife she hadn't needed a dime of it.

Now she was highly experienced in handing out crayon packets, art smocks and graham crackers, in mopping up glue and tears, in leading alphabet singalongs, and at the moment, feeling like the loser in a competition she'd been telling herself wasn't happening.

'How did you meet Lyle?' Another sip of the orange drink, then a pink tongue dragged luxuriously across pinker lips.

'At a college party.' Holly felt her back slumping. God, she was tired. It was getting harder to fight. 'A hot-tub party.'

'Ooh, you crazy Californians. I hear it's all about *naked* hot-tubbing out there.'

'Yes.'

Megan looked surprised, then recovered to nod with girl-to-girl understanding. 'And that's all it took.'

Holly allowed a faint smile. 'My eyes. He noticed my eyes.' She sounded sluggish, dreamy, felt detached from reality, drifting into memories of the night she and Lyle met, startlingly vivid, as if she'd time-traveled. Much laughter, cool air and warm water, the rumble-swish of ocean waves and the smell of chlorine. Then out of the darkness, a mysterious and unexpected guest to the party.

Someone guffawed, a woman. 'They all say that. Was he in the tub too? I bet it was a pretty hot night.'

Holly tried hard to rejoin the table, becoming aware of expectant stares. Had someone asked her a question? She couldn't remember. It took everything she had not to close her eyes and rest her head on her palms. 'And so . . . that's . . . all.'

Megan looked over at Caleb in alarm. 'Is she okay?'

Caleb stood and reached for Holly's cane. 'Listen, it was great to see you guys.'

'Yes. Sure.' Megan only glanced at him, staring at Holly in golden-eyed fascination.

Holly let Caleb help her up and hand her the cane. If only she hadn't met Megan tonight, when she was like this, at her very worst. 'Nice to meet you.'

'Same here.' Bodie only had eyes for the sandwich George was putting in front of him.

'Ooh, that looks good. Gimme half, Bodie-babe?'

'I thought you weren't hungry.'

'I am now. C'mon, give me a bite at least . . .'

'Let's go.' Tight-lipped, Caleb gallantly offered Holly his arm. 'Ma'am?'

'Thank you.' She managed to get out from behind the table, stumbling slightly. Why had she had so much champagne? It had only added to the confusion fatigue brought on. She knew better.

'Is she drunk?' The whisper behind them was ridiculously easy to hear.

Holly ignored it, let Caleb guide her out of the gazebo and on to the path back to the lodge, the stone trail ahead of them seeming to stretch for miles.

One step at a time.

She put one foot in front of the other, did it again and again, wondering what the man she knew so well could have valued so highly in that aggressive, blunt-spoken, unfeeling woman at the table, whose name Holly had already forgotten.

While behind her, poaching bits of her boyfriend's sandwich, watching Holly shuffle away like a woman half again as old, Lyle's third wife was undoubtedly wondering similarly unpleasant things about her.

Chapter 4

UC Santa Cruz
October 1, 1986

Dear Caleb,

How's freshman year treating you? Get laid yet? Seriously, hope you're loving Princeton. It takes a while to settle in so don't be discouraged if you feel out of whack. I had a few weeks not being sure what was up. Santa Cruz is way different from Milwaukee. I'm glad I spent the year abroad after high school or I would have felt like a hick when I got here. College falls into place, though, didn't take too long. It won't for you either.

Big news, brother, I met a girl. The girl. Go ahead, make fun of me, but I know. I felt it, like those unbelievable movie scenes. Cue swelling music, the rest of the world falls away, etc. etc. She was in a hot tub, no swimsuit . . . you're laughing, I can practically hear it. She was laughing, I can definitely hear that. But it wasn't her body that got me – though I sure noticed, I'm not stupid. It was her eyes, man, I couldn't look away. This laughing, beautiful girl had the saddest eyes I'd ever seen.

I barely slept, couldn't wait to find her the next day. We spent hours together, talking as if we'd always known and trusted each other, and I've seen her several times since. Her name is Holly Penny, and she's a dancer. She moves so gracefully

I feel like a klutz around her. She has incredible determination too, knows what she wants and goes after it. I admire that so much. Especially since I still have no idea what I want to do except be useful and not waste my life slaving after the almighty dollar like Dad. I want to focus on valuable things, worthwhile things that improve the human race, not enslave or oppress it.

As for Holly, I'm going to marry her. Get up off the floor, I'm serious. Some force in the universe, which I never believed in before I met her, has me thinking all these clichéd thoughts about destiny and fate and soulmates. You would gag so badly. Love at first sight, dude. It's real. I'm like Peter Pan (though much manlier), wanting to leap around and crow. (Remember as a kid you thought he was a terrifying human–rooster mix?) I want to propose to her next time we meet, I'm that sure. Don't worry, I won't, but she is it.

Enough babbling. I'm glad you're there, Caleb. If I talked about her like this to anyone else they'd think I was nuts.

Lyle

Princeton University
October 15, 1986

Dear Lyle,

You are completely nuts. One second around a naked woman and you want to marry her? I mean, I get it, but . . . that's sex, not love. And yes, I do know what sex is. Holly's a cool name, though. Makes me think of Audrey Hepburn in that movie Mom loves so much.

I'm doing okay here. Working hard. Playing intramural soccer, and got into an a cappella singing group, the Krokodiloes. Making friends. Mostly I'm glad to be out of the house. Mom and Dad's fighting and complaining are worse, and I'm sick of them not dealing with the real problem – that they shouldn't be married. I'm not sure I ever told you how bad it was. Some of it was about you. They were pissed that you deferred admission to Harvard for a year of 'frivolous' travel. When you came back and chose Santa Cruz instead? I thought they'd explode. You only heard some of it.

When I got into Princeton, it wasn't 'Well done, son, we're proud of you', it was 'At least you're going to an Ivy. Your brother got into one and pissed the chance away.' Maybe I shouldn't have told you, but there's freedom in being away from it all. I just hope Holly is white, rich, Catholic, and wants to live in Milwaukee to help you lead Frederick Industries into its glorious future as is your destiny. Or they'll hate her.

Princeton's a nice town, pretty, not much going on, but campus life makes up for that and New York is a quick train ride away. I like my roommate. He won't ever be my best friend, but we do fine. Some people weren't this lucky.

I teased you about meeting Holly, but I'm happy for you. Look forward to meeting her and seeing her beautiful . . . uh . . . eyes. Just don't tell her you're at the wrong college.

Caleb

'Naked? In front of each other? Like . . . coed naked?' The girl – Jill? Holly had met so many people this first week at UCSC, she couldn't keep track – looked so terrified Holly didn't know whether to put an arm around her or burst out laughing.

Truthfully, Holly was kinda taken aback herself, since the suggestion of naked hot-tubbing had come from their resident advisor, Mason, as a way for the freshmen still hanging out after an official mixer to very unofficially get to know each other better. But Holly wasn't going to let anyone see her rattled. She was going to let the Midwestern Jills do the freaking out and play the part of the cool Californian she was. Particularly easy tonight because it was midnight and she was that strange combination of hyper and exhausted from the intense stimulation of so many new experiences over so few days. Plus everyone was either stoned or drunk on Rainier Ale.

After a few hems, haws, bravado and outright chickening out, eight people had agreed to go, two girls and six guys in two cars. Holly climbed into a VW bug whose engine hadn't even started before John – or Seth – in the passenger seat lit a joint and passed it to the driver, Seth – or John. Those names Holly remembered because the two of them had grown up together, gone to Santa Cruz High together, and were also rooming together in college, which she thought was insecure and weird. Didn't they want their social horizons broadened? She thought of them as JohnSeth.

JohnSeth took a hit and passed the joint behind him to Holly, who thought it was a really stupid idea to drive stoned, and a stupider idea for her to smoke weed when she'd already had too much to drink. But something a little reckless was driving her tonight – actually every night since she'd been here – maybe the same impulse that made her think it was a great idea to get naked with strangers.

Pretending the situation was cool and not dangerous, like so many dumb kids had pretended before her and would after, she took a couple of decent-sized drags and passed the rest to her roommate, Sherry, a delicate perfectionist from San Diego who seemed nice enough but was clearly more interested in finding a boyfriend than in hanging out with Holly.

Ten mildly tense – if she'd been sober, ridiculously tense – minutes later, they arrived safely at Mason's friend's house, a sprawling Mediterranean on the coast. Eight inebriated bodies poured out of the cars and race-walked nervously around to the back through the chilly night air. The hot tub was huge, big enough for nearly all of them, sunk into a wooden deck, with the ocean tumbling over sand only a bunch of yards away, behind a wooden fence.

'Psych!' One of the guys was trying to take off his shirt while still holding the last of the joint. A couple more guys joined him undressing, not quite as enthusiastically, but with macho determination. Teenage chests started emerging.

'You really doin' this, Hol?' Sherry looked doubtfully at the tub, half-mast eyelids tinged pink.

'I abso-freakin'-lutely am.' For whatever reason, Sherry's hesitation spurred Holly on to put down her beer and yank her shirt over her head. 'Absooo-freakin'-loooootly.'

'Hello, ladies.' RA Mason appeared behind them, his surfer's body filling out a Hang Ten T-shirt in a way that made Sherry brighten. 'Not having second thoughts there, are ya?'

'Nope.' Holly beamed at him, currently in love with her surroundings and the night and the unimaginable totality of the universe.

'Yes to second thoughts.' Sherry blinked demurely. 'It's *freezing*.'

'Well the water ain't!' Holly hurled her shirt across the deck, then unzipped her shorts. 'That's why it's called a *hot* tub.'

That had to be the funniest thing anyone had ever said. Ever! A gust hit her bare skin, making her squeal and giggle harder.

'Hey, Sherry, you want to check out the house?' Mason's Operation Make-Out was clearly being put in motion. 'It's nice and warm inside.'

'Oh, ya, that'd be so great. Thanks.' Sherry shivered pitifully and let him escort her inside, throwing Holly an oh-my-God! look over her shoulder, like she was *totally* surprised at this completely predictable turn of events. Like she hadn't been inviting it by drooling over him all week.

Left the sole female on the deck, Holly undressed the rest of the way as fast as possible, grabbed up her beer and followed assorted bare male asses to the tub, covering her most private bits with one hand, clutching the bottle across her body so her forearm hid her breasts.

'Lemme in.' She nudged a pair of broad shoulders with her foot, shivering and cracking up. 'Lemme in, it's like total Arctic winter out here.'

The owner of the shoulders turned and stared dully, eyes nearly shut. 'Huh?'

Holly gave up and ran to the opposite side of the tub, where she climbed in, grateful for her strong legs and dancer's coordination, so she could slip quickly under the water and release the grip on her modesty.

'Aaaah.' Heated water on chilled skin was blissful. 'This is most excellent.'

'What's yer name again?' The guy next to her flung out a hand that she was able to block with her shoulder before it hit her breast.

'Holly.'

'Holly, man, you are hard-core. Let's hear it for Holly.'

The whoop that followed made her shout with laughter, lifting her mostly full Rainier Ale in acknowledgment. 'Thank you, thank you very much. Tell me your names. You're JohnSeth.' She pointed. 'Who are the rest of you?'

'José.'

'Mark.'

'Will.'

'Nice to meetcha, José, Mark and Will.'

'Hey, Holly, wanna sit on my lap?'

Holly held up her middle finger. 'Hey, José, wanna sit on this?'

The guys roared like some primeval beast, five bodies and one brain.

'You a dancer?' This from Will. She thought it was Will. Who cared? She'd figure it out as the year went on.

'How'd you guess?'

'You're built like one.'

She wrinkled her nose. 'Skinny, no boobs.'

'No, no way. You're a fox. I really mean—'

'Where you from, Holly?' Mark was trying to see through the water to her parts.

'Santa Monica.' She couldn't stop giggling. She'd never had so much male attention before. Maybe because she usually had her clothes on. Which didn't say much for guys. 'You?'

'New Jersey.'

General chorusing made it clear what people thought of New Jersey, drowning out the poor guy's protests.

'Can you do a split in mid-air, Holly?' That was Will, who spread two fingers, and made an obscene tongue gesture.

'Are you for *real*?' Holly spluttered the words, on one level having the time of her life, deep down uncomfortably aware she was out of control. 'Not doing one around *you*, dude.'

The roar sounded again. Will started splashing her. She turned to avoid the spray and caught sight of a guy, fully clothed, watching them. Watching her. She could only barely make out his face.

'Hey! Perv!' She sent over a polite splash of water that was sure not to reach him. 'What're you lookin' at?'

'You.'

She giggled. 'Yeah, well either get naked or go away. This is a private party.'

49

He didn't move, but he did smile, a generous grin, teeth catching the dimmed lights on the deck. Something about that smile, swear to God, made her insides go shivery. The guy was good-looking, decently built, but not her type. She liked dark, slender guys who gave off a hint of danger. This boyish dirty blond looked like he'd want to take her home to try his mom's tuna casserole.

'You all freshmen?' He had a slight accent she couldn't place any closer than some non-California part of the US.

'Nah, we're seniors.' John puffed out his meager chest. 'We know it all already.'

'Uh-huh.' The dude was completely relaxed, standing solidly in a green polo shirt and khakis, like a model from the *Preppy Handbook*.

'You at UCSC or a real person?' Holly asked. He was definitely not a freshman.

'I'm a senior. You all in the same dorm?' The question was addressed to Holly.

She lifted an eyebrow. 'Why d'you want to know?'

'Friendly curiosity.' He hadn't stopped staring, but she didn't get a threatening or predatory vibe. Course Ted Bundy's victims thought he was a charmer too. Holly had the feeling that if she told him her dorm name, he'd come find her, and that if she didn't, he still might try. Even weirder, she, who usually took a long time to notice and return a guy's interest, wanted him to find her as well.

Definitely out of control tonight.

'Dude!' A shout behind her, who knew which one. 'You're bogarting the party.'

'Sorry.' The guy nodded his apology, then started walking backwards, not taking his eyes off Holly. 'Have fun. Be careful.'

She watched the distance widening between them from a

place of muddled panic. She wanted him to be able to find her. Didn't she? Was she in any position to judge right now? What if every year he scouted freshmen girls and already had a list a mile long? What if when she woke up sober, she wished she'd never given the guy any encouragement at all?

He turned and stepped off the deck.

Holly rose to standing. '*Hey.*'

The guy turned back, a silhouette now at the corner of the house. 'Yes?'

'I'm in Galileo.'

The grin again, the merest flash through the darkness, but it was there. A hand waved, and he disappeared, leaving Holly to realize she was standing shivering, surrounded by five guys she didn't know, all of whom had been stunned into gaping silence by her totally forgotten nakedness.

The next morning, Holly woke up smelling of chlorine, with a thick pasty fog in her head, mouth and sinuses. Served her right. She'd been drinking too much every night since she arrived on campus, set free from the anger and resentment clouding her home. Without being around other people breathing the same foul atmosphere, it was easier to push the pain away, at least consciously. Dad had been back from jail for a year. First thing he did after walking into their new mini-home was find Holly and apologize. Thanks, Dad, but too little too late. He hadn't been there while she and Mom had the humiliating burden of packing up and selling their big, beautiful house in Santa Monica. Nor did he have to explain to their neighbors and friends that they were moving to a much less affluent neighborhood, and why. He also got out of the fun of choosing a tiny condo in Torrance, then having to sell two thirds of the stuff Holly had grown up with in order to squeeze into it. Even being here at UCSC was a reminder. Holly and her parents had battled for months. She wanted to be a professional dancer. They wanted her to go to college. The compromise was college at a place where dance was taken seriously. When Dad ruined the family, she not only had to give up her dreams, but had to take a year off while her friends all went off to college or ballet school, and work two utter shit jobs to be able to afford tuition and board at this place.

So maybe she was entitled to overdo the partying a little. Except that even though she was no longer majoring in dance, Holly still planned to do plenty of it, and should be taking better care of her body.

She dragged herself out of bed – apparently Sherry hadn't come home last night, ahem – and across the narrow white hallway into the empty bathroom, where she did her best to clean up and de-stink so at least she'd look better than she felt.

Food would help, and water. Coffee might, or it might make her stomach more sour. If that guy, the one outside the hot tub, actually came by today looking for her, half human would be the best she could do. More likely he wouldn't show up. Either he'd change his mind, he'd never meant to follow through in the first place, or he intended to wait a few days so he wouldn't look too eager. Above all else, guys needed to maintain their precious cool.

Outside the door, Holly stood blinking painfully in the scalding sunlight – as in scaldingly bright. The temperature was pleasant as usual. Santa Cruz didn't seem to know how to do bad weather.

She climbed gingerly down the stairs and headed toward the dining hall. Several yards later, she stopped short, thrills firing off inside her. He was sitting against one of the giant fir trees that grew all over campus, reading a book. As if he sensed her, he looked up, and that slow, sweet grin lit his face, making her thrill machine work harder.

'Hi.' He closed the book, picked up a cloth bag lying next to him and stood easily, not using his hands. 'I brought some coffee and muffins to share. You have time?'

His vowels were broader than hers, 'kah-fee'. Not an accent she'd heard before. Shyness made her look around for a few seconds, smiling in spite of wanting to pretend his showing up was no big deal, not even sure why it *was* such a big one. 'I guess, yeah. What's your name?'

'Lyle Frederick. You're Holly.'

'Yes.' She walked toward him, stopped about two yards away. Seen in broad daylight, he was even cuter than the night before. 'Holly Penny.'

'Nice to meet you again. We can stay here, or I can drive us to the beach. Which would you like?'

Holly considered, hand shielding her eyes from the sun. Beach was always tempting, but she wanted to get a better sense of Lyle Frederick before she committed to being in his car. 'Here is fine.'

'Sure.' He led them back on the path to the grassy Lower Quad, where they sat in the shade among other kids enjoying the late Saturday morning. 'How are you liking UCSC?'

'Good so far.' She was stupid-nervous, when all week long she'd done nothing but meet new people one after another and been fine. 'I like my roommate. My classes are okay.'

'You don't sound that thrilled.' He pulled a good-sized thermos out of his bag, then handed her a red mug, keeping a black one for himself. 'How do you like your coffee?'

'Black, please.' While she held the mug steady and Lyle Frederick poured, Holly studied his face. Good cheekbones, sharp, slender nose, well-shaped jaw, dynamite lips that would look feminine in a less masculine face. His thick wheat-colored hair had a cowlick in front that made it start up hopefully, then lose the battle to gravity and swoop in a smooth arc over his forehead. Every strand was in place, tempting her to reach over and tousle, just to see what he'd do.

'Tell me why you aren't more excited about our beautiful institution.' He handed her the mug and stretched out his nicely muscled legs.

'I'm sure I'll adjust.' She took a careful sip. 'This is delicious. Definitely not from the dining hall.'

'Nope. My private stash from Santa Cruz Coffee Roasting. Best in town.'

'What dorm are you in?'

'Off-campus.' He pointed west. 'Oceanview Apartments.'

'Literally? Ocean view, I mean?'

'Yup.'

'Holy high rent, Batman.'

He shrugged. 'I inherited a little money when my grandpa died. You haven't answered my question about UCSC.'

'Oh, right.' She lifted and resettled to avoid a lump in the grass, careful not to spill coffee on her favorite shorts. 'I do like it here, I'm probably being bratty. Santa Cruz wasn't my first choice.'

'What was?'

'NYU Tisch School of the Arts.'

'Didn't get in?'

'Didn't get to apply. My family dabbled in financial ruin.' And didn't she sound exactly like the bitter brat she'd just said she was? 'I'm working on my attitude, though.'

'By getting naked in hot tubs.'

His perceptiveness startled her. 'That was my first.'

'Whatever floats your boat.' He reached into the bag again. 'Blueberry muffin?'

'Sure, thanks.' She took one. They looked home-made and smelled buttery and delicious. 'Where are you from? You have an accent.'

'No, *you* have an accent.' He was teasing her. 'I'm from Milwaukee, Wisconsin.'

'Wis-kaaaahnsin,' she imitated. 'Beer town, right?'

'Beer, cheese, Green Bay Packers, *Laverne and*—'

'*Shirley*, yes! I forgot that series was set there. Goofy show.' She bit into the muffin, which tasted as good as it smelled and made her realize she was starving. 'What made you want to come here?'

He gestured around them with his cup. 'Look at it. Gorgeous campus. Gorgeous weather. Gorgeous location.'

'*That's* what mattered to you? Not academics?'

'That's what mattered to me.' He grinned, and she wasn't quite sure if he was teasing or serious. She hadn't pegged him as an intellectual lightweight. But maybe her fantasy brain was doing the thinking for her.

'These muffins are incredible, by the way.'

'Thanks.' He sipped more coffee, looking up at the trees in the courtyard. 'I believe that nurturing and enjoying beauty is the most important part of being alive.'

'Physical beauty?'

'Physical, natural, beauty of spirit, beauty of intention, beauty of caring. Beauty in art and music and architecture, in sports and literature and philosophy.'

'There's beauty in philosophy?'

He laughed. 'All things that contribute to the richness of life in a positive way. Good thoughts, good views, good friends, good food.'

'You're an aesthete.' She pretended not to think the word was cool. 'Or a hedonist.'

'Yeah, but not so much in a self-serving way, I hope. I believe in improving society at large, wherever I can reach.'

'Your parents were hippies. Or no, schoolteachers.'

'Definitely neither.' He carefully peeled off half the paper from his muffin. 'My dad is a serious capitalist, but his profit-centered version of life never felt real to me, or enough. When I graduated high school, my Grandpa Frederick sent me abroad to backpack through Europe. I lived in hostels and earned money when and where I could, just enough to keep me going. That year opened up the world, showed me how other people live and what they value. It also confirmed that my father's vision was not only small and twisted, but didn't fit me. I felt I could start a more vivid and useful life here in California than . . . somewhere else. And now you think I'm nuts.'

'Totally,' she agreed cheerfully. 'You can't ignore ugliness. It's as much part of life as anything else. You need to accept it.'

'I'm not ignoring it. I grew up studying and learning it – know thy enemy and all that. Now I want to work to negate whatever I can, and make sure I'm not contributing. I want to live generously, ask myself what I can bring to the world instead of how I can profit from it. How can I help someone else enjoy the world's beauty instead of internalizing its ugliness?'

He sounded way more California than Wisconsin. No wonder he liked it here. 'So what are you majoring in? Beauty studies?'

'English. What about you?'

'Mathematics.' She managed not to sound bitter that time. 'I'm going to be an actuary.'

'That can't have been your lifelong dream.'

'Why not?'

'Well is it?' He looked certain it wasn't.

'My lifelong dream was to be a dancer.' She ate the last bite of her muffin and crumpled the paper into the sack he offered, feeling much less like death warmed over.

'I'm not surprised. You move like a dancer. Why aren't you majoring in that?'

'Because . . .' she took care to sound breezy, not wanting him to feel sorry for her, 'I believe women should be financially independent.'

'Artists can't be?'

'Not as reliably as actuaries. I don't believe men should carry the financial burden of the whole family.'

His eyes narrowed; he cocked his head. 'There's a story behind that.'

She was taken aback, again, sure she'd not let her anger leak out. 'Well. Sort of.'

'I'm listening. If you want to tell me.'

'Well. No. I mean, it's fine. Sure.' She was rattled now, feeling he'd broken through a defense she'd been holding on to since she'd arrived on campus. The sensation made her feel both vulnerable and relieved. 'The short version. I grew up in a family with money, a spoiled only child, then Dad went to jail for some white-collar crap he was stupid, careless or amoral enough to get involved in. Mom had no job skills and fell apart, so there went everything. Our house, our boat, our vacations . . . and any hope of NYU. Everything.'

'Not everything.'

'I know, I know, I have my health, blah, blah, blah. But even you couldn't find beauty in sudden bankruptcy.'

'You're here, and you're determined to be independent, and you learned early about exactly the kind of ugliness I'm talking about. Greed for money, not only for itself, but to have more than other people. Greed for power, not only for itself, but to flaunt it over other people.'

Holly pretended horror, brows down, mouth wide. 'Are you a *communist*?'

'I'm a dreamer. A realistic dreamer.' He got to his feet without spilling coffee, and held out a hand to pull her up. 'Want to walk?'

'Sure.' She got up under her own power, to prove she didn't need a man's help to stand. They started south toward McLaughlin Drive, holding their mugs. 'What's your family like?'

'Mom, Dad and my Aunt Janet, who was like a second mom, sometimes better than the original, and my younger brother, Caleb. He's the good kid, I'm the black-sheep rebel. We have a family business, which my great-grandfather started as a small factory for industrial equipment. My dad got hold of it and now we manage and coordinate other manufacturers throughout this fine country and, if he gets his way, the rest of the world. I am supposed to inherit this miracle.'

'Not your thing?'

'Let's just say Mom and Dad are so far disappointed with my choices and decisions. All of them.' He held up a hand. 'No, actually, they approve of how I dress.'

She laughed. Cargo shorts, striped Izod shirt, loafers. 'You are very . . . neat.'

'Thank you. I think.' Their hands bumped. Bumped again. She found herself wondering what it would feel like to hold his, surprised by her reaction. She tended to be skittish with guys physically, even ones she was attracted to. What Sherry dove into last night with Mason would be impossible for Holly. Men always had to make the first move, and that first move almost always came too soon for her.

'I'm sorry about your relationship with your parents. Dad was my idol growing up. His implosion was devastating, doubly so since he took the rest of us with him. He told me he was just doing what he was told to do, what everyone was doing, in the company and the industry, but that he got stuck serving as the example.' That was the version she and her mother had dutifully spouted to everyone, and oh, the cruelty and unfairness of it all. Holly took a big breath. 'That might be true. But how would I know? Maybe he's a bad guy and I couldn't tell. Just because he's my dad and I love him and don't want him to be awful doesn't mean he's not. You know what I mean? It's totally confusing.'

Also confusing was that Holly was telling this man one of her darkest secrets fifteen minutes after they met. Was there such a thing as falling in trust at first sight?

'That's really hard.' Lyle touched the small of her back. 'I bet your dad is a little good, a little bad, like most people, and circumstances took care of the rest. I'm lucky. I knew my dad was a jerk from the very beginning.'

She snorted. 'Yeah, gee, that is totally lucky. I sure wish I was you.'

He stopped walking.

Holly turned back, afraid she'd offended him. 'What is it?'

'I was wondering.' He took a step toward her, with that same calculating but not predatory look in his eyes that had made her shivery the night before. It still did. 'Would you like to drive up to San Francisco with me? We can grab lunch for the ride, spend the day there, have dinner then come back tonight.'

She gave a short laugh, incredulous, but already calculating, thinking about the studying and dance practice she'd planned to do today, wondering if it would be so bad if she put it off until tomorrow. 'Today? Tonight? *San Francisco?*'

'Sure, why not?' Lyle took another step, his steady gaze hypnotic. 'There's a restaurant right on the water called Cliff House. It's a gorgeous spot.'

Holly felt her expression fall. 'I've been there. About five years ago. It's out of my budget now, sorry. But maybe we could—'

'No, no. My invitation.' He took another step. His clear light-brown eyes were making her a little wobbly, a little giddy. 'Everything's on me.'

'It's too much.'

'Not for me. I'm serious, Holly. It's not an extravagance at all. And I'd really like to get to know you better.'

'Oh . . . well . . . I mean . . . It sounds crazy.' And she sounded like a breathless dork.

'Maybe. But it will also be beautiful. Like all things worth doing if you know how to look at them. Like you.' He grinned his slow, warm grin, and just like that Holly fell so deeply into what she told herself was infatuation that she knew she'd say yes, even though she barely knew this guy and could never pay him back in kind. She also knew, in a burst of uncharacteristic and disconcerting intuition, that they'd have a wonderful evening, and that there would be more evenings like this one. Many more. Possibly a whole lifetime's worth.

Chapter 5

Holly half opened her eyes from the depths of sleepy comfort to find she wasn't in bed in her tiny guest-house bedroom in Santa Monica. Someone had replaced that with a spacious, luxurious suite whose curtained windows showed cheerful daylight trying to sneak inside. Instead of traffic, pedestrian voices and the distant roar of surf, she heard birds and . . . nothing. Senneck.

Drugged with sleep, lips curving in a contented smile, she idly moved her arm toward the other side of the bed, then realized with a jolt that she'd been reaching for Lyle.

That was weird, even for Holly. She might confuse more easily than she used to, but she'd never made a mistake like that.

She twisted to look at her phone, knowing it would take too long to read Senneck's wooden analog clock. The minute and hour hands no longer made sense to her. Numbers in general, once her close friends, had stopped behaving when she needed to interpret or manipulate them. At least she could tell time digitally.

Seven a.m. She'd slept deeply, twelve solid hours since Caleb had dropped her back at her room.

The memory of her humiliation in front of Megan danced a taunting jig. That had been one of the worst disorientation episodes she'd had in years, over a dozen at least. Life in California consisted of simple daily, weekly, monthly routines, and had done since Holly had finally been able to care for herself, and moved from her parents' condo into Melinda's place in the early 2000s. Understandable that there would be repercussions away from the familiar, especially entering this emotional terrain. Caleb had been very kind last night. For the rest of the weekend Holly would make sure to rest at regular intervals, and give her brain time to clear and refocus.

Yawning, she tossed off the covers and slid out of bed. After using the bathroom, she called for breakfast, which, she was assured, would be delivered shortly. Good, because having skipped dinner the night before, she was starving. Also good, because as much as Holly had fought hard to achieve and enjoy her current independence, it was utterly delicious, more than it had ever been, to produce a fabulous breakfast, well beyond her ability, by picking up the phone.

She'd never loved cooking the way Lyle had, was capable at following recipes, but not much for creative flair. Since The Change, following recipes had become a chore requiring so much energy Holly had finally given it up. Eating every meal alone didn't provide much inspiration for culinary brilliance anyway. Melinda helped immeasurably, bringing over fantastic meals as if Holly was doing her a favor: *I made way too much, we'd be eating leftovers forever . . .*

By the time Holly had showered and slipped into the ivory robe – because who didn't want to lounge around in silk once in a while, even if sweatpants were more comfortable? – a knock announced breakfast. What a breakfast. One perfect English muffin, made in-house, split, toasted and buttered, served with a pot of deeply flavorful strawberry jam, next to a glistening tumble of smoky ham and peppered scrambled eggs. Another plate bore a bowl of fragrant sliced peaches and deep crimson raspberries. And coffee, lots of it, black and strong.

The entire breakfast disappeared, leaving her in a food coma that nearly made her want to crawl back into the gorgeous bed, except coffee would keep her awake, and the day was beckoning.

Instead, she stepped out on to her balcony, into the cool warmth of a summer morning, and stretched out on the cushy chaise, gazing at the mountains while her body tackled the momentous job of digesting, until her phone rang and she was forced to move.

'Hey, Melinda!'

'Well? Is the place as incredible as you remember? Flunkeys ready to wipe your nose at every turn?'

'My nose is completely dry, yes.' She settled back on the chaise with a grin. Melinda's favorite sport, acting like one of the downtrodden when she'd be considered upper-middle class in Santa Monica, and filthy rich just about anywhere else. 'You'd love every second.'

'I'm sure I would. Have you seen Caleb? Is he still gorgeous? Still single?'

'I had champagne with him last night, yes and yes.'

Melinda sighed longingly. 'After my divorce comes through, I'm calling him. I truly believe his money and I are meant to be together.'

'So touching.' Holly laughed to cover her unease. Melinda had been manic since she and Matthew had finally agreed to split – him because he couldn't live without his latest sweet young thing, and Melinda because with empty nest looming, she'd finally run out of excuses to justify being maritally miserable. Mania was a fine coping mechanism for initial grief, but it didn't tend to last. 'I told him last night you were divorcing.'

'Did his eyes light with hope and love?'

'Uh . . .'

'I know, I know. I've got my work cut out for me. How are you doing? You haven't traveled in years. Emotionally okay, too?'

Holly cringed, thinking of the previous evening's disaster. 'I was tired last night, but I'm doing great.'

'Have you met the other wives?'

'Just Megan.'

'Ooh, the home-wrecker. What was she like?'

'Not what I expected.' Holly frowned, trying to think of a way to describe Megan. 'Beautiful, young, probably in her thirties, perfectly put together, but not in a classic way. A little in-your-face. Mom would call her "rough around the edges".'

'Ah.' Melinda chuckled. 'Lyle's Eliza Doolittle? Bring the girl out of the gutter and teach her to be a proper lady?'

Holly rolled her eyes. Melinda had adored everything about Lyle until they separated, at which point everything wonderful about him became suspect and bordering on evil. 'She doesn't strike me as the type who'd take instruction. I'm sure he fell for her for good reasons.'

'Uh-huh. Two, between her ribs and chin.'

That wouldn't have been enough for Lyle. But Melinda had the right to be cynical and bitter with divorce pending from a cheating jerk. 'You know what's weirder?'

'I'm not sure I want to.'

'Lyle hadn't told either of the wives about me. They didn't know he'd been married before Eliana.'

'You're *kidding*.' Melinda gasped. 'He wiped you clean? Just like that? What a buttmunch!'

Holly made a face. She missed the part of her brain that would have said 'Telling Melinda is a bad idea' *before* she told her. 'So what's going on today in Santa Monica? Must be a

64

completely different place after twenty-four hours.'

'Ugh. Hannah just found out who her roommates are going to be this fall at Stanford.'

'That's bad?'

'No, no, it's great. I'm just a wreck that my baby is going to college.'

'She's going awfully young. Isn't she still five?'

'I know, it's . . . actually, it's terrifying.' Melinda's cheerful act collapsed into a wail. 'I'll barely be a mom anymore. Or a wife. I'll be nothing.'

'You will *always* be a mom. And you will continue to be a sexy, fantastic, brilliant woman in front of whom men will prostrate themselves.' In Holly's opinion, what Melinda really needed was time away from both men and children to remember who she was.

'Of course, you're right.' Her friend laughed, but not like it was fun to do. 'So what's on the schedule today? Or should I call it a shed-yool?'

'There's a reception tonight before dinner. Most people arrive closer to the actual ceremony, so it will just be me, Caleb and the wives.'

'What? I don't know.' Melinda answered someone out of Holly's hearing. 'Listen, Hol, I gotta go. Hannah can't find her stupid soccer cleats.'

'And you will miss having her home how much?'

'Point taken. Have a good time, be careful, and call me when anything fun happens.'

'You can count on it.'

Holly hung up and noticed the message light blinking on the room's phone, which by default was set to voicemail instead of ringing so as not to bother guests. Caleb must have been checking on her.

She picked up the receiver and dialed into the system. A woman's voice, rich and musical.

'Holly, this is Eliana, Lyle's second wife. I wondered if you'd like to take a walk with me later this morning so we can get to know one another a little without everyone watching, if you know what I mean. You can reply through the hotel or text me.' She rattled off her number, thanked Holly – as if Holly had done something she should be grateful for – and hung up.

Holly squared her shoulders, lifted her chest, then indulged her centered self in some good healthy breathing. It was hard not to associate Eliana with pain and bitterness. After Holly and Lyle agreed to separate, he left LA to run his family's company foundation in Milwaukee, while Holly continued to work on her recovery. They kept in touch by phone at least weekly. Having been best friends since the day they met, they couldn't live without each other entirely. As she improved, Holly had started to believe they could make the marriage work again. Love like theirs could never be extinguished, even if it took ten more years, even if they dated other people.

Lyle had found Eliana fairly quickly in Milwaukee, and started dating her very casually. They were both lonely, he'd said. Fair enough. Holly was in no shape to date; she couldn't blame him for wanting company. If anything, his friendship with Eliana accelerated Holly's fight to recover far enough that they could realistically re-evaluate their future.

Mere months after they met – it was longer, of course, but it felt like no time at all – Lyle was on the phone telling her he was getting remarried, and the precious little left in Holly's life to look forward to shattered. And so did she.

None of that was Eliana's fault. She hadn't been aware that Lyle was so recently married. Meeting her now was a good idea. As she'd pointed out, much easier than at tonight's reception, with onlookers. Holly replayed her message twice, making sure she wrote down the number correctly before she texted Eliana suggesting they meet at the main building's side entrance in half an hour, and got a quick reply agreeing.

After several wasted minutes fretting over the outfits her mother had sent – she would not repeat the mistake of meeting a Lyle Wife looking like the Queen of Frump – Holly chose a colorful tropical-print skirt and teal top, and, since heels were part of her distant past, a pair of strappy natural sandals. The elasticized-waistband skirt didn't have a front or back – thanks, Mom! – so that went on easily, and she tried only once to get the right foot into the wrong shoe. Finally dressed, with ten minutes to spare, she put on light makeup and gathered her dancer's long hair, which she'd refused to cut no matter how often her mother commented, into a high ponytail, then checked out the look.

Pretty nice. Melinda didn't have a full-length mirror in her guest house, so it had been a while since Holly had gotten the whole picture. Maybe Senneck catered to its customers by installing new reflective technology that made guests look thinner, taller and younger. Or maybe Holly had been feeling so crappy last night, she'd woken up thinking she looked that way too.

Impulsively, she grabbed her phone and texted her mother: *Thanks for the clothes. You were right, I need them.*

Her mom wrote back immediately: *OF COURSE I WAS RIGHT.*

Holly grinned: *First time for everything.*

At the door, her cane hung patiently waiting. She pulled it off the handle, remembering the days when she could float downstairs with full-on dancer's grace, hardly seeming to touch each step.

Forcing herself into her pre-accident gait, she marched across the hall and took the elevator to the lobby, trying not to look as nervous as she felt. Before The Change, Holly had no problem chatting with strangers. Now, meeting someone was a grim reminder that this new, not-improved version of her was all they'd ever know.

Downstairs, Eliana was waiting. Tall, slender, dark hair and eyes – Lyle clearly had a type. But where Megan embodied edgy confidence and sexuality, on first impression at least, Eliana was all approachable elegance and, judging by her eyes and smile, genuine warmth. A glance at Holly's cane, the merest flicker, spoke also of good manners. And Eliana was only ten years Holly's junior instead of Megan's twenty.

Holly relaxed some.

'Hello, it's good to meet you.' Eliana extended her hand. 'In a totally bizarre situation.'

'Pretty strange.' Holly shook, pleased by the firmness of Eliana's grip. 'But it's nice to meet you, too. I even mean that.'

'We should survive this, then.' Eliana gestured toward the side door off the lobby, which led on to the grassy lawn cut with paths, some of which meandered toward and through woods before branching into steeper mountain trails. Others took gentler routes around and through the Senneck compound and its various offerings. 'You okay to walk the outer loop?'

'I'd love to. It's a beautiful day.'

Outside, the temperature was perfect, the air still dew-fresh. Drops sparkled here and there on the grass like ephemeral diamonds. The birds sang to the sun or trees or each other; bumblebees and butterflies investigated garden blooms. A scene straight out of Disney. Or Stephen King, right before something evil erupted through the earth and swallowed everything.

'Look at this place.' Eliana flung out her arms to encompass the resort grounds and the forested Adirondacks, glowing green in the sunlight. 'It's gorgeous, every bit of it, totally perfect.'

Holly fell into step beside Lyle's second wife. 'It's certainly that.'

'When Lyle and I came here . . .' Eliana glanced over. 'Do you mind me talking about him?'

'He *is* the point of the weekend.' Holly pressed her lips together, wishing that had come out sounding friendlier. 'Which means no, I don't mind at all. We should all be able to talk about him.'

'Good. I wasn't sure. He and I came here several times, probably seven or eight trips.' Another sidelong glance. 'You did too, right? With Lyle?'

'Yes.' The picture stung. Lyle and Eliana wallowing in boundless luxury and each other while Holly struggled to patch together some kind of meaningful life. 'Yes, of course. We came here often.'

'I don't want to assume anything.' Eliana's laughter was nervous and deep, at odds with her higher-pitched speaking voice. 'I didn't even know you existed.'

'So I've been told.' Holly spoke drily, hoping to convey that the topic wasn't her favorite.

'Anyway, he brought me here several times. Which I already said.' Eliana gave another brittle laugh. 'Sorry, I'm nervous. Meeting you is . . . a little terrifying.'

'No, don't worry. Lyle loved it here, of course he'd bring you.'

Holly made that sound *too* friendly. This was hard.

'He certainly did love it.' Eliana showed her exasperation. 'I couldn't stand it.'

'None of it?' Holly stopped walking. It didn't surprise her that Bodie Bauer-Baker was uncomfortable here, but, admittedly

69

based on nothing but appearance, Eliana seemed to fit right in, wearing subtle, flattering makeup and a beautifully made dress in a rose-colored fabric that hung perfectly on her slender body. Tortoiseshell combs neatly pulled back her rich brown hair. Unlike with Megan, Holly was not at all surprised Lyle had fallen for her. 'Not even the hiking and the lake and, I don't know, spontaneous cookies?'

'They are good cookies.' Eliana glanced toward the path. 'And I do love hiking and swimming, but not here. I don't judge anyone for enjoying it, but for me it's too *exclusive*. I'm using the word's literal meaning – most people are excluded.'

'Yes, but . . .' Holly stared at her feet, reaching for the right words to make her next point, luckily a familiar one she'd had plenty of practice wrestling with during her marriage to Lyle. 'Nearly everything in the world is beyond someone's reach. Home ownership, restaurant meals, electricity, enough food, a mattress, clean water, clean air even. I don't know where you draw the line between what's morally okay to indulge in and what's not.'

'You have a point.' Eliana gave the path another lingering glance.

'Senneck probably seems totally middle-class to some people. Lyle and I were at a resort once with tunnels for staff so guests wouldn't have to see the workers.'

'That is disgusting.' Eliana grimaced. 'I wouldn't have lasted a day. Like they were sewer rats.'

'In French Polynesia, there's an island resort that costs something like twenty grand a week. Each cottage has its own staff and pool. Senneck has nothing on that excess.'

'I see what you're saying.' Eliana's next glance at the path was accompanied by a gesture. 'Should we . . .'

'Oh, yes. Sorry.' Holly felt herself color, and lurched forward on her cane. They were out for a walk, and she'd not only forgotten herself enough to stop walking, but missed Eliana's broad hints that they get back to it. 'I have good memories of this place. It's nice to be back.'

'I didn't mean to whine. This weekend was what Lyle wanted, so being here now feels like a tribute, not self-indulgence.'

'True. Oh! The rose garden.' Holly pointed ahead, smiling rapturously. They'd rounded the first of the four private cottages, exposing an iron fence formed into a solid wall by cascades of climbing pink, white and red roses. In its center, an arched gate through which the visitor entered a remarkably scented garden of more roses in every color, brilliantly designed to look like a careless free-for-all. On one visit, Lyle had reserved the whole thing for an evening, and had asked for a CD of waltzes to be played over the sound system. The two of them had drunk champagne and danced, waltz after waltz, surrounded by darkness and the scent of roses.

'The reception's there tonight, isn't it? So pretty. Lyle always wanted to hang out there.'

'Yes, he did.' Holly didn't need to say that, but it came out anyway.

'I'm sorry. Of course you knew that.'

'Don't worry about it. As we said, awkward situation.' Holly inhaled hopefully, but the breeze was carrying any floral scents away toward the lucky mountains. She'd have to wait for tonight.

'So back to what I was saying. When we were here, I couldn't get past how much money we spent, and how much good that money could have done elsewhere.'

'Lyle gave away plenty. Both his personal money and through the family foundation. That was super-important to him.'

'Yes, it was.'

Touché. Holly grinned at her. 'Of course you knew that.'

They approached and greeted a beaming young couple holding hands. Eliana threw a pointed look over her shoulder as they passed.

'For example.' Eliana had lowered her voice, even though the couple was already out of earshot. 'How do they afford this place? They're babies!'

'Software geniuses? Mom and Dad's treat? Honeymoon?' Holly wondered where Eliana and Lyle had honeymooned. If it had been anywhere near Hawaii, the first thing she'd do if she ever saw Lyle again was sock him in the solar plexus.

Past the rose garden, from here discreetly camouflaged by trees, loomed the athletics center – a full-service spa, a state-of-the-art fitness complex, and tennis and squash courts. Lyle and Holly had visited dutifully when they weren't hiking or cross-country skiing. As Lyle would say, 'So we can eat more tonight.'

'Do you mind if I ask about your marriage to Lyle? I'm fine talking about ours too if there's anything you want to know.'

'Oh.' Holly was taken aback. What could she possibly want to know about Eliana's marriage to Lyle? 'If you want, sure. It was a long time ago.'

'There are so many things I never figured out. Pieces I still haven't put together. And I can't ask Megan.' Eliana made a sound of disgust. 'Everything's a competition with her.'

'Ah.' Holly wasn't adding anything to that. When it came to The Wives of Lyle, she was Switzerland. 'I don't mind a few questions. Unless you're going to start asking about our sex life.'

'What?' Eliana gasped. 'No! I would never—'

She caught sight of Holly's face and cracked up.

'Whoosh.' Eliana mimed the joke missing her. 'Not about

sex. More like "Were you happy with him?"'

'Oh yes. Very happy. We had a wonderful marriage.' Holly shouldn't have said that. She could already guess Eliana's next question.

What happened?

Friends and other people who deserved to know – like Holly's boss or her lawyer – were easy: she told them everything. Strangers were also easy: she told them nothing. Eliana occupied an untested middle ground.

'Can you talk about what happened? Why you divorced?'

'I . . . changed.' Holly pretended to be lost in admiring the athletics center, from this angle free of the camouflage that enabled lodge and cottage dwellers to pretend it wasn't there. 'Our marriage couldn't survive.'

'Oh. I see.' Said in a way that convinced Holly she didn't see at all. 'So it wasn't because of him?'

'You mean his fault? No, not at all. He lived – we lived – a beautiful life, full of travel and . . . I don't know if adventure is really the right word. We went everywhere.' She made herself pull back the enthusiasm. 'I'm sure you did too. To Lyle adventure could be as complicated as being flown by plane and dumped into the Alaskan wilderness, or as simple as . . . I don't know, wandering through the heart of a medieval Spanish city and discovering a place with incredible fried seafood.'

Eliana looked startled. 'Are you talking about a specific trip where he did that?'

'Sorry?' Holly stopped walking again, confused by the question.

'What city was that in? Where you found the seafood place? What kind of seafood?'

'Uh . . .' Holly stared into the hilly distance. The memory had jumped up, she'd pounced on it, who cared? Why did

Eliana want to know? 'The place . . . There was a big ruin. On a hill. I can't remember . . .'

'The Alhambra? In Granada? The seafood place was there?' The intensity of Eliana's questions was unnerving.

'I don't really remember. Probably. Spain is full of—'

'Was there a long counter and neon lighting? Fried anchovies and razor clams?'

Holly turned to face her, able to picture the place clearly now, smell the clean scent of perfectly fresh, perfectly fried fish and shellfish, hear the musical chatter of patrons, see the small glasses of beer offered to each customer gratis, watch the cooks dip fresh anchovies in milk, then flour. 'Yes. Yes, that was it.'

'Los Diamantes. We went there too.' Eliana's musical voice had lost its tune. 'I remember because the seafood was so amazing, and we'd just had too much wine at this fabulous little tapas place.'

'Bodegas Castañeda?' The name came out automatically, Holly wasn't sure from where, because once out of her mouth, the words became immediately unfamiliar.

'Yes.' Eliana looked disturbed. 'I remember all this because Lyle made a big deal about how he was discovering these places for the first time, and what finds they were, and how fun to stumble over places like that together, and on and on. It made an impression because it seemed . . . off.'

'Well.' Holly felt queasy. 'I guess he wanted to spare you the weirdness of having been there with his ex-wife. More to the point, I guess he wanted to spare you the weirdness of having *had* an ex-wife.'

'I would rather he'd been honest. Not that it really matters anymore. I remarried, maybe you knew?'

'I did know.' Caleb had told her somewhere along the way. They were approaching the final turn to the path before it

74

meandered down to the lake. The stables were here, and the paddock, now occupied by a half dozen grazing horses. Holly tried to find the chestnut with white socks she'd always chosen and Lyle's bay, before realizing – of course – those animals would be retired or dead by now. Before they met, Lyle had loved to ride, having taken lessons as a kid at Highland Hunters near Milwaukee, and spent a summer vacation with his family at a 'dude ranch'. Holly, on the other hand, had seen horses. That was it for her.

On their first ride together, she'd been nervous and clumsy on the chestnut. Lyle's directions and hints, meant to be helpful, felt constant and patronizing. *Now here's how you jump*. He'd cantered toward a low fence . . . where the horse stopped short, and Lyle sailed over. Holly had doubled over laughing. He'd gotten up grinning, brushing himself off. *See how it's done? Now you try*. Holly had learned quickly – no jumping! – and they'd taken several rides on trails up into the mountains for mouth-watering picnics packed by the Senneck staff.

'We're a much better fit than Lyle and me.' Eliana gave her deep nervous laugh. 'In case that . . . I don't know, in case it matters to you.'

Holly had to make an effort to remember what they'd been talking about. 'I'm happy for you, truly. How did you meet your husband?'

'I met Jeremy at synagogue.' They passed the middle-aged couple Holly had seen on the terrace the previous day, the wife walking a few steps behind her spouse, neither smiling. Holly offered a greeting, unreturned. She didn't understand. She and Lyle were lucky, granted, but why not ditch misery for happiness when you could? Even Melinda was finally doing it. 'He was a widower with two young sons.'

'And how did you meet Lyle?'

'In a coffee shop.' Eliana pointed to the path that led across more beautiful lawn and gardens to the gazebo where Holly and Lyle had been – no, Holly and *Caleb* – had been last night. 'Would you like to branch off here or keep going to the lake?'

'Oh, the lake. It's so pretty, and I haven't been down there yet.' They kept walking on the narrowed path, edged by lilies and ornamental grasses. 'You were telling me how you met Lyle.'

'Yes. I was working as a barista after I graduated college. I was a mess, no idea who I was or where I was heading.'

'Pretty typical for that age.'

'It was and it wasn't. I grew up in— Do you even want to hear this story?'

'Of course.' Holly said the polite thing automatically, bracing herself for images of Lyle meeting this beautiful woman and falling in love so soon after they'd separated. Just so damn soon.

'I grew up Conservative Orthodox Jewish. Pretty intense, but it was okay, and of course when you're little, the world is what your parents make it. When I was about to start high school, my dad decided my brother and I were being corrupted by contact with non-Jews and the amoral outside world, and converted to a different branch of Orthodox Judaism, which was *super* religious.

'I had to change from normal public school to an all-girls' Orthodox school that was so new, there were only five girls in my whole grade. I almost never saw my old friends or spent time with anyone who wasn't also stuffed away in this little community, strict rules and limitations on pretty much everything.'

Sounded like life with a brain injury. 'That must have been hard.'

'For me it was. My parents loved it, though honestly I always wondered how my mother really felt. She'd never contradict my father. My siblings loved it, too, but they were a lot younger than I was. I couldn't *wait* to get out of there. Senior year I was madly applying to colleges and found out my little school wasn't even accredited. I'd either have to make a special case or take catch-up classes. I pitched a fit at my parents, and Dad basically said, You're not going to college, we're picking out a husband so you can start pushing out as many Jewish babies as possible.'

'Good Lord.' The path started its descent; Holly slowed her step. 'What did you do?'

'I freaked out and ran away. My best friend's family took me in. My parents stopped speaking to me. I had to get a job, get my GED and put myself through University of Wisconsin at Milwaukee all on my own— Sorry, I didn't mean to start ranting about it all like that. I survived.'

'That took courage.' They were halfway down to the lake where the path grew steeper. Holly had to fight gravity's need to speed her up or she'd go ass over teakettle all the way into the water. 'You did a remarkable thing.'

'It felt more like a desperate thing.'

'So then you met Lyle . . .'

'Yes, so as I said, I was working at Stone Creek Coffee, not only cut off from everything I knew growing up, but now from the college community as well. I had no idea how to figure out what to do next. Then I met Lyle. He was very kind. He said he wanted to give me all the world I hadn't been able to experience.'

Yes. That would have been a strong instinct for him. Take the wounded bird from its cage, and heal it by introducing the beauty of freedom and discovery. Holly could picture how Eliana would have looked then. Young. Vulnerable. A bit lost. Irresistible to someone like Lyle, who couldn't bear unhappiness. Holly was grateful for having to concentrate on the steep slope in front of her. 'And he gave you the world?'

'He did, and it was wonderful. But then . . . I think the best way to put it is that I went from two very closed worlds to one that was totally open. Even though it was terrifying at first, I wanted to see everything, go everywhere, experience as much as I could. But solving an extreme problem by doing the extreme opposite isn't a long-term solution. I began to miss having a real home and stability. We limped along for a few years. Then he met Megan. Or rather Megan took aim at him.'

Holly made a non-committal sound. Swimming in dangerous waters there. Holly wasn't supposed to know Lyle met Megan while still married to Eliana.

If Lyle popped back into her life again, she was going to tease him over the soap-opera messes he'd made. She hoped he wasn't out there making more of them.

'I knew he wasn't happy. I wasn't happy either,' Eliana said. 'The marriage was essentially over. You'd think I'd be able to forgive her by now.'

Holly was distracted, working to keep her body weight back, steps slow. Nearly there.

'But the way she . . . I'm so sorry. Again. Here I was supposed to be asking about you and Lyle, and I've told you my entire life story instead.'

'I don't mind.' Holly would nearly always rather talk about other people than herself, and she was only a few feet from where the path leveled off. Victory was at hand.

'So where did you grow up, Holly? It's so strange coming here knowing nothing. Caleb was very cagey about you. I wasn't sure what to expect.'

'There's not a lot to know. I was born and raised in LA, met Lyle in college, and we moved back to LA, where I still live.'

'Oh, right. When Lyle and I met, he told me he'd been living in California. So that was true.'

'Well, yes.' The path was flat again; Holly had made it. She could now look at something besides her feet. 'He wouldn't lie.'

'No . . . he wasn't a liar.' The pause made it sound as if Eliana was searching for a different word, possibly not flattering either. 'I'm still having a hard time. We told each other everything, I thought. But he never mentioned you. This whole other part of his life . . . I can't make sense of it. I was hoping you could help me.'

They'd reached the sand at the edge of the lake. Holly looked out over the water, aware of Eliana's expectant gaze. She was remembering the late, late night about ten years into their marriage when she and Lyle had gone in naked, splashing and giggling, chasing each other like a couple of courting idiots. 'Until last night I didn't know Lyle hadn't mentioned me, so I'm not much help. I'm guessing he wanted to start over cleanly.'

Maybe.

Eliana kept her eyes on Holly, not appearing to register anything of the tranquil beauty surrounding them. 'How long were you married?'

'Twelve years.'

'*Twelve years!*' Her jaw dropped. 'He said nothing about you ever. Not even a slip. That is just so bizarre.'

Yes. It really was. Holly shrugged pleasantly, tired of the subject, knowing it would probably come up all weekend. 'Would you like to go wading?'

'Oh.' Eliana looked doubtfully at her leather sandals. 'I hate getting sand stuck between my toes. But you go ahead.'

Holly kept her smile pleasant. She'd expect anyone Lyle was with to be a plunge-right-in person. 'Sure.'

'One thing I do have to ask. Did you and Lyle . . . were you in touch after we met? After we married?'

'No, not at all. I cut off any contact. Even alimony. We had nothing to do with each other.' She couldn't hide all her bitterness, but . . . half-point for trying.

'Thank you.' Eliana sagged into relief. 'That would have hurt a lot.'

About as much as it hurt finding out Lyle had pushed Holly out of his heart in less than a year?

Eliana's forehead wrinkled again. 'Wait, you said *you* cut him off. So Lyle wanted to stay in contact?'

'As friends.' Holly turned so she could look her in the eye. 'We were not viable as a couple anymore and we both knew that.'

'Okay.' Eliana seemed to be letting something go. 'Well. We were wrong for each other too. Divorce is a brutal business.'

'Amen to that.' Holly spoke in a tone she hoped would close the discussion, then looked around for a seat. The tricky part of wading would be balancing while she took off her shoes.

'Have you met Megan?'

'Last night. Briefly.' Holly snorted. She didn't need a bench, she was wearing sandals. All she had to do was kick them off.

'I know, right?'

Holly took a moment to realize that Eliana had misinterpreted her snort as a sign she was on her side. 'We had a drink together. With Caleb and her boyfriend. She was pleasant enough.'

Holly managed to slide down the heel strap of one sandal and kick it off, anxious to get away from Eliana and into the coppery water of the lake, now shivering in tiny ripples from a sudden breeze.

'She's a snake. Don't trust her. Especially if she starts being friendly. She's capable of anything to get what she wants.'

'Oh dear.' Holly moved forward and tested the water. Blissfully cool and, unlike the Pacific, not rushing in waves eager to knock her over. She tipped her face up to the sky to catch the sun and sniff the sweet, clean air.

'She wanted Lyle for his money and his class and what she perceived as power.' Eliana's lovely voice thickened and shook. 'Never mind that he was married to me at the time. She came after him like a female Terminator.'

'I'm sorry.' As Switzerland, Holly didn't want to hear this. She wanted to enjoy the beautiful day, this beautiful spot, and fondly remember her Lyle, not this sordid story that had nothing to do with her or her memories of him.

'Did you know about the detective Megan sent?' Heavy sarcasm on the word *detective*. 'She said her goon could do better finding Lyle overseas than the State Department and the local police.'

'I didn't know, no.' Holly took another step out, planting her cane, swinging one leg gently back and forth, wondering why Caleb hadn't mentioned that. Maybe he'd intended to. Maybe it was such an obvious dead end he hadn't bothered.

'I met him. Rudy something. A friend of a friend of Megan and Bodie's, from a big Milwaukee mob family. The guy interviewed me and Caleb before he went. I swear, Holly, he was a hit man. A real one. I was terrified of him. Caleb was furious Megan was stirring up trouble all over again, after he'd done such a good job keeping on top of the search. They had a big fight – another one. He told her she was out of line. She yelled at him that she couldn't live on nothing, that she needed closure. She needed a body.'

'Ah.' Holly took another step, wanting distance between herself and this upsetting scenario. Such a beautiful day. Such a beautiful place. Soft sand under her feet. Tiny minnows investigating her ankles.

'Do you see, though? Megan told Caleb she needed Lyle's

body in order to claim his money.' Eliana spoke impatiently, as if disappointed that Holly hadn't made the connection fast enough. 'I think she sent this guy over to find Lyle, and if he was alive, to kill him.'

The accusation was absurdly out of place on such a gorgeous day in such a serene setting. 'Kind of a big leap from understandably wanting the estate settled to having her husband offed.'

'Megan will inherit a lot of money this weekend, money she's wanted very badly from the moment she laid eyes on him.'

'One big problem with the story.' Holly leaned down, made a swirling pattern on the water with her hand, then looked up at Eliana with a reassuring smile. 'Lyle isn't dead.'

'What?' Eliana's voice rose in shock. 'That's impossible. Of course he is.'

Holly was apparently naïve to think people who loved Lyle would be pleased, or at least intrigued, to hear he was still alive. She went back to swirling the water, clear and delicious over her skin. 'I know it sounds nutty, but . . . if he were dead, I would know.'

Eliana gasped. 'Oh Holly. Caleb never told you?'

Holly sighed and turned reluctantly to find Eliana looking stricken. 'Told me what?'

Eliana folded her arms, hugging herself. 'That this *thug* Megan found actually managed to discover where and how Lyle died, and where his body is buried.'

Chapter 6

Holly's mouth opened to ask *What body?* But while her tongue moved to form the words, no sound came out. Her brain felt as if it were filling up with sand.

'It's totally suspicious.' Eliana's lovely face twisted. 'This detective, Rudy, goes over to look for Lyle's body and finds it right away when the police and the US authorities couldn't for months? I think he killed Lyle. Now Megan might not only get away with murder, but inherit Lyle's fortune and live happily ever after.'

Holly's legs gave out. She sat abruptly into the lake, scattering minnows, staring up at Eliana, whose features had crumpled into distress.

'I'm so sorry.' She waded in, offered Holly her hands. 'I'm so, so sorry. I shouldn't have said anything.'

Holly stared at Eliana's fingers, no idea why they were in front of her.

Lyle was dead?

'Holly?' Eliana's voice sharpened; she reached down and cupped Holly's arms, gave them a gentle tug. 'Can you hear me?'

'Yes.' She made herself move. 'Yes. Of course. Are you sure he's dead? Did Caleb say so?'

'Yes.' Eliana gave her a pitying look. 'Let me help you up.'

83

Holly stood with difficulty. Lyle's body. They'd found Lyle's body. He'd died, and Holly hadn't felt a thing.

'Can you walk? Are you dizzy?' Eliana fumbled for her cell. 'I'll call Caleb.'

'*No*, don't call Caleb.' Holly's voice sounded strangely high. Things around her were too bright. She remembered this feeling, had had it before. The shock of finding out the family's money was gone, that Dad would go to jail. The shock of finding out she couldn't breathe when she was choking, the certainty that she was going to die. The shock of finding out Lyle was going to marry Eliana.

She was sick to death of this feeling.

'I don't need help. I was surprised and lost my balance.'

'Here comes someone, thank goodness. You're going to be fine.'

'I *know* I'm going to be fine. I never—' Oh crap. Two staff members were speeding toward them in one of Senneck's fancy golf carts.

Eliana leapt forward and flagged them down – as if they could be heading anywhere else. Holly did not want Eliana around during an actual emergency. An earthquake, say, or a fire. The only good part was that annoyance was re-centering Holly enough to make her function better.

'Everything okay?' Two buff young men with handsome, concerned faces climbed down from the vehicle and strode toward them.

'She fell. She had a serious shock.' Eliana was clasping and unclasping her hands. 'I'm worried she might have had some kind of attack.'

'I was wading and I stumbled.' *Where* had they found Lyle's body? *When*? *Why* hadn't Caleb told her?

'It's my fault. I'm so sorry. I thought she knew.'

'I'm okay. I'm not in shock.' As if to mock her, the next shock symptom showed up right on schedule – she started shaking, therefore looking very not-okay, and very in-shock.

Stud number one slung a blanket around her shoulders, clipped on an oxygen monitor and unrolled a blood pressure cuff. 'Would you like an ambulance?'

'No.' Holly shook her head. 'I found out something upsetting is all that happened.'

'Oxygen's fine, pulse eighty-five.' Said stud wrapped the blood pressure cuff around her arm and pumped while stud number two retrieved her cane and sandals. 'Dizziness? Blackout? Nausea? Numbness?'

'None of the above.'

'The nurse practitioner on staff can look you over.'

'Please, I just want to go to my room.'

Stud one peered at the pressure gauge. 'Blood pressure one-forty-five over eighty-five. Elevated, but not dangerous. You sure you're okay?'

'I'm sure.'

'All right, let's give you a hand here.'

Holly let the stud twins help her into the cart while Eliana wrung her hands and a few guests gathered to watch. This was *not* how this weekend was supposed to go. Back in LA she went weeks – *months!* – without more than a mild stumble; maybe a moment of confusion, probably several moments of radical indecision, but nothing worse. She'd barely been here a day and already mortified herself three times. Exactly what Mom and Melinda had worried about.

She gave the onlookers a shaky duchess's wave and as much of a smile as she could muster, then let herself be bundled, still dripping, into the annoying vehicle and whisked back to the lodge and up to her room, where she was left alone after repeatedly assuring the nice young men that if she dropped dead, she'd call immediately.

Barely after she'd closed her room door, before she'd even had time to exhale, her phone rang. Caleb. Holly groaned. Eliana must have called him. At this rate the incident would make the evening news: *A Senneck resort guest collapsed during her ex-husband's funeral weekend after discovering he was dead.*

As soon as she'd changed clothes and collected herself, she'd call back.

Halfway to the bathroom, a knock on the door. Aargh!

'Ms Penny? Maid service. I can take care of your wet clothes for you.'

Oh. That was nice. 'Just a second.'

Holly ditched the damp skirt and panties into a plastic laundry bag and handed them out the door. They'd probably be cleaned, dried and returned before she finished lunch.

By the time she'd re-dressed, Holly was less shaky, but still bewildered. She'd long ago accepted that as things stood, she and Lyle could no longer be a couple. She'd also long considered herself 'over him', whatever that meant when you'd truly loved someone. But she still believed they could sense each other. It seemed impossible that his remarkable life force could be extinguished without her knowing.

The voices of those who'd helped her through the last twenty years showed up to comment. Her mother. Melinda. Her therapist, Sue. They'd urged Holly to accept that Lyle was not The One Great Love; he was an ordinary guy she happened to meet, happened to get along with well, one of many she could have fallen for, one who'd made poor choices when their blissful life had turned so unexpectedly complicated. Just a man.

She couldn't bear to think they might have been right.

Another knock on her door. 'Holly?'

Holly drew in a quick breath, shuffled over and unlocked the door, meeting Caleb's eyes, not bothering to hide how she was feeling. 'Why didn't you tell me?'

'Can I come in?'

She nodded, stepped back, closed the door and stood with her arms folded, legs parted to keep herself solid, wishing she had grabbed her cane. 'I had to find out that Lyle died from Eliana.'

'I'm sorry. Truly.' He spoke quietly, sincerely, but his face was set. Apparently a grim job to have to disabuse your brain-injured ex-sister-in-law of her romantic notions. 'I know this has to be hard.'

'Tell me what happened.'

'Eliana said she told—'

'I want to hear it from you. I was upset when she told me; I don't remember anything except that there's proof Lyle died. You should have told me last night, Caleb. No, you should have told me when you found out.' Her body wanted to sway; Holly corrected the impulse. She should invite Caleb to sit down, but then she'd have to sit opposite him at the table with her honeymoon bouquet.

She felt stronger on her feet.

'Here's what we know. Lyle was last seen in a mountain village in northern Thailand, leaving his hotel in the car of a guy he'd met there. The owner said Lyle was on his way to visit a monastery farther south, and this guy had offered him a ride. That was the last time anyone heard from either of them. Megan hired a detective, who found that a wrecked car had been discovered some months earlier in a remote location about an hour from the hotel, with two burned bodies inside. At the site, he uncovered a charred piece of Lyle's custom-made backpack.

Locals had removed and buried the bodies. We have no idea what happened.'

'Why couldn't the police find this out?'

Caleb shrugged. 'Officials asking questions can make people nervous. The detective got people to talk to him.'

'Eliana thinks Megan had Lyle killed.'

'Yes, she does.'

Holly waited for more. Then realized there wasn't any coming. Lyle was dead. *We have no idea what happened.*

'You should sit down.'

She hesitated, then caught herself swaying again.

'Chair.' He pointed.

Holly sat, breathing deeply, the sweet smell of freesias making her want to scream.

'I'm sorry, Holly. I know you thought you . . . sensed him.' Caleb closed his eyes against obvious pain. 'Maybe you can believe now that what you felt was his spirit.'

'Or my imagination.' She was the worst kind of romantic fool.

'Would you like to go kayaking this afternoon?'

She stared as if he'd turned magenta, unable to shift gears that quickly. 'What?'

'Would you like to go kayaking after lunch? You've had a crappy morning, might do you some good to get out on the water.'

He was nuts. Completely nuts. 'Caleb, not only am I a mess right now, but I'm not able to do that stuff anymore.'

'Kayaking? Why, what is wrong with your arms?'

Holly gave him a look. 'Nothing is wrong with my arms.'

'So?'

Her annoyance grew, and an odd feeling of panic. 'I can't do sports stuff like that anymore. It's dangerous.'

Caleb was looking exactly the way her elementary school nurse looked when Holly tried to fake her way into a gym excuse, arms folded, skeptical scowl: *You're not fooling me, young lady.*

She folded her own arms, pushed away the panic and gave him scowl for scowl: *You're patronizing me, old man.*

'We'll stay in the shallows, at the edge of the lake. In a foot of water.'

'I've been in a foot of water already today.'

'And survived. I've made a reservation for us at two.'

'Will you cut the CEO act? I'm not yours to boss around.'

'Two o'clock. Have a good lunch, take a nap.' He strode toward the door. 'I'll be by at a quarter to.'

She gave a furious-lioness roar. 'For God's sake, I told you that I wasn't—'

'I've been where you are, Holly. This will help in ways you can't begin to imagine.' A long, searching look from dark eyes that softened enough to remind her of the last time they had dinner in Los Angeles. 'Trust me. Please.'

This was a pretty piss-poor morning for Caleb to be asking for trust. 'I'm not going.'

'Good. I'll see you then.' He pulled the door closed on a smile. Click.

Holly's lioness had another good roar. *Bully.* Caleb's injury had been purely physical. He had no idea how terrifying the world became when who you were all but disappeared. No idea how your brain could betray you in questions of distance or judgment or basic instinct.

He just strapped on a new leg and bingo, good as new. Until they invented prosthetic brains, Holly would have full responsibility for keeping herself safe.

What a godawful morning.

She couldn't even pace because she risked tangling her feet with abrupt direction changes. So she stomped around the suite for a while, until her anger was replaced by nightmarish images of Lyle's burned body in a stranger's car, buried by more strangers, visited by no one.

A wave of weeping overcame her. She threw herself on the big bed and gave in, a half-hour of loud sobs she stifled in the comforter, probably leaving a wet, snotty spot, but tough. The staff had undoubtedly dealt with worse.

Finally the pain and frustration relented; her sobs calmed. She rolled over and gazed at the ceiling, sniffling. A last tear rolled down her temple and into her ear, lukewarm and nasty. Holly sat bolt upright and wiggled in a finger until it stopped feeling so creepy.

At least that made her giggle. She reached for a tissue, filled that one, then another, and a third, before she gave a long, shuddering sigh and pronounced herself better. Poor Lyle. He'd been so miserable last time she saw him. What a ghastly way to meet his end.

A second later, seeking comfort, she scooched to the edge of the bed, opened the nightstand drawer and pulled out the roll of Life Savers, dragged one out and put it into her mouth.

Orange. Her favorite. She folded down the paper to cover the next candy in the pack, and noticed . . .

It was orange too.

She tore the paper back farther.

Orange.

Orange.

Orange.

Lyle.

Her eyes filled again, but not with anguish. The year Caleb's wife died – when had that been? At least ten years ago. That year Lyle had written the plan for this weekend, after he'd rushed into marriage with two more women, blocking out Holly as if she'd never existed. Yet he not only remembered every flower of Holly's bridal bouquet, and which Life Saver flavor was her favorite, but wanted to remind her of both after he was dead.

How did she reconcile those two parts of the same man?

She got off the bed, washed her blotchy face and redid her makeup until she looked less like a puffy-eyed disaster of a woman and more like a puffy-eyed disaster of a woman wearing makeup. Then she called for lunch – including a glass of wine, please – and ate it on her balcony, enjoying the bone-deep relaxation a hard cry can give.

By the time she finished her lobster roll, served with an exquisitely seasoned cabbage slaw, juicy sweet mango and a gorgeously chewy coconut blondie with a cup of the house's excellent coffee, she was revived and calm, ready to forgive Caleb for his high-handedness – just this once. He'd been trying to help her through a bad spot. She was even feeling conciliatory enough to agree to walk down to the lake with him and watch him go out on the water in the boat.

After coffee, she had a brief, lovely sit on her balcony, leafing through a cooking magazine, remembering with an affectionate smile how much she and Lyle had enjoyed making dinner together every evening. He'd been in charge of the menu and planning, the shopping and scheduling. She'd show up, bleary-eyed from studying or back from the office and a brutal LA highway commute, and would chop or stir or mix whatever needed chopping, stirring or mixing, while they chatted about their days, about world events, about music, movies, anything and everything important to them, or subjects that weren't remotely important but which amused or annoyed them.

Holly hadn't indulged in these memories for years. Maybe that was what Lyle had intended. Let bygones be bygones, remember the good times.

Okay, Lyle. She could do that.

At precisely 1.45, she was ready for Caleb's knock, and opened the door with a smile that made him visibly sag into relief.

'You're coming.'

'I'm walking down to the lake with you. I'll watch you kayak.'

His eyes narrowed, then he nodded. 'Fair enough.'

She became aware that he was wearing shorts, and couldn't help looking down at his prosthesis, managing not to flinch at proof that part of her brother-in-law's body, familiar from his LA beach visits, was missing. 'That is an awesome machine.'

'It's been a life-changer.'

'A life-change-back-er.'

'Yes.' He gave her his charming Caleb grin, which made her heart soften. She'd been upset by their disagreement, more than she realized. 'I'm sorry you can't get one of those for your head.'

'Funny, I was just thinking that.'

They smiled at one another, until Holly dropped her eyes.

'I wish you hadn't found out about Lyle that way, Holly. I should have told you last night, when you said you believed he was still alive.' Caleb put his hands on his hips, face somber again. 'I thought it would be enough to say I was sure he wasn't. I didn't want to upset you with details.'

'I suppose I've been in denial. It was easier to imagine he'd just gone off somewhere.' She heard the grief return to her voice and cleared her throat. 'How about we spend the rest of the afternoon not being hard on ourselves?'

'Deal.' He gestured toward the hallway. 'Ready?'

Holly grabbed her cane. 'I'm ready.'

'You really need that thing?'

She rolled her eyes and left the room ahead of him. 'Let's go.'

In the lobby, they were greeted by the young woman at the front desk who a few hours ago had seen Holly brought in soaking wet. She stared a little too long, maybe hoping Holly would do some other goofy thing she could pass along to staff-mates. Gossiping about guests must be a common pastime.

Holly would really like to get through the rest of this weekend without making an ass of herself again.

Down by the lake, a good distance from the boathouse, two kayaks waited, one blue, one green. Two paddles, two life vests and two pairs of water shoes, bringing back in a vivid, sensory way that mere memories couldn't match the times Holly and Lyle had kayaked together. Here, of course; on the Milwaukee River and Lake Michigan; on various Hawaiian islands; on their Galapagos cruise; in Alaska, Australia, Belize, Baja . . .

Holly looked out over the lake, rippling invitingly in the breeze. The wind had picked up since that morning. Little waves lunged at the sand, miniatures of the ocean, like tiny yipping dogs doing their best to be fierce.

Her heart sped; her cheeks heated. She missed being out on the water.

'Want to sit in the boat? Just for kicks?' Caleb spoke casually, shrugging into his navy life vest.

She glared suspiciously. 'Is this part of your evil plan?'

'Absolutely.'

'I don't know, Caleb.'

'Tell you what.' He handed her the smaller life vest, bright yellow. 'We'll take it one step at a time, and when it gets too much, you can use a code word.'

Holly burst out laughing. 'That has to be the weirdest thoughtful offer I've had in a while.'

'Just sit in it?'

He was playing her, the cad. 'You sound like what I used to hear in high school. "C'mon, Hol, just lie next to me, nothing's gonna happen, I swear . . ."'

'Guys are famous for the technique.' Caleb picked up the turquoise water shoes, the smaller pair, and held them out. 'I asked for the bench to be brought over here. Helps with balance.'

'Thanks.'

'Not just you.' He lifted his good leg and teetered dangerously.

Him too. Holly was used to being the center of her own disabled universe. Sharing the inconvenience – to put it politely – was nice.

The shoes fit perfectly. She pointed, flexed, waggled side to side, loving seeing them on her feet again, remembering the sand grains she could never quite evict from her own pair, the clammy chill of putting them on wet for a second outing or swim. The way they inevitably started to stink if they weren't allowed to dry between wearings. The way her hot-pink pair had looked so tiny next to Lyle's black behemoths. 'How did they know my size? Don't tell me your brother had that in his plan too.'

'Nope.' Caleb was grinning crookedly, sitting next to her. 'That was me.'

'You?'

'Yeah, it's stupid. One of those weird things that stick.' A blush crept up his cheek. He seemed very busy adjusting the laces on his shoes. 'When I came to visit you in California, that time we had dinner at Little Door. You mentioned your shoe size. For whatever reason, it stuck in my mind.'

'I talked about my shoe size?' She was distracted by the

memories, by his blush. It had been an . . . unexpected evening.
'Wow, I must have been a fascinating dinner companion.'

'You were.' He stood. 'You ever been back to that restaurant?
It was a great place.'

'Nope.'

'Why not?'

She stood too, stared down at her water shoes as if they were
the most fascinating things on the beach. Because she couldn't
afford it. Because no one invited her. Because it was a special
date-night place and she hadn't had any dates special enough.
'Never got around to it, I guess.'

'Okay.' He moved down the beach toward the kayaks and
stood by the green one, waiting for her to catch up. 'I'll hold
the boat steady, though on sand it probably won't move around
much.'

'Thanks.' She was stupidly nervous. Or excited. Worked up
anyway. All she was going to do was sit in the damn thing, not
compete in the Olympics.

She surprised herself by climbing in like a champ, no wobbles,
no need for Caleb's steadying hand on the boat, blessing her
dancer's legs and the work she did to keep them strong. The
second her ass hit the seat, it all came back to her. Her feet
found the rests along the boat's sides; her fingers itched to hold
the paddle.

As if he'd heard, Caleb handed her one. 'How does that
feel?'

'Good.' Classic understatement. She was giddy. Tried not to
show it, childishly, though she doubted Caleb was one for told-
you-so.

'How do you think you'd feel about floating?'

'I don't know . . .' She gazed out at the beckoning expanse
of water, bounded by lush forested hills along its opposite shore.

Very wide. Very deep. Probably cold. She hadn't practiced self-rescue from an overturned boat in years. Decades. She might not even be able to manage it anymore. 'I don't think so. Not today.'

'Just a little.' Caleb grasped the gunnel and gently, steadily slid the kayak farther into the water. Waves made the front bob slightly.

'That's enough. Enough.'

'Okay.' He kept pushing.

'*Stop*, Caleb.'

'Almost there.' The bow wavered. A wave caught it diagonally, tipping her to the right.

'*Caleb!*'

One more stronger shove and she was afloat, too afraid to breathe. Freed from the conflict between static sand and moving waves, the kayak stabilized, bobbing in the breaking waves near the shore, but gliding unimpeded.

Holly sat rigid, paddle clutched in her fingers, adrenaline pushing her breath. *Oh dear God*.

The breeze gusted her to the left. Any farther and she'd start catching the waves broadside, increasing the wobble.

Quick. She dipped her paddle, took a stroke with the left blade. The kayak responded immediately, straightened. She took another hard stroke, then another, using both blades now, propelling herself into deeper water where the waves no longer broke.

Safe now, heart still pounding, she turned the boat to glare at Caleb, shout at him for putting her in danger. For ignoring her fear and requests to let her be.

But one glance showed the waves that had so threatened and terrified her were barely three inches high. In her panic, they'd been tsunamis.

Holly turned back, considered the full lake, feeling her body solidly centered in the kayak. Habit took over. She dipped her paddle again, and again, then surrendered completely, the rhythm coming easily back.

Sweet Jesus. She was afloat. Balanced. In control of herself and the boat, moving across the water with almost no effort. Exactly the way it used to be.

Almost nothing left of her life after The Change was exactly the way it used to be.

She smiled; the smile turned into a grin. Her shoulders relaxed; she paddled faster, heading toward the cold, deep, dark middle, no longer afraid.

This she knew how to do. This had not changed.

Tears rolled down her cheeks, and she laughed out loud, then couldn't stop, smiling and laughing like a complete lunatic. But look! A complete lunatic who could *move*! Without effort, without bumping into anything or anyone, without falling, without shame. Without fear.

With grace! With purpose! With style!

'You look great, Holly.'

Her grin wouldn't let her scowl at Caleb as he deserved. 'I should hate you.'

'I know.' He gestured to his own boat. 'After my injury, kayaking was my first time, too.'

'First time?'

'To feel like you're feeling now, as if you're magically back to how you were. It was a huge moment for me. I wanted to get you there.'

She was touched. 'It was still a dirty trick.'

'Same one that got played on me. You did great.' He grimaced. 'I squealed like a little girl.'

Holly laughed, not believing him for a second, moving the

boat, turning, totally in control. Why wouldn't she be? Lake kayaking was easy. How had she forgotten that? She should look for places near LA where she could get out on calm water. Maybe Melinda would want to go with her. Or one of the women in her book group. A few of them were super-active.

'If I ask you something, will you tell me the truth, Holly?' His eyes were hidden behind sunglasses that probably cost more than her weekly grocery bill, but his jaw looked purposeful.

All Holly's banished tension resurfaced. She fixed her eyes on the opposite shore, made sure to keep her voice light. 'Well, you know me, lying comes easily, but I'll try.'

'What would you do if you woke up back to how you were? If you could do anything? What would be the first thing you'd want to get back to?'

She tried to laugh, but the relief at having been asked such an obvious question was squashed by the pain involved in her equally obvious answer.

'Dance.' She dipped her paddle, dipped it again, gunning now for the whole width of the lake, before she had to return to the evening, to the cocktail party, to Lyle's other wives and her own clumsy damaged existence. 'I'd drop everything and dance.'

Chapter 7

Santa Cruz, CA
October 31, 1989

Dear Caleb,

Happy Halloween. It's so surreal writing to you in the midst of this bizarre time. We're still doing okay. As I told you when I called, downtown is a mess. It's amazing how you can know something intellectually – earthquakes happen in California – and still be shocked and surprised, even outraged, when one does, especially one of this magnitude. Tornadoes and hurricanes at least you can see coming. But to have a disaster occur without warning on an otherwise normal day . . . it changes you. Or it changed me.

Californians have a strange oh-well mentality about the risks. I guess they consider it worth taking on for the privilege of living here. I'm still pretty shaken up, so I'm not sure I agree. Good old Milwaukee seems pretty stable and sane compared to having everything in your life turned upside down – in some cases literally – in fifteen seconds. I'm still amazed that there were so few deaths here in Santa Cruz. If you look at the damage and collapsed buildings, it seems even more of a miracle. I think of the dead, not only here, but all over, and what their families must be going through. A loved one in the wrong place, maybe *by inches, in one wrong moment. A son turned back for one second to get a stirrer for coffee. A mother delayed by a few seconds leaving work. Minuscule decisions we make all day long, that we never imagine could become the difference between normal life and injury or death.*

At the same time I am grieving, I am also insanely happy. As you pointed out, asking Holly to marry me was driven by the intensity of the moment, the fear and the relief that we both survived. And yet, as the quake recedes with the weeks, neither my certainty nor my joy has receded with them. Holly feels the same. Some things in life are too rare and precious to risk losing, and there seems no point waiting. Carpe diem! *I know Holly is the woman for me. Though I suspect, having watched you with her, that you are a little in love with her yourself. I don't blame you. She's like that.*

I've been thinking harder about my future. I'm giving up the idea of business school. I know Dad will flip out, but he's already flipped out so many times over my decisions, what's one more flip? At this rate, he'll be able to do gymnastics for the US. He and Mom were definitely lukewarm on the engagement. They had their heart set on a dutiful woman who'd be appropriate decoration at all the cocktail parties and board dinners being part of Frederick Industries requires. Holly has great plans of her own.

I know it's hard for them to adapt to their eldest being such a disappointment. You, on the other hand, can now roar ahead and conquer the company in my place. You were born for it. I can't think of anyone better.

What I want to do is bring beauty and . . . culture's the wrong word because people hear that and their noses turn up, like I'm some nineteenth-century missionary trying to 'civilize savages'. But it's not that. I have a firm conviction – I'm certainly not the only one – that the world would be a better place if we focused more on beauty and creativity.

I can hear you laughing, wanting to call me a hippy long after hippy times are over. It's an impossibly naïve task, I agree. Human nature tends too strongly toward power, competition and violence. And yet, if you don't try to leave your mark in some positive way, what is the point of being here?

I'm a hedonist, not in the modern sense of always seeking to gratify myself no matter the cost, but in the classical philosophical sense of believing that all humanity should be devoting itself to pleasure over pain, and that the only things with intrinsic value in our universe are those which provide good to the maximum number of people. Capitalism is inherently flawed in that all we pursue is money. Money does not provide happiness except in the pleasurable experiences it can provide for others. Communism, likewise, concerns itself with money, competition and power, but from the opposite perspective, which is just as bad.

All right, you got a free Lyle Philosophy Lecture there. I know you are so amazingly happy and grateful to get these big-brother crumbs of wisdom. I wrote this in a pensive mood obviously.

Love, Lyle

Princeton University
November 13, 1989

Dear Professor Lyle,

Your lecture changed my life. I'm no longer going to business school after I graduate, or to work for Dad, I'm going to sit by my window and blare Mozart while holding up a Picasso. Soon there won't be a single world problem left.

Yeah, I don't agree with you on all of it. But there are a lot worse things you could do, and as soon as I think of one, I'll let you know.

There are days I see my life mapped out ahead and feel like I'm embarking on a great journey. Other times I feel like I've already got my toes at the edge of a quicksand pool and am about to take my next step.

I had dinner with a girl from French class tonight. It was fine, we talked pretty easily, but golly gee willikers, she's no Holly Penny!

Yeah, that was sarcasm. Holly is cute, she's funny, she's got a great career ahead of her, and I'm happy for you. You're crazy to get engaged so young. Mom and Dad called me a few days ago and asked if you were still with 'that girl'. Why don't they just ask you? Yelling at me about stuff you do is their favorite pastime.

I don't know why you keep insisting I'm in love with Holly. It's like you want to win at something I'm not competing for. I only met her twice. She's great (okay, she's perfect). But she's in love with you. The end. Okay? I am disgusted that you'll be taking a honeymoon trip around the world after she graduates while I'll be sorting mail at Frederick Industries and answering more furious calls from Mom and Dad when they find out you eloped.

I'm in a shitty mood today. Maybe I just need to get stoned. Or laid. Or both.

Caleb

'Bye, Crystal, see you Thursday.' Holly passed DCD Insurance's reception desk, headed for the front door. She was cutting her usual Tuesday internship hours short to do errands before meeting Lyle that evening for his birthday celebration.

'Leaving already?' Crystal, the receptionist, looked up from her typing. She typed more than any other employee in the whole office. Their boss was constantly praising her for how hard she worked. Holly's private theory was that Crystal was writing a novel.

'It's Lyle's birthday.' Holly took another step, only half facing Crystal, keeping her body off balance, poised for flight. Crystal could talk the ear off a cornstalk. 'I still need to do some shopping downtown.'

'Ooh! Birthday boy.' Crystal's heavily lined eyes lit up. 'What are you getting him?'

'The new Linda Ronstadt album and his favorite coffee from Santa Cruz Roasting Company.'

'Nice. Are you going out tonight? Dinner? Dancing?' She aimed a sigh heavenward. 'You're so lucky to have a guy who likes dancing.'

'We're staying in. I made him dinner.' Holly pointed to the exit. 'I really need to . . .'

'Ooh, what did you make, all his favorites?' Crystal rested her chin on her hands, settling in for a long chat.

'No, not his favorites.' Holly edged farther away. The door was so close . . . 'His favorites are like foie gras and pizza from this one shop in Naples, and Viennese—'

'Florida?' Crystal looked astonished. 'Pizza from Florida?'

'No, Naples, Italy.'

'Oh!' She waved away her own silliness. 'I should've known. He probably flies you out there for dinner every other weekend.'

Holly laughed as if the idea was ridiculous, when one weekend not long ago they had done exactly that. Over-the-top even for Lyle, but what a crazy, fabulous time. 'I really should go.'

'Oh, sure, sure, don't let me keep you. What did you make him?'

Ack! She'd almost escaped. 'Spaghetti and meatballs, about all I can make.'

'My Italian grandma always says, "It's the love in the dish that counts." How long have you guys been dating?'

Holly groaned silently. She should have kept going, but she couldn't be rude to Crystal now. Despite the slave wages, Holly appreciated this chance to get to know the business. Her plan was to work for a larger insurance company after graduation, one that would pay for the classes and training she needed to earn her actuarial license. 'We started dating early my freshman year.'

'And you're a senior now, so . . . three years.' Crystal poised her hands over her typewriter, then dropped them back into her lap. 'This guy is it, though, I can tell by the way you look when you talk about him. I bet he proposes as soon as you graduate. If not sooner.'

Holly took another step toward the door. 'We haven't really talked about it.'

'I can't wait to meet *my* Lyle.' Crystal dreamily swayed her chair back and forth. 'I can't believe all the things you do together. He is the sweetest guy. And so cute. And *rich*! You're so lucky.'

'Thanks.'

'Does he have a brother?'

'Yup.'

Crystal's heavily shadowed eyes lit. 'Single?'

'So far.' Holly gestured desperately to the exit. 'I really gotta go.'

'Yes, of course, of course – what about a cake? Did you get him a—'

'Cake too.'

'What kind?'

Enough. 'Chocolate, bye, Crystal!'

'Have fun!' Crystal waved cheerfully. 'Don't do anything I wouldn't do!'

'Okay!' Whatever that meant.

Holly emerged on to the sidewalk to see the bus pulling away from the closest stop on Soquel Avenue. Too fidgety to wait for the next one, she decided to walk. Universe Records wasn't much more than a mile, the coffee shop farther along on the same street.

She couldn't wait to see Lyle tonight – well, she always couldn't wait to see Lyle – not only because of his birthday, but because today he'd had his first school performance of the year. A couple of years earlier, he'd cooked up a hilarious and brilliantly performed one-man piano, guitar, drum and sax routine to expose kids to classical and jazz music. That routine had grown into a series called SmArts, which introduced everything from painting and sculpture, to woodworking, architecture and drama. A tough sell at first, each year more and more schools and kid-centered organizations signed on.

After the performance, he was having lunch with friends at Shadowbrook Restaurant in Capitola, and hanging out with them for the afternoon.

Holly was so proud of him. Between those performances, the painting classes he was taking, music lessons – guitar and piano, both taking and teaching – and volunteer work as a Big Brother, high school tutor, and meal delivery for older Santa Cruz residents, plus all kinds of reading and research on everything from business to Buddhism, he was as busy as she was. Lyle didn't see being stinking rich as a license to goof off, rather as the freedom to concentrate on work he valued and cared passionately about.

The twenty-minute walk down Soquel to Universe Records on Pacific Avenue downtown took her fifteen. She'd been planning to hit the coffee shop first, but she absolutely had to get him the album. Lyle had been crazy in love with Linda Ronstadt since he was a kid. *Cry Like a Rainstorm, Howl Like the Wind* had only been out for a few weeks. When Holly left his apartment that morning, she'd double-checked that he didn't already have the record. You had to move fast to buy Lyle music. One wall of his apartment was floor-to-ceiling records, tapes and compact discs, carefully arranged according to genre, artist or composer, which she teased him about until she found out she ate apples in the exact same way every time, and always arranged her M&Ms in patterns by color.

They had ridiculous amounts in common.

Holly found the album without much trouble, took it to the register and handed the guy a twenty. He looked vaguely familiar. Maybe she'd seen him on campus. The shop was quiet enough to hear the occasional patter of feet from the ballet school upstairs, afternoon lessons in progress. She could picture the scene perfectly, tall, willowy instructor surrounded by earnest kids, like a swan among colts. Holly was resolute in her long-ago determination not to pursue dancing professionally, but there were still bittersweet times like these that gave her heart a squeeze. Who knew how far she could have gotten in that world? Would she have excelled or become one of the broken hearts and messed-up bodies, used and dumped still young with no training for anything else?

Or both?

'Here's your change.'

'Thanks.' Holly dropped it into her purse, glanced at her watch and grimaced. Shortly after five. She wanted to make it back to Lyle's place early enough to prepare before he got back. Maybe she should have gone to the coffee shop first, to avoid the after-work crush.

'That's a good album.' The kid gestured to the bag she'd picked up from the counter. 'My girlfriend got it last—'

The most godawful bang interrupted him, followed by a terrifying roar. Holly gasped, clutching the album to her chest. Something horrible must have happened upstairs. All those kids—

An instant later, the ground tipped and shook. Above them, fluorescent lights swung wildly from their chains. Tapes and CDs flew off shelves. The horrendous grinding roar continued, punctuated by terrifying pops and cracks as if the building were disintegrating around them.

Earthquake.

Holly staggered toward the exit over the pitching floor. The front window exploded, showering glass. The screams of customers could barely be heard over the noise.

Stop stop stop.

She grabbed the door frame at the same time as the cashier guy. A cloud of black dust gusted by from the west, as if it were being chased. Holly clung grimly, riding the heaving ground, too frightened for thought or breath.

Then the earth behaved again. The roar ceased into shocking silence, except for a chirping chorus of car alarms. Holly scrambled out on to the cracked, deformed sidewalk with the cashier and other customers.

The car alarms stopped, replaced by gasping breaths and moans around her, a ringing in her own ears. The city had become a marionette, strings jerked by a manic child, now dropped to lie in a collapsed heap. On Pacific Avenue, people were emerging from every other building, stunned, into a scene made nearly unrecognizable by the destruction. Windows missing, bricks piled in the street, store signs dangling, walls and ceilings collapsed.

Twenty or so sobbing little girls in pink leotards and ballet shoes poured into the street alongside their dazed instructors.

Holly's heart hammered in her chest; if she glanced down, she felt sure she'd see it pushing out her shirt with each beat, like a cartoon character in love.

Now what? What was she supposed to do?

Where was Lyle? Her parents? College friends? She couldn't bear to think what might have happened to any of them.

Around her, people started comparing experiences and emotions in breathless half-phrases. Holly caught the eye of a hysterical ballerina and thought about going over to comfort her. The girl stared back blankly, then turned again to reach for her teacher, hemmed in on all sides by young bodies seeking comfort.

What should she do? Holly turned helplessly. What *could* she do? The streets teemed with people. Stopped rush-hour cars packed the streets. She wouldn't be able to get Lyle his birthday coffee. She couldn't go indoors anywhere. Aftershocks would happen.

She had to get to Lyle.

Trying to calm her crazy pulse, Holly put one shaking foot in front of the other, heading down Pacific Avenue, feeling as if she were deserting fellow passengers on a sinking ship, except the whole city was the ship, and its citizens had no choice but to be on board. Glass underfoot everywhere, bricks everywhere, sidewalks buckled to crazy angles, building after building with walls or entrances destroyed.

The Ford's department store roof had caved in, one wall collapsed. People were digging, trying to clear rubble, calling for responses from any survivors.

Traffic lights were out, all power out. It would be dark soon. Darker than any of them had ever seen Santa Cruz.

She had to get to Lyle.

The next instant the pavers under her feet moved again, tossing and shaking, less than before, but bad. Holly had the absurd impulse to step off the sidewalk, as if it was a ride and she'd had enough, as if the street would somehow stay solid and safe.

Creaking, cracking around her as buildings endured another challenge. People screamed, again caught by surprise, furious that they had to go through more, terrified the weakened buildings would succumb this time and tip into the street.

Make it stop.

Holly braced herself, clutching the album like a shield, until the aftershock was over. She stayed, rigid, waiting, breaths hoarse and ragged. How many more structures had succumbed? How many more people had died, crushed by falling bricks and beams? How many more would die before they could be rescued? Here in the city? Farther out? It was hard to imagine anyone anywhere going about his or her day normally. Somewhere they must be. Here the day had ended.

Another half-block and Pacific Avenue became too much to bear, too many people, too much destruction, too many taller buildings that might go down any second. She struggled on to Lincoln, heading for Chestnut, past the Nickelodeon theater, now a shocking pile of rubble, people frantically trying to clear it, *Anyone in there? Can anyone hear me?*

Holly closed her eyes. No one could survive that many tons of bricks.

People had died. How many? Where?

Lyle. No, not Lyle. She could feel him out there, okay, alive.

Mom. Dad. Melinda, her roommate Carol and Carol's boyfriend John, and on and on . . . so many others.

Pressure built inside, as if Holly had an internal fault line destined for its own earthquake. She wanted to scream, to cry, but her tight chest and throat could manage neither. All she could do was stumble. Toward Chestnut. Toward Lyle. Once she found him, they could make plans together. Decide what to do, how to get through this.

Forward again, detouring around collapsed walls, around crying people, hugging people, people staring in shock, people sitting in the street or on the sidewalk, as if they no longer had energy to stand or anywhere to go. Holly helped a limping older woman maneuver past a fallen tree. She lifted a little girl, whose mother carried a toddler, over a chasm in the street.

Sirens started somewhere. Later, the smell of drifting smoke.

Fire. Dust. Glass. Rubble. Destruction. Death.

She kept going.

Where was Lyle?

What if he couldn't get home tonight? What if he'd gone looking for her at work or on campus? How would she find him? Where would she start searching? What rendezvous site would he choose? How would she find her parents and friends? What if one or more of them was lying in a collapsed building? What hospitals would she have to check? How could she get to them?

She wanted to run, to move faster, but the sidewalks were crowded, the pavements broken. So she walked on, knowing where she was and where she was going, but feeling as if she were traveling the wrong way on a moving walkway. Time passed too slowly. Her body felt too heavy. Still shaky. Still scared.

Right turn on Laurel. Daylight was already starting to fade. The sun would set. Without city lights the darkness would be absolute until the moon rose. Holly needed to hurry. She kept on, choosing the least destroyed streets, trying to find the safest, fastest way, seeing her pain and bewilderment mirrored in the expressions of everyone she passed. The farther she walked from downtown, the less devastating the destruction, giving her hope the death toll wouldn't be too high, praying that she'd find Lyle soon and that her family and friends had been spared injury or worse.

She'd been through quakes before. They were part of life in California. But not like this. Nothing like this.

'Holly. *Holly*.'

It took her a while to understand he was calling from across the street, and then it took her body a while to obey her brain's order to stop and to look.

Lyle. Emerging from a cluster of dazed people, crossing the street, weaving through stopped cars to reach her.

She gaped, unable to take in that he'd found her this fast, that he'd found her at all. He was dusty like she was, a scratch on his arm and on his forehead. But here, and okay.

'Lyle.' She barreled into his arms, embracing him frantically, whacking him on the back with the bag containing his album. 'How did you find me? How did you get to me? I was at work and then . . . the shaking . . . the noise. I couldn't believe—'

'You're okay. You're here.' He was holding her, but she could feel his heart going as hard as hers, feel him trembling. 'I knew nothing terrible had happened to you, I would have known. But thank God. You're here. You're—'

'How did you find me?' She pulled back to gaze into his face. 'How did you ever find me?'

'I don't know.' He looked ragged, confused, exhausted, but alive. It came to her with a rush of certainty that she could bear almost anything except losing him. He was part of her heart. He *was* her heart. 'I was on my way home. Walking outside. And I just . . . came to where I knew you'd be.'

'That makes no sense.'

'Oh Holly.' A tear leaked out of his eye. He laughed and brushed it away. 'Yes, it does.'

'The Nickelodeon is gone, Lyle. Ford's department store is gone. Pacific is destroyed. People must have died. What about Mom and Dad? What if our friends are—'

'We need to get home, then we'll figure it out.' He was rocking her; she clung to him, not sure who was comforting whom. 'Look around, the damage here isn't fatal. My apartment will be okay. It will still be there.'

'Downtown was much worse. Downtown is horrible.' She lifted her head from his chest, remembering. 'Oh Lyle, it's your birthday.'

He made a sound, halfway between a laugh and a sob. 'Yeah, happy birthday to me.'

'I made you dinner. I got you a cake.' She giggled, a little hysterically. 'Dinner's in your refrigerator. The cake is hiding in your closet. God knows what shape that's in.'

'Let's go.' Gently he set her away from him. 'Let's go eat my birthday dinner together.'

'We can't go inside. It won't be safe.'

'We'll figure it out.' He took her hands, trembling like his. 'Bit by bit, like everyone else is doing. We'll figure it out.'

'Yes.' She responded to his logic and reassuring presence, inhaled and exhaled, squeezing his fingers. 'We will.'

'Okay then.' His clear brown eyes crinkled into the grin that still made her insides go gooey, three years after they'd met, and in the middle of a citywide disaster. He pulled her next to him, arm around her shoulders. They started walking.

'I got one of your birthday presents.' Holly hoisted the bag with the album. 'I was at Universe Records when the quake hit. I hope I didn't break it.'

'If you did, we'll frame it as a tribute to our survival. It'll be important earthquake art.'

Holly managed a smile, loving that he could keep his humanity, his courage and his humor even in the worst circumstances. *You learn a lot about a man in the bad times*, Mom always said. She sure had plenty of bad times to learn about Dad.

They walked around Neary Lagoon Park, through neighborhoods that showed toppled chimneys or fences, occasional cracked walls, but thank God not the collapse of downtown. They matched strides, moved as a unit even though it slowed them, because Holly couldn't let go of Lyle and he didn't seem to want to let go of her. They stopped twice, once on Centennial Street to help an elderly man drag a chair and blankets out of his house, and again on National to hold a screaming baby while his mother darted into their home for food, diapers and supplies. Lyle made goofy squeaky noises and bizarre faces until the child became so fascinated he forgot to cry, staring up at Lyle as if he were the most magical toy he'd ever seen.

Holly didn't blame him.

As the sun met the ocean horizon, they reached Lyle's apartment complex, seemingly intact, including his building next to Lighthouse Field State Beach. Reassuringly normal, though distant sirens and smoke and groups of confused, frightened residents made it impossible to pretend anything was still the same.

Lyle and Holly joined a cluster standing across Pelton Avenue from the apartment building, debating whether it was safe to go inside for whatever they'd need for the night. There was no question of sleeping inside. They planned to bunk down in Lighthouse Field, where they'd be safe.

Gradually the consensus turned toward chancing a supply run. A group of brave souls headed toward the entrance, including Lyle, leaving partners and friends to watch, wait and worry. When Lyle disappeared inside, Holly was nearly overcome by a wave of panic.

'Mind if I bug you?' A man had moved to stand next to her. 'If I have to wait silently while they're in there, I'll lose what's left of my mind.'

'I'd love you to bug me, for the same reason.' Peripheral vision told her the guy hadn't taken his eyes off the building while he spoke. Their combined gazes had to be enough to keep it secure, right? 'This is really hard.'

'Where were you?'

She didn't have to ask what he meant. 'Downtown. Universe Records on Pacific. It was bad. Pacific was bad. Much worse than here.'

'Yeah, I was just talking to someone who was walking out of Santa Cruz Roasting Company when it hit. The whole building collapsed. There were people in there. Customers. Staff.' His voice broke. 'I don't even want to think about it.'

Holly closed her eyes, trying to process the awful news. Some people could still be trapped in there. Alive? Injured? Dead? She prayed they were all alive.

Then the obvious took her breath away. If Crystal's chatter hadn't delayed her, Holly might have been in there getting Lyle's coffee when the building went.

The man was still talking. 'Downtown is basically gone. It's going to take years to get this city back to where it was. My roommate and I are moving back to Illinois as soon as we can pack. This earthquake stuff is bullshit.'

His statement gave Holly back her tongue. Was he nuts? 'No, no, don't leave because of this. It won't happen again. Not this big. You shouldn't leave because of this. California is fantastic. Illinois?'

'In Illinois the ground does this cool thing. It stays where you last saw it. As far as we're concerned, that makes it paradise.'

As if to prove his point, an aftershock made the palm trees lining the street shimmy. Holly stifled a shriek and grabbed the guy's shoulder, eyes glued to the three floors and balconies of Lyle's building. *Stay up. Stay up. Stay up.*

The shock passed. The building stayed up. Holly released her grip, finally turning to take in a vaguely familiar man she might have passed in Lyle's courtyard or seen by the pool. Thinning hair, dark mustache, glasses, stocky. 'I'm sorry I attacked you.'

'Do not apologize.' He shuddered. 'I practically crap my pants every time one of those hits.'

'Did I leave claw marks?'

'Not one.'

She stuck out her hand. 'I'm Holly.'

'Glenn.' As if on cue, they both turned anxiously back to their watch. 'Who do you have in there? Boyfriend?'

'Yes.' She folded her arms, wishing Lyle would hurry. 'Guy in the blue polo. You?'

'Same. Guy in the red shirt.'

'Ah.' Holly nodded, searching for the words to show him she had nothing against gay people that wouldn't come out sounding as if she were trying to show him she had nothing against gay people. 'Wish they'd hurry up. It feels like they've been in there an hour.'

'No kidding.'

Glenn's boyfriend was first to appear from the building, triggering a whoop from Holly and a prayer of relief from Glenn, who darted across the street and touched the man's arm, a far cry from what he must want to do. The two turned and walked into the park, shoulders bumping. It sucked that they didn't feel they could demonstrate affection, even in such a crisis. If her arms would reach, she'd wrap them three times around Lyle when he showed up.

One by one, others returned from their foraging and followed Glenn and his boyfriend into Lighthouse Field, either alone or joined by a relieved member or two of the waiting group.

Holly didn't relax until Lyle reappeared, wearing a stuffed backpack and carrying a large canvas tote and a suitcase, one of which he told her was full of bedding and toiletries, the other of food and wine, including the meatballs and the flourless chocolate cake she'd bought for his birthday. Damage in his apartment had been light, and he'd been able to call his family and to leave a message with Holly's parents that she was fine. After trying several numbers, he was also able to reach a friend at UCSC who said damage to the college had been minimal, and that an emergency generator was providing electricity to the campus.

They joined the other Oceanview Apartments refugees in the park, some of whom they'd said occasional hellos to, but nothing more. For the next couple of hours, they made new friends, chatting, sharing food, including Lyle's birthday meatballs and sauce, which were delicious even cold, and passing around bottles and cans of whatever alcohol people had grabbed to bring out. After Holly led a tipsy round of 'Happy Birthday', Lyle divided his cake into enough small pieces that everyone got a taste.

They traded earthquake stories, some mundane, some remarkable. Now and then, newcomers would arrive from wherever they'd been when the quake hit, and share their information. One neighbor had an old-fashioned transistor radio and checked news regularly, relaying the nightmares unfolding up north in San Francisco and farther south in the Santa Cruz County community of Watsonville.

A running loop through everyone's minds, the same questions: how many had died? How many still would? How to get in touch with friends and family? How many of their old haunts would they find intact in the morning? How much time would it take to rebuild? How much of their lives would go on as usual, and how much would have to change?

Talking, tied together by having survived a common enemy, helped take away the overwhelming feeling of being so small, so isolated from everyone and everything familiar, huddled in a moonlit park in a terribly damaged city with the entirety of space pressing down from above.

As time went on, the stories and conversation moved away from tragedy and disaster. People wrapped up in blankets and took turns playing favorite tapes on a player someone had retrieved. Candles flickered. Camping lanterns glowed. Aftershocks were suffered through with tears, frozen fear or grim tolerance. Silences brought to the foreground the comforting normalcy of rolling ocean surf, like the earth resuming regular breathing after a grand mal seizure.

Around one in the morning, a few people went back inside to grab instruments: Lyle brought his guitar and the group started with a series of improvised, sometimes badly remembered, sometimes surprisingly good renditions of songs, ranging from James Taylor to 'Mother Goose', until a large aftershock stunned them back into silence.

Peggy, on their left, started crying. 'I'm so tired of this. I want it to be over.'

Her friend hugged her, stroking her back, reminding her how lucky they were.

Lyle started strumming again, de Falla's Spanish Dance, a classical piece with irresistible energy and flair, one of Holly's favorite pieces, one she'd been toying with choreographing for a campus show she'd been invited to participate in.

'Holly.' He spoke over a riff of the song's dominant harmonies. 'Dance for us.'

'You're a dancer?' Glenn was a few people away, knee to knee with his blond boyfriend, odd shadows thrown on their faces by the lantern in front of them. 'I should have guessed by the way you moved. What kind?'

'I trained in ballet, but I'm more interested in modern now.'

'I'd love to see you dance.'

'C'mon.' Lyle nudged her. 'It'll cheer people up.'

She glanced around the circle to find people watching with curiosity, with interest. Even Weeping Peggy looked hopeful, as if she thought dancing could somehow ease this nightmare. Holly shrugged and got to her feet, pleased when a couple of people applauded. 'I have no idea what my dancing will be like after an earthquake and a couple of glasses of wine, but I'll try.'

She moved to the center of the circle, did a quick couple of shoulder and neck rolls, shook out her arms and legs, and stretched briefly, trying to shoo out the tension and invite in the dancer, reminding herself of some of the steps she'd been practicing. Then she lifted her chin, centered her body, filled her ribcage with sea air tinged with smoke and exhaled.

Lyle flexed his fingers, picked out a few notes, then nodded to her, eyes shining with pride. He loved her for her dancing, respected her reasons for giving it up. He loved her for her strengths and for her weaknesses. She loved him the same way, no more so than at this moment, when his quiet natural leadership came through, seeing past himself to what needed to be done, and doing it not with fanfare, but with kindness and generosity. 'Ready?'

Holly nodded.

'I'll be playing a piece by Spanish composer Manuel de Falla, from his one-act opera *La Vida Breve*, or *Life is Short*. Kind of a good message for today.'

Holly let the music go a few measures while she swayed in place, re-tasting its flavor, feeling its rhythms in her body. She took a few tentative steps, then a few more. Gradually the lively beat and muscle memory took over; her movements became more fluid, broader. Rarely did she manage to think more than a beat or two ahead, yet her body seemed to know the music, know this dance, even the parts she hadn't finalized or planned, as if she were channeling all those who had danced to it before, helping her overcome fear and uncertainty, honoring with her those who had and would suffer from today. Holly gave the best way she knew how.

Only once did the ground quiver under her feet. Her first instinct was to stop, react, tense, but Lyle's fingers didn't miss a note, and the soft gasps and cries around her only encouraged her to let the earth's liquid trembling become part of how she responded to the music.

She had no idea how long the piece went on – Lyle might have played it twice? – but she emerged from her trance to recognize the final chords, and forced herself away from the hypnotic effort and joy of movement, back to their small human circle in the midst of a terribly scarred and scared city.

A beat after Lyle lifted his fingers from the instrument, applause started and went on and on, from strangers who had shared this surreal night. Holly gave a brief curtsy and went back to Lyle, breathing hard, smiling her first effortless smile of the evening.

The look in his eyes as he watched her approach made her heart swell to fill her chest. She dropped down next to him as he put his guitar back in its case. 'You played like a god, Lyle.'

'You were incredible.' His voice was husky. 'I've never seen you dance like that.'

Her pleasure emerged in a breathy laugh. 'I guess trauma agrees with me.'

'Too bad. We're not doing trauma again.' He pulled her close, wrapped his arm around her shoulders, leaned his head against hers. 'After the quake, you were all I thought about, Holly. You are so deeply in my soul that I will never, ever be able to remove you. I love you more than anyone I've ever known, anyone I will ever know.'

She closed her eyes to let his words embrace her, trying to find a way to respond, knowing she could never say enough. 'I didn't know it was possible to love someone as much as I love you, to be as happy with someone as I am with you, to fit so perfectly with another person.'

He leaned forward so their eyes could meet, rested his hand tenderly against her cheek. 'Will you marry me? Will you spend the rest of your life with me, Holly Penny?'

She had no hesitation, no doubt, humbled and awed by the power of what lay between them. 'Yes. Yes, I will.'

They let their secret cocoon them, settling together on to the unstable earth, whispering, making plans, until exhaustion robbed them of the energy to speak. Holly drifted off in Lyle's arms, with their city burned, collapsed and ragged around them, thinking she'd never before felt so happy and so safe.

Chapter 8

Holly walked through the bloom- and vine-tangled gateway into Senneck's lush rose garden, stopping for a moment to savor being back and to remember a few truly beautiful times spent here with Lyle. She was early for the evening's party, but it had been such a remarkable feat not to be late and in a panicked rush that she'd decided to enjoy the small victory and go. The weather was perfect for the gathering, softly cooling toward evening after a warm, dry day. In spite of the difficult morning and the excitement of the afternoon kayaking, Holly felt energetic and centered, confident that her injury wouldn't dictate her behavior tonight.

A good nap and afternoon tea had helped.

The fact of Lyle's death still weighted her stomach, like something indigestible she hadn't wanted to swallow in the first place; but alongside the pain had crept in unexpected lightness. Holly must have been constantly reaching out, searching for Lyle's signal, like humankind's ongoing attempts to scan the universe for alien communication.

Tonight she looked forward to speaking about Lyle with those who had loved him, free of her parents' and Melinda's sneering and sarcasm. She was curious what Lyle had been to Eliana and Megan, how their marriages had functioned. Even if it hurt a little. Even if it made her want to pull their hair out with her teeth.

At the sound of her footsteps on the stone walk, Caleb turned, eyes lighting at the sight of her. Holly had worn one of her nicer dresses tonight, a jewel-green linen-blend sheath, more festive than the restrained outfit she'd wear to the service Saturday. The obvious reason was to honor Lyle and the occasion, but she'd admit to wanting to hold her own around Megan and Eliana as well.

Enticing Caleb had not been part of her plan.

He watched her approach down the middle path to the central paved circle where water tumbled and chased itself over an artful pile of rocks before sliding into a small pool. Around the cascading fountain, staff had set up two white-clothed tables, one for the bar, one for the food. Caleb looked relaxed and welcoming, hair damp from a shower, wearing shades of black and gray that tastefully rode the line between formal and casual.

'You look beautiful.' He kissed her cheek, staying close to smile at her. 'What would you call that color, emerald?'

'Emerald, yes.' She felt self-conscious, grateful for her cane or she would have had trouble figuring out what to do with her hands.

'It's your color. But you also look . . .' he tipped his head, 'I don't know, different. Vibrant, strong. You got some sun today.'

'So did you.' The faint color livened his complexion and set off his dark eyes. The evening light flattered him. He also smelled good.

She remembered him tasting good as well.

Stop. Holly needed to keep thinking about Lyle. And his wives.

'How are you holding out? It's been a long day for you.'

She wasn't going to disagree. 'I'm okay. The morning was

hard. But Lyle has been out of my life for decades, so nothing really changes except knowing.'

Caleb touched her bare elbow. 'I should have paid more attention, thought harder about how much to share with you. I wanted to protect you, but I also wasn't sure . . . what Lyle might still mean to you.'

The statement hung in the air like a question.

'You were being kind. You've always been kind to me.' She took a step back, pretending to re-explore the garden she knew so well. 'It's so beautiful here. As always.'

He looked around as if seeing it for the first time. 'Lotta roses.'

'Lotta.' They were everywhere, clustering in beds, climbing walls and trellises. Tiny tea roses edged the walkways; larger varieties stuck together in multicolored groups or twined stems to form tree-like topiaries. Simple single roses, elaborate multi-petal. Reds, pinks, corals, yellows – the smell was enchanting. Like entering a perfumed fairyland.

'I talked to the concierge today. Whenever you'd like to, Daniel can have a harness set up in one of the rooms at the gym, the type gymnasts use to train, with a wire attached to the ceiling. He can arrange private time for you whenever you'd like.'

Holly straightened from smelling a magenta beauty. 'Kayaking wasn't enough? You want me to do gymnastics now?'

Caleb grinned, the slow, sexy spread of his mouth that so reminded Holly of his brother. 'Not gymnastics. You'll be able to dance again. With the harness it'll be impossible for you to fall.'

Holly gaped at him while her cheeks reddened to a degree that, if natural, would indicate sunburn. She couldn't dance anymore. Her body was in decent shape, but dancing required a whole different set of muscles used in a whole different way. Not to mention her brain would no longer be able to keep up with complex movements and footwork. He might as well walk up to Nadia Comăneci next week and demand she repeat her perfect-score 1976 Olympic gymnastics routine.

'Is this why you asked me this afternoon on the lake what I would do if I could do anything safely?'

'Yes.'

Her mind went on protesting the idea, while inside another awareness grew, of a quiet warmth. This was an extraordinarily generous and thoughtful gesture on Caleb's part. It had been a long, long time since someone had gone out of their way to make any of her dreams come true.

Holly gave him a look. 'I seem to be your project this weekend.'

'Absolutely.' He nodded soberly. 'I also have a total makeover scheduled for you tomorrow at four a.m., followed by an assigned daily workout routine, and at noon a brainwashing session that will—'

'Okay, okay.' She held up a hand in surrender. 'I deserved that.'

'All I'm doing . . .' He touched her arm again. 'No, let me put it this way. After a life-limiting accident, it's easy to focus too much on what you can't manage anymore instead of pushing yourself to explore what you can.'

Holly's eyebrows headed for her hairline. 'You think that's what I do?'

'Yes.' He spoke without blame. 'And I want you to grab life by the balls and swing like Tarzan.'

She nearly choked. 'Yikes.'

'The world likes us compromised people better when we're noble and uncomplaining, when it can reward us for courageously

124

accepting the dung heap life threw at us. For being determined to go on at all costs. For being so gosh darn grateful every day for what we still have.' Caleb gestured at his missing leg. 'I think we need to say "Screw that, this sucks" and grab for whatever normalcy we can, even if it's cheating.'

'I'm damaged as hell and I'm not going to take it anymore?'

'Exactly.'

'"You're doing great, Holly."' Holly mimicked her well-meaning father's deep voice. '"There were days after the accident when we weren't even sure you'd be able to swallow on your own. Now look at you!" Yeah, Dad, now look at me.' She gestured to her cane. 'My marriage and career are gone, I can barely get through the simplest day, but darned if I can't swallow! All the day long!'

'Yeah, you get it,' Caleb said. 'There's always someone you can point to and say "Thank God I'm not like that", but who wants to live that way?'

Holly managed another discreet step back, annoyed to miss the scent of his aftershave. 'Thank you for the chance to dance again, Caleb. That was really sweet.'

'You're welcome.' Caleb smiled crookedly, looking uncharacteristically vulnerable, sending through Holly both a warning and a thrill. Their eyes held. The silence grew electric.

This could *not* happen. She couldn't handle a fling at her age, especially not at Lyle's funeral. For heaven's sakes. And if Caleb was thinking of finishing what they'd started more than ten years ago, he was living a fantasy. He'd have no idea what a relationship with a brain-damaged woman would entail. As CEO of Frederick Industries, he needed a whole high-functioning person by his side.

'Holly . . .'

No no no.

She searched frantically for how to send a not-now-not-ever message. Her gaze landed behind him on the bench where she and Lyle had enjoyed some pretty heated moments. Not subtle, but it was all she could come up with.

She gave what was supposed to sound like a wistful sigh. 'I'm so pleased with this whole weekend. All the perfect details. You know what I found in my room today?'

'What?' He was amused now, as if he knew why she was babbling, which made him even cuter.

Help.

'The five-flavor Life Savers in my nightstand were all orange. Lyle did that once for my birthday, because orange is my favorite flavor. I can't remember which year, but it was so thoughtful—'

Her vocal cords locked on a convulsive swallow. Caleb's face had turned to rock; his eyes narrowed and chilled. Holly took an involuntary step back, breath leaping into her throat. What had she said?

'I need a drink.' He turned abruptly and stalked over to the bar. 'You?'

Holly followed slowly, trying to take in what had just happened, searching for what might have startled him. All she could come up with was that she and Caleb had been having a moment, and she'd reacted by throwing her special relationship with his brother into his face.

No, that made no sense. A little jealousy might be enough of a trigger for a different man, but not one with Caleb's self-control.

From the neat rows of bottles on the table, Caleb yanked up the Scotch, poured himself a healthy dose and threw back a swallow. Not offering her a drink first was a major sign of his upset.

'What can I get you?' He drank again, not meeting her eyes. 'Anything that's not here we can order.'

Holly stared at the array of bottles, deeply shaken, wondering if they should talk about what had happened before the others showed up, or if she should let the weirdness pass. 'Gin and tonic, please. Easy on the gin.'

'Coming up.'

She watched him compose the drink with mechanical movements. Botanist gin, a special house-mix tonic, one slender, flawlessly clear obelisk of ice, a thin slice of lime twisted into a perfect spiral.

Caleb handed her the drink without a hint of his usual smile.

'Cheers.' She aimed her glass toward his, not sure he'd clink with her. He didn't hesitate. A relief.

'Cheers.' Caleb's smile was tight, but at least it was there, and it helped loosen the knot in her stomach.

'Can I ask . . .' Holly forced herself to continue, afraid of reawakening his anger, 'what happened just now?'

'I gave you a drink?'

'Caleb . . .' She waited, neck muscles aching with tension.

'Nothing that should have happened.' Another of those humorless smiles.

'It would help if you could tell me what—'

'It wasn't your fault, Holly.' He spoke as if the words were blocking his breath. 'We need to leave it at that.'

'Okay.' She looked down at the lime spiraled over her drink, trying to figure out how to maneuver through a bewildering and complicated situation with a brain that didn't calculate that kind of thing well anymore.

He took another large sip of his Scotch, Lagavulin 16 Year, the brand Lyle preferred, the kind their father drank and had allowed his boys to taste from adolescence, already planning his mini-me Frederick legacy. Caleb tossed off the rest of his drink and scowled toward the garden entrance. 'Eliana and Megan should be here soon.'

Please. 'Not Bodie?'

'He comes attached.' Caleb swung toward the bar table and picked up the Lagavulin. 'I hope this event doesn't turn out to be a disaster.'

'Did Lyle say why he thought it would be a good idea to have all three wives at one party?'

'Believe it or not, this was my idea.' Scotch glugged into his glass. 'Maybe I'm an optimistic fool.'

'No, I'm sure not.' She wasn't sure at all. 'I promise I'll behave.'

'You're not the one I'm worried about.' He looked again toward the rose-covered entranceway at the same time Holly heard voices. Thank God. 'Here they are.'

Eliana appeared first, in a black strapless sheath with a sheer floral overlay that billowed and swirled as she walked, emphasizing her slender grace, making her look younger than her forty-whatever years. Her dark hair was piled on top of her head, showing off her high forehead and the pale perfection of her skin. Behind her, expertly maneuvering on white stiletto sandals, came Megan, outrageously sexy in a skin-tight white lace dress, hair loose in auburn waves just past her shoulders. Next to her, Bodie's physique had been poured into jeans and a white shirt, over which he wore a teal jacket and a skinny black tie he was pulling at.

Holly's welcoming smile faltered. She'd misplaced the idea that Eliana thought Megan and Bodie had Lyle murdered. It was hard to imagine such beautiful people capable of such ugliness. But then few murderers probably looked like the central casting prototype in her mind – scarred faces, blank eyes and cruel mouths prone to diabolic chortling.

Stilted hellos were exchanged, drinks poured for the new-comers. Caleb proved to be a knowledgeable and efficient bartender, a skill he said he'd learned during his fraternity days at Princeton. He even managed to be patient explaining to Megan that he'd wanted the event to be private when she demanded to know why there were no Senneck staff members on hand to tend bar and serve food.

While Caleb mixed drinks, Holly took a refuge moment to study the food table. Plates of miniature caviar and cream tarts, halved fresh figs with bacon crumbles and a balsamic drizzle, small lengths of Belgian endive stuffed with blue cheese and grapefruit, fresh mozzarella-topped flatbread with mashed fava beans, lemon and mint. She was half tempted to park herself there for the duration and stuff.

'How was your afternoon, Holly?' Eliana wandered over and reached for a caviar tart. 'I hope better than the morning I gave you.'

'It was fine, don't worry. I had a good cry, a better lunch, and then Caleb and I went kayaking.' She loved that, *I went kayaking*, tossing the words into conversation as if she could still take being active for granted. 'It was fun. Nice weather for it.'

'I'm so glad.' Eliana sipped her drink and dabbed at her mouth with a rose-strewn cocktail napkin. 'I still feel awful about what I did.'

'No, you shouldn't.' Holly suppressed a smile, savoring the fact that Eliana hadn't said, *You went kayaking? Really? Oh my God, it's amazing you survived.* 'I should have been told sooner that Lyle was gone. That wasn't your problem.'

'What wasn't your problem?' Megan gently removed Bodie's hand from the diminished tray of flatbread and whispered something to him that made Holly think he'd been treating them like dinner. 'What happened?'

'Nothing important.' Eliana spoke frostily. 'Not your concern.'

'I don't mind if she knows.' Holly turned to include Megan, wanting to see her reaction. 'I didn't realize they had found Lyle's body. I thought he might still be alive somewhere.'

'Ah.' Megan's perfectly plucked brows quivered, as if they were trying to frown but something was stopping them. Was she trying hard to look unconcerned? Wrestling with guilt? Fighting Botox? 'If I'd known you existed, I would have made sure you knew. Rudy found him, you know, our detective. Or found where he died and where they buried what was left of him.'

'Megan, please.' Eliana put a hand to her chest, a picture of distress. 'People are eating.'

Megan's expression faltered before a quick recovery. 'Oh, relax. They're not eating *him*.'

Eliana's nostrils flared. 'You know, I've been wondering. It is pretty remarkable that *so* many people searched for Lyle for *so* long, but your Rudy found him almost right away. Amazing, really.'

'I know, right?' Megan shook her head, eyes wide. 'Like what are the odds?'

Holly shot a look over at Caleb to find him scowling across the garden. She was on her own here. 'Sounds like it was a lucky break.'

'It was a lucky break all right.' Eliana smiled acid. 'Megan had a lot to gain from finding him quickly.'

'Yes, you are right. I did.' Megan matched acid and countered with venom. 'But it was also agonizing not knowing what had happened to my husband. Those idiot authorities clearly did nothing right, or they would have found out as fast as Rudy did.'

'Rudy was amazing.' Bodie had abandoned the food to stand next to Megan and pull on a bottle of Genesee Cream Ale. 'It was kind of a desperation move hiring him, you know? But Rudy could literally find a flea in a haystack, I'm not kidding.'

Megan nudged him with her shoulder, smiling affectionately. 'Needle in a haystack.'

'Right, needle.' He blushed. 'The point is, the guy was good. He not only figured out where Lyle had been but also where he was going.'

'I forget where he was going.' Caleb had mentioned a place, but Holly had been too upset to take it in.

'Some monastery in Thailand,' Megan said. 'I can never remember the name. Something like Wappa Nanochat.'

'Nanachat. I remember that because it makes me think of talking with my grandma.' Bodie laughed, a high yuk-yuk-yuk that was absurd emerging from his massive body. 'Get it? Nana—'

'I can't imagine Lyle in a place like that,' Megan said. 'I mean, those monks do absolutely nothing he liked. In fact, they do nothing all day long.'

'Not exactly true,' Eliana said.

'Maybe he wanted a life change.' Holly sipped her drink. Lyle had told her as much on that final surprise visit, though she couldn't imagine him choosing a monk's life either.

'Sure, change, but *that*? Can you imagine Lyle Frederick eating two vegan meals a day and drinking nothing but tea and water or whatever?' Megan rolled her eyes. 'No gourmet anything? No exploring to find the best of the best of whatever it was? He'd go nuts. And sitting in silent meditation for hours at a time? Please.'

'I can't imagine him sitting in silent *anything*, even for *minutes* at a time. He was always going going, doing doing.'

Eliana chuckled fondly. 'I was exhausted half the time.'

'I loved every second.' Megan managed to insinuate *therefore I'm better than you*, which made Eliana stiffen like a corpse. 'All adventure all the time.'

Holly sighed. This party might not go as she or Caleb had hoped.

Caleb rejoined them, his glass refilled . . . for the third time? Holly had never seen him drink like this. 'Thanks for coming, everyone. Meeting here was my idea. I wanted us to get together before the service this weekend. You already know how much Lyle loved Senneck. He wanted the three of you to arrive a few days early so you could have the experience one more time on his dime.'

Eliana bent close to Holly's ear. 'After Saturday, Megan will be able to buy the entire resort on his dime.'

'Share with the class, Eliana?' Megan asked.

'I was saying how generous of Lyle, and how typical.' Eliana jumped in so smoothly Holly was impressed. Even before The Change, she wouldn't have been able to cover her ass that convincingly. 'Sorry, Caleb. Go on.'

'As I was saying . . . I thought it would be nice if we got together tonight, before the others show up tomorrow evening, to share personal remembrances. The service is programmed, so we won't be able to speak then.'

'Who's on the final list for the service?' Megan asked. 'I lost track.'

'Aunt Janet is coming, Fred and Liz Gaveson – Liz worked closely with Lyle at the Frederick Foundation. Then John and Carol Leafwood, good friends from Santa Cruz . . .'

John and Carol. Holly should have tried harder to stay in touch with a lot of people. Casual friends had understandably drifted away after her accident, and around the few who had stayed, she'd felt the difference in herself and their friendship so keenly that she'd withdrawn for the most part. But John and Carol had done the disappearing themselves. It would be good to see them. She hoped.

'. . . . and Lyle's best buddy from kindergarten on, Norman Godfrey, and his wife.'

'Norman?' Megan covered a laugh with her fingertips. 'Really? Bare Butt Boy at Senneck?'

Eliana looked aghast. 'Oh, very tolerant.'

'I am tolerant. Just wondering if he'll be wearing clothes here.'

'Yes,' Caleb said. 'He dresses in public.'

Holly blinked. 'Norman Godfrey is a nudist?'

'As a jaybird. Or the day he was born.' Megan giggled again, ignoring Eliana. 'He met this woman, Beatrice, and she converted him. They live in this whole nudie community. No one wears a thing, and let me tell you, it is seldom pretty.'

'Wow.' Holly couldn't imagine Lyle's sweet, nerdy friend frolicking around in the buff.

'Who's coming to officiate at the memorial?' Eliana asked. 'Father Crowley?'

'Oh, Father Crowley. He married us.' Megan was beaming. Bodie wasn't. 'You too, right, Eliana?'

'Yes. We had a rabbi there as well, but—'

'Oh, right, Jewish.' Megan pretended to whack her forehead. 'Who married you, Holly?'

Everyone turned to look, Eliana last, after glaring at Megan. Holly smiled, anticipating their reaction. 'The guy who ran the B&B we were staying at in Hawaii.'

Eliana's jaw dropped. 'You didn't have a church wedding?'

'We got married on Carlsmith Beach, on the Big Island, near Hilo.'

'I wasn't given that choice.' Megan rolled her eyes. 'How did you pull that off?'

'We eloped, went to Hawaii and grabbed a couple of people as witnesses. It was beautiful.'

'I can't believe Lyle didn't insist on church.' Eliana stared as if Holly was capable of magic. 'He certainly insisted with me.'

'For my parents' sakes,' Caleb said. 'They were not happy about missing his first wedding, and doubly unhappy that it wasn't in a Catholic church.'

'And triply that it was me he married,' Holly said.

'You had no dress, no bridesmaids, no *presents*?' Megan was appalled. 'Nothing?'

'None of it.' Holly smiled, enjoying the memory and their surprise.

Megan tsk-tsked. 'You need to get married again and do it right.'

'I did do it right. It was the rightest thing I ever did,' Holly answered firmly. 'A totally perfect wedding. We never regretted it for a second.'

Silence for several beats except the gurgle of the tumbling fountain. Apparently that was tough to swallow for this crowd.

Eliana moved first. 'Caleb, you are trying to eulogize your brother and we keep interrupting you.'

'Yes. Right.' He dragged his hand over his forehead, eyes not in their usual sharp focus. 'Where was I?'

'You were talking about why we're here tonight,' Holly said.

'Yeah. So the idea was that . . .' Caleb sighed, then stood taller and looked around their little circle with a steadier gaze. 'I miss my brother. I'm sure you all miss him as well, in your own ways. I wanted the four of us to have the chance to talk about Lyle this evening. To remember him good and bad, talk about how he affected us, what he brought to our lives, what he took away, whatever comes to mind. I deliberately didn't warn you about this in advance because I didn't want speeches. Just words that come straight from the heart, whatever's there. If there's nothing you want to say, that's fine too. We're not all struggling with the same grief in the same intensity at the same time, but we've all been through it.'

'It's a lovely idea, Caleb.' Holly hoisted her glass toward him. After the bad news that morning, she was eager to share stories of Lyle's integrity, optimism and energy with others who had also loved him. The good times.

'It is,' Eliana said. 'Thank you for doing this.'

'I'm totally up for it.' Megan put a warning hand on Bodie's arm as he was about to speak, which was good because Holly was pretty sure none of them wanted to hear what Bodie had thought of Lyle. 'It will be good for all of us to remember him. Caleb, you start.'

'Anyone need anything to drink or eat, go ahead whenever you want. These aren't lectures.' Caleb rubbed his jaw, posture still too upright, too unbending. Holly had seen him speak at Frederick Industries events, both large and small. He had the perfect knack, always hitting the right degree of formal authority while still projecting the kind of relaxed, funny guy you could see yourself inviting over for beer and peanuts.

'Lyle was a remarkable person, a Renaissance man, a type all too rare today. He fought hard to spread passionately held ideas about manners, culture and arts education, ideas many rejected as a waste of time. Ironically, emerging neuroscience research has been proving that Lyle's theories are important for young brain development.

'I'd like to read a compiled excerpt from his years of writing to me.' He unfolded a bit of paper from his pocket, peered at it, then moved it farther away. '"Art is the means to a richer, greater, better quality of life. To live for art – and by this I include music, literature and architecture – is to live for so much more than self-gratification or material worship. Additionally, thoughts and relationships must not be treated as stepping stones or transactions, but deep and spiritually sustaining necessities. Teaching our children at home and in schools to blend creativity with kindness and with respect toward the importance of being part of a productive society can and will create a more perfect world."

'Lyle and I were brought up at the altars of the Almighty and the almighty dollar.' Caleb put the paper back in his pocket. 'We were taught to measure our self-worth by our attendance at church and our success in business. We were taught that there were two ways of approaching everything we did: the right way and the wrong.

'I bought into it, the dutiful son. But not Lyle. He didn't make scenes, was never rude or angry. His rebellion was a quiet, determined and joyful declaration of who he was and what he believed.' Caleb flashed a wry smile. 'It made my parents completely insane.'

He waited during their quiet laughter. 'Through the extra-ordinary life he lived, my brother taught me to question many lessons I'd internalized, to broaden my world, and to take risks I never would have taken without him for inspiration.

'Though some might say we were competitive as brothers, we—'

All three women snorted. Caleb looked sheepish.

'Apparently *all* might say we were competitive. But when it counted, especially through times of some pretty remarkable tragedy . . .' he moved his gaze to Holly, who nodded her acknowledgment, annoyed to see Megan glancing between them, 'during those times in particular, we were unfailingly there for one another.

'And though I disagreed strongly with his decision to leave the country after the blow that defeated his optimism . . .' Caleb all but hurled the words at Megan, 'and though we had bitter words before he left, I am fully confident that he died knowing how deeply I and so many others loved him. I will be grateful to my big brother for the rest of my life.'

His voice broke; he put a fist to his mouth, then let it drop.

'Ultimately, I was to discover, however, that forgiveness has its limits, and that there are things I am not able to get past where Lyle was concerned. Foremost among them . . .' he looked up into the electric silence, 'foremost among them, stealing my lunch pickle the summer I was three and throwing it into the neighbor's yard.'

Startled laughter. Everyone could move again. A breeze distributed jumbled rose scents among them.

Caleb acknowledged the laughter with the hint of a smile. 'I don't believe in life after death. But if there is one, I would like to think Lyle is living well, drinking good wine, eating good food, painting, playing music, and bringing happiness and beauty to those around him, as he did while he was on this earth.'

His solid male shape shifted and wavered through Holly's tears, as something shifted and wavered in her heart.

She closed her eyes, let the tears spill, telling herself firmly that the evocative and emotional circumstances of being back at Senneck were making these feelings happen, and that they'd vanish when she got back to California and found a new place in which she could settle into her old routines.

The idea wasn't soothing.

'Who'd like to go next?'

'Are you kidding?' Megan wiped away a tear that Holly couldn't quite see. 'Who wants to follow that? You should have gone last.'

'I'll go next.' Eliana stepped back to separate herself from the group. 'But everyone should freshen up drinks or get more to eat so I can think for another minute.'

Caleb crossed over to speak to Holly. 'You don't have to take a turn if you don't want to.'

Megan overheard and pounced. 'Why is she special?'

'Oh for God's sake, Megan.' Caleb blew out a breath and mumbled something. 'I'm getting another drink.'

'Fine. Whatever. Don't tell me.' Megan pouted until he turned, then surprised Holly with a wink. 'I drive him crazy. He loves me, though.'

'Ah.' Holly lifted her eyebrows, not about to touch that one. 'He's a good guy.'

'Sure, if you like the thoughtful, liberated, brilliant, totally hot rich ones.' She gazed after him, then turned back to Holly. 'He's into you. Did you ever . . . you know?'

Holly gasped, traitorous color flooding her face. 'Are you kidding me? My husband's brother?'

'No, no. I meant after, while you were both single.'

'Megan.' Holly gripped her arm and leaned in so they wouldn't be overheard. 'Even if you and I were alone at the North Pole that would be an inappropriate question, but it's double that this weekend. We are old friends meeting again during an emotional time, and that's it.'

The words came out with strength and fluidity. Holly was triumphant . . . until she realized Megan hadn't implied there was anything going on now, so why had she made a point of denying it?

She was bad at this.

Megan made no effort to pull away, but her gaze held no calculation; her eyes were wide and sincere. 'I'm so sorry. Whatever goes on in my head comes out my mouth. I didn't mean to imply anything ugly. Just trying for . . . I don't know, a girl-connection. We should be friends, right?'

Maybe. Holly released Megan's arm. 'We're all a little on edge.'

'Tell me about it.' Megan put a hand to her flat abdomen. 'I've used enough Gas-X this week to deflate the Goodyear blimp.'

Holly strangled her laughter, wanting to avoid attention. After Eliana's alternating anxiety and reserve, she could see how Lyle would be drawn to Megan's bluntness and edgy humor. He'd had a goofy-kid streak a mile wide. 'It's good that we're all here for Lyle.'

'Ugh, Bodie's snorting up the food again. I'm glad you're not mad at me.' Megan squeezed Holly's shoulder and hurried over to her boyfriend just as Caleb returned with his glass full again – of water this time, and whew.

He jerked his head back toward Megan. 'Everything okay?'

'Fine. You did a wonderful job speaking.' Holly made a show of wiping her damp eyes, not about to admit they were still wet because of Megan's potty humor. 'As you can see.'

'Thanks. That means a lot.' He looked around as if he'd lost something. 'I didn't ask for chairs. Are you okay standing, or would you rather sit on one of the benches? We can move—'

'No, no.' Holly brandished her cane. She was dying for a chair but wanted to stay part of the group; the first one she'd been part of in a while where few people knew what had happened to her. 'This is all I need.'

'I'm ready. If everyone else is.' Eliana waited until Bodie and Megan quietened down, then smiled around the circle, radiant and poised. 'What I loved most about Lyle was how much being alive meant to him. I grew up in a community that had little contact with the outside world. There was a feeling of safety there. You knew exactly what was expected of you, you knew that you would be taken care of. I did go to college, but I was still ridiculously sheltered when we met. Lyle showed me so much, with so much patience. The poor guy had to teach me everything about traveling. I'd never been on a plane, never had a passport, never had contact with other cultures, except in a classroom.

'We went to so many remarkable places and had so many amazing experiences it made my head spin. Lyle opened up the world to me, a world I was taught very little about. You'd have to grow up as I did to understand how profound that gift was.

'What always struck me was that for all his money, and as much as he loved the things it could buy . . .' she gestured to the garden, eyes lit, cheeks pink, 'like trips to Senneck and other places outside the reach of normal people, Lyle didn't need luxury to be happy. He was just as excited about really good . . . I don't know, anything, peanut butter, let's say, as he was about caviar.'

'Chunky style, in a sandwich with honey and raisins,' Holly called out.

'Creamy style with banana,' Caleb added.

'Both of them right out of the jar,' said Megan.

'Reese's Pieces!' Bodie shouted.

Eliana looked confused. 'He didn't like those.'

'Oh. Him.' Bodie's face fell. 'I thought we were listing *our* favorite ways to—'

'We're not.' Megan gave him her glass and a gentle shove toward the bar. 'Can you get me another drink, babe?'

'Sure, yeah, okay.' He ambled away, looking disappointed.

'Go on, Eliana,' Megan said.

'Uh . . . Oh, yes.' Eliana's face cleared. 'In spite of Lyle taking so much delight in so many things, I couldn't help feeling there was deep dissatisfaction in him, a longing for something that he could never seem to find and that I couldn't give him. I was less surprised than Caleb when I found out he'd gone abroad. Definitely less disapproving – not judging you, Caleb.'

He inclined his head. 'No problem.'

Holly was still trying to work out what Eliana had said. Lyle restless and searching? Enthusiastic for experiences, sure, energetic, yes, sometimes to an exasperating degree. But he'd been as fulfilled and contented by their life as she could possibly imagine or want.

'Even while we were married, I used to wonder if he was after a deeper spiritual component without realizing that was what his life needed. Maybe because Judaism and my relationship to its laws and to God have always fed me so richly and borne me through so much. Lyle rejected the idea of worshiping God, an entity he considered mankind's creation, shaped from our ignorance and insecurity. I found that ironic, since he worshiped every other beautiful thing created by humanity.

'But I always suspected that deep down in his most honest soul, there was a being trapped by skepticism who wanted to burst free and dive into spiritualism. I'd like to think that in the temples he visited abroad, he finally found some peace.'

'Amen to peace.' Bodie handed Megan a glass of something pink. 'Especially there in the Middle East.'

'We're talking about the Far East, babe. Thanks for the drink.' She toasted Eliana. 'Pray continue.'

'Right.' Eliana looked down, her color intensifying. 'You all might disagree, but I felt that what Lyle needed most, what would have brought him that same measure of peace, was committing to staying in one place and raising children. He resisted it, always, said he wasn't cut out for being a family man.'

Holly held her breath. *What* had he said?

'Didn't you discuss this before you were married?' Megan asked.

'Of course,' Eliana shot back. 'I agreed at first, but it was a knee-jerk rebellion against the life I would have been trapped in if I'd stayed in my community. I underestimated how important it was to me to have children and pass my faith to a new generation. It was naïve. But I was so immature for so long, I didn't really understand who I was yet.'

Holly resumed breathing but couldn't believe what she'd heard. Lyle told Eliana he hadn't wanted a family? He and Holly had been trying for a baby for months when The Change happened, both of them excited beyond words at the idea of bringing their child into the world. Holly was the one who'd kept putting him off before that, wanting to finish her actuary certification.

'I called his resistance to settling down "denial". He called it "avoiding stagnation". Whichever it was, it finally broke us up.' Eliana gave Megan a sidelong glance. 'In spite of what some people seem to think.'

'No, you're right.' Megan was standing tall, again with that guileless, unguarded look. 'If Lyle had really loved you and been happy with you, I wouldn't have stood a chance. That's what love is.'

Eliana looked unsure whether she'd just been complimented or insulted. 'To this day I think Lyle would have been happy if he'd allowed himself to slow down, stay home for more than a month at a time, have kids to love and be loved by.'

'Mmm, no.' Megan shook her head, halfway through her

second drink. 'I hear what you're saying, but I can't picture Lyle tied down with kids. He was too into his own needs and causes to think of anyone else.'

Holly had to bite her tongue. The Lyle she knew was caring, intuitive and empathetic, always working to balance his needs with those around him.

'I'm almost finished, Megan. Then you get a turn.'

Megan made a zipping motion across her mouth. 'Sorry.'

'Part of me will always love Lyle, the way you love someone who awed you a little too much for it to be real.' Eliana lifted her glass. 'I meant it sincerely when I wished for him to be resting in peace.'

Holly joined the rest of the group with smiles and appreciative murmurs, but inside she was in turmoil. Had both these women been unable to understand who Lyle was? Or had he changed that much?

'You want to go next?' Megan asked her.

'No, you next,' Caleb said.

'Okay by me.' Megan took a sip of her drink and clutched it next to her shoulder. 'Well, so as we all know, I'm the horrible home-wrecker. Like I said, I couldn't have landed him if Lyle wasn't ready to go, but I do admit that when I saw him and decided I wanted him, I went after him the way I've gone after pretty much everything else I've wanted. That kind of determination comes from growing up with virtually nothing. You know no one will be handing you anything. If you want something, you figure out how to get it yourself.

'Growing up, I lied about my age so I could get jobs, so I could buy clothes that made me look classier. I listened to the TV and radio and worked my ass off practicing to get rid of my Wisconsin accent.'

'What's rang with a Wis-kahnsin yaccent?' Bodie's deliberately thick version made everyone crack up, which delighted him.

Megan blew him a kiss and faced center again. 'My friends accused me of trying to be better than they were. I'd tell them guilty as charged. I'd tell them it was fine if they wanted to stay in the pithole, but I was going places. I paid for college classes myself until I got my degree, first one in my family. It was a bitch, too. I have dyslexia, so reading was hell for me, but I wasn't going to let anything stop me.' She spoke proudly. 'I graduated at twenty-four knowing how to dress, how to speak, and that I was ready. But I couldn't do any more without help. So I started looking, hanging out at galleries, museums, concerts, knowing I'd find him. And I did. I wasn't looking to bust up a marriage, but that's what happened.'

She turned to Eliana. 'I'm sorry for the pain I caused you. In case I never said that.'

'You never did.'

'Okay, well. I'm saying it now, and I mean it.' She lifted her chin as if defying anyone to contradict her. 'I was a different person then. None of you except Bodie knows what it's like not to have enough money.'

Caleb turned toward Holly, who shook her head. Her family experience was not the same. Her dad was well connected and educated; a definite edge for climbing back out of a financial dive. Even with a prison record.

'But maybe some of you know what it's like not to have enough of something else you need to survive – approval, sex, affection, validation; you go long enough without it and you start changing, your morals start shifting until your ideas of right and wrong are completely overwhelmed by whatever it is you need. Like a mom stealing food for her starving kids. She knows stealing is wrong, but it's like who cares, right? I was starving my whole life, and starving when I met Lyle.' She looked around at each of them, then dropped her eyes to her drink. 'And I know none of you believe this, but . . . I did love him.'

Bodie's arm jerked and beer splashed on his shirt; he glowered down at the spreading stain.

'Our marriage was not perfect. We fought like dogs. The thing about Lyle was, he wanted everything his way. No compromises. But I'm sure I don't need to tell you ladies that.'

Holly stared at her, trying to remember a single time she and Lyle had raised their voices to each other before their world fell apart.

'He did like to be in charge . . .' Eliana ventured.

'You can say that again.' Megan laughed and tossed her hair back. 'He was sneaky about it. Don't get me wrong, I'm sure it was unconscious. But like, perfect example. He was always coming up with surprises. Like "Surprise, I got us tickets to this" or "We're going there for the weekend" or whatever. He never asked me if that was what I wanted, or whether I was tired or wanted to be alone sometimes.'

Holly stared at her. How could she categorize Lyle's delight in giving people wonderful experiences as manipulative?

'That said, it was amazing what I learned from him.' Megan glanced at Bodie's scowling face. 'As I said, I'm literally a different person now than I used to be. There is stuff about being human I didn't learn from my family. Like how to treat people with respect even when you disagree with them. Like that there are productive ways of solving conflicts that don't involve your middle finger. Like that you can approach anyone with trust, even those different from you in whatever way, while still asking questions and keeping your eyes open.

'Lyle gave me that and . . . well, he gave me everything I am today. Everything I will be tomorrow and for the rest of my life. And I will always be grateful.' She sent Caleb a wide smile. 'Thanks for arranging this, Caleb. I wasn't sure, but it's ended up being really good talking about him.'

'She only talked about herself,' Eliana murmured.

'Oh, one more thing I want to say. In all honesty, I don't think our marriage would have lasted.' Megan gave Bodie a quick smile. 'Things were so bad that when Lyle told me he was leaving the country, I felt relief, I admit it. But those long months when we didn't know what had happened, or where he was . . . that was agony.

'And I want you all to know that I still feel guilty, every day and every night, because . . .' her voice wavered, 'I sorta had a hand in his death.'

Eliana whipped her head around. 'What are you saying?'

'I'm saying I feel guilty.' Megan gave her a look. 'What didn't you understand?'

'You said you had a hand in his death.'

'Eliana.' Caleb spoke sharply, stepping forward. 'She didn't mean—'

'What?' Megan's face crumpled in horror. 'Are you kidding me? You think I had something to do with *that*?'

'You just said you did.'

'You think I snuck over to Thailand and pushed that car into—'

'You sent Rudy.' Eliana had turned white. 'Did *he* do it?'

'Of course he didn't.' Bodie looked like he could tear Eliana into bits.

Caleb made a soothing motion toward Eliana, who was clearly not in the mood to be soothed. 'I think she meant that if she and Lyle had been happier, he might have stayed Stateside.'

'He might have gone abroad anyway.' Holly couldn't keep

her eyes off Megan, who looked as if she'd just been punched in the stomach. 'Seems like he was on a pilgrimage of some kind.'

Eliana turned on Holly and Caleb, clearly considering them traitors. 'Look what she'll inherit with no questions asked. What if she and Bodie are getting away with murder?'

'You're out of line, Eliana,' Caleb said. 'We can't prove anything.'

'That's it? That's all I get from you, Caleb?' Megan stared incredulously. 'That you can't prove it?'

'I can't prove it.' He held her gaze. 'Or disprove it. So I choose to believe he died by accident.'

'Oh *thank you*, that is so generous.'

'Calm. We need calm.' Caleb's outstretched hand was shaking. 'Lyle wouldn't have wanted this.'

'Lyle didn't want this whole party,' Megan snapped. 'It was your idea.'

'It's my turn now!' Holly shouted. All eyes traveled to her. 'I'd like to speak. It's my turn.'

A few breaths, people moving, sipping drinks, but no one objected.

Holly took weight off her cane, stood taller and balanced on her own, having only a small idea of what she wanted to say, trusting that her feelings for Lyle and her need to set the record straight would carry her through, even if her concentration failed. For the second time that day she felt him, half expected him to appear in the garden as she'd expected him to be in her bed that morning.

'Go ahead, Holly.' Caleb stepped back into the circle, which had widened as people moved, though Megan and Bodie remained a unit.

'First, I want to say that it was very weird coming here to

share Lyle, and finding out only Caleb knew I existed. I'm still not sure why Lyle didn't mention me. Our breakup was painful, and I suppose he wanted to start over completely.' She summoned a smile for Eliana, who stared stonily back. 'I can't pretend it doesn't hurt, but as you know, Lyle had strong ideas about how things worked best.'

Snort from Megan, who had just sent Bodie to the bar for a third drink. An eye roll from Eliana. These women had loved Lyle, but they hadn't known him. For his sake, she would tell them.

'His love of beauty and kindness, his strongly felt responsibility to promote a greater good by living for both made him a remarkable person in what is too often an ugly and careless world. For this ideal he was willing to sacrifice not only those he loved, but eventually his own happiness. Like a tragic hero, his fatal flaw was that he wanted too much to win the battle to change the world.

'The restlessness you spoke of, Eliana . . .' Holly took a moment to focus her thoughts, elated to find them secure in her mind's grasp. She felt strong and sure, closer to her old self in challenging circumstances than she had in a long time. 'Europe came closest to Lyle's ideal of what the world should be. This country is too disparate and too young to compete. He wanted to travel there often, partly to explore and experience what he most—'

Megan blew a raspberry, having gotten an enthusiastic start on her third drink. 'Are you kidding me? I couldn't get him to go to save my life. I was dying to see the great European capitals. He always wanted to go somewhere weird, like Vietnam or Korea.'

'Weird?' Eliana said acidly. 'Did you mean to choose another word?'

'Sorry, ma'am, how about *exotic*. Better?'

'Slightly.'

Caleb held up his hand. 'You're both interrupting.'

'Uh . . .' Holly wasn't sure where she'd left off. 'I think . . . that . . .'

'You were talking about how Lyle liked Europe better than here,' Bodie prompted.

'Thank you.' Holly smiled gratefully. 'He was in awe of the natural beauty of this country. But I think what he craved most in the places we went overseas was a kind of safety. Beauty is restful, ugliness is challenging and demands a response; for Lyle it was a call to action. One of the places I remember he felt the most relaxed and at peace was in a tiny, very inexpensive house we used to rent on the Greek island of Milos. He always—'

Megan gasped. Everyone swung to look.

'I'm sorry. I'm so sorry, interrupting again. But we went there. He never mentioned he'd been there before.' She shook her head. 'Oh my God, he was in a foul mood the whole time. I thought he *hated* it.'

'Babe.' Bodie nudged her. 'You gotta wait till she's done.'

'I know, but it's so weird that he'd take me where they went and not say anything.'

'He did that to me too,' Eliana said. 'A restaurant in Spain. He never told me he'd been there. In fact he made a big deal out of how it was our little discovery.'

All eyes returned to Holly, as if she owed them an explanation.

'Well.' She took a deep breath. 'Okay. Maybe that was a bad example. Let me think a minute.'

Of course the more she tried, the less she could think. She closed her eyes, picturing Lyle smiling his biggest smile, lazing . . . where? In a chair? On a beach?

The image came as if he'd heard her and answered.

'There was a little inn on the coast of Portugal in a tiny fishing village where every day the owner would cook us—'

This time the gasp came from Eliana.

'Oh my God. You went there, too, didn't you.' Megan's mouth was open in disbelief. 'I bet he never told you he'd been there before either.'

Eliana shook her head, looking uneasy. 'That is freaky weird stuff.'

'No, no, it's not,' Holly protested. 'Places like that made him incredibly happy. Of course he'd want to go back.'

'But he wasn't happy,' Eliana said. 'He was miserable there. I couldn't do anything right as far as he was concerned. It was horrible.'

'In Greece, too. We fought the whole time. He was being a total bully.'

'Will you shut up and let Holly finish?' Caleb snapped.

'I am finished.' Holly took in a deep breath, trying to lessen her frustration, confusion and grief. 'I am finished. Because the Lyle I knew isn't the same man either of you two married.'

Chapter 9

Subject: Foundation director job
Date: September 12, 1999
From: Caleb@FrederickIndustries.com
To: LyleFred@aol.com

Great to talk to you yesterday, Lyle. I just wanted to follow up in writing to make it official.

As I told you, Ed Jaskiewicz is leaving as director of the Frederick Foundation. Obviously I'm hoping you'll take the job permanently, but right now the offer is for acting director.

The Foundation's current focus is on supporting local businesses, but you'd have a somewhat free hand in broadening the scope to include some of your own ideas and projects. We've recently installed new board members who are open to change.

The job is tailor-made for your strengths and passions. You've mentioned a couple of times wanting to get away from Los Angeles. I know Holly is happy there and impressively employed, but maybe she'd be willing to try Milwaukee? You've hung in there a lot of years while she worked toward her certification. Maybe it's your turn. Or maybe not! Obviously you'd know better than I do what she'd tolerate.

Another thing to consider, which I didn't mention on the phone. Dad is showing his age. It would mean a lot to him to see you attached to Frederick Industries before he goes. Not that you owe him that, God knows, but if it turned out you were interested in the job, that would be a nice side benefit. Mom keeps trying to push a move to a retirement community, but of course he refuses. 'Give up a mansion on two acres in River Hills with a pool and tennis court for a urine-smelling two-hundred-square-foot apartment someone just croaked in? Screw that!'

I'm not sure how we survived him.

Salary is $146K with full benefits. I'm sure Holly could get a job here in a snap. Hell, I'd hire her if she wanted to work for us.

As I mentioned, I'll be coming through LA in a couple of weeks. Think it over, run it by Holly, and we can talk more in person.

Can't wait to see you both.
Caleb

Caleb J. Frederick
VP, Frederick Industries

Subject: re: Foundation director job
Date: September 13, 1999
From: LyleFred@aol.com
To: Caleb@FrederickIndustries.com

Thanks for the follow-up note. I'm pleased with what I've been able to contribute here to the LA arts scene, but being The Boss of Money would give me more clout and free me up from all the begging. I spend so much time flattering and cajoling rich locals, all of whom are simultaneously being flattered and cajoled by every other worthy cause in town. It's time I would rather be spending on developing and implementing programs.

I was cringing the other day, thinking back to my twenties when I thought all I had to do to make people change their lives and the world was expose them to everything I valued. I needed more educating than they did. My current ideas have much more to do with sharing the heights and breadths of creativity achieved across countries, cultures, races and religions. I can do more good toward my mission by giving the world to those without access to it, then letting them choose what excites them. That's been my main thrust of late. The problem I've encountered is that even in this relatively liberal town, those with the bucks still want dead white guys taught as the pinnacle of accomplishment and the way forward. I need to bring people around, but I can't do that with the little power I have here.

So yes, I am thinking about it. And thinking about it. And thinking about it . . .

Can't wait to see you either! I know you'll be tied up in company business, but give us whatever time you can.

Lyle

'Who's Aunt Janet?' Melinda tilted her head, precipitating a cascade of long blond hair, while she gazed hungrily at Caleb. Holly didn't blame her. Caleb did amazing things to a business suit, even minus the jacket, which hung from the chair behind him.

'My Uncle Jack's wife.' Caleb dipped up some of Lyle's famous – at least among their many friends – guacamole. 'Our dad's sister-in-law.'

The four of them were sitting around the table on Lyle and Holly's second-floor deck for pre-dinner drinks before Caleb had to go to the airport and Melinda to free up her after-school babysitter.

'She did this weird thing in our family called parenting.' Lyle gestured with a loaded chip. 'Ingenious concept.'

'Mom and Dad tried,' Caleb said. 'They weren't cut out for the job, but they did try.'

'They lived their lives exactly as they had always lived them and expected us to adjust.'

'Yeah, but . . .' Caleb looked pained. 'Okay, that's a fair point.'

'Janet is a piece of work,' Holly told Melinda. 'I love her. You would too. She says exactly what she thinks, dresses exactly the way she pleases, does exactly what she wants, and manages to offend nobody.'

Caleb chuckled. 'Perfect description. You nailed it, Holly. Everyone's business is hers, but she only wants good things for each person.'

'My inspiration in many ways,' Lyle said. 'She's in her seventies now, and has the same energy she did forty years ago.'

'Is she from Milwaukee?' Melinda asked Caleb.

'No, her family was Boston Society. She went to school at some . . . what was the name, Lyle? Miss Something.'

'Miss Porter's School for young ladies, founded in the nineteenth century.' Lyle lifted his chin, embellishing the words with his idea of a highbrow Boston accent. 'A finishing school for the best of the best. But also a solid education. After graduation, Uncle Jack dragged her away from all that was holy to the misery of the Midwest, which she never lets anyone forget.'

'She and Jack couldn't have children, so she "adopted" us.' Caleb nodded to his brother, eyes soft and amused. Melinda clearly couldn't look anywhere else. 'Our parents took us to museums and churches, where we got lectures on the benefits of colonialism and missionary work. Aunt Janet took us to zoos and beaches, where we got cotton candy and sand in our bathing suits.'

'She gave us a childhood,' Lyle said.

'I hope I meet her someday!' Melinda was two thirds of the way through her second margarita from the batch Lyle had whipped up for the occasion. 'I could give her *my* children!'

'We'll take your children.' Lyle stood with the drink pitcher. 'Caleb? Another one?'

'Nope. Stopping here, thanks.'

'You mean it, Lyle?' Melinda half rose from her chair. 'I'll go get the little darlings now.'

'How many do you have?' Caleb asked.

'So far three, Alyssa is two, Gavin is four and Charlotte is six.' She continued counting on her fingers. 'Which means I have . . . *sixteen years* to empty nest. Unless I have more, and then it will be pretty much forever.'

'They're great kids.' Lyle offered Melinda a top-off. 'Smart, all of them, funny and polite. Total charmers.'

'Around *other* people.' Melinda smiled thanks to Lyle, then turned back to Caleb. 'They're crazy about their "Uncle" Lyle. When he comes over, he turns into a human jungle gym. Patience of a saint.'

'Aw, but think of everything you'll get to do after they're all in college.' Holly turned down more margarita. Today was the thirteenth anniversary of her and Lyle's first meeting, and before they celebrated, she had asset/liability projections to run for an upcoming regulatory filing – better done sober. 'You and Matthew will be able to go anywhere on a moment's notice.'

'That would be nice. He's always so busy. We used to sail to Catalina almost once a month.' She shifted casually so she could lean closer to Caleb and smolder. 'Do you sail, Caleb?'

'I have sailed . . .'

'Maybe the four of us could go!' She smiled hopefully. 'Or five. Matthew was going to come tonight, but he had a stroke.'

Caleb's eyes shot wide. 'He had a—'

'No, no.' Holly waved frantically as if to erase the comment. 'Someone else had the stroke.'

'Yes, sorry! Matthew's a neurosurgeon. He has to operate. I'm so used to saying stuff like that.' Melinda rolled her eyes. 'He's got a stroke, he's got a brain injury. You must have thought I was a horrible person partying here while he was in the ICU.'

Caleb looked lost how to react to that one.

Holly rode in for the rescue. 'How's the fundraiser going for the Studers?'

'Amazingly.' Melinda straightened, eyes lit with enthusiasm. 'Our community has rallied. The Studers are a family at school, Caleb, who lost their house to a fire. Everything's gone. Furniture, jewelry, clothes, pictures, documents, everything.'

'They were lucky not to go with it,' Caleb said.

'They know that for sure. But Cherry was saying the experience taught her how much we feel that what we own defines us. How big is your house, how expensive are your clothes, how many carats in your engagement ring? She said when the stuff is gone, you realize you're just a body with memories. I'm telling you, this has made me think. Fires are not rare in California, but it's different when you know the person.'

'Like they always say, you can hear about ten thousand children dying and feel sad, but hear about one, see a picture, hear his or her story, and you'll be flattened.' Lyle lifted an eyebrow. 'Used to advantage in fundraising brochures.'

'How is the family coping?' Caleb asked.

'This is the best part.' Melinda dipped up some guacamole. 'People are coming out of the woodwork. Donating cash, furniture, clothing, you name it. People dropping by meals, people offering their own homes while the Studers rebuild. I know it sounds trite, but besides the shock, it has given me a lift to remember that people aren't all selfish buttheads.'

'I'm going to contribute. I keep forgetting.' Holly shook her head as Lyle poised the pitcher over her empty glass. 'Do not leave without taking a check with you.'

'You're a doll.' Melinda peered at her gold bracelet watch. 'Ugh, I have to go. It's been so blissful having a grown-up conversation.' She grabbed her bag, which caught on the chair, her drink tilting perilously. 'Where do you go next, Caleb? Back home to Milwaukee?'

'The other direction.' He reached behind her to free her purse. 'I'm on my way to a conference in Sydney. Then I'm taking a couple of weeks to visit some of Frederick Industries' partners there and do as much touristing as I can fit in.'

'I am so envious. I'd *love* to visit Australia.' Melinda sighed dreamily. 'Hell, I'd love to visit Wisconsin.'

'Why don't you?' Lyle asked. 'Milwaukee's a great town. Gorgeous lake, beautiful architecture, and all the sausage, beer and cheese curds you can eat.'

Holly sent him a look. He loved setting Melinda up. She was so easy.

'Because I am ass-deep in rugrats.' Melinda set down the rest of her drink. 'Do you have time for that sail before you go, Caleb?'

He grimaced his regret. 'Unfortunately I'm going straight to the airport from here.'

'Ah, bummer.' Melinda got to her feet, tanned, sleek and gorgeous in a navy spaghetti-strap sundress. 'I know Lyle and Holly will miss you.'

'Sure you don't want another drink?' Lyle held up the pitcher.

Holly kicked him under the table. He was legendary for his

157

hospitality and she loved him for it, but Melinda did not need more before she drove home.

'No no no.' Melinda held up a perfectly manicured hand. 'I'm going to be a good girl and get back to the babysitter before I am gone three times as long as I said instead of two. Caleb, it was great to meet you finally. Holly and Lyle have been bragging about how perfect you are for a long time. Good to see it's all true.'

'Not sure about that, but thanks. It was nice to meet you too.' Caleb stood to shake her hand, smiling broadly, startled when she ignored his hand and went in for a hug. 'If you and Matthew ever make it to Milwaukee, which no one ever does, for some reason . . .'

Holly gestured to the spectacular view of the LA basin and the Pacific from their perch atop the Palos Verdes peninsula. 'Well, *obviously* . . .'

Caleb and Lyle exchanged glances.

'Who knows, maybe I'll ditch my kids with the husband someday and take to the road on my own.' Melinda slid her purse over her shoulder. 'More likely I'll tag along on one of Holly and Lyle's adventures, which they go on practically every week.'

'We haven't gone anywhere in a while.' Holly stood, wondering what the look between the brothers had been about. 'Work is crazy. The usual load plus all the panic over what will happen when the century turns over to 2000.'

'And you got a promotion, which you probably haven't bragged about yet.' Lyle took her hand, beaming proudly. 'She's now a manager at US Life.'

Holly waved away his praise. 'Pretty much everyone who certifies gets a manager position.'

'Certified after passing *ten* exams. Incredibly difficult ones,'

Melinda told Caleb. 'All of which she studied for and passed *while* she was employed full-time.'

'That's how it works for everyone. C'mon, Melinda, I'll write you that check.' Holly shooed her toward the kitchen.

The second they were safely out of earshot, Melinda turned and gripped Holly's forearm. 'God, Holly, if I ever get a divorce, I am flying to Milwaukee naked and having my way with him. I mean, Lyle is a total catch, but *that* guy . . . major hunk.'

'He's a sweetheart too.' Holly rummaged distractedly in the kitchen junk drawer for her checkbook. 'You've been bringing up the D word more and more often, Mel. Is it time?'

'No, no, it's not that bad.' Melinda folded her arms across her middle. 'I have three kids under ten and a husband married to his job. Of course it isn't easy. But the early kid years are hardest on any marriage. Any *normal* marriage, that is. When you and Lyle have kids, you'll probably fight over who gets to do more for the other person.'

'Nah, we'll have our troubles too.' Holly ripped off the check and handed it to Melinda, thrills running through her thinking of the present she'd give Lyle that night. He'd been wanting kids for so many years. Holly was finally ready to try. 'But you are taking on way too much beyond motherhood.'

'Maybe. Problem is, if I slow down, I have time to realize my life is crap.' Melinda turned at the door and gave Holly a hug. 'Don't listen to me, I'm fine. Thanks for having me over, and don't let Caleb marry anyone else before I get a shot at him. Two hours is all I need.'

Holly cracked up and pointed outside. 'Go home to your children.'

'I'm going. I'm going. Be good.'

Holly's smile dropped as the door closed. Melinda had been singing the I'm Unhappy song ever since Charlotte was born, but kept finding herself 'oops, pregnant' again. Holly wouldn't be surprised if there were more little ones in the future. Over the years, she'd made suggestions ranging from daycare to therapy to divorce. Melinda invariably countered with excuses, and went on wearing her misery like a badge of honor.

The two of them had first bonded over Weebles in kindergarten, then proceeded through Cabbage Patch Kids, ballet and boys before they separated to attend different colleges. After Holly and Lyle's move back to LA, they'd picked up effortlessly where they left off. It had been hard watching the sunny, intelligent woman Holly loved so much sink into this self-imposed deterioration, but there wasn't much more she could do until Melinda was ready to make changes herself.

Back through the kitchen, Holly paused at the sliding screen framing Lyle and Caleb, standing at the deck railing, twin broad-shouldered, tapered builds. They were talking earnestly, Caleb slightly taller, darker, solid and still, Lyle lighter, lithe and graceful, gesturing as he spoke. So alike, and so different.

Surf was high tonight; its rush could be heard even up here atop the peninsula. Holly and Lyle had fallen in love with the view before they'd even set foot inside the house. On clear nights, they could lie in bed next to their wall of windows, listen to the muted roar of the Pacific and watch the stars and the lights of Los Angeles twinkling all the way across the sky and the vast city beneath.

How would it feel after building such a rich, rewarding life for so many years to lose it overnight? How deeply people fooled themselves into thinking their bodies and circumstances were anything but fragile and temporal. Holly was as guilty as everyone else of taking too much for granted.

She pushed out on to the deck and went to stand between the brothers.

Lyle put his arm around her waist. 'Melinda okay driving back?'

'Yes. She can handle it.' Holly looked over to Caleb. 'Someone made quite a conquest.'

'Huh.' He quirked an eyebrow. 'She'd be perfect if I was looking for an unhappy married woman with three small children.'

'Yeah, why aren't you?' Lyle asked.

'She's in a rough patch.' Holly spoke dismissively to hide her worry. 'Sorry I interrupted you two. Looked like a serious conversation.'

'I was hoping your husband had decided by now— Look.' Caleb pointed. 'A hawk.'

'Red-tailed.' Lyle shielded his eyes to follow its flight to the topmost branch of one of their spruce trees.

Holly glanced at the bird. 'Decided what by now?'

'About Ed Jaskiewicz's retirement from the Foundation.' Caleb turned from watching the hawk. 'Lyle has the experience, energy and creativity for the job, and of course is uniquely qualified because he's a Frederick.'

Holly whipped around to Lyle so fast she got a twinge in her neck. 'What the hell?'

Behind her Caleb inhaled, but if he was going to say anything, he changed his mind.

Lyle's Adam's apple bobbed in a sudden swallow. 'I haven't told you yet.'

'No kidding.' Holly started to feel queasy. 'Are you considering this, Lyle? How long ago did you hear about it?'

'Sorry, Holly,' Caleb said quietly. 'I screwed up. I thought you knew.'

'It's not your fault, Caleb.' She pinned Lyle with her fiercest stare, comically to keep the atmosphere light, but he'd get the message. 'Of *course* you would assume my husband would discuss a critically important decision with me, right, *darling*?'

Lyle pretended to cower. 'Yes, your husband should have discussed a critically important decision with you. But he knew the idea would upset you, so he thought he'd try it on for size first, and only drive you to insanity with worry if it seemed like something he'd really do.'

Okay. She could see that. 'And?'

Lyle sighed and looked away, toward the city. 'It's a huge foundation. Someone could do a lot of good with that money.'

'In Milwaukee.' Holly felt as if a trapdoor was set to open under her feet and cannonball her into their pool. 'Half a country away from here.'

'My hometown.' He still wasn't looking at her, a slight frown visible on his profile. 'It's not such a bad place.'

It sure as hell wasn't California. Holly swept her arm across their expansive view, mountains, ocean, city, trees, flowers and sunshine all year round. 'You'd consider leaving all *this*?' It took everything she had to ask the question conversationally when she wanted to shriek it and add, *for Milwaukee!?*

'You and I have talked about it.'

'We talked San Francisco, or Vancouver, or Seattle in ten or fifteen years, not Wisconsin, not *now*.' She was losing the battle to sound calm.

'I'm the bad guy here.' Caleb touched the small of her back. 'Lyle isn't going to drag you somewhere you don't want to go.'

'At this point it's a fantasy.' Lyle turned to her, brow and eyes clear, lifting his hand as if he were holding something between his thumb and index finger. 'Like someone dangling a big chocolate donut you get all excited about until you realize it will make you fat and gassy.'

Holly exhaled slowly, trying to get herself to stop being panicky and process what he'd said.

'Okay. Okay, yes, I see.' Maybe she had overreacted. 'Melinda bringing up the Studers just now made me think about how much I love our life here, and how nightmarish it would be if it all disappeared. Bad timing, I guess.'

'Subject tabled.' Lyle kissed her cheek warmly.

Tabled? She wanted it closed. But fair was fair. Her job was the only reason they'd moved to Los Angeles. Lyle had fended for himself admirably, building a new life in an unfamiliar city. Holly could get a job anywhere. Her skills were in high demand. They could afford to come back here often to visit family and friends. They could even rent out this house and keep ownership, maybe move back in five to ten years. If this job would really give Lyle what he wanted and needed to be happy, she couldn't stand in his way.

Even the thought made her want to throw up.

'So, Caleb . . .' Lyle's body tensed beside her. 'How's Dad doing?'

'Tired.' Caleb leaned his arms on the railing. A breeze did its best to mess up what Lyle called Caleb's 'corporate cut'. 'Heart's not in the business anymore, I don't think.'

'I can't imagine Dad's heart anywhere else. Is his health okay?'

Caleb shrugged. 'Like he'd tell me?'

'Any talk of . . . retirement?' Lyle sounded way too casual.

'None yet. But he's nearing seventy. It has to happen soon.'

'You'll take over, of course.'

'Not for a long while.'

'But someday.'

Caleb turned from the view to examine his brother. 'Unless you want a crack at it, yes. Someday.'

'Nah. You're welcome to the whole show.' Lyle's arm had become a band around Holly. 'I'd lose sanity in about a week.'

'I understand.'

And in a proverbial aha! moment, so did Holly. This wasn't about being unhappy in LA. This was about Frederick Industries, about Lyle's heritage, going back generations, and its hold on her husband, in spite of his declared rejection of everything it stood for. She believed he didn't want to run the place. That job was a perfect fit for Caleb. But watching his younger brother being groomed to take complete control someday . . . Lyle's worm was turning.

'I should visit Mom and Dad soon. *We* should.' Lyle gave her shoulders a squeeze, then loosened his grip.

Holly felt the sun on her cheek, thought of the cold gray city of her husband's childhood. The only way she'd survived past visits was knowing they'd be able to escape back here to paradise. The idea of being trapped there, raising kids in a dark German house in provincial and unremarkable surroundings . . .

Caleb's phone deedle-deedled. He hauled it out and peered at the display.

'My driver's here.'

Lyle started chuckling. 'Your *driver*?'

Caleb gave him an uncharacteristically severe look. 'None of your *guff*, now, young man.'

Lyle cracked up. 'Perfect imitation.'

'Your father?' Holly dragged herself back to the present.

'To a T.' Lyle ushered Holly and Caleb into the house. 'We tried to name one of our dogs Guff, remember?'

'I'd forgotten that. Mom refused. It would have been a great name.' Caleb stopped by the front door, where his suitcase stood ready, his expression warm and wistful. 'Thanks so much for the last couple of days. It was great to stay with family. Not to sound like a country song, but the road gets lonely.'

'We loved having you.' Holly went to him for a goodbye hug. Caleb held her for several seconds, pressing his cheek to her temple.

'Be safe, be well. Come back soon.' Lyle embraced his brother, then opened the door to the view of a huge black Cadillac dominating the driveway. 'Send us a postcard from Down Under.'

'Will do.' Caleb waved and climbed into the car while the driver put his bags in the trunk.

Holly and Lyle waited in the doorway until the Cadillac purred out of sight, then stepped back inside, Holly determined to salvage the mood for their anniversary. They could fight out the job issue another time. 'It was great to see him, Lyle. I'm crazy about your brother.'

'Yeah?' Lyle pulled her into his arms. 'Not as crazy as he is about you.'

She blew a raspberry. 'Oh, c'mon. You always say that.'

'I always mean that. Did you see how he was looking at you?'

She pressed close to him, thigh to thigh, chest to chest. 'Like he was glad I make his brother happy?'

'Like Melinda was looking at him. I'll feel better when he falls for someone else.' He kissed her, then rocked her gently back and forth. 'Hey. I'm sorry the job thing was dropped on you tonight, Hol. Caleb was right, you know. You have absolute veto power.'

'Give me time to get used to the idea.' She burrowed against his chest, not sure she'd ever get used to the idea. Their house hadn't burned down, but their life here felt suddenly on shaky ground – of course in Los Angeles sooner or later everything was on shaky ground.

'Are you hungry?'

'Starved.' Holly lifted her head eagerly. 'What are we having?'

'A surprise. Give me half an hour. We'll take dinner down to the beach.'

Her face fell. 'I can't, Lyle. I've got work to do still tonight, and— Mmph.'

He kissed her again when she tried to object, and again, until she gave up and started laughing. 'No work tonight, Holly. Special occasion.'

'Compromise?' She looked at him pleadingly. 'Eat a fancy dinner at home, and I work while you get it ready, then just a little more before bed?'

Lyle looked deeply aggrieved. 'You are messing with perfection here.'

'Yes, I know.' She moved suggestively against him. 'I'll make it up to you later.'

'Mmm. Okay, we can eat here. Out in the garden.'

'Deal.' She stepped back. 'I'll get started, you do your magic.'

'Half an hour.'

She was already rushing toward her study, relieved the evening seemed to be back on track. 'You're on.'

Half an hour later – Lyle was freaky-good at estimating how long he'd need – Holly begged another fifteen minutes, then joined him in the garden by the patio set they'd arranged in a spot perfect for catching the best of the sunset. Lyle had the table set with a white cloth, yellow plates, her favorite pink, yellow and blue napkins, and blue votives with candles for when darkness fell. Holly had his gift stuffed under her arm.

The meal was classic, simple and delicious: a Caprese salad with fresh imported mozzarella, and basil and tomatoes from their vegetable garden; poached lobster salad with tarragon;

French cheeses served with a fresh baguette from La Brea bakery, and chilled Taittinger champagne.

'Oh Lyle, how gorgeous.' She looked longingly at the bottle. 'Though I shouldn't have champagne on top of a margarita.'

'Why not?' Lyle was already twisting off the wire cage.

'I still have work to do. I told you.'

'So do it tipsy. You know what you're doing.' He eased out the cork with a soft pop, waited a moment, then poured into glasses she held at an angle. 'Better yet, surrender to the romance and do it tomorrow.'

'One glass.' Holly raised hers, knowing she'd give in and have more. It was such a beautiful evening, and he was right, her work would keep until tomorrow. Anxiety kept her at it, and a touch of her mother's control-freak personality. Lyle had been so good for her, prodding her to slow down, teasing her into enjoying what she could. She always got the work done. 'Here's to our first meeting, Lyle.'

'When you were so prickly.'

'And you were so weird.' She faked a shudder. 'Staring at me in a hot tub, then showing up the next day outside my dorm? Creepy!'

'Look at you. You're gorgeous. How could I help staring?'

They toasted with the beautiful champagne, then sat, Holly only slightly awkwardly, in order to let the package slip on to her chair. Then they settled in to eat where they'd shared so many delicious dinners on so many nights before Holly would have to hurry back to her office to study for the next exam. She felt wistful tonight in the soft air, with daylight fading and fall on the way, as if she were already facing a dreaded move and the prospect of a snowy dark winter with pushy in-laws constantly in their business.

'This looks so delicious.' She whipped open her napkin,

shooing away the thoughts. 'Thank you for spoiling me once again.'

'It's my pleasure. As it has been for thirteen years. I'm so glad you went naked hot-tubbing with strangers that night.'

Holly lifted her glass to him. All these years later, she still got first-date fizzy when Lyle looked at her that way. Open and loving, the absolute connection she'd felt from the first time their eyes met.

'That was a strange experience.' She served him some of each salad, then filled her own plate. 'It's funny to look back on a younger me as if she was a different person.'

'You *were* a different person. We're all changing all the time.'

'Yes, but it's hard to remember why taking my clothes off in front of a bunch of guys I didn't know seemed like a good idea.' She picked up her fork. 'I don't feel like a person who ever could have done that.'

Lyle shrugged. 'You were trying stuff. It's what we do when we're young. Experimenting to figure out what fits, what doesn't. And you were still working through grief over your dad's disaster.'

'Yes.' She tried a bite of the lobster salad. 'Oh, that is good. Tell me you didn't have these overnighted from Maine.'

'I might have . . .'

Holly shook her head, pretending disapproval. 'You are such a hedonist.'

'Guilty. Isn't it fun?' The rosy sunlight emerged from behind a tree and found his beloved handsome face, lighting his brown eyes and smooth gold skin, his grin showing faint lines that hadn't been there when they met, that would deepen over time. When they were old, would they still be having dinners here in this beautiful place?

'You were talking about your dad,' Lyle prompted gently.

'Yes.' Holly took a sip of champagne, which was so good she had to have one more. 'I was thinking about his time in jail. I wonder if he feels now the way I do about young me in the hot tub. Like, who was that guy?'

'Ever ask him?'

'God, no. The Pennys Do Not Talk About That Time.'

'Like The Fredericks Do Not Talk About Mom's Drinking.' He took a bite of the Caprese salad and his eyes rolled back. 'There is no reason for supermarket tomatoes to exist.'

'I'll drink to that.' Holly hoisted her glass, by now thoroughly convinced that work could wait until tomorrow. Once again, Lyle had saved her from herself.

They ate the rest of their meal, chatting about old times on campus and the horrible day of the earthquake, their move to LA and the progress they'd both made professionally. Movies they wanted to see, restaurants they wanted to try, people they wanted to invite for dinner. Holly's worries eased further. Lyle was invested in the community here. He was happy. They'd raise children and grow old right here in this house.

Holly waited until Lyle had taken his last bite, suppressing a sly grin, then sat back and pretended to be surprised. 'What is *this*? What am I sitting on?'

'What?' He stood to see.

Holly made a big show of turning around to check, and came up with the small, slightly squashed package she'd wrapped three days earlier in white tissue paper. 'Well if this isn't the gosh darnedest thing.'

Lyle caught on, put one hand on the table and struck an outrageously cheesy pose.

'Why, you clever little minx,' he growled. 'What have you got there?'

'Oh sir, if my brain cells still worked in your magnetic and powerful man-presence, I could tell you.' She tossed the soft package so it hit him in the chest. 'Happy anniversary, Lyle.'

'Thank you, Holly my love.' He blew her a kiss and sat, pulling at the pink and blue ribbons.

Holly clasped her trembling hands under her chin and watched him unwrap the baby onesie and impossibly tiny booties, both in purest white.

Lyle's grin faded into awe as he held them up. His eyes reddened. 'Holly?'

'If you don't have anything . . .' she could barely get the words out, 'better to do this weekend, I'd like us to start trying for a baby.'

Lyle nearly upset the table coming toward her, hauled her out of her chair and kissed her over and over, soft delicious kisses that went on until he laid his forehead against hers. 'If we hadn't had so much champagne, I'd say to hell with it, let's try now.'

'Ooh, bad idea.' Holly giggled euphorically. Lyle had waited so long for this, and been so supportive and patient with her delays and worries. 'We'd have a mutant.'

'But it would be *our* mutant.' He kissed her again, brown eyes glowing with joy. 'We're going to be parents.'

'Assuming everything works. All the parts.'

'Of course they will. Everything will work.' He let her go, raced to pull an envelope from under his seat cushion and raced back. 'Here's your present. Another perfect way to celebrate.'

Holly spread her arms to embrace the garden they'd worked so hard to restore, the glistening pool, the sunset and soft clear air, the distant city. 'This is pretty perfect right now.'

'Open.' He handed her the envelope, face lit with anticipation. 'Happy thirteenth anniversary, Holly.'

'Why thank you.' She opened the envelope, pulled out a sheet of paper, unfolded it and scanned the print. 'Oh my gosh, Lyle! Hawaii? *Japan?*'

'Thought you might like it.'

'Like it? This is—' Her eyes landed on the dates. She gasped. 'This is in *two weeks*. I can't pick up and go that soon.'

'I called your boss,' Lyle said triumphantly. 'It's fine for you to take the time off. Everything is arranged. We'll drop in on Hawaii, then on to Tokyo.'

'*What?*' Holly dropped her hands, still holding the itinerary. 'You spoke to my boss?'

'Sure.' His grin faded at the look on her face. 'I had to make sure you could take the time off.'

'But it's . . . my job.'

Lyle looked confused. 'I don't understand.'

'You . . .' She closed her eyes to think. He . . . what? Arranged a dream vacation and carefully made sure the trip wouldn't interfere with her work, all done so the gift would be a fabulous surprise? What did she have to complain about?

She wasn't even sure how to articulate it except that on some level her territory had been invaded. Matters that involved her had been discussed without her knowledge. Again.

No. This was different. This was about Lyle arranging a badly needed vacation that she never would have allowed herself. He was doing this for her.

She opened her eyes to Lyle's worried ones. 'I'm so sorry. I'm being ridiculous. Control-freaky, in fact.'

'No. No, you are not.' His face relaxed into tenderness and he took her hand. 'I got so excited about surprising you, I didn't stop to think how it might feel if I went over your head. I'm sorry, Hol. Real apology.'

'It's fine. Don't worry.' She forced a laugh and examined the

171

itinerary again, trying to let go of the uneasy feelings. Hawaii, Tokyo, Kyoto, Hiroshima . . . It would be an incredible time. She needed this break. They'd be adding to a lifetime of happy memories. Much more important than another three weeks on the job. Sometimes she thought she'd never learn to treat herself better. Without him to remind her, she might end up working herself into missing the best parts of life. 'Thank you, Lyle. The trip will be perfect.'

Chapter 10

Holly stopped outside the lodge, overfull and sleepy, anxious to get back to her room. She and Eliana had just finished a gorgeous lakeside picnic of poached salmon set up by the Senneck staff. After a halting start, they'd managed to have a good conversation, comparing hometowns Milwaukee and Santa Monica over the decades, sharing tastes in music, books and travel destinations, not mentioning Lyle except on the way to Eliana's glowing description of her current marriage and thriving stepsons. Holly had been surprised by the invitation after the weirdness at the previous evening's rose garden party. Eliana apparently didn't hold grudges; she'd been pleasant company and fun to talk to. Back in California, Holly occasionally had coffee with a co-worker, but apart from Melinda, most of her socializing happened in groups. She should make a point of nurturing more one-on-one friendships, though providing half the conversation today had been draining. 'I better get back to my room. Thank you for lunch, Eliana. It was nice getting to know you a little better.'

'You're welcome. I'm glad you wanted to come. Last night . . .' Eliana lifted her arm and let it float back to her navy pants, 'I let my emotions get the better of me.'

Holly stiffened. She did not have energy left for more Lyle drama. There would be plenty tomorrow during the service.

'Don't worry about it. It's a hard weekend for all of us.'

'I also wanted you to know . . .' Eliana glanced around to make sure they were alone, sleek ponytail swishing across her bare shoulders. Effortlessly classy in a sleeveless white top with navy and white jewelry, she made Holly feel their ten-year age gap. Eliana fresh and blooming, Holly withering fast. 'Lyle and I weren't right for each other, we wanted different things, but I loved and respected him. Megan has no idea what she had. That still makes me angry.'

'She seems . . .' through her sleepy fog, Holly searched for a neutral word, 'complicated.'

'Yes, which isn't her fault. She makes me furious, but that's not her fault either. None of those are excuses for my behavior yesterday. I wanted you to understand.'

'Ah.' Holly barely took in what Eliana was saying. She really, really wanted that nap. 'We're all who we are.'

'True.' Eliana looked dubious. 'Anyway, Holly, I enjoyed our talk. I'll see you tonight when the crowds descend?'

The idea of crowds made Holly want to crawl into a hole for the rest of the weekend.

'Yes, I'll see you there.' She raised a hand in farewell, and turned back toward the cottage. She'd be much better able to face the day if she rested. The idea of that gorgeous four-poster was making her crave sleep even more.

Eliana called her name.

Exasperated – she'd been so close to getting away – Holly turned back to find Eliana looking confused. 'Yes?'

'Sorry, but . . . you're not going back to your room?'

'No, I am.' Holly wasn't sure what her problem was. She gestured behind her. 'The cottage. We always get the same . . .'

Crap.

Eliana walked toward her with that look on her face, the one

Holly knew too well. The oh-dear-something-is-wrong-with-you look. 'You're in the lodge, right? Second floor? We all are.'

'Yes.' Holly reversed course, leaning heavily on her cane. 'Yes, I know.'

Eliana came to meet her and took her arm. 'Is there anything I can do to help?'

'No. Thank you.' Holly resisted the urge to shake herself free. 'I just have . . . get confused sometimes.'

'Oh.' Eliana's gentle voice was full of pain. 'Is it . . . Do you know why?'

Polite code for *Got Alzheimer's?*

Holly stopped under the grape arbor leading to the lodge entrance. She'd rather have this loathed conversation out here than in the lobby. 'Brain injury. When I'm tired, the gray matter doesn't work well.'

'Oh no.' Eliana looked stricken. Lyle would have loved her for her empathy, equal to his own. 'What happened, if you don't mind me asking?'

'Lack of oxygen for too long. Generally a bad idea.'

'I'm so sorry.' Eliana bit her lip, wondering, Holly guessed, whether to ask any or all of the juicy questions spinning in her head. 'When did this happen?'

'Twenty-three years ago.'

Eliana looked to one side, working it out. She might as well have been counting out loud on her fingers.

In the midst of her exhaustion and impatience, Holly took pity. 'I was still married to Lyle. My accident was part if not most of the reason our marriage broke up. I really need a nap right now.'

Eliana's beautiful eyes widened; she gasped. 'I'm so sorry, Holly. This is all none of my business and you're tired. Let me walk you to the elevator.'

175

Another guest came up behind them. Even though it was the last thing Holly wanted, she let Eliana take her arm and parade her disabled new friend through the lobby, Good Samaritan keeping inept Holly from falling on her face.

All the best intentions, Holly knew that. But being treated like a helpless, fragile being only made her feel more like one. Caleb would understand.

Happily, Eliana's room was on the third floor, and since Holly's room was only a few steps from the elevator, Holly was permitted to exit it under her own power. She managed a friendly goodbye smile and another round of thanks for lunch before the doors slid shut and she could let herself into her room, toss aside her cane and climb on to the bed.

Ten minutes after she'd dropped into a blissful doze, her eyelids flew open. Somehow in her sleep she'd remembered what she'd remembered and forgotten and remembered again throughout the morning.

Dancing.

In half an hour she was signed up to execute Caleb's very kind and utterly idiotic gift of hooking herself on to wires like a marionette and lumbering around a private gym room as if she were dancing again. Dancing! With a brain injury! After more than twenty years! She let out a groan that grew into a roar she cut off before its volume brought staff running to investigate.

Okay.

Gone were the days when ten minutes was all she needed for ready-set-go. Coffee would have to replace her beautiful nap for now.

Holly picked up the phone. Usually she'd go down to the lobby and help herself to the excellent brew available throughout the day, but screw that. Within two minutes a steaming mug appeared at the door on a small silver tray, its rich aroma enticing her part way out of her massive grump.

She'd been planning to call her parents this afternoon, but now she needed to save her energy for the miserable gym adventure. So she plunked herself into the green and tan chair by the window and texted them about all the wonderful fun she was having, not mentioning the part about discovering Lyle had died a ghastly, fiery death, and that one of his wives suspected the other of murdering him, and that Caleb might be crushing on her and she on him. Because that would only make them more sure that she shouldn't have come.

Holly was starting to wonder if she agreed.

Melinda had texted earlier, wanting details. Holly answered her in much the same way, feeling guilty for not telling her bestie the truth. However, the truth would take too long right now, and the truth would make Melinda call to offer support and a shoulder, and if Holly didn't answer, she'd worry. So it was lies all the way today, to the people she loved and trusted most.

Whee.

The facts would come out eventually. Since Holly might never travel again, this would become her big adventure story, one people would hear over and over because she'd forget she'd already told them. The weird story that weird Holly always tells.

As soon as she hit send to Melinda, another text came in, from Caleb. *Drink before the dinner tonight?*

Holly groaned. This was not the time to answer, when she was this tired and discouraged, because her knee-jerk reaction would be *No, absolutely not, leave me alone, you and every other human.* Telling someone about The Change always put her in a foul mood. She felt invaded, too wide open, as if she'd been forced to strip naked in front of a horrified public, all her most private bits revealed and judged.

The coffee helped, but the acid left her craving a Life Saver the way some craved cigarettes. Hard as it was to get back on to her feet, she'd have to start putting together an outfit suitable for fake-dancing anyway, so she forced herself.

The nightstand drawer slid out easily. Holly stared inside, hand poised over her favorite candy. Next to the Life Savers, a CD, pink, with cover art of a bulbous-nosed cartoon creature holding a banjo. On his head, a nest with an egg out of which burst an adorable baby robin, wings extended, beak open to sing.

Songs of the Pogo.

Holly picked up the CD; it trembled in her unsteady hands. Mom and Dad had given her this album when she was a girl. Holly had adored it, asked for it to be played on the turntable she wasn't allowed to touch over and over until she had memorized every one of the nonsense songs it contained, and had choreographed steps to each tune, including what she'd considered a sultry seduction number to the blues-style song 'Don't Sugar Me'. Holly had never met anyone else who had the album or who'd even heard of it – not that she made a habit of asking.

She turned the CD over, peering at the sweetly familiar song list. 'Go-Go Pogo', 'Whence That Wince?', 'Slopposition', 'The Keen and the Quing'. All so clever, so funny, and so impenetrably weird.

One night . . . when was that? She couldn't remember. Before the accident, certainly. She and Lyle had been lying in bed and something they were talking about had reminded her of the album. Predictably, Lyle had never heard of it. Had they had wine that night? She couldn't remember that either. But she did remember rising up in the middle of the bed and performing the entire 'Don't Sugar Me' routine, imitating her non-sexual twelve-year-old self's idea of seduction, and reducing them both to crazy laughter. Lyle had immediately tried to find a copy for her, but the recording had long been out of print. She'd called her parents, but they no longer had the album, neither did the library or anywhere else they'd searched.

How had he managed this? Where had he found it? How had this one nutty idea come to his mind all those years later when he was planning for a funeral he must have been sure wouldn't happen for many more decades, one he couldn't be sure she'd survive him to attend? She loved that he'd thought of such happy things to remind her of on such a sad occasion. Their wedding bouquet, the orange Life Savers, now this. Would there be something else tomorrow?

Holly chuckled. Of course there would be. Lyle would never set up expectations like this and not follow through. She wondered what reminders Eliana and Megan were getting in their rooms, or if Caleb was, though she wouldn't ask him after the way he reacted to the Life Savers.

She ran her fingernail along the edge of the CD to open it, eager to listen. Then her stomach sank as she remembered again. Dancing. By the time she found the room's CD player and got it working, she'd have lost more precious minutes she needed to get dressed and out the door.

Reluctantly, she put down the case, humming a few bars from 'Potlucky', and promised herself that if she could get dressed in a decent amount of time, she'd play at least one track before she left.

The task, however, proved an exercise in frustration. What should she wear? Had she packed workout clothes? She couldn't remember. She hunted through drawers, choosing and discarding items, finally settling on black leggings and a casual white T-shirt. For her feet . . . more hunting, more indecision.

This was going to be a disaster. She couldn't reschedule; there wasn't enough free time left in the weekend, and she definitely did not want to deal with this tomorrow, the day of Lyle's service. Though she did enjoy the idea of the ceremony going on while Holly appeared and disappeared from the wings at the end of a wire, butchering *Swan Lake*.

Better to get it over with. Caleb had been so thoughtful, if misguided.

Eventually she managed to get the damn leggings on correctly, after having to pull them all the way on and then all the way off, at which point they were inside out and had to be righted. Utter pain in the ass. Her scoop-neck white shirt went on fine, but only after she tried to put her head through a sleeve hole. Finally, late and in a panic, she shoved her feet into black sandals that caught on the rug on her way to the door and tripped her. She saved herself by grabbing at the bed, made so perfectly the quilt barely gave.

And then she couldn't find her cane.

By the time she got to the gym building, ten minutes late for her hour, Holly had decided that once someone had hooked her up to the stupid wire, she'd send that someone away and dangle, pouting, for the next forty-five minutes, like a body in a noose.

At the front desk, Holly blurted out her name to the pretty young woman, who grinned as if she'd been waiting her entire life for that very moment, then summoned another beaming employee, who could qualify for a gold medal in Macho Enthusiasm.

'Hi, Ms Penny! I'm Andrew! Let me show you to the room we have ready for you!' He led the way, not offering to take her arm or bring her a wheelchair or carry her himself. Points for that.

'The room' was a surprisingly large area, about the size of a basketball half-court, with painted walls and a wooden floor Holly would bet represented the latest in athletic technology, firm underfoot but with the sense that it would easily and safely absorb the force of a jump or a grand jeté. Or a catastrophic fall.

On a small table near the entrance sat a basket containing a towel, bottles of water and a sports drink, energy gels and bars, dried fruit and dark chocolates, next to a large bouquet of red camellias, yellow tulips and fragrant white gardenias – nice touch to put strongly scented flowers in a place where people generally smelled bad.

'Those are for you!' Mr Enthusiasm was pretty excited about this, bounding over and extracting a piece of paper from among some leaves. 'There's a card!'

Holly's eyes narrowed, glaring as if the flowers were straight out of the *Little Shop of Horrors* musical. 'Oh?'

They better not be from Caleb.

She opened the card.

They were from Caleb.

Thought you might have had your fill of roses last night. These are for your triumphant re-entry into the dance world. I know it will feel impossible at first. Relax and have fun. Surprise yourself.

Holly was about to roll her eyes over Caleb's self-appointed role as her disability guru, when she remembered the kid was watching oh-so-enthusiastically.

'How sweet.' She forced a smile and went to put the little note in her pocket, trying a few times before she realized her leggings didn't have a pocket and she looked as if she was standing there wiping the card on her butt.

Sigh. Holly'd had such a gorgeously restful morning – reading and lounging on her balcony, then a leisurely stroll around the grounds and down to the lake for lunch. The rest of the day had turned annoying.

'When you're ready, I'll help you into the harness!' Andrew jogged over to one of the walls, on which was painted in large slanted letters words like 'peace' and 'tranquility' and 'serenity'. Apparently she was in the yoga room.

He grabbed the harness from where it hung from a hook. Fabric strips buckled around each thigh, her waist, and across her chest and shoulders. From the ceiling dangled a wire cable with a hook on its end, which Andrew clipped to a harness ring in the center of her upper back. He gave the cable a good couple of yanks then jogged back – did he ever walk? – to another wall and dragged a portable barre a few feet out into the room.

'Okay, you're set! The wire is on a track that runs most of the length of the room. You can get a sense of how far you can go, but pretty far! Anything else you need?'

Holly thought for a second. 'A mat for warming up?'

'Sure!' Another brisk jaunt took him to a closet, from which he extracted a hot-pink yoga mat that he unrolled on to the floor near the barre. 'Okay?'

'Perfect. Thank you.' *Goodbye and good—*

'Before you start, you need to learn to trust the equipment.' Avid Andrew put his hands on his hips, looking so happy she wanted to kick him. 'I want you to try to fall down.'

Holly was pretty sure she'd never hear that phrase again.

The task should be easy enough – by now it was one of her real strengths. But it was one thing to fall out of clumsiness or inattention, and another to let herself go enough to make herself do what every cell in her body had been terrified of for the past twenty-plus years.

Several attempts later, while she couldn't say she'd lost all her fear that the wire would snap or come undone, she had come to accept that as long as the equipment functioned, it would bear her weight.

However, she also couldn't summon any excitement about trying to dance. She might not be able to fall, she might not be able to hurt herself, but she was pretty certain she would not enjoy any of this bizarre artifice. Joy in dancing was something you took from the emotion, the music, the spontaneity, the chance to communicate a story or emotion or character.

Right now, Holly's story was disaster, her emotion was cranky and her character was full-on bitch.

'If you want music, we have full audio equipment!' Andrew opened a cabinet on the wall painted to look like a sunny meadow. 'You can use Bluetooth or plug in your phone.'

Another screw-up. 'I forgot my phone.'

'A CD would work . . .' He trailed off, realizing she had nothing in her hands and no pockets and very little brain. If she'd thought, she could have brought the *Pogo* CD, all songs pre-choreographed for her convenience, though she probably couldn't remember a single step. 'No problem, we have Sirius XM, so you can get whatever kind of music you want. They've got everything. I'll show you.'

He went through the procedure, which was simple enough and included a remote she could use to change the channels then tuck under one of the straps, since the wire wouldn't let her reach the radio unit.

'All set! I'll stay and see if you need—'

'No.' Holly checked herself. 'Thank you. I need to be alone to do this. If you stay, I will stand here without moving until the hour is up, and then you'll just have to take this thing off.'

Andrew almost said something, but maybe she managed to look terrifying, because he stopped looking quite so enthusiastic. But he did fumble in his back pocket and come up with a buzzer-thing, which he fitted to the strap across her chest. 'If you need me, if you're done early, or whatever, just press it and I'll come in.'

'Isn't this what old people wear when they fall and can't get up?'

'Standard issue.' He obviously hadn't seen the commercial. 'For liability reasons. It's smart too. Have fun!'

Yeah. 'Thank you.'

Holly waited until he left, then studied the remote, feeling like a horse in tackle, foolish and exposed, as if there were cameras all over and people lined up pointing and laughing at the trussed-up middle-aged lady who thought she was a dancer. A quick scan of the peaceful room didn't reveal any telltale lenses trained on her, but that didn't mean there weren't any.

She scrolled down the list of Sirius XM channels, ruling out the options under the Pop category. Those songs would be too short. She'd barely get started before she'd have to change mood and tempo and start over again. Too much to keep track of.

The Jazz and Classical list looked more promising. 'Real Jazz' promised a classic sound of 'the original American art form'. That would be good, at least for a warm-up. She selected the channel and waited. A Dave Brubeck piece whispered into the room, volume clearly set for a yoga soundtrack. Holly increased it until the music filled the space, replacing its sterile emptiness with life and aural color.

Her warm-up started the same as her warm-up for any exercise, brisk marching in place holding the barre until her heart rate accelerated and muscles warmed, then careful gentle stretches on the mat. Back at the barre, with a combination of anticipation and dread, she moved on to dance-specific exercises: pliés, relevés, développés . . .

The moves felt strange, her body heavy and sluggish, hips, ankles and feet no longer flexible. As she worked, images came back to her, of her years of classes and teachers at Westside Ballet in Santa Monica, of performances and the annual competition among the kids for parts in the company's *Nutcracker* production. Her pride buying her first pair of toe shoes, how magical they looked, pink and shiny in the box, and how hideously uncomfortable they turned out to be, no matter how short she trimmed her nails or how much lambswool she packed into the tips – discomfort that became familiar and bearable the longer she practiced. The thrill of her first costume, her first tutu, her first solo role. So many memories, so far away, belonging to a different woman.

Even having kept her body and muscles in good shape, Holly's turnout was shot; she could no longer hold her leg straight out or up to the side for more than a few seconds before it started quivering. Her knees cracked through each plié, her ankles resisted each relevé, her arms felt stiff, heavy and uncooperative.

After fifteen minutes, experience told her that her body was warm enough, ready to move, but she took five more because her mind was still telling her she didn't really have to do this, that just because Caleb thought hooking herself up to a wire leash could help her didn't make it true. That even though she couldn't fall as far as the floor, she could turn an ankle or strain a muscle, and be in pain or incapacitated tomorrow for the service if not the rest of the weekend, or longer.

Underneath her hesitation lurked the not-very-well-hidden

fear that she might be really, really bad at something she'd been so passionate about, so wedded to. Until the reality of what her father had done to her future hit, she had been totally committed to spending the rest of her life doing it. Giving up that dream had been the right decision; she had no regrets. But it had also been like giving up part of herself – a wrenching experience she had to do a second time after the accident.

Why did she want to put herself through this? What was the point?

Holly closed her eyes and blew out a breath. There was no point except pleasing Caleb. But not having a good point didn't make it impossible to get through. If she was careful, she could improvise a few steps, tell Caleb it had been the joy of her life, and be done with it.

She started clumsily, not sure what to do, no choreography in mind, moving tentatively, using her arms more than her feet. That felt okay, and brought a tiny distant fraction of the pure satisfaction she used to feel bringing the illusion of effortless grace to movements requiring strength, focus and precision. Simple steps, feet on the floor, not really dancing, but moving with some grace.

Then somewhere up from her subconscious emerged the very first step sequence she'd learned at Westside. How old had she been? Seven? Eight? *Plié, tendu devant, chassé arabesque, balancé, soutenu, passés left and right, and révérence.* She got through it, a little wobbly, and did it again, happy to have a definite trail to follow, remembering the sound of little-girl feet swishing across wooden boards, trying to make their still uncoordinated bodies mimic the perfection of their teacher. *Plié, tendu devant, chassé arabesque, balancé, soutenu, passés left and right, and révérence.*

She tried again, moving faster with larger steps, too slow for the music's energy but some satisfaction in it. Some. Then she went for the arabesque, kicked her own leg and tripped, yelling in panic before she realized she'd only end up dangling stupidly from the wire, feet scrabbling over the shiny floor to regain purchase.

The piece ended. The announcer came on. A wacky jazz experimental piece started. Holly stood listening, heart still hammering from the terror over her non-fall. More? Stop? Maybe a little longer, but different music.

Holly checked the channel list again, and decided on Symphony Pops, currently playing the last movement of a Haydn symphony. Back in the center of the room, she started again, tried to build on the baby routine she remembered, and somehow came up with the part she'd danced as an older girl in *The Nutcracker*, one of the lead flowers. She was still going through the motions more than dancing, but she didn't stumble or trip this time, so that was something. Haydn finished. Holly stood again, feeling foolish. Now what? Limp through a few more half-remembered roles?

This was stupid. Holly knew it would be. Twenty minutes left, and really, what was she accomplishing by looking like someone's crippled grandma attempting to recapture her youth?

Another piece started: Gershwin's *American in Paris*, a piece Holly knew well. First time she heard it, she and Lyle had been watching the movie on a visit to Milwaukee, Holly's first white Christmas. Lyle's parents had been in a decent holiday mood and had thawed a little toward their disappointment of a daughter-in-law. Caleb had brought his then-girlfriend, whose name Holly couldn't remember – a pretty and pretty dull person. They'd watched the film on a VHS cassette in his parents' sunroom, the windows on three sides strung with Christmas lights. Holly remembered being mesmerized by the flakes drifting at the mercy of the wind, sparkling on the yard, mounded on the bushes, shading bare branches, thinking how magical it was, and how desperately she wanted to be back in California because she couldn't stop shivering.

The movie, however, she'd loved, and the dance sequence had been so superb that back home she'd bought a VHS copy and watched it numerous times.

While she stood listening to the lilting phrases, so familiar it was impossible not to smile, a miracle happened. The familiar itch, first in her toes and feet, then traveling up her legs, stimulating her fingers, her arms, her torso and up to the top of her head, until Holly simply *had* to move. The song continued, forced her to go with it. Twice she lost her footing, twice she was left dangling, flailing with her feet until she found solid ground. Twice she swore to herself to stop before she got hurt, and twice kept going, becoming more and more reckless, moving – almost dancing – with fierce, panting joy that felt close to anger. Since she couldn't fall, she hurled herself into the music with a body decades past a dancer's prime, but that body did the best it could. Even more miraculous, the more she danced, the more that body remembered – steps from a recital she did in college, steps from the dance she did for the crowd after the Loma Prieta earthquake, steps her body had internalized so thoroughly they were jumping out now, fully formed, like Athena from Zeus's head. The old familiar euphoria built, the feeling that she was in her element and all was right with the universe.

Gershwin called a halt. Holly likewise came to a stop at one end of the room, breathing hard, sweating, nearly out of her allotted time. The best she could do had turned out to be enough. More than enough. How wonderful to be able to end this crazy experience on a happy note, literally and figuratively.

Caleb would be pleased, yes, but she'd enjoy being able to report truthfully that he'd scored a hit.

Another glance at the clock, and Holly turned off the music. She had one minute left, then Andrew would be coming back in to take off the harness, to strip her of this one blessed defense against falling.

One minute.

She grinned at the room, then took off running as fast as she could, which wasn't very fast given that she hadn't run anywhere for any distance in twenty years. At the end of her tether, she made a grand leap into the air, soaring for one . . . two seconds, then turning to land, pushing off again, riding the wire with her legs off the ground, swing-flying back across the length of the room, a liberating rush.

Then she did it again.

And again, back and forth until she was whooping and laughing, happier than she could remember being in decades. Again and again, until Andrew returned, beaming his enthusiasm, and it was time for Holly to return to reality, to relative immobility, like one of the catatonic patients in the movie *Awakenings*, given back movement and freedom only to have to surrender it again.

But she would not forget. For a brief time, careless, carefree, reckless motion had been returned to her present rather than existing only in torturous memories from her past. Taking root in her exhaustion was hunger for more, to test and push against other boundaries she'd taken for granted were do-not-pass-go permanent. She wanted to swim across the lake, go to Paris and climb the Arc de Triomphe, zipline through the Amazon . . .

The exhilaration and feeling of reclaimed power wouldn't last. Holly wasn't that naïve. Without the wire, she was still exactly what she'd been for the past two decades.

But she saw now what Caleb had given her, what he'd wanted so badly for her to understand. Not just kayaking, not just dancing, but a gift that went beyond the experiences themselves. He'd given Holly the determination to find out what else this damaged middle-aged body could do that she'd never had the courage or confidence to try.

Chapter 11

Subject: Holly
Date: December 12, 1999
From: LyleFred@aol.com
To: Caleb@FrederickIndustries.com

Still in the coma, on a ventilator. The first forty-eight hours are the most dangerous. Don't come yet. Her parents are here. Our friends are here. I'm taken care of. Wait until she's awake and can appreciate your visit.

Subject: re: Holly
Date: December 13, 1999
From: LyleFred@aol.com
To: Caleb@FrederickIndustries.com

No change.

Subject: re: Holly
Date: December 14, 1999
From: LyleFred@aol.com
To: Caleb@FrederickIndustries.com

No change. The strain is crushing. I did this to her by surprising her. I might have killed her, or worse, made her into an alive but unconscious being, unable to perceive beauty or experience pleasure. What is the point of a life like that? She wouldn't want to live it. But how can I contemplate anything else? It's too early, I know. There is still plenty of hope. But the doctors don't know what will happen, they don't know how far she'll come back. My only option is to wait and see. She's young, they say, the brain is an amazing organ, they say. But she was without oxygen for a dangerous number of minutes. People have not recovered in similar situations. People have recovered totally in similar situations. Most likely she will fall somewhere in the middle. It is daily, hourly agony. She is my life.

Subject: re: Holly
Date: December 15, 1999
From: LyleFred@aol.com
To: Caleb@FrederickIndustries.com

No change. Yes, by all means call her, call as often as you want. I'll hold the phone to her ear. I talk to her every day, all of us do, but have no idea if she understands.

Subject: re: Holly
Date: December 16, 1999
From: LyleFred@aol.com
To: Caleb@FrederickIndustries.com

No change. How could I have done this? How can I get that one moment back? If I lose her, I lose me.

Subject: re: Holly
Date: December 17, 1999
From: LyleFred@aol.com
To: Caleb@FrederickIndustries.com

No change.

Subject: re: Holly
Date: December 18, 1999
From: LyleFred@aol.com
To: Caleb@FrederickIndustries.com

No change. Despair is getting harder to keep at bay. At times it feels like each tick of the clock is taking away more and more of my beautiful Holly's chances to come out of this.

Subject: re: Holly
Date: December 19, 1999
From: LyleFred@aol.com
To: Caleb@FrederickIndustries.com

No change.

Subject: re: Holly
Date: December 20, 1999
From: LyleFred@aol.com
To: Caleb@FrederickIndustries.com

She's awake! She knows me. She knows who she is, though not where or what happened. I can't stop crying. There is life again in her eyes.

Subject: re: Holly
Date: December 20, 1999
From: Caleb@FrederickIndustries.com
To: LyleFred@aol.com

I'm cancelling everything. I'll be there tonight.

'Pillow?' Lyle offered one from his side of the bed.

'Thank you, sir.' Holly tucked it under her butt to help tilt up her pelvis, hoping gravity would help Lyle's little tadpole-sperm guys find her egg. They'd been trying for a baby for three months now, with no luck, but the way Holly figured it, every month only brought them closer to success. She'd waited until age thirty-two to feel ready for this overwhelming responsibility, and now that she'd finally made such a huge decision, she was impatient, as if the world and her body should fall in line with her schedule. A few months of failure was nothing, though it didn't stop her occasionally worrying that she'd put off baby-making for too long. Any earlier, however, and she'd also be worried that she was working too hard to be the mother she wanted to be.

She figured all this worry was good training.

Lyle stretched out next to her and put a tender hand on her belly, rubbing gently. 'Swim, swim, faster, faster. Only one winner in this race.'

'Not hoping for twins?'

He considered, hand pausing. 'Twins would be a challenge. But if that's what we get, okay, bring 'em on.'

Holly pretended a shudder. 'I'd rather have that work spread out over a few years.'

'Yeah, but twins would give us a good start on our Frederick Family volleyball team.'

'Dream on, boy.' She brushed up his widow's peak to watch the hair fall back. 'I hated a lot of things about being an only child, but I'm not pushing out six.'

'No.' Lyle gave her a final pat. 'But kids do need at least one sibling to complain to about their parents.'

'Even though you and I will be perfect in every way.'

'Of course we will be.' He yawned and settled back, adjusted his hand under his head and gave a contented sigh. 'I like when you ovulate on a weekend.'

'Relaxing, isn't it?' She gazed dreamily at the budding orange tree outside their window, imagining her and Lyle and their children cuddled in this bed, maybe on a rare rainy morning. They'd tell stories, roughhouse a little, laugh a lot. Yes, there would be sleepless nights, stinky diapers, helpless frustration – she'd lived it through Melinda. But those picture-perfect moments would balance all that, enriching the love she and Lyle already had.

'Sex is different when we're trying,' Lyle said. 'Don't you think?'

'Nice different or not nice different?'

'Nice different. Meaningful.'

'Sex with you is always meaningful.' She touched the smooth, hard muscle of his shoulder. 'Even crazed-beast sex.'

'Ah, I sure do like me some crazed-beast sex.' His growling noises made Holly giggle – carefully, so she wouldn't disrupt her internal swim team. 'But maybe-a-baby sex is really awesome. I'm using the word literally, as in it fills me with awe.'

Holly wrinkled her nose. 'There needs to be a different word that means filled with awe.'

'Awe-full?'

Holly groaned. 'Awful is right.'

Lyle turned and nuzzled her neck. 'When do we get to try again?'

'Not until your depleted sperm have once again amassed a mighty army.'

'Lunchtime?'

She giggled and brought him over for a kiss that turned into another and then another. She loved his mouth, the shape of his full lips and the way they felt on her mouth and body. For the millionth time she thought about how lucky they were to have found each other and to fit so well.

'Think she'll look like you or me?'

'If he's lucky, he'll look like you.' She smiled, imagining a little Lyle running around after his father, drinking in everything his hero did. A little girl would be fine too. Lyle could spoil her like crazy, and Holly could teach her about being strong and fighting for equality.

Inevitably, both would then grow into teenagers who'd hate everything about Mom and Dad.

'Maybe next year we'll have a baby around for Christmas.'

'Wouldn't that be fabulous? Though wait . . .' Holly wrinkled her nose. 'Would we still have to spend the holidays at one of our parents' houses?'

'Do we have to worry about this now?'

'Of course we have to worry about this now!' She made her hands into claws and grabbed at her temples. 'Why would we put off such superb worry for later when we can enjoy it together right here?'

'Hey, I know! Let's invite both families here for Christmas! There's plenty of room. You could do all the cooking and nurse the baby and I'll pour the drinks and watch a lot of TV. Deal?'

Holly opened her mouth in a silent scream.

'Maybe not.' Lyle kissed her hand, massaged her fingers. 'We'll figure it out later. I'd love to stay here and start our own family traditions.'

'Me too.' She smiled adoringly at her husband. Her stomach gurgled loudly.

Lyle gasped in pretend astonishment. 'Baby's talking to us!'

'Sounds pretty hungry.'

'I'll start breakfast.' He sat up, exposing the long, muscled lines of his back, covered with golden skin that always made her want to taste it. 'Have you been lying there long enough?'

'Uh . . .' She peered at the clock. 'Three and a half more minutes.'

'Yes, Ms Precision.' He shook his head, smiling affectionately. 'I'll go make the OJ.'

Five minutes later, she joined him, wrapped in a bathrobe. Coffee was brewing and Lyle was cutting up oranges, ready to juice them into a small crystal pitcher their friends Ed and Doris had sent after their elopement. Next he'd start in on their standard Saturday-morning breakfast of pancakes, whatever recipe he'd come across lately. Holly was spoiled rotten. If she ever had to cook for herself, she'd starve.

She headed to the refrigerator and pulled out grapes, raspberries, apples and apricots for a fruit salad, then set up a cutting board at the table by the door so she could look outside while she worked. A little chilly this morning, but they often had breakfast on the deck bundled up and further warmed by food and coffee. She loved their weekend mornings.

'So what did Melinda call about so late last night?'

Holly's languorous mood evaporated. 'Ugh. She thinks Matthew is cheating on her.'

'What?' Lyle sounded as horrified as she had been when Melinda told her.

Holly twisted around to face him. 'I know. I can't believe it.'

'When the hell would he have *time*? He's always working.' Lyle's face fell. 'Oh. As in not home.'

'She's a mess over it.'

Lyle frowned down at the whisk he was holding, dripping batter into a bowl. 'I can't imagine Matthew . . . What makes her think he is?'

'A feeling.' Holly shrugged and popped a grape into her mouth, enjoying its crunchy sweetness.

'A *feeling*?' Lyle shook his head and turned to light their flat-top grill. 'She needs better evidence than that.'

'Yeah, maybe.' Holly cut an apricot into bite-sized wedges.

'I wouldn't let it get to you until you know for sure. Melinda gets . . . dramatic sometimes. Maybe her imagination went wild.'

Or maybe she was a wife who knew her husband. Holly finished chopping fruit, aware of the back door opening and Lyle stepping outside. If Melinda was right, she'd be lost. Her marriage and kids had been her whole life for so long. At the same time . . . maybe this would be the push she needed to finally escape her unhappiness.

She swiped apple and apricot pieces from the cutting board into the bowl, then added a handful of raspberries and started picking grapes off the stem. For fun, she tossed one into the air to catch. Mouth open, grape on its way in for a three-pointer, she was startled by a pair of cheerful yellow daffodils thrust into view. 'Mood lifter!'

Holly gasped. She hadn't heard Lyle come back in. The grape shot down her throat and lodged.

'These are the first from the bulbs we planted last fall across from the pool. I've been checking them every day. Can you believe they're blooming already?'

She couldn't breathe. She got up from the table and signaled to Lyle, shaking her head, pointing into her mouth.

He looked startled. 'What is it? What's wrong?'

She pointed again, to her diaphragm, then laid her hands on her ribs, shaking her head.

'Holly . . .'

She spun around, pointed to the grapes, pointed to her throat, shook her head again, mimed a clumsy Heimlich.

'Oh my God.' Lyle turned her away from him, put his arms

198

around her, fist just under her ribs, palm covering it. He jerked in and upward.

Nothing.

He tried again.

Nothing.

Again.

The grape wouldn't budge.

Holly told herself to stay calm. Barely thirty seconds had passed; she still had a big lungful she'd taken in with her gasp. Lyle would keep trying, the obstruction would come out and she'd be fine. Their lives would go on and they could laugh about her brush with death-by-grape.

Five Heimlichs later, Lyle's breathing was starting to sound panicked, and Holly was starting to starve for air. The thought of dying from a grape was no longer funny.

'Holly? I'm going to call 911, then I'll be back and we'll get this out, okay? I want them on the way. They're at the bottom of the hill, they'll be here in minutes.'

Holly nodded, staring at him sprinting to the phone, working her chest, feeling desperate for air now, incredulous that it was being denied to her. It was a gorgeous sunny Saturday, they were making breakfast, there was plenty of air all around her, her lungs worked fine. This was *ridiculous*.

She remembered something, dimly, and attempted a solo Heimlich over the back of one of their kitchen chairs, while behind her Lyle was on the phone, voice strained and unfamiliar, talking, then silent, then talking. *Please hurry. Please hurry.*

The edges of her vision fuzzed and faded. She didn't understand why she couldn't breathe when it was so easy. The first thing she'd done as a baby, the last thing she'd do as an old, old woman. There was no reason she shouldn't be able to breathe. *She had to breathe.*

Her skin cooled, she became dizzy, no longer sure what was happening. Dimly she could feel Lyle behind her, his strong arms around her, pushing, pushing, swearing, sounding as if he was about to cry, then his voice got farther and farther away, and Holly left him to the terror and frustration and plunged into a trance-like calm. She was going to die. She could not die faced away from Lyle.

In a burst of strength, she tore Lyle's hands away and turned, took his face in her hands to stop his objection, barely able to make him out, forced herself to mouth the only words left to her. *I love you.*

There were strange noises after that. Lights. Strangers' voices. People moved her, washed her. There was pain sometimes, but also soothing touches. Lyle was often there, his voice comforting, though he wasn't speaking in a way she understood. Sometimes her parents came, and Melinda, too, though they were all using languages she didn't know, and she couldn't seem to explain how frustrating that was.

One week she and Lyle went on a cruise down and around South America, a fabulous time, though she had trouble trying to pack for that many different climates in one trip. Another time, the two of them and their seven children put on a play of Holly's favorite movie, *The Sound of Music*. The kids were so talented. She and Lyle were so proud!

But terrible things happened, too. A doctor with robot claws for hands tried to tear out her baby, and she couldn't move, couldn't scream, just had to lie there and let him try until Lyle burst into the room and stopped him. Once a horrible insect crawled out from a log she was sitting on up in the mountains and pierced her all over with its stinger. She had to run for a mile before she could shake it.

Then one day she could see Lyle differently, somehow more

concretely, as if she'd been perceiving him only in two dimensions for a while. He was bending over her looking worried, holding her hand. This time he spoke to her in English, asking if she could hear him, which made her want to laugh. Of course she could hear him, stupid question! But for some reason she couldn't answer; there was something wrong with her throat. So she winked at him to show she understood his joke, then stared as he started to cry. She wanted to ask him what was wrong. Was he okay? Did he not have fun on their cruise? Did something happen to one of their children? But before she could figure out what was wrong with her voice, he faded away like a mirage.

She wasn't sure where she was. It didn't seem to be home, but where else could she be? She hadn't gone anywhere, though she did seem to have slept for a long time. Maybe she was still dreaming? She felt awake, but . . . different. The room was definitely not in their house.

More people started speaking English, and eventually the problem with her throat was fixed and she was able to talk. She understood by then that she was in the hospital, that something bad had happened to her, something she couldn't remember at all.

She remembered the cruise and the doctor trying to take her baby, but when she asked if that was the problem, the bad thing, the reason she was here, people didn't seem to understand what she was talking about. *Where is my baby?* Even Lyle didn't know. No one seemed worried, which reassured her some. If they weren't worried, the child must still be okay, still growing inside her in spite of this accident she must have had. Was she in a car? Was anyone else hurt? It was very hard to work anything out. Much easier to slide back into sleep.

Eventually that room changed into another room, and she was able to sit up, speak and stay awake longer, though everything was so foggy and strange in her mind, so many blank places. Hospital staff asked her questions. What season was it? What year was it? Who was president? Ridiculous questions! And yet she had no answers, which frightened her. How could she not know something so simple? They had to tell her the answers! Winter. It was winter.

They'd come back again and ask her again, the same questions. Or they seemed like the same questions. Sometimes she remembered the answers she'd been told. It was winter. Sometimes she had no idea all over again, and the humiliation would burn. How had this happened? She'd been without air for too long. The medics had been able to clear the obstruction and revive her, but she'd been in a coma for a week.

Holly didn't believe them. A week? How could she be in a coma for a week? What about all the things that had happened? The cruise and their children . . .

And then she'd get confused all over again. So much confusion.

From that room she was put in another room, with more people, some of whom made horrible groaning noises or spoke nonsense, seeming more animal than human. She found this deeply distressing and depressing. Why wasn't she home yet?

They told her she could go home when she could climb stairs. They told her to put the green square on top of the red circle. They told her to try to make macaroni and cheese from a mix. The words on the box were in English, she must know them, but they didn't always make sense. They put her in a walker and walked her around the corridors. They'd ask her what a three-digit room number was, and she'd get it wrong.

They'd ask her what time it was on a clock, and she couldn't tell.

Lyle would show up with puzzles and games, which she'd thank him for and put aside. They made no sense to her. It was exhausting and humiliating even to try. He'd read to her. The sound of his voice was so comforting, soothing, relaxing, but trying to concentrate on his words was too much.

Gradually her headaches grew fewer. Words in print started making sense again, though when she was tired they still confounded her. Little bits of her life would peek through the fog now and then and decide it was safe to stay. She remembered winter, she remembered the year, she remembered the president and their address. She remembered she was an actuary and that she and Lyle wanted babies. She couldn't remember choking or anything after that. How long had she been in this rehab place? It felt like forever.

She had to slowly and painstakingly accept which of her experiences had been dreams and which were realities. She was never pregnant. She hadn't been on a cruise; there was no family *Sound of Music* play. She'd been in a coma.

Finally, she mastered the toilet and the stairs, and was allowed to go home. But home was a maze of obstacles and complications, and her life wasn't her life. She couldn't go back to work. She couldn't read. She couldn't do puzzles or play games. She couldn't move without her walker or cane. She could sit. She could sit on their deck and watch the pines and the view with the sea. She could sit on the beach and watch bobbing surfers. She could sit in their living room and watch Lyle.

People visited. Friends of hers and Lyle's. Melinda. Mom and Dad. John and Carol. She could have conversations, though people were more confusing than they used to be, spoke faster, and always stayed too long. One day a man walked in she'd worked with for five years, and until he spoke, she had no idea who he was.

Every day was a supreme effort. Getting out of bed was a marathon. Staying awake all day was impossible. This was not her life. This wasn't even her. Somehow she had turned into an old woman, unable to move or think quickly. She wasn't sure how it happened. When she looked at the backs of her hands, they were still smooth, not ridged with veins and lines like her mother's, like her grandmother's. But she was no longer young, with half her hair fallen out and the rest laced with sudden strands of gray. She was more miserable than she could ever remember being.

Summer dragged on, fall dragged on. She improved. She could make macaroni and cheese. She could put the red square on the blue rectangle. She could read and follow conversations. She still misplaced things. She still had balance issues. She still got confused. She still got headaches. She still got tired easily. The rare times she and Lyle made love, she cried bitterly. There was no more talk of babies.

Lyle was loving and supportive and wonderful, always doing things for her, never complaining. But weeks and weeks went by, and then months and months, and he started getting impatient when she couldn't find her reading glasses or her purse or her cane, when she forgot what day it was, or where her shoes were for the third time that day. His desire, his need to get back to life as they knew it was palpable, a pressure that weighed heavily when she was just trying to make it through each hour.

Some days were better, others worse. Then there were the days that would sink her into the blackest despair.

The day she resigned her job, understanding even through

the you'll-always-have-a-place-here murmurs that there was no hope of going back or ever having a career she could be proud of.

The day she resigned her position on the Westside Ballet board of directors, forever severing her relationship with dance.

The day she admitted to herself that she would never be able to have children.

The day close to a year after the accident when she realized she was not going to recover fully. That she'd always be helpless. That the independence she'd vowed to acquire and maintain through her life, that she'd fought and studied so hard for, was now impossible. She would always be more burden than partner to her husband. Their lives and their marriage would never be the same again.

Over those same months and those same black despairing days, Lyle wanted to go to the desert. Lyle wanted to go to Milwaukee. Lyle wanted to go to Senneck. Lyle wanted to go on a European cruise.

No, no, no. It was too soon. She couldn't handle it. He'd need to give her more time.

Lyle thought she was selling herself short. He thought she wasn't fighting hard enough.

She told him he didn't understand.

He said he was trying to.

She wanted him to try harder, to imagine his entire life disappearing.

He said her entire life hadn't disappeared, that he was still there.

She couldn't tell him that he wasn't enough.

They had Thanksgiving at her parents' house, but Lyle insisted they fly to Milwaukee for Christmas. Holly had forced him to stay in one place probably longer than he'd ever been in one place since he graduated high school. She owed this to him. The idea of packing, of flying, of coping with different surroundings, even familiar ones, panicked her. But she couldn't keep him from his family, so she agreed, smiling. Of course they could go.

The trip was a nightmare. Crowds terrified her. One jostle the wrong way, one person's foot interfering with her cane, and she could fall. If she hit her head, disaster. LAX overwhelmed her with noise and motion, colors and smells. She didn't understand the gates, the seat numbers. She clung to Lyle, trying not to cry, wanting to be home curled up in bed. Lyle was solicitous, but she could sense his impatience. He was sick of her like this. She didn't blame him. She was too.

His parents treated her like the village idiot she was, speaking too loudly and too slowly, not asking for or accepting her help with anything, exchanging told-you-so glances. Their precious son had saddled himself with a brain-damaged wife. As if they could have seen this coming.

Christmas Eve dinner, she spilled soup down her front, called several people by the wrong name, and knocked red wine on to the white linen tablecloth that had been in the family for generations. Lyle's mother gasped, then caught herself, insisted it didn't matter and clamped her mouth in tight disapproval. The Head of the Family raised an eyebrow and kept eating. Lyle told her to try to be more careful.

Caleb looked at his brother as if he wanted to sock him, tossed his napkin on the table, banged into the kitchen and came back with a dish towel, which he spread over the stain in front of Holly with a waiterly flourish, then replaced Holly's plate and silverware on top and poured her more wine.

'All set. We'll throw the tablecloth in the washing machine right after dinner. It's had worse. It'll come out fine.'

Caleb was sweet. But Caleb had no clue. He didn't have to live with her day after day after day . . .

Lyle squeezed her hand under the table, contrite. He'd apologize when they were alone. Holly knew he felt terrible. But it was more of the same, and the longer it went on, the more slowly she would improve, and the slower she improved, the more impatient he would become.

Christmas morning – mornings were her worst time – the whole family was gathered around the tree, showered, dressed and ready, frozen where've-you-been smiles in place by the time Holly made it out of bed, into a robe and slippers and on to Lyle's arm down the stairs.

Lyle had done all the shopping and signed her name on tags and cards. She received thanks from everyone for gifts she'd had no part in choosing or wrapping, and gave thanks for those she got, half of which she would not be able to read or use without help.

Halfway through the event, Lyle plucked up an envelope from under the tree and handed it to her. 'Merry Christmas, wife.'

'Thank you, husband.' She didn't want to open it, remembering the last envelope.

Inside was the itinerary for a Mediterranean cruise, leaving April 4.

Oohs and aahs filled the room.

Holly sat there holding the paper, forcing a delighted smile, afraid she was going to throw up Mrs Frederick's oversweet Stollen. 'Lyle!'

He beamed at her, wearing his most determined husband-knows-best look. 'Excited?'

All eyes were on her, parents proud of their thoughtful son, Caleb wary, watching her, seeing her, Lyle exultant at his triumph, believing with every bit of his soul that this form of torture was the very best thing for her.

'I'm . . . Of course.'

'You're ready. I know you are.'

'Yes.' She wasn't ready. 'I'm so thrilled.'

Caleb's all-seeing sympathy made her act even harder to maintain. She wished he'd look at someone else.

In bed that night, she lay awake until Lyle came upstairs from where he'd been drinking and laughing with his family.

'You're still awake.' He smiled, leaned over to kiss her. 'Merry Christmas, darling.'

'I can't go on a cruise, Lyle.'

His smile sagged, but into tenderness, not disappointment. 'You can, my love. I know you can.'

'Lyle . . .'

'I understand that you're afraid. But I promise you that you can do this. You're going to keep getting better. You're going to come back. The doctor said the more you hang back, the less you challenge yourself, the less you will improve. Use it or lose it. That's how brains work.'

Her brain no longer worked. Why couldn't he understand that?

'We're going to fight this together, sweetheart.' He was whispering so sweetly, that voice she knew so well, kissing one white knuckle after another as she clenched the covers to her chest. 'We'll start small. The trip here to Milwaukee this month. Next month, I don't know, maybe a weekend at a resort in the desert. We'll drive. In March, somewhere else warm and calm. We'll give you plenty of practice. Then . . . a cruise is like staying at a hotel. You'll do great.

'After that, we can start on shorter touring trips here in the States until you're back to where you were.' He kissed her again, sweet brandy flavoring his mouth. 'And then the world. There'll be no stopping us.'

Holly smiled up at him, too tired to go through the same argument all over again, wondering how long he could maintain his illusion that she was going to get better, and what would happen to their marriage when he realized he no longer could.

Chapter 12

Holly was going to be late to tonight's party, the big Friday-night dinner before Lyle's service, with more of the weekend's cast present. After her marionette session at the gym and her initial excitement over discovering new horizons, she'd come back to her room drained and mildly depressed by memories of Lyle during her recovery urging her over and over to do more, to try harder. His frustration and her insistence that she was unable had eventually driven them apart.

If she'd tried harder from the beginning, could they have stayed together?

Moot point. She hadn't. They didn't.

In the midst of her self-torture, she'd conked out on the bed, waking an hour later groggy and confused to find herself for the second time that day in the position she hated most – having to rush to get ready.

Instead, Holly had decided the party could start fine without her. She'd show up when she was ready. In fact, she was going to have the staff deliver a half-caf cup of coffee, and take her damn time getting dressed, using her new *Songs of the Pogo* CD as a goofy soundtrack.

Perfect choice. The *Pogo* songs made her laugh, bringing back forgotten scenes, smells and sounds of her childhood, and her tongue-in-cheek seduction of Lyle. *Don't Sugar Me!* Coffee kicked her out of her post-nap fatigue, and not having to hurry helped her function more efficiently.

For the party, she chose a simple sleeveless red knit dress with a faux-turtleneck collar over which she slipped a silver multi-strand necklace that flowed around her neck. Silver earrings, red sandals – reds were hard to match, but these came close – and a black silk shawl, since the day had clouded over while she slept and a light rain was enlivening the varying greens of the mountains. As pleasant as the day had been, the evening temperature would drop as a result.

At quarter of six her phone rang. Caleb's deep voice was annoyingly thrilling. 'You need an escort?'

Holly rolled her eyes over a smile. Helicopter brother-in-law. 'I'm not ready yet.'

'I didn't mean we'd go yet. I was wondering if you wanted a quick drink before we crash the bash.'

She snickered. 'Did you really just say crash the—'

'No. Absolutely not. You imagined it.' She could hear the grin in his voice. 'I'm looking forward to and dreading tonight; thought you might be too. How about I bring up a bottle of Green Spot Irish whiskey and a couple of glasses?'

She thought a whiskey shot for bravery sounded like a great idea, and told him so, wondering if along with her shoe size, he'd remembered her fondness for the brand. Being able to walk into the party with a drink in her and a gorgeous man on her arm would do a lot to help her get through the ordeal of seeing so many people who'd only known her Before. 'Give me ten minutes.'

Exactly ten minutes later – both brothers had been absurdly punctual – a light tap on her door. Holly had surprised herself; aside from cane and shoes, she'd managed to get the rest of the way dressed and made up.

'Hi, Caleb.' She smiled affectionately, teeth clenched, trying not to swoon. The bastard was wearing a tuxedo. He was absolutely edible. 'You look so handsome.'

She nailed the perfect maternal tone so the words didn't come out as a drooling homage to his manliness.

'Thanks.' He put the bottle of Green Spot and shot glasses on her table and tugged at his bow tie. 'The tux is probably overkill, but Lyle would have liked it.'

'He would have liked it very much.' She was sure of that. Lyle always made a point of dressing a little more finely than the occasion required as a show of respect to hosts or performers. Holly sometimes wished she could throw on comfortably worn jeans like so many others, but she agreed on principle. If she'd spent countless hours rehearsing or preparing food for a party, she liked to feel guests or audience members were also anticipating a special evening.

'Is a small shot of whiskey okay, or would you rather have wine?'

'Whiskey. Green Spot is one of my favorites. I haven't had any in a long time.' Not since the last time she saw Lyle.

'How come?'

'Not much occasion for it. And it's a little out of my budget.'

'Ah.' Caleb looked contrite, which he should be. Rich people had no idea. Lyle had been pretty good about giving himself reality checks, but even he was clueless sometimes.

'How was the dancing today?' He poured her a half-shot, handed her the glass and poured his own.

'Oh Caleb! I should have said something right away.' She was ashamed to have forgotten. 'I had so much fun.'

'You did? It worked out?' Holly had been bracing for a told-you-so, but he sounded delighted.

'It was fantastic.' She sat opposite him at the table, her refreshed wedding bouquet shedding fragrance between them. 'If you'd been there, you would have thought Anna Pavlova had come to life.'

His brows shot up. 'Well done, Pavlova!'

'Pavlova at eighty years old with crippling arthritis.'

His laugh made her evening. 'I'm thrilled, Holly. Skydiving next?'

Her turn to laugh. 'Uh . . .'

'I'll go with you. It'll be great.' He clinked glasses with her; they both sipped. 'What could go wrong?'

'Splat?'

'Ah, splat.' His smile was making her a little crazy. A reckless demon had been unleashed on that gym floor as she danced. She needed to get the little imp back in his lair before something happened either she or Caleb would regret.

'I hate to admit this, but you're probably right that I've been too hesitant to take risks, or rather, seen too many things as risky that aren't. After this weekend, I'll try to shake things up a little.'

'That is great news, Holly. I'm glad.' Caleb moved uncomfortably in the chair, the groove deepening between his brows. 'So, change of subject. I have something I want to talk to you about.'

Uh-oh. Holly put down the shot glass. 'A new way to reorganize my life, Mr Frederick?'

'Another change, yes. But I won't order you to do this one, just putting it out there. You're going to start thinking I'm a meddling pain in the ass.'

'No, I'm not going to start thinking that.' She batted her eyes. 'I already do think that.'

'Ha.' Caleb tossed back his whiskey. 'This is about your

living situation. I know you have to move, and . . . my house is really big for one person.'

Holly's gauzy playfulness dropped like it had turned to chain mail. 'You want me to move in with you?'

'Yes.' He stood and walked over to the French doors that gave on to her balcony, the glass striped and dotted with traveling drops of rain. 'I've also been thinking for some time about retiring early. I feel as if I've done all I can do for Frederick Industries.'

'You're kidding.' She couldn't imagine Caleb without Frederick Industries. Or vice versa.

'I have a replacement in mind who has all the good ideas I don't, so I can leave the company in capable hands, with a clear conscience.'

'What would you do?' Holly was still trying to wrap her brain around him suggesting they live together.

'This weekend I've been thinking a lot about Lyle, about what he valued and the joy it brought him. For the past year or so I've been doing some consulting, mentoring, whatever you want to call it, for start-ups in neighborhoods that need more local businesses. I've been loving it, and want to do more. Before that becomes full-time, though, I want to travel. I've done plenty of that for business, but I'd like to go for pleasure. Not alone.'

Holly stared at his broad back, framed against the dripping glass by pale linen drapes. She had no idea which of the thoughts merry-go-rounding in her head would get the brass ring.

Caleb turned and grinned at her. 'Am I terrifying you?'

'No. My brain doesn't react that quickly. But in the middle of the night . . .' she opened her eyes wide, 'scared out of my gourd.'

'Fair enough.' He walked back and picked up the bottle. 'I

know this is out of the blue for you. I've been contemplating my next chapter for years. Take time to process. Take time to weigh the pros and cons. You'd lose California. You'd win a lot more freedom. You can pay me rent if you'd like to, not if you don't. There's a whole floor you can have to yourself. We'd share a kitchen.'

She was touched by the way he spoke, quickly, forehead furrowed, not his usual cool. He must have put a lot of thought into making the offer comfortable for her. Except for one thing. 'So you're inviting me . . . as your sister?'

'I'm inviting you . . .' he looked away, 'as a housemate. You need a place to stay. I'd love the company and a traveling companion. It seemed like a practical solution. As I said, you are free to think it over for as long as you like.'

'Okay.' She let him pour her a refill, heart thumping with nerves, no idea what she thought of the idea except it both excited and frightened her. 'Thank you.'

'Sure.' He tossed back his shot and thunked the glass down in a gesture of exaggerated nonchalance that betrayed his nerves. 'Ready to party, babe?'

'You know it, dude.' She stood holding her shot, looking around her without taking anything in. 'All I need is my cane . . .'

'And your shoes.'

Holly glanced down at her stockinged feet. 'Oh. And my shoes. Are you sure you know what you'd be getting into?'

Caleb handed over her cane with a warm grin. 'Who ever does? All I know is that I could stand to see a lot more of you. Like every day.'

Holly's cheeks heated. He was making it hard for her to stay rational. 'I'd like to see more of you too. But—'

'No answering now. Much too soon.' He gestured to the

215

door, back to calm confidence, as if he asked women to live with him every day. 'Let's go.'

They went downstairs and toward the lodge's main hall, where Holly and Lyle had attended concerts and occasional movie screenings or social events, though they'd preferred to spend most nights alone in their cottage, reading or talking as they made their way through a bottle of wine, making love whenever and wherever the impulse took them.

They were met outside the entrance by a black-clad member of the staff, who asked to speak with Caleb. Holly paused at the doorway to the familiar room, this evening warmed by a fire blazing in the stone hearth. Colorful art still decorated the walls, done by local artists if she remembered correctly. Windows provided generous views of the rain now pelting the gardens and their distant mountain backdrop. Next to those windows, between potted ficus trees and flowers, dinner tables for six, each already assigned its quota of china, crystal, silver and linens. On the other side of the room, rugs and comfortable chairs, a bar with bartender, and waitstaff circulating small trays of hors d'oeuvres among the knot of guests.

John and Carol spotted her first, friends of hers and Lyle's from UC Santa Cruz, whom they used to see regularly, there and after both couples moved to Los Angeles. They'd disappeared after Lyle left town, either unable to decide whose side to be on or unwilling to hang out with the brain-damaged shade of their former friend. Holly had given them the benefit of the doubt and chosen to believe the former. Divorce was hard on a lot of friendships.

They came at her full tilt, eyes hyper-wide in delight, arms extended for hugs, a ginger one from John, as if he were afraid she'd break, and an all-out love-fest from Carol.

'Holly! It is completely insane that we had to travel to New

York to see you when you're practically next door!'

'I'm glad you're here.' She felt odd, stiff, as if they were strangers after so many years of such close friendship.

'You look fabulous. You really do.' Carol still had hold of her arm, standing at a reasonable distance – she must have finally corrected her nearsightedness. 'It's terrible that we haven't been in touch. We've thought about having you over so many times. Haven't we, John?'

'You bet.' He rocked on his heels, laughing his dorky, nervous laugh, which Holly had always loved. John was a rocket scientist – or close, an aerospace big shot at RAND Corporation – a deep thinker and an all-around sweetheart. But not great at cocktail party chatter.

'No, you shouldn't worry.' Holly freed her arm gently. 'I'm sure the kids have kept you plenty occupied.'

'Absolutely.' John smiled indulgently while Carol caught Holly up on their kids and her new – since Holly had last seen her – career in real estate.

'So what are *you* doing? Back at the insurance company?'

Holly's stomach knotted. 'No . . . I'm working at McKinley school now. I'm a kindergarten teacher's aide.'

Shocked, then pitying faces. Expected. Loathed.

'Oh. Well that must be . . .' Carol trailed off with a silent plea to her husband.

'I'm sorry,' he said quietly. 'What a comedown.'

'John!'

'No, no.' Holly shifted on her cane, much preferring his directness. 'He's right. But it's not a bad job, the people are nice, the kids are great, and best of all, I can handle it.'

'Right. Right. It's what makes you happy that matters.' Carol took a deep breath, looking around with signs of desperation. 'Well. This place is incredible, isn't it?'

217

'Incredible.' John nodded too hard. 'We're loving it.'

Holly pointed to a rain-streaked window. 'You'll love it even more when you can get outside.'

'Oh, we've been here before,' John said.

Holly caught the tail end of a warning glance from his wife. 'Really? When—'

'Hello, everyone.' Eliana joined the circle, wearing a royal-blue pantsuit that looked – no surprise – fantastic on her.

'Hi, Eliana. You own that color.' Holly gestured to her old friends. 'Have you met John and Carol?'

'Oh yes.' Eliana hugged them, eyes sparkling. 'Many times. Here, and in California, and we had them to Milwaukee. We also took a trip together to Paris. One of the best trips ever.'

Horrible silence while Holly's chest contracted in pain. *Many times.* John and Carol had chosen Lyle.

'Crab appetizer?' Saved by a ponytailed waitperson with a tray of tiny phyllo nests stuffed with fresh crabmeat. 'Can I get you something to drink, ma'am?'

'Yes.' God, yes. 'Green Spot Irish whiskey please. Over ice.' Because why the hell not? If the rest of this evening went anything like the beginning, Holly might as well go for it.

'Right away.' Ponytail passed around the tray and left Holly with the job of trying to extricate herself from John and Carol without being rude.

Though rude was tempting.

She glanced to her right and locked eyes with a giant of a man wearing a flowing caftan – with, if she had her guess, nothing on underneath.

'Holly Penny!' Norman bellowed. He charged her. 'It's you! As gorgeous as ever.'

Holly almost gasped. The Norman she'd known mumbled most of his sentences into his chest, and generally acted as if he wished he were invisible. 'Norman Godfrey, you look wonderful.'

'Beatrice! Come meet Holly.'

Beatrice, wearing a similarly non-binding outfit, smiled but lifted a please-wait finger, deep in conversation with someone Holly didn't recognize, which made him the husband of the woman Lyle worked with at the Frederick Foundation, the only couple Holly didn't know here tonight.

'She'll be by soon. Holly Penny, you are a feast for the eyes!' Norman hugged her again. 'Where are you living?'

'I'm still in LA. What about you, still a Milwaukee Cheesehead?'

'No, not us. I met Beatrice a little over fifteen years ago, and we moved to Florida, to a little town north of Tampa.' He turned to gaze adoringly at his wife. 'After a few years getting used to the humidity, I have adapted. You can't beat over two hundred days of sunshine. When we miss snow, we just go home for a while.'

'Sounds perfect.' Holly was astounded by the change in him. If that was what being naked all day did to a person, maybe she should try it. 'You seem so happy.'

'A totally new life. When I met Beatrice, I was reborn.' A few worry lines appeared on his forehead. 'I don't know if you knew . . . we're both nudists.' He waited for her reaction.

'No kidding.' She was grateful to Megan for preparing her. 'That sounds . . . freeing.'

'You have no idea. Our home is in a nudist community. Total immersion.'

'Like a development?' That time she was surprised. 'How does that work?'

'Good high walls.' His laugh was an infectious bass chuckle. 'Beatrice was always a nudist. I came to it late.'

'She converted you?' Holly was surprised how much she loved the idea of tightly held Norman letting it all hang out. Literally.

'Kicking and screaming at first, but I was crazy enough about her to try. After the first few times, I was hooked. It's changed me. Living this way reminds me of Lyle. Being anti-textile is a way of being an environmentalist, which he cared a lot about; and the way people are together, so friendly, so open, it's his beautiful, loving world.'

Holly touched his arm. 'I'm so happy for you. Are you still doing tech stuff?'

'Yes, we're computer people, so we can work from home, which is perfect for the bare-butted among us.'

She cracked up. 'Hilarious.'

'Isn't it?' He was grinning, his brown eyes crinkling at the corners, looking tanned – undoubtedly all over – and robust. She couldn't get over the change. The Norman she knew had the complexion of a rice noodle. Beatrice must be a remarkable woman.

Holly's whiskey arrived with a discreet touch to her elbow. She thanked the server and held the glass up to Norman. 'Here's to your new life, new to me anyway, and to your happiness. It is so great to see you.'

'Thank you, and likewise. It's been way too many years.' He drank a gulp of beer to toast their reunion. 'Now tell me about you. Are you happy? Still leading the charge in actuarial science? Remarried?'

'I am content. Single. With a different job now.' She didn't want to have to repeat the details of her fall. 'It's so nice we can all get together here for Lyle.'

Norman shook his head, pain evident in his face. 'I still can't believe he's gone. We met in kindergarten. He's been my best friend my whole life. The hole is there all the time, something precious missing. I keep wanting to pick up the phone and call him.'

'Yes, it's been difficult.' She said the polite, expected thing, not wanting to explain that until yesterday, she'd thought Lyle was still out there, reachable by phone somehow.

'You know, Holly, I never got to tell you how sorry I was about your injury and what happened with Lyle. You two were so perfect together. Lyle was never the same again.'

Holly snorted. 'Yeah, me neither.'

Norman looked contrite. 'No, I didn't mean—'

'For one thing, I don't like grapes anymore.'

He gave a trumpet blast of a laugh. 'I meant that Lyle never got over you. I've never seen a man in so much pain.'

She stared at him, wondering what version of Lyle he was talking about. There seemed to be an awful lot of them flying around. 'So much pain he got engaged within a year of our divorce?'

'Yes.' He was totally serious. 'That much pain. He did what he could, but it never left him.'

'I see.' He did what he could except come back willing to try without his rosy glasses so firmly in place.

Norman bent toward her. 'It must be strange meeting the other wives.'

'Only because they didn't know I existed.' She tried not to sound bitter, but wasn't sure it went that well. This second whiskey probably wasn't a good idea.

'Lyle never spoke of you even to me, it was too painful. Except once.'

Holly couldn't believe the way her heart leapt. 'When was that?'

'Not long before he left the country. He called me in a total state, saying he'd made a big mess of his life. I'd never heard him talk like that. He asked me what he should do.' Norman took a breath. 'I told him to go find you. Talk to you.'

Holly's breath came faster. Lyle showed up that last time because his friend told him to? 'What could *I* do to help him?'

Norman looked surprised. 'He wanted you back. He never stopped wanting you back.'

She tried not to look skeptical. Lyle hadn't said anything like that, only something about wanting to be in touch, as if she were a long-lost friend and he wanted them to be buddies again.

'He might have wanted the old me back, Norman, but not this version.'

'What version? You look great, and you sound great. If I didn't know, I would never be able to tell.' He nodded briefly to acknowledge someone behind her. 'Anyway, Lyle never did take my advice to go talk to you. It kills me to think you two might have worked out if he had.'

Holly pretended to sip her drink while she tried to sort that out. Strange that Lyle hadn't told Norman he'd come to LA. 'It wouldn't have worked, Norman. Too much time, too much pain. Don't torture yourself.'

'You're a sweetheart. I hate that it's been so long since I've seen you.' He lit up suddenly. 'You should come visit us! Clothing optional for guests, but you might find you love nudism as much as we do.'

Holly laughed without meaning to, remembering her hot-tub experience in college – she'd never expected another chance to be naked around strangers. 'It sounds great, but I don't really travel anymore.'

Norman's eyebrows rose. 'You're here now.'

'Yes, but not . . .' Something stopped her – it took her a few seconds to identify. *No no no*, said on autopilot, without ever thinking through the possibilities. She'd lived like that for decades. 'Who knows? Maybe I will.'

Even if she never did go, the words felt daring and thrilling to say. Maybe Melinda would come with her. Holly couldn't think of anyone more fun around a nudist community. Or anyone more likely to ditch her clothes if she and Holly decided to go for it.

'Excellent! I guarantee you will love the place, naked or not. Though a nudist vacation means packing is ridiculously easy.' Norman pulled out his phone. 'Give me your contact information and I'll be in touch. I mean it.'

She gave him her number, wondering what Caleb would say if she announced that a naked visit to Norman was next on her agenda.

'Hello, Norman.' Megan bent in for an air-kiss, half-empty martini in hand, looking a little unsteady. 'Good t'see you.'

'You too, Megan.' Norman's warmth cooled. 'You look beautiful as always.'

'You look clothed, as not-always.'

'Where's Bodie?' Holly pretended to look for him, hoping to distract Megan in case she was into Norman-baiting. 'I don't see him.'

'Not. Coming.' Megan made the grand announcement, then waved it away as inconsequential. 'We had a fight. He's up pouting in our room. Hates me. Join the club, I say. Lotsa people already in it.'

Holly and Norman exchanged glances. *Well . . . yes.*

'Norman, tell me something.'

'Yes, Megan.' He turned back to his wife, and made a surreptitious sign that Megan missed because she was trying to extricate her stiletto from the braided edge of a rug. 'What is it?'

'I wanna know what clothes feel like when you wear them after so long not.'

'Well, Megan.' Norman looked slightly devilish. 'Right now, they feel exactly like a situation I can't wait to get out of.'

Holly suppressed a snort, relieved when the jab whooshed right over Megan's head.

'Hello there.' Beatrice joined the group, responding to her husband's signal. 'You must be Holly.'

'Yes.' Holly took the woman's soft, plump hand. Beatrice was tiny, barely over five feet, with graying blond hair in a loose braid down her back and startlingly blue eyes.

'It is so nice to meet you.' She held Holly's hand in both of hers and gave it a pat. 'I am looking forward to getting to know you, but I'm going to have to borrow Norman for a moment. We need his expertise. I'll send him right back.'

'Of course.' Holly grinned at Norman, tickled by the perfectly coordinated rescue operation. 'Look forward to chatting later.'

'Same here.' Beatrice led Norman off toward whatsisname.

'He hates me,' Megan said glumly. 'She does too.'

'Really?' Holly looked at Lyle's third wife with amused tolerance. 'Why do you think that is?'

'Because I'm hateful? I dunno, I piss people off.' Megan emptied another half-inch of her drink. 'You just met me, you tell me.'

Holly shrugged. 'You say what you think. That's threatening to some people.' *And you cheated on Lyle and drove him to his death, which would not make you super-popular around here.*

'You know why Bodie's mad at me? Because I told everyone I loved Lyle at that rose garden party thing. Is that stupid or what? Like I couldn't love Lyle and him both? Like we only get one person to love in our whole lives? That would be so sad.'

No comment. Holly only got one.

'Plus he hates this place. I worry about that. Because when I inherit, I'll be able to come to places like this a lot. We're already planning to stay here into next week. I *love* this life, but if he doesn't . . .' Megan rolled her head around as if the anticipated weight of her incoming fortune was crushing. 'I feel trapped between two worlds, ya know? The one Bodie and I grew up in, and then Lyle's. Maybe you can't really leave where you came from. What do you think?'

Holly took a moment to pick through Megan's jabber for something to respond to. 'I don't think we can escape our basic personalities. But we can change some.'

'Tell me.' Megan leaned in until Holly could smell her perfume, sweetly floral. 'Tell me what happened to you. Lyle wouldn't have married— I mean, something obviously happened to you.'

Holly reminded herself that Megan was drunk, probably in pain from whatever tiff she and Bodie had, and upset on who knew how many levels over the death of her husband. Because otherwise, Holly would be tempted to waste her delicious whiskey all over Megan's green lace-up dress. 'I have brain damage from an accident I suffered in my early thirties.'

Megan gasped in horror. 'Omigod. Omigod! That so *sucks*, Holly.'

Holly glanced around, hoping she wasn't attracting attention. 'I'm used to it by now.'

As if.

'Sorry, sorry. Nosy question, me and my lack of filter. But oh my God.' Megan frowned slowly, looking as if her mental faculties were moving at Holly's pace. 'So you're not who you were when you and Lyle married.'

'Nope.' Holly's mouth snapped shut on the word. She wanted her own Beatrice Rescue.

'Did he leave you after the . . . thing?'

Holly forced herself to breathe deeply, relax her shoulders, telling herself the questions were natural curiosity. 'He didn't leave me. We ended the marriage mutually.'

'*What?*' Megan did a double-take. 'You wanted out? In that shape? I mean . . . damaged like that? Why?'

'Why does anyone end a marriage? Because it was no longer working.' Holly was grasping for patience. Why did it feel ruder to say *none of your business* than to submit to questions this woman had no right to ask?

'I bet I know why he left.' Megan touched Holly's arm with the hand holding her martini, only just managing not to slosh any over the rim. 'Because you weren't his idea of perfect anymore. Lyle Frederick was all about perfection.'

As happened sometimes, temper brought Holly's thoughts into clear focus. 'Let me explain something to you. Our marriage was the most amazing meeting of soulmates you can imagine. We were everything to each other, everything we needed each other to be. When it changed, it changed for both of us. Lyle didn't want to spend the rest of his life trying to keep me organized and having to finish my sentences. And I didn't want to spend the rest of my life imagining all the "poor Lyles" from people who felt sorry for him having to carry such a pathetic burden.'

Instead of snapping back, Megan nodded, genuine sympathy in her eyes. 'I totally get it, honey. I really do. When we were married, I was always terrified of acting wrong and making people think Lyle married beneath him. It totally sucks being on the wrong end of a snotty stare that makes you feel like something a horse stepped in. There is *nothing* worse. I should know.'

Just when Holly most wanted to kick this woman, Megan

managed to surprise. They did have this in common. 'That is very true.'

'Anyway, don't listen to me. I'm drunk and probably being inappropriate as usual.' Megan finished her martini and held her glass high, looking around for a refill. 'I hope you at least took the bastard for everything you could. Everyone must have been on your side, the poor brain-damaged woman whose husband was leaving her. Like fish in a barrel.'

Holly shook her head, disgusted again. 'It was an amicable divorce. I didn't sue. I had enough of my own money saved.'

Megan gasped in horror. 'Not even alimony?'

'I stopped that when he married Eliana.'

'You—' Megan froze with the martini glass still up in the air, then turned on Holly so excitedly she stepped back. 'Oh my God, Holly. I figured it out. I finally figured it out. Your initials are HEP, right?'

'Yes.'

'Ha!' Megan pumped her fist. 'That's it. The HEP Trust is for you.'

She was making Holly tired. 'What are you talking about?'

'Right, so, when Lyle disappeared . . .' She handed her empty glass to Ponytail. 'Another please . . . I had to go through his asset records, because I needed to—'

'I thought they were frozen.'

'Yes, but . . . No, so I spoke to his financial advisor, actually, about how much he—'

'Trent? Nope.' Holly shook her head. 'Trent would never disclose confidential information.'

'Okay, okay.' Megan looked supremely annoyed. 'I found his tax stuff.'

'After searching under mattresses and floorboards?' Holly

put on a disapproving schoolmarm face. 'Trying every possible password online?'

Megan blushed. 'Leave me alone, that part doesn't matter. This HEP Trust had monthly payments into it starting from 2002. Was that the year you stopped taking his checks?'

'Yes.' Holly couldn't follow what Megan was getting at.

'Well, he saved them for you, honey, in your name. Once-a-month deposits for twenty years.' Megan named the amount. Not a lot for a Frederick, but enough to secure Holly's retirement. 'It's a nice chunk o' change, and baby, it is *yours*.'

'Why would he do that? I told him I didn't want the money.'

Megan accepted her next martini. Holly didn't want to know how many she'd had before that one. 'You know Lyle. Integrity up the wazoo. In his mind it was your money; you wouldn't take it, okay, but *he* wasn't going to keep it. 'Cuz . . . yours! See?'

Holly wasn't sure how to take the news. Pity money? Guilt money?

One thought did emerge. Once a year when Lyle signed his tax return, unavoidably he'd stumble over her: HEP.

'Oh man, they make a killer 'tini here.' Megan wiggled her hand to throw off some spilled gin. 'I'm so glad that mystery is solved. I couldn't ask anyone because I wasn't s'posed to know. I thought maybe Lyle had a love child or a mistress somewhere. It was kinda eating at me, you know? Anyway, I'm super glad you're getting something, Holly, 'cuz you totally deserve—'

'Well look who it is.' Aunt Janet appeared next to Holly. 'Stirring up more trouble, Megan?'

Megan's shoulders hunched. 'Hi, Janet.'

'How are *you*, Holly? My dear, it's so good to see you.' Janet took Holly's shoulders and kissed her on both cheeks, smelling of makeup and Chanel No. 5 as always, looking svelte in a boxy teal suit and silk scarf with a matching pillbox hat. On her feet, teal sneakers with teal socks that featured knitted goldfish swimming up her ankles. Her neck, wrists and fingers were still covered with gold jewelry, though the skin they rested against had slackened considerably since Holly last saw her.

'Hello, Janet. You look elegant as ever.'

'I *am* elegant as ever.' She lifted her skirt to show off the running shoes. 'Foot trouble. They don't make a single damn shoe that is elegant *and* comfortable, so I said to hell with it and had a pair of these posh babies custom-made for every outfit.'

'They're great, Janet.' Megan seemed to have deflated some. 'You rock them.'

Janet turned to her, leaving one hand on Holly's shoulder. 'How is our little gold-digger today? You must be excited about the will being opened tomorrow, yes? After all that waiting?'

Holly cringed, waiting for the return volley.

To her surprise, Megan took a wobbly step back. 'I don't see any point in pretending not to be excited. I'm sure everyone is hoping for something. I'm just the only one honest enough to admit it.'

'Really.' Janet could make the word sound like an obscenity. 'I'm not hoping. Caleb's not hoping. I doubt Eliana is. Are *you* hoping for money, Holly?'

'Uh . . .' Best to leave it at that.

'Looks like it's just you, Megan.' Janet shook her head despairingly. 'Didn't you know lottery winners are some of the most wretched people in the world? Money doesn't buy happiness, my dear. Experience and kindness and *honesty* are what—'

'Says every rich person. From the deck of their yacht.' Megan smiled sweetly, listing starboard. 'Then they spit on you.'

'Rich people say it because they're the only ones who know

it's true. And if you ask me, you'd better go easy on that drink, young lady.'

Megan took the martini glass away from her mouth, looking guilty. 'You're probably right.'

'For one thing, there's good wine with dinner. Now go away. I want Holly all to myself.'

Megan dipped the suggestion of a curtsy – with surprisingly little irony – and lurched away toward the cheese plate.

'What a pain in the buttocks that woman is. Though I don't know what's wrong with me, I can't quite hate her, as much as I try.' Janet took hold of Holly's other shoulder, tipping her head back to get the best view through teal bifocals with rhinestones liberally sprinkled around the frames. 'How are you, dear? You've aged wonderfully.'

'I'm doing fine, Janet, thank—'

'What's it been, twenty years?' She clucked her disapproval. 'You've never come to see me. Not once.'

'I don't travel. It's hard for me.'

'Oh dear Lord. Of course.' Janet's face scrunched into pain. 'I find it hard to believe in God after what happened to you and what happened to Lyle. Two such wonderful people who made each other so happy. You'd think He'd go pick on someone else for His disasters. I can come up with several perfect candidates.'

Holly nodded dumbly; she was becoming tired and disheartened for reasons she couldn't pin down.

'Lyle was absolutely miserable after your marriage ended, Holly. Eliana is lovely, but she wasn't strong enough for him. He should have known that. And that other one . . . don't get me started. Lyle was always my favorite, but after her . . . Well, it was a huge blow to realize he was a man after all. Marrying her was the stupidest thing he ever did. I told him so myself.'

'Hello, ladies.' Caleb stepped into their group. Holly wilted with relief. She couldn't bear to hear any more about Lyle.

'Here's the one you *should* have married.' Janet grabbed Caleb's arm and hung on, beaming up at him adoringly.

Caleb turned to look at Holly at the same moment she looked up at him. Both of them started turning pink.

'Dinner's ready,' Caleb said.

'Oh good,' Holly said.

'Well, well.' Janet looked from one red face to the other. 'We may not be too late.'

By the time Holly got back to her room, the whiskey and a never-ending glass of wine at dinner – refilled after practically every other sip – plus the noise and the effort of conversation and the emotional nature of the evening had drained her tank to fumes.

Nice party, nice food, nice people, nice toasts and remembrances, but by now it was all Holly could do to kick off her shoes and wash her face. She wasn't even sure she had the energy to undress. As a compromise, she took off her clothes, but didn't bother with her monkey pajamas. Lights out, she snuggled down under the covers, finally able to relax.

Except she couldn't. Too much had happened today. She'd sorta-danced, she'd gotten the *Pogo* CD and sorta-sung, she'd laughed, she'd cried, she'd made a vow to continue pushing the limits of her disability, she'd gotten an invitation to move in with a man she found inappropriately attractive, and she'd had three separate conversations that challenged her understanding of Lyle's state of mind after their divorce and left her in more turmoil. If Lyle had suffered so deeply without her, why had he never tried to come back?

All that would still be around tomorrow. She needed to sleep now, because Lyle's service would be emotional times three.

Sleep, however, didn't listen to her. Her body had been forcing adrenaline for so long to get through the day, it had forgotten how to stop.

And also . . .

All through dinner, and even now, she'd felt Lyle, not in the way she'd gotten used to over the years, fondly distant with a twist of wistful. But strongly again, a real presence.

Leave me alone.

She closed her eyes and went through a progressive relaxation routine that often helped, slowing her breathing, letting go of muscles from her toes to her—

A small sound, something dropping on to the floor. Must be the chocolate left on her pillow. She'd been so bleary-eyed, she hadn't even seen it.

Her eyes opened. Chocolate meant the staff had been here. Had something been left in the drawer tonight, prescribed by Lyle so many years ago?

She turned on the light, pulled open the drawer . . .

Yes, there was something. A votive candle in a blue holder, a near-exact match of the ones she and Lyle had on their outdoor dinner table in Palos Verdes Estates. Lying neatly next to it, a matchbook.

She grinned and held the candle up to the lamplight, remembering all those wonderful evenings, some lasting nearly to midnight even on a weeknight, a bottle of wine slowly sipped while they enjoyed the night air and each other, talking about their days, planning future trips and, not long before the accident, imagining kids at the table with them.

Oh Lyle.

Holly curled her fingers around the candle. Tears filled her eyes and leaked down toward her chin. She picked up the matchbook and struggled to sitting, wanting to light the candle and go to sleep with its flame flickering next to her bed.

The matchbook cover gave her pause. Bar Chloe, Santa Monica. It took her about a minute to remember – the bar where she and Lyle had met that final time, six years earlier, not long before he disappeared. The meeting at which Norman said Lyle had intended to ask her to come back to him.

After Lyle had run, not walked, into his relationship with Eliana, Holly had assumed his near-mythical devotion was less about Holly and more about whoever he was with.

Could she have been wrong?

Her hands trembled as she lit the match and touched it to the wick. The small shimmering flame started round, then stretched upwards, reaching into the darkness it was pushing aside.

Holly set the holder carefully on the night table and turned out the lamp, burrowing back under the covers, watching the glow flicker liquidly on the ceiling.

She tried again to relax, remembering what it had been like seeing Lyle at Bar Chloe after so many years, and how complicated her feelings had—

Holly sat bolt upright, trying to force herself to calculate the sequence of years, one of her most damaged functions, over and over again until she was sure, absolutely sure.

Caleb said Lyle had written extensive details of what he wanted for his funeral after Clarissa died. Holly couldn't come up with the actual year of that tragedy, but she was positive it was more than five years ago, closer to ten.

She screwed up her face to retrace the logic, force it to behave in an orderly manner.

Lyle couldn't have designated that Holly receive this matchbook in the original document for Caleb, because when he wrote it, that meeting hadn't happened.

In seconds, her lamp was back on, the candle blown out. Holly grabbed her phone and dialed Caleb. He picked up on the second ring. From the relative quiet, she could assume either he'd ditched the party or it was over.

'Hi, Holly. You ready for a nightcap?'

Ordinarily she would have laughed – he knew how tired she was; he'd practically had to carry her back to the elevator. 'I need you to answer something.'

'Okay . . .' He sounded wary. 'What's up?'

'Did Lyle ever send you a new version of what he wanted at his funeral? Or revise the document somehow? Maybe right before he left the country?'

'No. There's always been only this one original. Why?'

'I was curious. We can talk tomorrow. Goodnight.'

Holly hung up and lay back on the bed. She couldn't move, could barely make herself comprehend what this meant.

The matches were a signal only she would understand. No one else knew about that final date, not even Norman, whose idea it had been for Lyle to come see her.

Only Holly. And Lyle.

Her heart started pounding so hard she rose up on her elbows. *Breathe, Holly. Breathe.*

And then she felt him again, so strongly she got out of bed and threw open the doors to her balcony, as if he might be standing there waiting for her. Out in the chilly night air, wind-driven rain pelting her naked body, Holly stretched her arms wide and started to cry.

She'd been right all along. Lyle was alive.

Chapter 13

Subject: Back
Date: April 20, 2001
From: LyleFred@aol.com
To: Caleb@FrederickIndustries.com

Hi, Caleb

We're back. The cruise was a disaster. Worst Christmas present I ever gave anyone. It was too much too soon. Instead of rallying to meet the constant demands of the trip, Holly was crushed by them.

I thought she'd come out of this nightmare furious and fighting. Holly is tough! Nothing keeps her from what she wants to achieve!

I thought this trip would remind her of what we had, and spur her to work harder on her recovery. But everything defeats her. The hospital gave her exercises, mental and physical, that will strengthen her body, improve her balance and co-ordination and help rewire her cognition. She doesn't do them. She says they make her feel stupid. And so she doesn't progress.

I thought getting her away from all that would help. I thought feeling the Mediterranean sun and wind on her face and body, doing together what we love best, would help.

If that didn't help, if she still won't do what it takes to get back on track . . . what the hell is left to try?

Subject: re: Back
Date: April 20, 2001
From: Caleb@FrederickIndustries.com
To: LyleFred@aol.com

Your wife is still recovering from one of the most shattering injuries anyone can sustain. Our brains are who we are. Who she is has been injured. I can't imagine how terrifying and disorienting that must be. Give her time to grieve. Give her space to heal at her own pace. It's too early to say whether she's fighting hard enough – leave her the hell alone. I know it's easy for me to say, I'm not in the trenches day after day, but Jesus, Lyle. I saw her face at Christmas when you gave her the cruise ticket like it was an award from God Almighty. She was dismayed, but she put on a brave face, wanting to please you. I'd say the fact that she went along with this stupid idea of yours is putting up a pretty big fight. And you're complaining that you didn't have enough fun?

Subject: re: Back
Date: April 21, 2001
From: LyleFred@aol.com
To: Caleb@FrederickIndustries.com

You're right, Caleb. That was hard to read, but you're right. My email was a blast of inappropriate frustration. Most of the time I'm more patient. It was so hard to be on this trip and watch her struggle, knowing her struggles are my fault. I know it's just fate, I know I didn't do anything wrong, but the bottom line is that she choked because of me.

Subject: re: Back
Date: April 21, 2001
From: Caleb@FrederickIndustries.com
To: LyleFred@aol.com

Sorry here too. You got me on a bad day. It's easy for me to preach patience, I'm not the one having to be a 24/7 caretaker.

You and Holly had the kind of marriage everyone dreams about and few get, and she's different now. You are doing grieving of your own. It's got to be unnerving and frightening. Give her time. Keep nudging her to do whatever will help her get better, but maybe back down for a while, or suggest something so easy that she has successes instead of failures. I assume she's in therapy? Not a bad idea. You might want to it try too. My heart goes out to you both. If anyone can make it through this, the two of you can.

Subject: re: Back
Date: April 21, 2001
From: LyleFred@aol.com
To: Caleb@FrederickIndustries.com

Yes, Holly is in therapy, has been for some time, and on depression and anxiety meds. They don't seem to do much. It's hard not to panic. I'm trying. Thanks for being there as always.

Holly heard the purr of the garage door opening. Adrenaline flooded her. Lyle was back from his day: lunch with a donor, afternoon meetings with the arts council he'd helped start, then a trip to the supermarket. He was gradually reconnecting with commitments he'd had to give up while Holly needed constant care.

She sat up, pushing off the blankets, embarrassed to be

237

caught in bed. If she could make it to the closet for a robe, at least he might think she'd been up but hadn't bothered getting dressed yet. Her energy level had been crap since they'd returned from their cruise, supposed to be the triumphant return of Life As They Knew It.

Holly knew it wouldn't be. There would be no more such life. Because of a grape. If it wasn't so horrible, it would be hilarious.

She'd taken a few shuffling steps toward the closet, trying to speed them up, when she heard the back door open and Lyle's cheery voice. 'Hey, I'm back. Vons was a zoo of Friday-afternoon shoppers, but I made it out alive.'

'That's good.' She wasn't sure her voice had carried to the kitchen. Too much effort. But she'd found the robe now, pink silk Lyle had bought her in Madrid, and pulled it toward her. It stuck on the hanger and pulled back, nearly overbalancing her.

Holly grabbed at the closet's louvered door and hung on, yanking the robe until it slipped free. The first sleeve went on fine, but the robe hung wrong and she couldn't find the other armhole.

'Hi.' Lyle's eyes ran over her, registered disappointment. 'You were still in bed.'

'Yes.' She stared helplessly at the material draping her body. The opening was supposed to be in front.

'You have the wrong arm in the wrong arm.' Patient, patient and so gentle. God, he must be sick of this. 'Let me help, sweetheart.'

'Thanks.' Holly fought to keep down the tears, throat aching with the effort. A year and four months had gone by since her accident. That crucial first-year mark, when most of the improvement took place, had long passed. She still couldn't dress herself.

'There you go. You're gorgeous.' Lyle kissed her, smiling, but his eyes were lined and anxious. This year had been hell for both of them. 'You'll never guess who I bumped into at Vons.'

'You're probably right.'

'John and Carol. Remember they took a ski trip to Switzerland? After they got back, we left on our cruise. Haven't seen them in a long time. I invited them up to have dinner with us tonight.'

Panic started. 'I can't, Lyle. I—'

'It'll be fine. We'll do steaks and salad; they're bringing wine and an appetizer. Simple. You won't have to do anything but show up.' He took her shoulders. Patient, patient and so gentle, with exhausted eyes. 'Sweetheart, it'll do you good to see old friends. They've been so supportive of you, of both of us, over the last year. We need to do this.'

'Yes. Yes. You're right.' She nodded, suffering the burn of resentment. Lyle didn't mean it to, but his reasoning always made her feel guilty. Always she acquiesced, in the hope that he was right, that doing this would work, that doing that would help. Going on this errand, doing that puzzle, attempting the simplest tasks: laundry, errands, gardening. All of it only made her feel stupider and more clumsy.

She was so tired. Jet lag was always harder east to west, but weighing her down further were the implications from their disaster trip. A few months earlier, in therapy and out, Holly had begun the horrendously painful process of trying to accept what Lyle seemed unable to acknowledge. She was not going to get back to normal, and their marriage was forever changed, from a seamless mesh of values, attitudes, energy and desires into two people who no longer wanted the same thing. There was no way to reconcile, no way to make one of them happy without making the other miserable. She couldn't keep pretending she enjoyed being busy and traveling, and Lyle couldn't pretend he loved staying home doing next to nothing.

As much as Holly couldn't imagine life without him, as little as she could imagine launching herself into the suddenly frightening and confusing world alone, a damaged, helpless puppy, it was clear that clinging to Lyle, to his undimmed capabilities and to his cheerful strength, was eventually going to drag them both under. Lyle deserved to continue living the way he was born to live. And Holly deserved to exist comfortably within the narrowed confines of her new life without the constant stress of being pushed toward being someone she no longer was.

One of these days, soon, Holly would have to work up the courage to point out the enormous elephant in their room.

'I'll get stuff ready for dinner.' Lyle took a step toward the kitchen, then looked back. 'Maybe . . . you could shower?'

Holly felt herself color. She must smell as bad as she looked, in all her bedheaded, un-made-up glory. Maybe a shower would lift her spirits, give her some energy. She did love John and Carol. She and Lyle had introduced them to each other at UC Santa Cruz, and they'd been a fearsome foursome from then on, except for a couple of years after Lyle and Holly moved to LA, before John and Carol followed them.

But it was so hard to talk to people, to follow conversations, and to last through an evening.

Tears welled. Holly turned toward the bathroom to hide them, aware of Lyle sighing deeply as he left the room. Those tip-of-the-iceberg hints of his exasperation, his impatience, his pain, were fueling her determination that something had to change. She loved him enough not to want him to live in exasperation, impatience and pain, especially when she was causing it.

Mom had once told Holly about a divorcing friend who'd

said simply that the bad days became more numerous than the good ones. Holly and Lyle hadn't had a good day since her accident.

'Holly?'

She turned, instinctively grabbing at the wall when she lurched off balance. 'Yes?'

Lyle smelled deliciously of cinnamon. 'Sorry. I just . . . didn't hear the shower.'

Holly blinked at him. Had she done it again? She could have sworn she'd been standing there only a minute or two. Whole days seemed to evaporate with very little memory or awareness of what she'd accomplished or spent time on. Lyle was constantly having to show up with nudges, reminders.

Patient, patient and so gentle.

'Yes. Shower. I'm on my way.' She shuffled into the bathroom and turned on the water, determined to stay on track so she could help him prepare for tonight's dinner.

Showers these days consisted of carefully climbing into the stall using newly mounted grab bars and sitting in a plastic chair while the water cascaded over her. Once seated, Holly shampooed her hair and soaped her body, having to rock back and then forward to do the naughty bits, a move that had taken a while to figure out.

Maybe she'd go whole hog, shave her legs and wear a dress, if she could find one that still fit. She'd gained weight since her activity level had been so badly reduced. The fat rolls on her stomach disgusted her dancer brain, but she couldn't figure out what exercise to do. Swim, Lyle had suggested. Ride the stationary bike.

But she didn't, even though Lyle had bought her the bike, and they had a pool. Everything took too much effort. Everything seemed fraught with danger.

Holly lathered up her legs and started in with the razor, one long stripe at a time, until she was smooth-skinned again.

'Everything okay?' Lyle poked his head into the shower. 'Finished?'

She tried not to show her exasperation. 'I've been ten minutes, Lyle. Max.'

His expression fell for that brief flash she'd become accustomed to, before he bolstered it back into cheer. 'About twenty, sweetheart. I thought I'd check on you. No big deal.'

He turned the water off, started to hold out his hand to help, then retracted it. 'You really don't need that chair anymore. You can grab on to the bar if you—'

'I feel safer this way.' Same old arguments. The chair reminded him of his parents' decline, his dad's final days. Holly was still young, therefore Holly didn't need it. Warped logic that made sense to him.

While Lyle blasted Steely Dan's *Aja* album – a sure sign he was in a good mood – and worked on dinner prep, Holly dried herself off, then put on a floral halter dress that was considerably tighter than it used to be but still wearable, and a matching cardigan, since the temperature would lower soon. She couldn't seem to decide if she should bother with a new wardrobe to go with her new weight, but then she had trouble deciding pretty much anything. She needed a simpler life, one of easy daily routines that she could slip into without having to think too hard about anything. In that existence, Lyle would suffocate within three weeks.

Earrings, sandals, mascara, lip gloss, a little blush, not much, but it felt good to have made the effort.

Finally ready, she found her cane behind the door – Lyle had put her walker in the attic, claiming she no longer needed it – and made her way to the kitchen, where Lyle had already made oatmeal apricot bars, coleslaw, and a mixed fruit bowl – without grapes.

'What can I do to help?' She stared at the clock on the wall, willing herself to understand what it said. 'When are they coming?'

'At six thirty.'

Holly hated asking. 'What time is it now?'

'Quarter of.'

Quarter of what, Lyle!? 'So . . .' She tried to work it out, hating that he made her thrash around like an idiot. He said working at challenges was the only way her brain would come back. But Holly couldn't bear the constant humiliation and the constant failure. 'How long is that from now?'

He relented. Patient, patient . . . 'About forty-five minutes.'

Holly recoiled. Already evening, and all she'd done today was shower, read a few chapters of . . . she couldn't remember the book, or magazine or whatever, and . . . something else? She had to have done something else. Quality brooding anyway.

'Headache?'

She opened her eyes, shook her head, tired of being examined so minutely for every twinge, every sign of forward or backward progress. And yet she didn't blame him. He loved her. He worried about her. He'd been through the hell of her near-death, long weeks she blessedly couldn't remember. He wanted her to keep getting better.

Her throat tightened again at the thought of what she'd have to say to him. One day. Maybe today. Maybe next month. Maybe next year. But they couldn't go on like this. They shouldn't go on like this.

By the time John and Carol's car pulled up at the house, Holly had managed to set the table outside with votive candles for when the late-April darkness descended, and the rest only after Lyle loaded up everything they'd need so she wouldn't spend half an hour trying to figure it all out, and carried the tray outside so she wouldn't stumble and shatter their plates and wine glasses.

Lyle was a fabulous cook and a wonderful, generous host, fully capable of putting on a dinner party by himself, but Holly loathed that she couldn't help the way she used to. When she tried, she often ended up making more work for him by screwing something up. He was caught in a terrible place, wanting to give her more responsibility for this so-called brain rewiring theory he was so fond of, while in reality finding it much easier and faster to do everything himself.

John and Carol burst in with two bottles of wine, grilled marinated shrimp and loud enthusiasm. Lyle shepherded them outside to sit by the pool and served gin and tonics all around while he started the charcoal in the grill.

'This is so nice.' Carol pulled her cotton sweater more closely around her. 'I love what you've done with the garden.'

Her husband gave her a look. 'Like you've never been here before?'

'I'm just noticing it again, John. Okay with you?'

'Sure. Have at it.'

Holly stared down at a green leaf floating in the glassy water. Carol and John bickered seemingly without thinking, certainly without realizing how uncomfortable their squabbles made people around them. Exactly the type of marriage she refused to have. Exactly the type of marriage she and Lyle could be headed for.

'Tell us about your trip.' Lyle took the plastic off the shrimp and passed them, in his element surrounded by people he loved. How he must have hated being home so many, many nights without friends to host. 'We'll tell you about ours later.'

Holly sipped her drink, light on the gin, heavy on tonic and lime, hoping he meant much later, like never. She was not looking forward to reliving any of it.

'We had a fantastic time.' Carol leaned toward Lyle, who was back in his seat, nearly tipping her chair to bring him into focus – she couldn't wear contacts and refused to wear glasses except for reading. 'Perfect time of year, not very crowded. We skied at Zermatt. My God, the views. We live with gorgeous views every day here, but wow. The Swiss Alps are stupendous.'

'Skiing was good too.' John spoke in the deep, announcer-like voice that made Holly feel he should say only things that were uniquely important.

'It was perfect, perfect, perfect.' Carol thumped her chest on each word. 'We worried, since March is late in the season. But that made it cheaper.'

'And less crowded,' boomed John.

'Oh! And we skied down to Italy for lunch one day,' Carol said. 'I *love* telling people that.'

'Which is why everyone we know has heard it by now.'

'And they all loved it, John.' Carol rolled her eyes at Lyle as if her husband was Just Too Much.

Holly listened, aching with envy. She'd grown up skiing at Tahoe and Alpine Meadows, and had introduced Lyle to downhill – he'd skied in Wisconsin, but cross-country only.

'I just had the best idea!' Carol planted a hand on Lyle's shoulder. 'You guys should come with us next year. We're going back in February. It was that good.'

'We'd love to.' Lyle spoke decisively. 'It sounds incredible. We haven't skied for a while, but if there are easy slopes to warm up on, we're in.'

'Yes, there are plenty.' Carol practically sparkled with excitement. Holly had long suspected she had a crush on Lyle, which Holly had never blamed her for or been bothered by. Until tonight. 'Oh, we will have so much *fun*!'

'I can't.' Holly couldn't understand what Lyle was thinking. 'I can't ski anymore.'

Carol looked over as if Holly had said she no longer spoke English.

'You don't know that,' Lyle said. 'It's early days still.'

She wanted to smack him: *Wake up!* 'It's been over a year. I won't improve much more. And I certainly can't ski now. I can barely walk.'

Lyle looked shaken. Carol and John exchanged glances. The breeze blew scents of eucalyptus and jasmine past them to mingle with charcoal smoke.

'Well.' Lyle cleared his throat. 'We'll see. But thanks for inviting us. So glad you had a good time.'

'We did.' Carol continued with more details, which left Holly to wonder if she'd always talked that much, and how Holly had ever enjoyed such a torrent.

She tuned out the chatter, staring past the group at the neat garden she and Lyle had worked so hard on since they moved in, though her main contribution this year had been to crush most of a flat of marigolds with a misplaced step and then topple over on to her face.

'However, we do have an announcement.' Carol turned away from Lyle and reached for John's hand. 'We told our families, but besides them, you are first.'

Holly knew before Carol said the words.

'We're going to have a baby!'

Lyle erupted into cheers and congratulations. Holly joined, then stood carefully for hugs all around. She was happy for John and Carol. At the same time, she felt as if someone had just fed her a hearty meal of ground glass.

'I wondered why you hadn't touched your drink. Can I get you something else?' Lyle waited, brows raised expectantly.

'No, no, Lyle, I'm fine. There's water here.'

'So . . . details!' Lyle took his seat again, looking years younger, so much like his old self that Holly was shocked to realize how unhappiness had changed him. 'How far along are you?'

'Due end of October.' Carol couldn't stop smiling. 'The twenty-eighth.'

'Are they going to let you take time off when the baby comes, John?' Lyle asked.

'Yes. I'll take saved personal and sick time, plus some vacation.'

'He'll be home for the first month. My mom will be helping, too, and John's parents are also super-anxious to be part of it all.'

'We are too.' Holly raised her glass, hating the black envy eating at her. 'Here's to the little one.'

John chuckled, shaking his head. 'End of life as we know it.'

'Oh you. Always the pessimist. It's going to be fantastic.' Carol put a hand to her midsection. 'One more person in the family to love. I can't wait.'

Lyle stared at Carol's belly with such deep hunger that Holly felt a physical jolt of pain. Lyle would have no children with Holly. There would be no more carefree travel. No more spontaneous picnics or weekends out of town. John's words rang in her head. Life as she and Lyle knew it had been over for a long time. It would not make a miraculous return. That look on his face had been the final sign.

She had to let him go.

For the rest of the evening, Holly kept on her autopilot face, attentive, reacting, smiling, laughing when others did, contributing almost nothing. No one seemed to mind or notice; it was as if she'd been written out of the picture already. Carol bloomed under Lyle's attention. Lyle bloomed under hers. Finally he could talk to someone who could answer quickly, banter, keep her mind on whatever they were discussing.

The shrimp was eaten, steaks and salad served and devoured. Candles were lit as darkness fell, their light embracing the quartet of old friends, as the space narrowed around them. Holly wanted to slink off to bed and sleep for the rest of her life.

Conversation stopped abruptly. Her three friends were staring at her.

'Holly?' Lyle said. Patient, patient and so gentle.

She found herself on her feet, wine glass in hand, without having been aware that she'd moved. Her marriage would all but end tonight.

'I'm . . .' she swallowed, 'cold. Going to get a jacket.'

'I'll get it for you.' Lyle jumped up. 'I have to get dessert anyway.'

'No, Lyle.' She needed to escape from everyone, just for a while. 'I'll get it.'

'I don't mind. I should have reminded you to bring one out earlier.' He looked at her dress. 'You want the blue fleece?'

Holly stared pleadingly. 'I'll go, Lyle.'

'I don't want you walking in the dark.'

She gestured to the well-lit path. 'It's not dark.'

'Lyle?' Carol held up her glass. 'I'd love some more water. Actually, I'd love more *wine*, but baby shouldn't have it. Would you mind?'

'Not at all.' He turned and went toward the house.

Holly sat down with a *whump* of defeat. Denied. Again.

Half the time he was pushing her past her ability, the other half not letting her do what she could.

'How are you, Hol?' Carol leaned too close. 'You seem tired.'

'Yes.' The word was all she could get out. If she said any more, she'd start crying.

'Well, no wonder. I mean, really. What you've been through . . .' Carol's face, alarmingly near, drooped into pity and affection. 'But you are so amazingly better, Holly. That's something to celebrate.'

'Yes.'

Carol squeezed her wrist. 'I know, easy for me to say. But remember, we saw you when you were in a coma, all those horrible tubes and lines sticking out of you. We weren't even sure you'd wake up. Then we weren't sure you could breathe on your own. Then we worried you wouldn't be able to walk on your own, all those weeks and weeks you don't even remember that we had to live through. So now to us, hell, you're a freaking miracle.'

Holly smiled fondly at her friend. She and Carol had roomed together sophomore through senior year. They knew each other inside out. But since the accident, Carol had acquired an edge of nerves around Holly that didn't feel so much like friendship.

'Well.' Holly held up her wine, determined not to be any more of a drag on the evening. 'I'm glad I can still drink.'

John and Carol laughed more than the joke deserved, which was kind of them.

Then Lyle was back with the dessert tray, draping the sweater around Holly's shoulders, handing Carol her water, garnished with a lemon slice, sitting with his easy grace and smile, features shadowed in the candlelight.

'So, guys.' Carol angled her body toward Lyle. 'We've been

talking so hard I completely forgot. Tell us all about *your* trip.'

Lyle told them all about the trip. Except the awful parts. Like when Holly had gone to the bathroom at the airport and been unable to find her way back to the gate. When she'd realized that she'd forgotten to pack any underwear. How she'd been overwhelmed on the ship by the people, the noise, the different decks and staircases, the constant requirements of schedules she couldn't keep track of, always having to be some-where, always behind on whatever time it took to get ready, always working to pretend she was having a good time.

How she'd stammered like an idiot every time someone spoke to her in a foreign language, the words and phrases in Italian and Spanish and French that she'd mastered hidden deep in her brain. How she'd tripped over a cobblestone and hit her head against the side of a building, then spent the rest of the day overcome by terror that she'd sustained more damage.

How when she was lolling in the Mediterranean one day, she'd been nearly overtaken by the desire to end her life.

Lyle had lost the rest of his strained patience the last day, when they nearly missed their flight home because Holly had forgotten her passport in the hotel safe, after he'd reminded her 'a million times' to have it with her.

She had never been so glad to be back home in her life.

Mere days later, Lyle was talking about their next trip, sometime in late summer or early fall, when Holly would be so much *better*.

Poor Lyle. Poor sweet, optimistic, earnest, wonderful Lyle.

'I need to use the restroom.' Holly interrupted his saga with the only thing Lyle absolutely could not do for her, and picked up her cane, hoping he wouldn't offer to escort her. 'Be right back.'

He didn't.

Inside, she used the bathroom, let out a few tears to relieve the pressure, then wiped her cheeks dry, peering in the mirror to make sure her face didn't betray her.

She took in a long, long breath, let it out slowly and decided for sure. She would speak to Lyle tonight.

Back outside, hushed murmurs, then Carol's too-bright voice. 'Well, Lyle. That sounds like a fantastic trip! Where are you and Holly off to next?'

Holly moved toward her seat, cheeks burning. They'd been discussing her.

'I'm hoping this summer we can take some shorter trips.' Lyle watched Holly shuffle past, poised to leap to her rescue even though it was only two more feet to her chair. 'We'll take it slowly until Holly can handle a full schedule.'

Holly settled in the chair and put down her cane, feeling like she was a guest at her own wake. For the next . . . she had no idea how long . . . she was a dismal hostess, either half or not paying attention, stifling yawns until John and Carol finally took the hint and got up, pleading Carol's pregnancy as the reason they were leaving so early.

So early? It felt like the middle of the night.

Back inside – Lyle wouldn't let her clear the table – Holly washed some dishes, hands trembling over what lay ahead, nerves strung so taut she felt like screaming. Then Lyle shooed her away from that job too, and sent her to their bedroom to lie down.

Holly went, too tired to argue, too tired to do anything, but determined to have this conversation so it would be over. She and Lyle could no longer limp along pretending that a parallel-play marriage was what either of them wanted. In an ironic twist, it was the extraordinary intimacy of their relationship that made this new state so impossible to bear. If they'd been in a more average marriage, with lots of independent interests and friends, her change might not have had as devastating an effect.

'That was fun.' Lyle came into their room, stretching his tall frame with a yawn. He went over to peer through the window at the vast spread of LA. 'It was so good to see them.'

'Yes.' Holly sat up, still unable to decide how to launch into this unthinkable topic.

'Holly.' His tone made her catch her breath. 'I want to talk to you about something.'

She didn't exhale. If it was the same thing she wanted to discuss . . . My God, it would be so much easier. No less painful, but so much easier. 'Sure.'

'I've been talking to Caleb. About the job in Milwaukee.'

Her shoulders slumped. Not what she'd hoped. 'Yes?'

'I'm . . . Well let's put it this way.' Lyle folded his arms, put them back down at his sides. 'We live in a ridiculously expensive area.'

'Agreed.'

'And . . .' Arms folded. Arms down. 'We took a financial hit when you stopped working.'

Guilt bit deeply. Holly hadn't given a thought to money – they'd always had plenty. Lyle must have been using his trust fund to support her all year. He wouldn't inherit the rest of the Frederick fortune until his mother died. Holly would pay him back out of her savings.

'I'm thinking it might be smart to take the job in Milwaukee.'

She gaped at him, the way she often caught herself staring these days. The perfect, agonizing, ghastly solution had fallen into her lap. 'Yes. I think you should.'

His face registered shock. 'Really?'

Holly nodded, trying to look calm while her whole body wanted to shake.

'Wait.' Lyle's brow furrowed. 'You understand what I'm say—'

'*Yes*, I understand. Jeez, Lyle.'

'Sorry.' He laughed, elated and relieved. 'But wow, that is completely unexpected. I know how much you love California. And how you feel about Milwaukee. But I've been thinking a lot about this. We can start over in a new place where you won't keep having to butt up against—'

'Lyle.' Her lips had turned to lead. 'I meant you should take the job. I'm staying here.'

'What?' He laughed again, not in either elation or relief. 'What do you mean? I don't want a commuter marriage.'

'No.' From a distance came the roar of surf pounding the beach. 'I don't either.'

'So what . . .'

They stared at each other, as they had done so often, but this time entirely, painfully different.

Shock registered on his face. Poor Lyle.

'Holly.' His voice came out hoarse. 'What are you saying?'

She couldn't say the words. Not yet. 'I can't go on any more trips. I can't be any kind of decent wife to you.'

'Sweetheart.' He crossed the room, sat on the bed, put a warm hand on her calf. 'I know how hellish this has been, and how hellish it is. But—'

'No you don't.'

'Let me finish.' He started stroking her with his long, strong fingers. 'But what you don't seem to realize is that you are going to get better. The doctor said—'

'The doctor said most of the improvement comes in the first year. It's been a lot longer than that. That last trip was hell for me, Lyle.'

'That was my fault.' He got up from the bed, went back over

to the window. 'I pushed you too hard, too soon. I should have waited until you were better.'

'This *is* better.' Her voice broke. She needed him to face this, and she didn't know any other way than to keep saying it until he let himself understand. 'As better as it gets.'

'No. You need to work harder. The puzzles are supposed to build back your brain. You're not doing them. The exercises are supposed to help stabilize your . . . your balance, and strengthen your muscles, and you're not doing those either. I want you to get better. I don't understand why you don't want that too.'

'I do. But wanting isn't going to make it happen. The only thing I can do well anymore is be a drag on your life.'

'Holly, sweetheart . . .' The grief on his face made waves of love wash over her. It was so tempting to let them carry her along. But no matter how often she lay back into their rolling embrace, she'd still wash up on the same stinking beach. 'That is not how I look at it.'

'I know it's not how you look at it. That's the whole problem: you're not seeing what's in front of you. This is me from now on, Lyle.' She gestured up and down, damaged brain to untrustworthy legs. 'I am no longer the person you married.'

'You are plenty you. This is crazy talk, Holly. Get some sleep. Everything will look better tomorrow.'

She couldn't believe he'd said that. 'Do not patronize me. I am a grown woman who has made a valid life decision.'

Lyle froze as if Holly were about to vomit up baby devils. She'd never spoken to him like that. 'Are you . . . Is your head . . . I mean, is it hurting? Or are you feeling—'

'You are not listening to me.'

'I am listening. But you aren't acting like yourself. I'm terrified you're having some kind of—'

'*Now* you notice I'm not acting like myself? I haven't been for some time. Our marriage will never be the same as it used to be either. Never, Lyle. You need to stop living in a happy-ending fantasy and accept the ugly truth.'

He paced from one end of the room to the other, trapped in a cage that wasn't his.

'So . . . you want us to live in different cities?' He looked incredulous. 'You think that will help?'

She still couldn't say the word. There was no need to. Once they separated, things would evolve naturally. 'I think it's best, Lyle. I can start a new life not constantly reminded that I'm not what I used to be. And you can start a new life not constantly reminded that I'm not what I used to be.'

'No.' He resumed pacing, hands clamped on his head, as if he was trying to keep it from exploding. 'No. This is not . . . No.'

'If we don't do this now, we will keep going in this . . . this slow decay.' Her face contorted. 'I can't bear that.'

'Decay? *Us*?' He'd turned to ice, his face not moving, only his mouth. 'My God. No. This is depression talking. I'll call Dr Blum. Maybe you can get a change in your medica—'

'You need to face it.' This time it was her turn: patient, so patient and so, so gentle. 'We aren't right for each other anymore.'

He stayed in that horrible icy pose, fists at his sides, Los Angeles twinkling behind him in a wide array on his right, the dark of the Pacific on his left, his beautiful healthy body straddling bright lights, big city and an endless black void. She expected more arguments, more denial, but he only stared.

And she knew with sickening certainty that it was only a matter of time before he gave in.

Chapter 14

Holly sat up in bed, defeated by the last couple of hours' useless attempts to relax, let alone sleep. The initial thrill of realizing Lyle must still be alive had given way to a horrifying whirl of now-whats?

What did she do with this information? What if she was mistaken thinking the secret was meant only for her, and Lyle had sent messages to his other wives? And to Caleb? And Janet and Norman and the whole gang, and all of them were keeping it private? Should she go downstairs and see if anyone was left at the party to ask? *Hey, show of hands: who knows Lyle is alive?*

More to the point, how was she supposed to sit through Lyle's funeral tomorrow knowing he wasn't dead? How could he allow the service to go on if he wasn't dead? How could she? How could he let his half of the Frederick fortune go to Megan? Would he reclaim it once she got what she wanted?

Holly's breath halted. Back on Wednesday, she'd joked to Caleb that Lyle might crash his own funeral. What if he did?

She pictured the mourners gathered in the rose garden. Lyle lowered from a helicopter into their midst. Lyle sailing over the floral wall, shot out of a cannon. Hoofbeats in the distance, then Lyle riding in on a white steed.

Holly closed her eyes. It was very possible she was losing it.

Maybe the matches were just matches. Maybe Senneck had some freaky-coincidental tie to Bar Chloe.

Or maybe she'd still felt Lyle's presence for all these years because they really did have a special connection and he really wasn't gone.

Her Ferris wheel of thoughts brought her back full circle. Should she tell someone what she knew? Caleb? Eliana? Megan? They'd think she was crazy. Norman? Janet?

They'd think she was crazy too.

Melinda picked up on the first ring. 'It's late; have you been out drinking Cristal champagne and eating beluga caviar?'

'Of course, haven't you?'

Melinda blew a tremendous Raspberry of Sarcasm. 'I wish. I'm browsing dating apps and becoming convinced I'll either be alone forever or have to turn gay.'

'You're not even divorced yet.'

'I know, just entertaining myself. It's going to be a long time before I'll feel like a relationship again. Sex would not be bad, however.'

Holly let her head whoosh back on to the pillows, refusing to think how long it had been for her. 'I need to discuss weirdness. Bear in mind I'm exhausted and freaked out, okay?'

'Oh Holly,' Melinda wailed. 'I wish you hadn't gone to this stupid—'

'Lyle is still alive.'

Holly grinned maniacally into the silence. It took nothing less than an atomic bombshell to knock the chatter out of Melinda.

'*What?*'

She explained as clearly as she could, leaving out the part where her sense of his presence had never stopped and lately seemed to be growing stronger.

More silence while Melinda digested the information. Or maybe she'd switched lines to call Holly's psychiatrist, Dr Blum.

'Run that by me again. Because on first hearing it is very tempting to say you have left the land of the sane.'

'I know. But no one except you knew that Lyle and I met that day in Santa Monica.' She spoke slowly, making sure fatigue didn't jumble her words or give Melinda any reason to doubt her clarity. 'And I never told you where we went.'

'So you're saying Lyle is sneaking into your room to plant bizarre memorabilia on his funeral weekend when pretty much everyone in the place knows who he is? And no one has seen him?'

'I assumed he got the staff to put—'

'Why doesn't he just call you? Why play games?'

Holly's ability to reason was fading into exhaustion. Logic trails ran on ahead of her, forking into too many routes to follow. 'I don't know.'

Muffled sounds came over the phone. Melinda had gotten up and was moving around. 'Maybe he's trying to soften you up with the bouquet and all the cute memories before he actually contacts you. Maybe he's trying to prepare you gradually for the shock of finding out he's still alive.'

Holly stifled a yawn, still zinging with nerves. Even her body couldn't figure out what to do. 'I think that's the kindest thing you've said about Lyle in twenty years.'

'I think you're right.' Ice clanked into a glass. Liquid poured. 'It's all too nutty, though, Holly. Why would he want everyone to think he was dead?'

'I don't know.'

'Is he sending lovey-dovey messages to all his women?'

A jolt. 'I don't— Wait, he can't be. His wife is going to inherit tomorrow. If she knew, she'd be devastated.'

'That her husband is alive? How sweet.'

Holly put a hand to her head. 'I know. It's . . . I don't—'

'Shh. You're going to get off the phone now. You've done enough thinking today.'

'I need to know what to do.'

'Nothing. You're going to do nothing. If Lyle wants everyone to know he's still alive, you'll find out. If he doesn't, if it's just you, you'll find that out too. Right now you don't need to do anything except go to bed and rest that excellent brain of yours. And one more thing, sweetie.' Sound of liquid being sipped, swallowed. 'For tomorrow, not now. Tomorrow, when you are refreshed and dewy with beauty, remind yourself that this guy left you at your worst. I know, you sent him away, but you didn't really mean it to be The End or you wouldn't have fallen apart so completely when he married Eliana. Whatever happens now, my sweet Holly, this is not going to be your happy ending. Please.'

Holly heard her words, but could barely comprehend them. Too much was happening, too quickly. 'Yes.'

'And on the other side of the . . . of whatever the hell this is, you need to keep in mind that you might be wrong about all of it and the matchbook is just a matchbook. Maybe Caleb ate there once and thought it would be fun to recommend their hamburgers or something. Lyle might stay dead after all.'

That much she got. 'Caleb wouldn't do that. He'd just say, "This is a good bar, you should try it."'

'Yeah, you're right, that was lame.' A faint tinkle of ice moving against the walls of a glass. 'But someone might have found out you met there. Someone who was close to Lyle might know. A wife, or another wife, or he had a secret girlfriend who is tormenting you, or Aunt Janet, or who knows. I'm throwing out anything right now. I'm so terrified this guy has the ability to hurt you again, alive or dead. I wish I had not let you go to this funeral.'

Holly barely listened after the first couple of sentences, had given up trying.

'Never mind. Sleep. Oh, wait, one simple and good thing, because you have plenty of bad and complicated. A friend is evicting her tenant in Malibu. Cushy situation, adorable tiny house. It's definitely not going to be free, but it's available if you want it.'

'Thanks.'

'Now, this is Mommy Melinda speaking. Put the dude out of your mind and sleep.'

She wouldn't be able to do either. 'I will.'

'And call me the second anything happens. Even if it's the middle of the service. Even if you have to stand up, tell everyone to wait and do it right then.'

'M'kay.' Holly's eyes were already closed, heart still thumping. She owed it to her body and brain to reset, to recharge, but all she could think was that the man she had loved more than her own life, a man she'd been trying forget for the past twenty years, had reappeared in her life just as she was preparing for yet another final goodbye.

Which made her wonder if for her and Lyle, goodbyes were never meant to happen.

Lyle's service was held in the rose garden at noon, filled with sunshine that made the foliage and flowers glow and shed warmth on the busy bees and butterflies. The garden's privacy was perfect for the event, and also meant that Norman and Beatrice felt free to show up in sheer full-length caftans, Norman in black, Beatrice in a dusky rose.

Seeing them – so much of them – put Holly off-balance, but

only for a minute or two. They were so kind, taking her over as soon as she walked through the rose-strewn gate. She had a feeling the strain of the past twenty-four hours and last night's nearly complete lack of sleep showed on her face. Most likely it was the raccoon circles around slitted eyes that gave her away. Under any circumstances she'd attend Lyle's memorial service in deep turmoil, but the situation she found herself in now was like being plunged into the mid-Atlantic and given a biodegradable paper straw to breathe through.

'Sit with us.' Beatrice took her arm. 'Isn't it a gorgeous day? Lyle would have been so pleased.'

He undoubtedly was. Holly couldn't help darting nervous glances around for him, even though she'd decided he'd never subject people to such theatrics. Heart attacks could result.

The few new arrivals who'd driven up today to attend the service were all people Lyle must have met after their divorce. Holly was relieved. She couldn't manage any more loaded reunions or questions about her marriage or her health. She still wasn't sure how she could sit through this sham of a memorial without standing up and blurting out the truth. It weighed heavily, a guilty secret she wasn't absolutely certain was really a secret to everyone.

She put a stop to her thoughts, head spinning through the same questions that had kept her awake last night, wondering when or if Lyle would try to contact her more directly, wondering if she'd get to see him again, wishing that thought didn't make her heart take off like a drag racer.

'Hi there.' Eliana joined them as they headed for seats, looking appropriately somber in a black dress with a muted floral print. 'Anyone get any sleep last night?'

'Not much,' Norman admitted. 'I finally got up and went into another room to spare Beatrice the tossing and turning.

You'd think after so many years we'd be more used to Lyle being gone. But today feels like I'm finally having to admit to myself that he's dead.'

Norman didn't know. Either that or he deserved an Oscar for that speech.

Eliana touched his shoulder. 'There's a Jewish saying that the only people who truly die are those who are forgotten. Lyle is still very much alive in our hearts and memories.'

And somewhere else, where there's a post office and/or phone. Holly swallowed a crazed and inappropriate giggle. 'That's a beautiful way to think about it, Eliana.'

'It's comforting anyway.' She bowed her head. A tear dripped off her nose.

Eliana didn't know either.

Holly gave her a hug. It was nearly unbearable having to watch this grief, knowing it was unnecessary. Lyle better have a really, really good reason to be dead.

They took their seats, about a dozen of them, the chairs set up at the end of the garden closest to the main entrance, the other side reserved for the luncheon tables they'd migrate to later. Caleb stepped up to the lectern, looking suave in a light summer suit, but not rested either.

'Thank you for coming, everyone.' His voice came over the sound system, muted, but with so few of them there, the volume didn't need to be louder. 'If you'd all take your seats, we can start.'

He waited a minute, calm and steady, until everyone was obediently settled. Holly's heart tugged. Lyle and Caleb had been so close. This must be tearing him apart.

Unless he knew too?

'I'm so pleased we have such nice weather today in this beautiful setting. Many thanks to the hard-working Senneck staff for putting on such a great event for my brother.'

Scattered applause, mostly from those who'd been enjoying several days of free unlimited luxury.

'Lyle composed his own service in 2011 when I asked him to write down what he'd like. I never dreamed we'd need those plans so soon. Rather than a mass or remembrances, Lyle wanted a performance of readings and music he'd selected. I'm happy to honor his wishes. If any of you would like to share personal stories about Lyle, there will be plenty of opportunity when we gather after the service for lunch.

'He asked that we open the program with the two pieces bookending Wagner's romantic tragedy *Tristan und Isolde*: the prelude, and an orchestral version of the soprano's final aria, the "Liebestod", or "Love-Death". Our parents exposed us to classical music at an early age, and though I admit Lyle got that bug a lot worse than I did, it's hard not to be carried away by the beauty of this piece. I hope you enjoy it.' Caleb sat in a chair next to the lectern, facing the audience.

'Darn.' Norman nudged Holly. 'This always makes me cry.'

'Me too,' she whispered back.

Lyle had worked to introduce Holly to opera, watching her eagerly as she listened, pointing out his favorite parts, telling her the stories. Holly couldn't call herself an enthusiastic convert, but you'd have to be made of wood not to respond to this music.

When the first notes started, she closed her eyes, found herself swaying as the lush harmonic landscape grew and blossomed, making her ache with the sensual, wrenching beauty of it. Melodies flowed, tension grew and pulled until the orchestra swelled to an ethereal climax impossible to hear without grief and yearning, but also joy. Given the suspicious sniffles around her as the music ended, Holly wasn't the only one affected. Had she already mentioned that Lyle better have a good reason for putting them through this painful charade?

'Our first reading is from Kahlil Gibran's *The Prophet*.' Back at the lectern, Caleb opened a small book. '"Only when you drink from the river of silence shall you indeed sing. And when you have reached the mountaintop, then you shall begin to climb. And when the earth shall claim your limbs, then shall you truly dance."' Caleb's smile was strained. He closed the book with an aggressive snap and sat back down.

The next piece came on without introduction. After three notes, Holly's heart thrilled. Joni Mitchell, 'A Case of You', from her *Blue* album, one of Holly's favorite songs of all time, so evocative, so rich in love and poignancy, the singer still on her feet even after drinking a case of her loved one.

She stared down at her folded hands, letting the song wash over her, its melody bringing back Lyle's apartment in Santa Cruz, their love still so new, both of them so sure it would last forever. She'd been eager to play him the song, hoping he'd love it as much as she did. He had! They'd both known that it meant something deep and important.

When Lyle chose this for his service, was he thinking of that day too?

She looked up as the song ended to find Caleb watching her. Holly managed a smile through tears she couldn't help, shed for that beautiful, hopeful beginning, and those two young people who could never have imagined what lay in store for them.

If Lyle had picked that song to elicit those exact feelings from her, she was going to kick his ass.

'Now we turn to wisdom that Lyle chose from a variety of Native American tribes. First from Chief Luther Standing Bear of the Lakota: "Never rail at the storms, the furious winds, the biting frosts and snows. Bright days and dark days are both expressions of the great mystery."'

Caleb waited, letting the meaning settle over the crowd.

'From the Cherokee: "When you were born, you cried, and the world rejoiced. Live your life so that when you die, the world cries and you rejoice."'

Another perfectly paced pause. Caleb looked as if he were clenching his teeth.

'From the Dakota: "We will be known forever by the tracks we leave."'

A few beats, then he moved gracefully away from the lectern and sat back down.

Next up, a selection from *Aja*, Lyle's favorite Steely Dan album, a somewhat outrageous homecoming celebration song called 'Josie' that Lyle and Holly would dance wildly to wherever they heard it, once outside a restaurant in Paris, rocking out all over the sidewalk with such enthusiasm that a small crowd joined in until a gendarme came by and broke up the party.

On her left, Norman hummed along in a cracking voice, while Holly bounced and gyrated to the infectious beat.

Eliana leaned closer from her right. 'I've never heard any of these. Did this song mean something to Lyle?'

Holly nodded mutely. It had meant a lot to both of them.

'So you know it too.'

Another nod.

'And the other ones? You and he knew them together?'

'They've all been special, yes.'

'I've never heard *any* of these pieces. I had no idea he liked them.' Eliana pursed her lips. 'I wonder if he plans to remember the years he was married to Megan and me.'

Holly was definitely going to kick Lyle's ass.

Caleb rose again to read a teaching from the Buddha extolling the virtue of generosity, the joy inherent in giving and in the satisfaction of having given, then waited his gracious moment for the words to leave their mark.

'Now another of Lyle's favorite pieces, *Metamorphosen* by Richard Strauss, during which he asks you as much as possible not to think, but to let the music flow over you like a meditation.'

Holly braced herself. This was going to be hard, too. She and Lyle had adored this piece, a rich harmonic blanket that folded listeners inside and transported them to a spectacular world of colors and sounds. It also made you want to rip your own heart out.

She must have sighed or made an appreciative noise, because Eliana leaned close again.

'You know this one too, I bet.'

Yes, Eliana, this one too.

Except when the music came on, it wasn't Strauss; it was the Beatles song 'In My Life'.

Caleb's head whipped around in the direction of the speakers. The audience rustled and murmured. At first Holly assumed, along with everyone else, that there had merely been a mix-up in the order and Caleb was upset that the service wasn't perfect.

But when he turned front again, he looked right at Holly, looking nearly as furious as two nights ago when they'd been alone here in this same garden.

An instant later, he bowed his head. There were more whisperings, people shifting, uncomfortably aware that something had happened beyond just the wrong track playing at the wrong time.

Eliana nudged her. 'What was that about?'

Norman leaned in. 'Did someone switch the music?'

Holly was trying to put pieces together. Something niggled at her telling her it made sense, but she couldn't find it.

The lyrics went on, bringing back another memory – of Lyle crooning the words into Holly's hair as he danced her slowly around their kitchen.

She could feel him there with her as he'd been with her that night, warm breath in her hair as he sang, his arms strong and loving around her, moving their bodies together over the floor.

Of all the memories, people and places he'd loved in his life, there was one he had loved above the rest.

Oh Lyle.

Holly started to cry, aching sobs that convulsed her body and dripped tears into her lap, using every bit of her strength not to howl out loud.

He'd loved her so much. And God, how she had loved him, still loved him, would always love him. What a fool she'd been to deny it for so many years. Melinda understood. Her parents understood. Caleb understood. Probably even people who didn't know her understood, it was that obvious.

Caleb looked up again, and her pain was reflected in his face, along with remnants of that terrible, cold anger.

Life Savers. That evening in the rose garden, she'd been telling him about the roll of all-orange Life Savers she'd found in her room, and he'd become exactly that angry.

The truth hit with a certainty that stopped Holly's tears as suddenly as they'd started. Lyle had left the bouquet and the orange Life Savers and the *Pogo* CD in her room to remind her of their happy life together.

He'd left the matches so she'd know he was still alive.

He'd inserted a surprise song into the service today to let her know that all these years later, he still loved her.

The song ended. Caleb got up and started the next reading, the familiar Bible passage from Corinthians about the beauty and power of love, about the emptiness of life without it, his voice raspy, the printed pages trembling in his hands.

Caleb had seen the document Lyle had written for his memorial – the one he'd sent to the Senneck staff to work with. He would have seen that there was no mention of orange Life Savers. That the song 'In My Life' was not on the program. He would have realized that only one person could have made those changes.

Caleb knew.

Now he and Holly would have to figure out what to do next.

Chapter 15

Subject: Eliana
Date: October 17, 2002
From: Caleb@FrederickIndustries.com
To: LyleFred@aol.com

I'm sorry I hung up on you, but I would have said things I regretted. I've taken a couple of hours to cool off, but I'm not cooling off. What the hell are you doing? I'm sure Eliana is a very nice woman and I get that you want company, but you have got to be kidding me. What about Holly? You think she deserves this slap in the face after you left her when she was depressed and helpless? 'Oh well, that marriage hit a tough spot, let's jump into another?' How can you want anyone after what you had with Holly? I've been to see her twice since you left, and I have no idea what is so changed and awful about her that you can't try again.

In case you can't tell, I am furious.

Subject: re: Eliana
Date: October 17, 2002
From: LyleFred@aol.com
To: Caleb@FrederickIndustries.com

I did not leave Holly. She sent me away. She wanted this separation. It was all I could do to keep her from rushing straight into divorce. I left because I thought leaving would show her how much we belonged together, how much it would be worth working to find a new way to stay married and be happy, but it backfired. Every time I speak to her she sounds stronger and happier. Without me. I can't begin to describe the agony.

Maybe I was alone in loving that much. Why else would she be so much better with me out of the picture? The only way, the only way I can survive this without ending up drooling on a straitjacket is to move on. Try to forget that the most beautiful and remarkable woman I've known ever existed. Try to look ahead instead of behind, and try to recapture some sad shreds of what I used to think was so wonderful about the world.

If you'd rather I dive back into torturous grief over losing the love of my life, that's your right. But until you've found yourself lying in bed night after night contemplating suicide because the pain of being alive without her is unbearable, and death seems like the ideal solution, you can't tell me about being shallow by trying to build myself even a fraction of the happiness I once thought I would have until my death or hers.

Subject: re: Eliana
Date: October 17, 2002
From: Caleb@FrederickIndustries.com
To: LyleFred@aol.com

God, Lyle. Okay if I come over?

Subject: re: Eliana
Date: October 17, 2002
From: LyleFred@aol.com
To: Caleb@FrederickIndustries.com

I'll leave the door unlocked.

Holly trudged around the smooth-like-glass pool toward her new home, Melinda's fully furnished guest house. She had been living here for four months, since . . . June? She couldn't count months backwards yet. Not a brand-new home, but it still felt that way; not only unfamiliar surroundings, but Holly had lived with Lyle since she was a college kid, before marriage spending more time at his place than in her dorm room, which suited roommate Carol fine since she'd already been dating John.

Carol and John had been collateral damage in the fallout from Holly's accident. She hadn't seen either one since Lyle moved to Milwaukee. Granted, they were both busy tending to their little one, but they'd made enough lame excuses when Holly called that she'd given up. They weren't the only friends who'd disappeared, but they hurt the most.

She spent a few minutes trying to unlock the door before realizing it was already unlocked. Had she forgotten? She tried to be so careful.

Inside it was cool and breezy – Holly distinctly remembered locking the sliding doors to the patio when she left.

'That you, Holly-Polly?' Her mother's voice emerged from the little kitchen, along with a savory aroma.

'Yes, hi, Mom.' She loved her mother's visits, but she was tired after a long week. The school days still wiped her out, especially this first month getting used to the new routine. She'd been looking forward to a relaxing Friday night. 'Something smells really good.'

'I brought enchiladas for your dinner later.' Her mother appeared in the doorway to the kitchen. Alison Penny had aged too quickly over the past couple of years. Holly's fault for putting her in hell, all this time after Dad had forced the first visit. So many people had suffered so much. Because of a grape – absurdity worthy of farce. 'Chicken salsa verde, your favorite.'

'Fantastic, thank you.' Holly dropped her backpack on the green brocade sofa's tautly upholstered seat. Nearly all the furniture in the place had once belonged to Melinda's aunt, absorbed by Melinda after her death when Melinda's mother couldn't bear to let go of her family's antiques. The result was a charming anachronism of dark Victorian pieces – swoop-backed sofa, fat-seated chairs, bow-legged marble table, roll-top desk, grandfather clock, and a glass-doored bookcase crowned by a bust of William Shakespeare – stuffed into a Mediterranean one-bedroom.

'How was your week?'

'Good. Tiring.' She walked over to give her beautiful salsa-verde-smelling mother a hug. 'But I'm getting the hang of it.'

'Of course you are.' Her mother pushed back a fringe of bangs at Holly's hairline that refused to grow longer than two inches, requiring globs of foamy mousse back in her dancing days. 'You look good. Better every time I see you.'

'Thanks, Mom.' Holly had continued to recover over this past year, to her delight. After medication did wonders to lift the worst of her depression, she also found herself more willing to work at her recovery.

Along the way, Melinda had been a lifesaver, cheerleading Holly through those dark, horrible days after Lyle agreed to the separation. They'd had to sell the house and nearly everything in it, their belongings poignantly and often agonizingly tied to so many stories and memories. Lyle had taken the Frederick Foundation job, and a floundering Holly had moved in with her parents until Melinda deemed her ready and dragged her out to where she could still keep a best friend's watchful eye, but where Holly was no longer in danger of strangling her well-meaning but smothering parents.

Melinda had also convinced her friend Constance Ether at

McKinley Elementary to give Holly a chance. Holly and Constance had hit it off and Holly was hired. Having to get up and out the door every day to a place where the focus was on the kids' growth, skills and social development kept Holly from dwelling on her own. That alone had probably accounted for a huge percentage of her progress. There was no longer any question of spending the day in bed wishing things were different. She had somewhere to be, a place where she was required to be cheerful and supportive every single day.

'You need anything to drink? Hungry?'

'Oh no.' Holly gave Mom a look. 'You're about to fix me an after-school snack, aren't you?'

Her mother laughed, showing large white teeth that made her smile light up a room. Holly had always envied that smile. There was much to envy about Alison Penny. She was tall, with the bearing and carriage of a dancer, if not the skill. Nearing sixty, her dark eyes showed shadows and her skin had lost its firmness, but she moved with determination and spirit, dedicated to her morning walk, yoga classes, gardening and tennis.

'I should make you ants on a log. Your favorite, remember? For years I could barely get anything down you but peanut butter.'

'Peanut butter is a perfect food.' Holly lowered herself on to the prissy sofa and leaned back, trying to find a comfortable place for her head against the carved wooden frame.

'I made iced tea and I brought some pecan sandies. Will that do instead?'

'Absolutely.' Holly knew better than to protest being over-mothered or she'd get the I-just-want-to-be-useful speech. And frankly, it was a luxury to have help. Holly cherished her relative independence, but she moved so slowly, it seemed like magic to want iced tea and have it appear within a minute.

'You must have walked home today.' Mom handed her the tea and put a plate of cookies on the coffee table. 'That's a long haul.'

'Less than two miles.' Holly sipped the dark tea, subtly flavored with mint. 'Exercise is good for me.'

'Constance is still picking you up in the morning?'

'She drives me home sometimes too, but I like the walk when I'm in the mood.'

'That job really is the perfect solution.' Her mother settled on to one of the wide-hipped chairs, tea in one hand, a cookie in the other. 'At least for now.'

Holly squinted at her. 'For now?'

'Well, I mean, you—' Her mother flushed. 'You are capable of much more than assistant kindergarten teacher. I assume someday you'll—'

She stopped when Holly growled. 'Mom, we've talked about this.'

'We have. But I think you're selling yourself short. Last year you thought you couldn't even get this far.'

Et tu, Mom? 'Tell you what, I'll become a neurologist and fix my own brain.'

'Now, now. You weren't there when we all thought you weren't going to make it. I remember praying that you'd be able to know who I was again. Now look at you.' Alison gestured proudly, as if approving her own handiwork. 'I'm happy you're working and able to care for yourself. I truly am. But I worry. It's what mothers do. After the life you and Lyle had, I can't see this satisfying you for long.'

'One day at a time.'

'Yes. Yes.' She spoke briskly, aware she'd overstepped.

Holly tried to think of another subject before her mother went back to—

'I was so proud of what you accomplished in your previous career. Not to mention envious. I hate to see you
now—'

'Envious?' Holly lifted her head from the sofa back. That
was new. 'You wanted to work? Why didn't you?'

'In my generation, not everyone did.'

'But some.'

'Some.' Alison bit daintily into her cookie, cupping her hand
underneath to catch crumbs. 'Work was considered a man's
world back then. I remember my friends gossiping about ladies
in our circle who had jobs as if they were traitors to our sex.
Women weren't supposed to be powerful or smart. I wasn't one
to rock the boat or take risks, and your father wouldn't have it,
so I stayed home.'

It struck Holly that her mother had never opened up about
her life before. Their relationship had changed since Holly's
accident, as if the tragedy qualified her for greater maturity.
'You never felt like you could change your mind?'

'I thought about it, especially after your father went to jail
and ruined us.' Alison shook her head mournfully as if it had
happened last week. 'Those were dark, dark years.'

So Holly remembered, and had heard again from Mom
many times since. She had made uneasy peace with Dad's
weakness. Or at least Holly didn't see the point of punishing
him for it any longer. 'Why didn't you go to work then?'

Bad question. Her mother sat up straighter, face locked into
the outrage she fled to when talking about Dad's screw-up.
'*He'd* made the mess of our lives. It wasn't up to *me* to get us
out of it.'

Ah.

Holly decided the best response to that passive-aggressive
bull was to stuff an entire pecan sandie into her mouth. Speaking

while chewing made her mother's Forbidden List, so she'd be off the hook for comment.

'I miss Santa Monica.' Mom picked something invisible off her sweater and put it in the palm holding crumbs. 'I miss our money and the things it allowed me to do.'

'Yes.' Holly washed down the cookie with more tea, coping with the same combination of sympathy and irritation her mother's sadness always engendered, promising herself never to inflict her own grief on others, especially seventeen years later. 'It's hard to start over.'

Mom gave another approving nod. 'You know now.'

Sigh. Holly was not into spending this beautiful sunny afternoon comparing scars. 'Do you want to sit outside by the pool?'

'Oh, I'd love that.' Her mother emptied her palm-trash into a napkin and stood. 'Melinda and Matthew have such a lovely property. I want to cry every time I think of that house we sold. Prices are way out of our reach these days. We could never afford to buy here again.'

'California is expensive.' A fact Holly was particularly aware of these days. She was startled by how little she earned, and uncomfortable having to rely on Lyle's monthly checks to build up her retirement fund. She was lucky not to pay rent – Melinda wouldn't accept a cent.

She and her mom went outside into the bright sunshine, and settled on side-by-side blue chaises by the pool. Holly relaxed back blissfully, ignoring traffic and mowers to concentrate on the breeze and good garden smells.

'Another reason I never worked . . .' Her mother was speaking down to her glass of tea in a way that made Holly pay attention. 'I always hoped there would be more babies after you. The doctor said no, but I hadn't given up. Maybe I should have listened.'

'I didn't know that. I assumed once you'd had a perfect child, there was no point going on.'

Her mother smiled distractedly. 'I hope you can find someone to share your life with again. As much as your father made my life hell for a time, being alone is . . . well, it's no kind of life for a woman.'

For a woman?

'We'll see.' Holly gave a shrug, not ready to share her secret. Lately she'd been having sneaky, daring thoughts that maybe Lyle had been right about her giving up too soon on her recovery and on their relationship.

'I hate that you're cooped up in that . . . museum.' Her mother pointed to the guest house. 'If I had the money, I would buy you a house. But of course *that's* not going to happen. When your father retires – which at this point we won't be able to afford until he's about seventy-five – we'll probably have to move out of LA. We won't be able to afford it on a fixed income.'

'What? Where would you go?' Holly heard herself reacting as if her mother had said they'd have to leave Planet Earth.

'Probably over the mountains. Palmdale or Lancaster. Or maybe Arizona.'

Holly wrinkled her nose. Desolate deserts. 'I hope it won't come to that.'

'It will. You don't know what it's like to struggle for so long. You had Lyle.' Alison's fingers were pressed white on her glass. 'I'll never forgive that man for leaving you. I'll never forgive myself for not seeing through him, for loving him like my own son all those years. Both of us loved him.'

Holly groaned, not bothering to hide the sound.

'I don't care what you say. He was your husband. He should have stayed.' Alison skewered Holly with her sharpest mom-stare. 'I stayed with your father.'

'You didn't have to.'

'Of course I did. That was my responsibility as his wife. I didn't run out of town and start seeing someone else ten minutes later.'

Holly groaned louder. She should never have mentioned that Lyle was dating. She'd been hurt at first, but deep down she understood. Lyle wasn't good at being alone. He still called her regularly. In a weird twist no one else would understand, they'd been each other's best support through their own separation. Eliana was a pastime, someone he went to concerts and shows with, someone he could try new restaurants and bars with, not someone who had truly touched his heart. Lately Lyle hadn't even bothered mentioning her, and had been sounding more and more hesitant and melancholy. A month or so ago he'd even hinted that he might like to come to California for a visit.

At the time, Holly had put him off, but since then, the idea of seeing him again had taken hold. Life was brutal when they weren't together. He must also be exploring the possibility of trying again.

She'd relished his calls even more after that, but in between the highs of reconnecting with her soulmate, Holly had forced herself to think realistically, take her time weighing possible outcomes, good and bad, if they tried again, gauging whether she was strong enough to handle whatever happened. Time was on her side. Holly had rejected the idea of a visit once; Lyle wouldn't risk suggesting it again. The next move was up to her, and they both knew it. So she remained warm, friendly, but took pains to let him know how much her strength, skills and optimism were improving, so he could read between the lines. *Enough that we might be able to share a life together again someday.*

Baby steps.

She had almost, *almost*, brought up the subject during their call last week, when Lyle had sounded particularly down, but as much as she fantasized about a joyful reunion, there was still too much fear attached to the idea, enough that Holly knew she wasn't ready.

But getting close.

'Lyle was the perfect husband until the first sign of trouble, then he fled. Men are doomed to disappoint us, Holly. They're not capable of the kind of love we are capable of. It's simple biology. Male lions will kill their own young! But I am sure not a single species' females are capable of such—'

'Hey, did I tell you the news?' Holly interrupted without guilt, tired of the same looping complaints.

'No!' Her mother snapped into eagerness for gossip. 'What is it?'

'Caleb is engaged.'

Alison clapped her hands, eyes alight. She loved Caleb. It was hard not to love Caleb. 'Oh how lovely. What do you know about her?'

'Not much. Her name is Clarissa. She has a son from another marriage. Lyle said they make a good couple. Maybe not the most passionate, but he thinks they'll be good for each other, and he's thrilled for Caleb.'

'The brothers are still close?'

'Why wouldn't they be?'

Her mother looked confused. 'I thought Caleb was angry at Lyle for leaving you.'

'They're family. They're mature adults. They get mad, they get over it.' Holly drank her tea, hoping that had sounded as pointed as she meant it. 'No wedding date yet. But I'm happy for him.'

Happy, but also a little uneasy for reasons she couldn't identify. Maybe it had been Lyle's not-complete-enthusiasm

279

about the match. The fact that he'd said, 'They're not us,' to describe it. Holly wanted Caleb to have something that good.

'You could do with new clothes.' Mom was looking her up and down. 'I should send around a few more things. You've had that skirt for decades.'

'So? People still wear skirts.'

'No, no, let me pick something out. It gives me pleasure. Let me spoil my girl.'

'I'm thirty-four!' Holly rolled her eyes, but they exchanged grins. 'If it would make you happy, thanks. Shopping is a disaster. I can't decide on a thing, and the clothes on-and-off in the dressing room is hopeless.'

'You need something for fall. Something washable. And clothes for dating.' Alison waggled her finger. 'Don't look at me like that. You're not meant to spend life alone.'

'*Mom.*' Nothing made an adult feel or sound more childlike than a parent. 'I'm not ready for—'

'You will be. Something in a good plummy purple. You are a knockout in that color. Remember the velvet you had in junior high? You'd wear it to dancing school on the special nights.'

'Ugh, dancing school.' Holly made what her father had referred to as her spinach face. 'Who decided seventies kids needed to know how to waltz?'

'You loved it. We could afford those things for you then. All those ballet lessons . . .' She sat upright and looked at her watch. 'Oops. I'm meeting Char and Lisa at five for a catch-up cocktail, I need to bolt. No, don't get up.'

'I should get out of the sun.' Holly swung her legs over to one side.

'I'll walk you back to the house.'

'You don't need to.'

Her mother looked worried. 'You didn't bring your cane out. I'll feel better. Call me an old worrywart.'

'You're an old worrywart.' Holly hugged her. Unusual to have forgotten her stick. She rarely went anywhere without it. 'You can watch me all the way to the door. Thank you for coming by, and thanks for dinner. Give Dad a hug, tell him I'll call soon.'

'I will. Any plans for the weekend?'

'Melinda and I are taking the kids to the beach.'

'Oh, that will be fun. I'm glad she's here to keep you from being lonely.' Mom made shooing motions toward the house. 'Go on now. I'll watch you.'

Holly walked as fast as she could, as steadily as she could, tottering once but able to push off against a handy palm tree. At her door, she turned and waved her mother off to her ladies' cocktail event, looking forward to a quiet evening.

Upstairs, she rested for a while, then did some of her puzzle exercises. She'd been working diligently on rewiring her brain, wishing depression hadn't so paralyzed her after rehab, and that she'd been able to fight her new disabilities this resolutely when Lyle was still around.

At least she had time to make up for that mistake.

Hungry by 6.30, she pulled her mother's famously delicious enchiladas out of the refrigerator and served up a portion to microwave. Left on her own, Holly subsisted on salads and sandwiches, too tired at the end of each day to concentrate even on the simplest recipes. Melinda was a godsend, regularly shipping leftovers across the yard to 'Aunt Holly' via one of her little ones. To pay her back at least in some small way, Holly had bought her a gift membership to a wine-of-the-month club, though the way Melinda put away booze these days, Holly thought next year she'd switch to fruit.

After dinner and cleanup, she plopped into a chair to watch TV, all she could manage by that hour. During the day, when she was still fresh, she was able to read again. Getting better. Getting stronger. Hang on, Lyle . . .

About ten minutes into *America's Funniest Home Videos*, her phone rang. Unfortunately for her comfort and relaxation, that would require moving to answer it. Another ring, and something made her heft herself up from the settee and head over to check caller ID.

Even before she saw proof, Holly knew it was him.

'Did I catch you at a bad time?'

It's never a bad time when you call. She was grinning like a fool. Lyle didn't usually call on a weekend night. It was just after 10 p.m. in Milwaukee, two hours ahead of Pacific Time. Obviously he wasn't with Eliana. 'Just winding down from the day.'

'Was it a good day?'

Her smile dimmed. He sounded nervous. Tense. 'Average. Mom came by for a visit.'

'That's nice. How is she?'

He definitely didn't sound like himself. 'Same as ever. What's up?'

'I wanted to talk to you . . .'

She closed her eyes, hope rising like an iridescent bubble inside her, fragile but so beautiful. He was going to say he missed her. He was going to ask to see her. He was thinking they could try again. And if he wasn't going to put himself out quite that far, maybe he'd open the door enough that Holly could slip right through. 'I'm here. Go ahead.'

'I wanted to tell you.' He exhaled impatiently. 'So . . . you know I've been seeing Eliana?'

'Yes.' Holly was breathless, clutching the phone to her ear

with one hand, a fistful of her Santa Cruz sweatshirt with the other. 'How is that going?'

We broke up?

'Not what I expected.'

Holly stifled a burst of laughter, joy threatening to spill over. How could he be happy with anyone else? She and Lyle were meant to be. 'No?'

'Things started casually, I told you that. Just two lonely people hanging out.'

'Sure.' Had Eliana met someone else? Had Lyle grown tired of her?

'And then we started getting serious.'

Holly turned around abruptly, as if a logical explanation might be waiting behind her. 'Serious?'

'Yes.' He cleared his throat. 'Quite serious.'

Her brows drew together. She had a sudden, horrible fear that her shimmering hope-bubble was headed for a pin. 'How quite-serious, Lyle?'

'I wanted you to hear it from me.'

'Hear *what* from you?' She sounded as if she were strangling on the words, confused now, annoyed, not able to shift gears quickly enough. Were he and Eliana back together? Or still broken up? Or . . . wait . . .

'I'm thinking about asking her to marry me.'

Holly had nothing to say to that, though she could hear herself breathing too loud. Too hard. He was joking. He had to be joking. There was no way Lyle could marry someone else. *Someone else?!* Not when he'd just asked to come visit. Not when he missed her. Not when they were on the verge of getting back together.

'Holly . . .'

She started to shake. He loved her, this woman who was

283

supposed to be a temporary distraction. He *loved* her.

Impossible. Lyle loved Holly. Holly loved Lyle. It was a cliché, a Mother Goose nursery rhyme, a deep truth etched in the universe.

'But . . . *we're* married.' She unclutched her sweatshirt and grabbed at her head. That could be changed. She knew that. This was her at her worst and most muddled. He'd have absolutely no reason to come back to her. Why would he? She wasn't even a whole person anymore.

'Holly?'

'You want a divorce, then. Yes. Sure.'

'Yes? Sure? Just like that?'

'You'd rather I said no, no divorce, you can't remarry?'

'I . . . I'm sorry, it's—'

'It's *what*, Lyle?' Beautiful clean anger cleared her head, snapped her thoughts into order. 'Difficult? Surprising? Complicated?'

'Yes. All those.' He sounded as if he was going to cry. 'I was hoping we could—'

'Do not say that.' Hoping we could be friends? *Friends!* 'No chance.'

'No.' He let out another pained breath, the complete *moron* who thought he was in love with someone else. There *was* no one else!

Holly closed her eyes, panting now, sounding like an injured dog.

There *was* someone else. Eliana. Lyle's bride-to-be.

'Are you all right? Do you need to call someone?'

Holly was not all right. She had no more brains, and now she had no more hope. But she did have one thing: pride. So she forced a laugh, which came out furious and creepy, like an arch-villain cackling at torture. 'Why would I call someone? You think I'm going to collapse because you've moved on?'

'No. Of course not. I'm just worried about you.'

Patronizing son of a bitch. Marrying someone else!

'I'm fine.' Bullshit, he knew her too well. 'I will be fine. I hope the two of you are really happy.'

'Holly . . .'

More panting, raspy with unshed tears, sounding now like a bulldog with pneumonia. 'I need to go.'

'Can I call later tonight to check on you?'

'No!' She gave another ugly shout of laughter. 'You have *Eliana* now to check on. In fact, don't call me again. For her sake and mine. I no longer want you in my life.'

'You don't mean that.'

No, she didn't. But she told him she absolutely did and slammed the phone down, aware she might not have handled that in the most mature fashion possible.

Not caring.

What a fool she'd been. Thinking she and Lyle could be together again. Thinking he would understand that her depression and her trauma and her despair had sent him away. That their love was so deep and wide, an *ocean* of love, *two* oceans, the *universe's* oceans. How naïve, how ridiculous. He was a man. Holly was out of sight, and look, there's a brand-new shiny Eliana-toy that isn't broken, that doesn't need so much maintenance. Toss out the old! Bring on the new! Mom was dead-on right about men and about Lyle, Melinda too. Holly was the only pathetic sap who'd believed in the impossible down to the depths of her Pollyanna soul, that True Love would conquer all.

Lyle hadn't loved Holly the way she believed with everything in her soul that he did. Nothing at all like the way she loved him.

Chapter 16

'Lyle didn't include this in his service, but I think before we play the final piece, the recessional if you will, I'd like to propose a minute or two of silence so we can remember him in our own ways.'

Caleb bowed his head. Holly bowed hers, late, since what was required of her took a few seconds to penetrate her shock. Caleb knew Lyle was alive. This wasn't a special husband–wife secret. This was something else, something darker. Why hadn't Caleb told her? Holly had brought up her certainty that Lyle was still alive on her first evening here, when they'd had champagne together. Caleb had been unusually brusque in his denial. At the time Holly had assumed he thought she was grasping at straws. Had he known even then?

She felt sick with the weight of all this deception, and she'd only just realized. What did Caleb know that made him able to stomach this? Why wasn't he telling everyone to go home, that this had been a terrible mistake?

'Thank you all for coming today. Please join us at the other end of the garden for lunch.'

The noise of moving, murmuring guests broke what had been peaceful silence. Glenn Miller's 'Moonlight Serenade' came on to escort the attendees to lunch.

Holly's first attempt at rising only half worked; she fell back on to her chair with a *whump* that provoked gasps around her.

Face burning, she bent for her cane under the seat. When she came up with it to try again, Norman and Eliana hooked arms through hers and lifted. She couldn't have stayed seated if she tried.

Another of life's little humiliations.

'Thank you.' She nodded left and right to her rescuers, the duchess bestowing blessings, trying to keep her body from trembling. How was she going to make it through this lunch?

'That was such a nice service, wasn't it?' Norman led her semi-nakedly down the short row of chairs to the main path, then took her arm again to escort her toward the luncheon area. Holly shuffled along beside him, where it was easier to know where to look. 'So like Lyle to put together such a great program. No boring speeches, no long odes to his wonderfulness.'

'He *was* wonderful, though,' Beatrice said from the other side of Norman. 'I did want someone to acknowledge that.'

'I agree.' Eliana was walking on Holly's other side. 'It felt like the service wasn't even about Lyle.'

'We'll spend the whole lunch saying how wonderful he was. How's that?' Norman boomed laughter at his own plan.

'It's a great idea, Norm.' Beatrice nodded politely to a startled server, whose eyes darted away as he welcomed the group.

Through her misery, Holly had a quick flash of what Norman and Beatrice's wedding must have looked like. *And the bride wore . . .*

The lunch tables were draped with coral linen that brought out certain rose bushes surrounding them and complemented the rest. White napkins and low vase with a single perfect white rose among ivy and baby ferns completed each setting.

Holly, Megan and Brodie, Eliana, Janet, Norman and Beatrice found their place names at one of the circular tables.

Holly sat between Janet and Megan, relieved that Caleb wasn't seated with them, hoping the two women wouldn't spend the whole lunch sniping at each other. Then hoping they would, so she wouldn't have to talk.

Waitstaff descended on the guests, asking for drink orders. Beatrice and Eliana asked for white wine while Norman stuck with water and lime, and Bodie with beer. Janet and Megan went hardcore with martinis. Holly sensibly ordered iced tea.

'Here's to Lyle.' Norman held up his glass. 'A gentleman and a scholar, whose loyalty and capacity for love were extraordinary.'

'Hear hear.' Beatrice clinked with him and swooped her glass in a circle to virtual-clink with everyone else.

'By capacity for love . . .' Janet looked pointedly at the three wives, 'did you mean quality or quantity?'

'I'll let other people decide that for themselves,' Norman said. 'As far as I was concerned, Lyle was one of the rare few who'd give you the proverbial shirt from his back.'

'Which you'd never need.' Megan threw a wink over the rim of her martini.

'Proverbial shirt.' Norman chuckled. 'Metaphorical. Figurative.'

'So tell me, Norman.' Janet put down her martini and curled her hand protectively around its stem. 'What's with the nudie thing? As a kid, you were terrified of everything. Bees, fireworks, clowns . . . What made you brave enough to go starkers in front of the world? By the way, your wife – Beatrice, is it? – yes, Beatrice, you have the most beautiful breasts for a woman your age. And you don't wear a bra. It's remarkable.'

Everyone at the table who wasn't Janet, Norman or Beatrice froze in horror.

'Thank you so much.' Beatrice glowed at the compliment as if Janet had been admiring a necklace or hairstyle.

Norman patted her hand proudly. 'And they're not even what attracted me to her.'

'No.' Janet lifted her chin and regarded him through her glasses, pink cat's eyes today, which matched her distinctly not funereal orange and pink suit. 'You have more depth than that.'

'Why, thank you, Janet.' Norman inclined his head. 'As for "the nudie thing", it was gradual for me, but freeing in a way you can't understand until you try it. You're no longer the sum of your appearance or trappings; you're all gloriously and equally human. I lay my personal growth at Beatrice's lovely feet. Our marriage made me a happier, better person.'

Holly leaned to one side as a waitress set a bowl of vibrant green soup in front of her.

'Marriage made me a happier person too, in some ways.' Megan nudged Bodie up from sniffing suspiciously at his soup. 'But not others. I loved the life, and I upped my emotional IQ. But we butted heads a lot, and I didn't like that. I'm definitely a better person around Bodie.'

A pause while they all probably wondered how awful she had to have been without him.

'I learned a lot from Lyle,' Eliana chimed in. 'He got me out of a terrible rut and depression, and I'm so grateful. But with Jeremy my self-confidence is stronger. I'm able to be me, instead of trying to be Lyle. I like myself better now.'

All eyes turned to Holly, who nearly spilled the glass of tea she was lifting to her mouth. Being ignored had suited her fine. This recitation of how much everyone loved and appreciated Lyle was making her secret even harder to bear. What would they all think of him if they knew?

'Uh . . . Lyle and I were very happy. We were lucky. We fit together as we were.' To show that was all they were getting out of her, Holly dropped her eyes and took a leisurely spoonful of soup, cool and fresh-tasting with a pleasant acidity. She wished she had more of an appetite.

'I was heavily medicated during most of my marriage to Jack.' Janet ignored the first course in favor of polishing off her martini. 'Valium in the early days. Then antidepressants.'

'Oh dear.' Beatrice's face was lined with concern. 'That bad?'

'Best present Jack ever gave me was his early death.' Janet giggled over the rim of her glass. 'I'm kidding. Mostly. We were married thirty-five years, and for thirty-five of those years, the marriage was about his political career. My job was to smile and agree with whoever I was talking to, unless they didn't agree with him, and then I was to shut up entirely.

'I've spent the decades since his death coming out with everything I wasn't able to say during that time.' She surveyed the table triumphantly. 'Maybe you noticed.'

'Yup,' Megan said.

'I love that about you,' Eliana said. 'It's refreshing.'

'Like a polar plunge.' Megan bared her teeth in a mocking smile that made Janet giggle again.

Holly ate more soup. Everyone at this table had suffered over Lyle's disappearance and 'death'. Did she owe it to Lyle to keep his secret? Or did she owe it to these people who loved him to let them know the truth?

Caleb made his way to their table, playing his perfect-host role with a generic smile. 'Everyone doing okay?'

'Delightful.' Janet rested her chin on the hand not holding her near-empty drink. 'We were grading spouses.'

'There's a good topic. No hurry eating lunch, but when you're finished, wives and Janet please head to the front of the garden.' He pointed to a corner. 'Lyle's lawyer is due at two. That's about forty-five minutes from now.'

His announcement cast a pall over the table. Megan immediately ordered a second martini. Holly felt her queasiness inten-
sify. How could she sit through this ordeal in good conscience?
What if Megan inherited and then Lyle popped up and said,
sorry, still mine? She couldn't imagine him being that cruel. If
only she knew what he was thinking, why he was doing this to
so many people he loved. Did he intend to stay dead? For how
long?

She barely touched the lamb chops, hardly able to taste a
thing. Dessert was a tiny, perfect passion-fruit flan flanked by
slices of ripe kiwi and papaya, refreshing and delicious. She
managed to eat most of that, but turned down the chocolate-
dipped almond tuile. Conversation slowed further as the hour
for the will release neared. Eliana went quiet. Norman and
Beatrice murmured to each other. Megan and Janet chatted up
an alcohol-fueled storm, even finding a few things they agreed
on, like that bowling had gotten ridiculously expensive and that
camping was out of the question.

Finally as the minutes ticked by, silence fell. Holly was
miserable. Whom did she betray? The man she loved, who'd
betrayed her decades ago? Or these innocent people around her,
all of whom Lyle was betraying now?

'I think I might die of tension.' Megan looked desperate.
'Even the martinis aren't helping.'

'Have another,' Janet said. 'Martinis help everything.'

'I don't think I should.' Megan gripped Bodie's beefy hand,
face crumpling. 'What if I don't inherit? I mean who knows,
right? Just because I was his latest wife? I don't know what's
going to—'

'You'll do fine, no matter what. We've been doing fine. We'll
keep doing fine.' Bodie tried unsuccessfully to extricate his
hand. Given his strength, it made Megan's panic all the more

impressive. 'You and me are good as we are. Money messes everything up.'

Megan turned on him. 'What are you *talking* about?'

'I'm telling you.' The tenderness in his hazel eyes was adorable. 'Lyle's money isn't going to magically fix your whole world, that's all I'm saying.'

'He's right, dear,' Janet said. 'I was telling you the same thing.'

Norman and Beatrice nodded their agreement. Holly felt ready to explode. How could Lyle do this? How could he put them all through this?

'Oh, come *on*!' If Megan had been a super-villain, this would be the perfect moment for her skin to melt off and reveal the demon inside. It certainly looked as if she were trying to keep that from happening. 'You have no idea.'

Holly put down her spoon. 'Did any of you find things in your room from Lyle? Little mementos? Reminders of your relationship with him?'

Blank faces around the table.

'Well I did. Things only he and I would have known about. One item referred to something that happened *after* he wrote out what he wanted this weekend.'

Nervous glances were exchanged. They thought she was losing it. Holly didn't care. She needed to get this dreadful burden off her chest. 'For a while I believed he was still alive. Some of you knew that. I'm not sure what to think now.'

Icy silence.

There. She'd done it. As much of a warning as her conscience would let her deliver until she could talk to Caleb and find out what was going on.

'That is fascinating.' Janet put one elbow on the table and turned toward Holly. 'The things just appeared?'

'Yes.'

'Well obviously the *staff* put them there,' Megan huffed. 'Per his *instructions*.'

'His ghost,' Janet announced. 'Wouldn't surprise me in the least. You marry a Frederick, you have to give up your soul to him. Lyle must be trying to reclaim yours. If you're not here in the morning, we'll know what happened.'

'You don't really believe that, do you?' Beatrice chewed her lip.

'The hell I don't.' Janet pointed a ringed finger. 'Mark my words. One day Jack's ghost is going to show up and say, "Get out your pearls, honey, I'm running for president of Hell."'

'We know Lyle's dead,' Megan snapped. 'We have Rudy's report, the proof. Bodies in the burned car. The bits of Lyle's backpack.'

Holly shrugged, legs trembling under the table. 'I'm just saying.'

'Or maybe,' Janet was getting very enthusiastic, 'maybe it's like that movie, what was it called? They remade it in the seventies or eighties . . . Oh yes! *Here Comes Mr Jordan*, remade as *Heaven Can Wait*, with Warren Beatty. About the guy who dies before his time, so his soul gets a chance in a new body.'

'Ooh, I loved that movie,' Beatrice said. 'With Dyan Cannon and Charles Grodin.'

'And Julie Christie,' Norman said. 'Delicious.'

'I've got it.' Janet slammed her hand down on the table. 'Lyle's soul is now in Caleb's body. That's why he's so in love with Holly.'

Holly closed her eyes to shut out the shocked faces turning toward her. *Thanks, Janet.*

'Oh dear.' Eliana's voice. 'The lawyer's here.'

Holly's eyes shot open.

'Oh God!' Megan rose to her feet.

Caleb came back to their table, his limp in evidence, still not making eye contact with Holly. 'Everyone ready?'

Janet gestured to Megan. 'Don't need to ask *her*.'

'Be nice to me.' Megan grabbed Bodie's arm. 'Five years I've been waiting, and now it's finally here. I'm terrified.'

'This way.' Caleb motioned them toward the other side of the garden with a choppy gesture, more traffic cop than gracious host. 'Let's get this done.'

Holly understood exactly how he was feeling. She found her cane and leaned on it heavily, grateful when Eliana offered an arm. 'Holding up okay?'

'Are any of us?'

'Nope.' Eliana matched Holly's slow pace toward the appointed corner, where Megan and Bodie already waited alongside a short man with a briefcase. 'You don't really believe Lyle is leaving you things, do you? Surely Caleb is doing it, or—'

'I have no explanation. So right now I'm choosing to believe that I have no explanation.'

Eliana laughed her lovely musical laugh, unconvinced, unconcerned. 'That sounds about right. I'm not looking forward to this part of the weekend, I admit.'

'Join the club.' Holly wondered if Lyle was hiding somewhere nearby with high-powered binoculars, enjoying the mess he'd created. If she felt him close by, she'd track him down and drag him in here by his ears.

The group gathered. The lawyer, Ned McGowan, was younger than Holly expected, probably about her age, mid fifties. He had an impressively full head of salt-and-pepper hair that stood straight up like a frightened cartoon character's. The rest of his face looked as if it had slipped too far down the slope of his forehead and landed just above his chin.

'Hello, everyone. I'm sorry for your loss, and for interrupting what looks like a delicious lunch in such a beautiful setting.'

'Thank you for coming,' Caleb said. 'There's plenty left over if you're hungry.'

'Thank you.' Ned gave a geeky little bow. 'I might take you up on that.'

'The soup was weird,' Megan said. 'Sour.'

'Sorrel,' Janet said.

Megan looked incredulous. 'You pronounce it "sore"? Not "sour"?'

'*Sorrel*,' Eliana said. 'The plant the soup was made from.'

Ned cleared his throat. 'As you know, I represent the deceased, Lyle Frederick.'

'Yes, we do know,' Megan said.

'As you also know, Lyle was officially declared dead on the fifteenth of this month, after the required five years had passed since he'd gone missing. As executor of his estate, his brother Caleb is permitted to make public the pertinent contents of his will to family before the estate has been officially probated. As he said, you've all waited long enough.

'Therefore, I have outlined the basics of how Mr Frederick wished his assets and personal property to be distributed in the event that those present here were still alive after his death. You will each get a copy – they're all identical – in a sealed envelope. I would urge you to take these back to your rooms and open them privately as Lyle wished. I am here today as Lyle's guest and friend, but will also be available this afternoon for any questions. In each of your envelopes I have also included my details in case you need to contact me after this weekend.'

'So.' Caleb clapped his hands, then rubbed them together.

'That's it. You're all free to go back to the party or wherever else. Thank you, Ned, for being here, and for dealing with an incredibly complicated situation so ethically and efficiently over the past five years and before.'

Scattered applause while Ned handed out the envelopes, and a chorus of thanks. Holly received her envelope and turned, wanting nothing more than to get back to her room, lie down and block out the universe until the next difficult moment had to happen: the conversation with Caleb.

Around her people were likewise moving away. The sound of tearing paper stopped them. Megan had ripped open her envelope and was unfolding the enclosure.

'Babe, you're supposed to wait,' Bodie pleaded.

'I've waited five years to find out if I get to live the way I've worked toward all my life. I can't wait any longer.' She started scanning the page. No one moved. It was like not being able to turn away from a skydiver without a parachute, a car heading for a pedestrian. Would there be a happy ending or not?

'So, yada yada, will and testament dated . . .' She gasped. 'Wait, this isn't the date we made our wills.'

'Yes, uh . . .' Ned cleared his throat again. 'Lyle changed it shortly before he left the country.'

Megan's face went white. 'Okay. Okay, well that doesn't have to be bad, does it?'

'Shh, babe, we'll be okay.' Bodie hugged her to him so tightly Holly found herself waiting for Megan's shoulder bones to snap. 'We'll be okay. No matter what.'

'I don't know, Bodie. This is freaking me out.'

'You want me to read it?' He held out his big hand.

'No. I've got this. I'm tough.' She sniffed, then bent her head to read. '"To my brother, Caleb . . ." Ha! Caleb, he left you five dollars to buy pickles. To replace the one he stole from you. You just told us that story! So funny.'

Caleb gave a lopsided smile. 'Kind of him.'

'Megan, I don't think this is right.' Eliana looked around for support.

Janet took a step toward Megan, eyes laser-focused. 'Go on.'

To her shame, Holly couldn't tear herself away either.

'"To my aunt, Janet Frederick, I leave all my love and gratitude, and my mother's Victorian embroidered chair, which she always coveted. Don't try to deny it, Janet."' Megan looked up at her. 'Those are all his words. I didn't add that.'

'Oh, funny.' Janet gave a teary cackle. 'That sweet boy, to think of me. I do love that chair.'

Megan read on. '"To Eliana Adler of Milwaukee County, I leave sufficient funds in a 529 account to put her stepsons through four-year private colleges or whatever education they choose."'

'Oh.' Eliana flushed with pleasure. 'What a sweetheart. Oh my gosh, Lyle. That is so generous. I never expected—'

She burst into tears. Holly patted her shoulder awkwardly. If sitting through the fake funeral was bad, sitting through this fake – illegal, actually – distribution of assets was worse. By the dark look on Caleb's face, he was enjoying it as much as she was.

'"To Megan Frederick, of Milwaukee County,"' Megan's voice sped, trembling, '"I leave the house at 3560 North Lake Drive . . ."' Where's the rest?'

'No money?' Bodie had gone as pale as Megan. Holly didn't blame him. Either version of Megan, super-rich or super-disappointed, would be hell to live with.

'No, wait, here. "The rest of the entirety of my estate I leave to—"' Megan's head jerked up. She stared at Holly.

Everyone else turned to stare as well. A bird lit on a nearby rose tree and sang gaily. Norman's laughter thundered from the other end of the garden.

'*You.*' Megan said the word as if she wished it was fatal. 'Holly fucking Penny of fucking Los Angeles County gets fucking *everything else.*'

Holly gasped into the beat of silence before the uproar. Megan furious, Bodie trying to console her, Janet and Eliana cheering so loudly Holly suspected they were sticking it to Megan. Through it all, Caleb stood silent, wearing his anger and disgust.

What was Lyle thinking? Leaving his fortune to her when he'd already left her plenty? Was this to punish Megan for cheating?

No, wait. She put a hand to her head. He was alive. None of this will could be valid or enforced. He hadn't really left her anything. So why . . .

A burst of horror-adrenaline gave her the clarity she needed to follow the rest of the sickening logic. Lyle had surreptitiously communicated to Holly that he was still alive, that he still loved her. He hadn't appeared this weekend, presumably because he wanted to stay 'dead'. If she was right, the next step he took would be to let her know how and where to find him.

Did he want Holly back? His money? Or both?

Holly turned and walked blindly away from the crowd, shaking off offers of help from Eliana and Caleb. She didn't want to talk to anyone. She wanted to get back to her room.

On the way, she stumbled twice, so tired she had to consciously tell her legs how to move. One step, another step, letting the cane do its work.

Inside, she managed to keep walking, grateful when Tom, the young man who'd greeted her on her first day here, what seemed like six months ago, handed over her room key, then came around the desk to escort her across the lobby, and made a gallant show of pressing the elevator button for her. Yes, it was a lovely day, Tom. Yes, the service had been perfect, lovely and so moving, and the rose garden had been the most perfect setting. Perfect and lovely, lovely and perfect, and a total freaking nightmare.

The elevator rose and deposited her opposite her door. It took Holly three tries to get the key in the right way and turn it. Inside, she marched straight to the bedroom and opened the night-table drawer, praying there was nothing more there, that the musical love letter during the service would be Lyle's final word.

An envelope with her name on it. Lyle's handwriting? Maybe, but changed. Holly wasn't sure.

She stood holding the envelope in her hands, heart trying to escape her chest to the point where she worried she'd have a stroke. Taking deep breaths, she forced herself to cross the room, drink a glass of water, sit down at the table on which her bridal bouquet scented the room with the aroma of long-ago love on a warm Hawaiian beach.

Inside the envelope, on a single sheet of notepaper, written in the same maybe-Lyle hand, were two lines.

An address.

Chapter 17

Subject: Clarissa
Date: June 12, 2006
From: LyleFred@aol.com
To: Caleb@FrederickIndustries.com

Sorry, I had to bolt to a meeting. Just wanted to follow up on our conversation with a note, because I think better on paper, or more accurately these days, on keyboard. I told you the truth – it's great that you are finally thinking about planning a wedding but it bothers me that you need my opinion. Have you discussed it with Clarissa? She's been married before, so she probably doesn't need the fancy ceremony and huge party. (Though maybe you do? Nothing wrong with that.) Sounds like you need to think this through out loud, whether that means in an email to me or another phone conversation, or over dinner, your choice.

Subject: re: Clarissa
Date: June 12, 2006
From: Caleb@FrederickIndustries.com
To: LyleFred@aol.com

She's great. Active and ambitious, beautiful and totally at ease both in her world and as a supportive partner in mine. Mom

300

loves her. Her kid, Ryan, is really cool. He and I are bonding slowly. His father remarried and moved out of state, so Ryan doesn't see him much, which is hard on him, but it helps my case attempting to become a father figure. Clarissa doesn't want more kids because her career is taking off, so I'm grateful to have this experience. I remember so often the things Janet did for us. It cracks me up to be in the position of doing the same for him. The circus sure seems like a different animal than when we were young. Is it different or are we? Anyway, I know we would make a good family, so I'm not sure why I'm hesitating.

Subject: re: Clarissa
Date: June 12, 2006
From: LyleFred@aol.com
To: Caleb@FrederickIndustries.com

In all that paragraph, you only have a couple of sentences about her – great, active, ambitious, etc. – but nothing about your feelings for her. Nothing about love. Are you really sure?

Subject: re: Clarissa
Date: June 12, 2006
From: Caleb@FrederickIndustries.com
To: LyleFred@aol.com

We can't all have Holly.

Subject: re: Clarissa
Date: June 12, 2006
From: Caleb@FrederickIndustries.com
To: LyleFred@aol.com

I can't believe I sent that. Sorry. That was low.

Subject: re: Clarissa
Date: June 12, 2006
From: LyleFred@aol.com
To: Caleb@FrederickIndustries.com

You have no idea.

Subject: More Congrats and Your Upcoming Trip
Date: September 25, 2009
From: LyleFred@aol.com
To: Caleb@FrederickIndustries.com

I left congratulations on your voicemail, but that was a hell of a great moment watching you take over the company, Caleb. I'm so proud of you – I know I said that, but I'm saying it again. The business will do incredibly well in your hands, I have no doubt. Even better, now you can start shoveling cash toward the Foundation by the boatload. Right? Right? Hello?

Also am looking forward to your wedding anniversary party next week (two years, can't believe it!) – thanks for the invite. And for the pep talk by the way re: Eliana. Badly needed.

I wonder if you wouldn't mind taking something with you to Los Angeles when you go next week. I'd rather it came from you.

Holly sat on the prissy green sofa in her living room, hands folded in her lap, fingers twisting. Any second, Caleb would arrive to take her out to dinner. Since her divorce from Lyle – seven years already – she'd seen Caleb numerous times, though only once since his marriage. Last visit he'd been a newly-wed and treated her to pictures of Clarissa – gorgeous, but in an unexpected Barbie way – and her son, Ryan, who was dark, dimpled and adorable.

He and Clarissa had waited three years to get married. Her son apparently needed time to come around to the idea, then Lyle and Caleb's mother died and they inherited the Frederick fortune, which probably entailed a prenup the size of the Manhattan phone book.

As much as Holly loved spending time with Caleb, every time she'd seen him, Lyle's ghost had always been lurking in the background. She was anxious that tonight's meal be between two old friends, without Lyle and the pain of their past haunting her.

Holly liked her life pretty well these days. She'd made new friends among the staff at school, in her book group and her volunteer job at the local animal shelter. Melinda regularly included her at dinner parties, and Holly had even been on a few dates, though the bar set by Lyle was so high she eventually stopped, wondering why she bothered hoping for lightning to strike twice. She'd rather be alone than settle for less.

A noise outside made her strain her ears. Caleb's deep voice, deeper than Lyle's, followed by Melinda's giggle. Adrenaline flowing, Holly half rose from the couch, feeling for her cane, which she'd left lying next to her.

No she hadn't.

She looked wildly around the room. There, hanging from the front door so she wouldn't lose track of it. Ahem.

Holly unhooked it and slipped outside, annoyed at herself for being so nervous. Worst case, she missed Lyle. That didn't mean she'd failed some test, just that the grief hadn't quite run its course, though it felt like high time.

'There she is!' Caleb strode toward her, grinning, picked up all five foot eight inches of her in a bear hug and swung her around, making Holly squeal like a teenager. Then he kissed both cheeks and drew back to gaze as if he'd found her after misplacing her somewhere. 'You look fantastic. I've missed you.'

'Wow.' She was breathless, touched by his emotion and buoyed by her own. He looked as tall-dark-handsome as ever, though tired. Undoubtedly working too hard, as usual. 'It's great to see you, Caleb. I was trying to figure out how many years, but my calculator is broken.' She pointed to her head, making him chuckle.

'A couple? Too long.'

'Where are you two going for dinner tonight?' Melinda strolled over to join them, already nursing a glass of a Central Coast Chardonnay she'd recommended Holly try.

'I made reservations at Little Door,' Caleb said.

Melinda flicked him a surprised glance before recovering her poise. 'Very nice, very romantic. Matthew and I went there for our anniversary. It's that kind of place.'

'Uh-oh. Am I too casual?' Holly's heart sank. It had taken her forever to choose this skirt and top and then get them on. Another outfit would make them too late for anything but dessert.

'You're perfect.' Caleb was still devouring her with his eyes in a way that made her just the teeniest bit uncomfortable, and made Melinda raise an eyebrow.

'Thanks.' She tried to think of something to say to cover her embarrassment. 'The shoes are Melinda's. We both wear a seven.'

'Nice.' He admired the perfectly ordinary pumps, then grinned at her again. 'You're a sight for sore eyes, Holly.'

'Apparently *quite* sore.' Melinda looked startled. 'Sorry, that shouldn't have popped out.'

No, it shouldn't. Melinda had been thrashing around in fresh marital hell, convinced again that Matthew was cheating but again refusing to confront him. Horrible, but didn't give her license to be bitchy.

Caleb turned to Melinda with his wide, easy grin, the one he needed to use more often, the one so like his brother's. 'You have a problem with me being crazy about your tenant?'

'Of course not.' Melinda forced a mortified smile toward both of them. 'I'm just jealous. Sad housewife drowning in wine, laundry and burgers instead of wine, roses and filet mignon.'

'*Mom?*' The female wail came from the house. 'Have you seen my pink jacket?'

'Coming.' Melinda backed toward the house, looking as if she was about to cry. 'Have fun. See you later.'

'Bye, Melinda.' Caleb waited until she went inside, then turned toward Holly. 'That was weird. Is she okay?'

'I don't think she'll be okay until she really wants to be. I hope soon.' Holly grimaced, gazing after her friend. 'I love her, but I also want to make her start over somewhere new.'

'You're a good person.' He touched her shoulder. 'She'll need you when she's ready.'

'She's certainly been there for me.' Holly brightened, determined not to let Melinda haunt their evening either. 'Ready to go?'

'I am.' Caleb offered his arm.

Holly took it happily. She hadn't been out to a fancy dinner in ages, let alone with such a handsome escort. Melinda had taken her to Sago for her fortieth birthday a couple of years earlier. Matthew was supposed to come but ditched last minute, which had pissed Melinda off no end, so the beginning of Holly's birthday dinner was spent hearing Melinda complain about her lonely marriage, followed by Melinda apologizing and promising to stop, then launching into more, and repeat.

Happily she'd gotten it out of her system before the main course came, and they'd chatted and laughed like old times, then finished the evening with a drink at the Beverly Hills Hotel's Bar Nineteen 12, where they had a blast listening to music, drinking crazy-expensive cocktails on Melinda's dime, and pretending not to be watching out for celebrities.

A black Mercedes waited out front. As Caleb and Holly approached, the driver started the engine, but thank goodness didn't do the big show of getting out to open their doors for them. Caleb did that job, waiting patiently while Holly turned sideways to sit on the leather upholstery before pulling her legs into the huge interior. 'I feel as if I'm being dragged off for questioning.'

'I won't cuff you if you promise not to struggle.'

Holly snorted. 'So kind.'

Caleb tucked in a fold of her skirt before he shut the door and went around to the other side. They made awkward conversation on the way, but traffic wasn't impossible, so the trip passed quickly. On Third Street, the car pulled up opposite a double wooden door set into walls painted bright blue. Holly took Caleb's offered hand to exit the Mercedes, grateful to be spared the worry of tripping over the curb or getting her legs and cane tangled. So many things she'd taken for granted when getting around was as easy as wanting to.

'Have you been here before?' Caleb had to shout over a roaring motorcycle. He'd paused by the door, wearing a mischievous half-smile. 'Seen pictures?'

'No to both. You?'

'I've seen pictures.' He opened the door with a flourish and let her precede him.

Stepping in, Holly felt like Dorothy leaving her black and white farmhouse for the Technicolor wonder of Oz. Their table was on the patio, where two trees reached for the starry sky, branches draped with glowing lanterns and tiny sparkling lights. Additional candles flickered on each white-clothed table. The same blue of the exterior found its way inside, creating an intimate, peaceful and richly colored interior.

'This is magical. I feel like I went through a portal and came out somewhere in Europe.' She sat opposite Caleb, cane hooked on the back of her chair. He looked even more gorgeous in the candlelight, which warmed his skin tone and softened the stark contrast between his white shirt and his dark jacket and coloring.

Two waiters approached, carrying a wine bucket, a tray with two glasses and a bottle of champagne from a vineyard Holly didn't recognize.

'I hope you don't mind . . . ?' Caleb looked sure she wouldn't. 'I pre-ordered.'

'I think I'll be able to get it down.' Holly grinned, delighted to be spoiled again, doubly delighted that she hadn't seen a trace of Lyle's ghost yet, even around the champagne. 'Someone has to make the tough sacrifices.'

They watched the waiter pour, a glorious initial rush of foam that settled into fizzy gold.

Caleb lifted his flute. 'Here's to you, Holly. You seem better every time I see you. I'm in awe of what you've accomplished.'

'Thank you, Caleb.' Holly returned the toast. 'Here's to your ascension to the CEO throne at Frederick. And to lifelong happiness with Clarissa and little Ryan.'

She took the first taste of her champagne, hoping she'd imagined his face falling at the mention of his wife. The wine was perfectly chilled, with typical French clarity. Holly closed her eyes to savor the flavors traveling over her tongue, then opened them to Caleb watching her with amusement.

'Something tells me you don't get to drink the good stuff often enough.'

'What is often enough?' She cocked her head teasingly. 'It's out of my budget for one. And better shared.'

'You don't have anyone to share it with?'

'Does Melinda count?'

'Nope.'

'Mom and Dad?'

'Sorry.'

'Then no.'

'Hmm.' Caleb leaned back, hands folded around his glass. 'I hope that changes. I still haven't forgiven Lyle for leaving you.'

'Our separation and divorce were mutual.' She braced herself for the inevitable pain. 'Isn't that what he told you?'

'Yes, that's what he told me.'

'And? You thought he was lying?'

'No.' He spoke quietly, eyes steady across the table, tree lights twinkling behind him. 'But if you were my wife in the state you were in back then, there is no way I would – or could – ever leave you.'

Oh . . . my . . . goodness.

Holly found nothing to say, just stared back while butterflies and impossible attraction chased each other around her insides. Good Lord. What an aphrodisiac.

Luckily the waiter showed up to take their orders and saved Holly from politely requesting that Caleb drag her into a back storage room and ravish her among sacks of flour and canned vegetables.

The thought made her want to giggle, which was good. Really good. Usually when she discussed Lyle, at some point she wanted to drive a knife through her heart. Apparently emotional pain could be blown out of the water by inappropriate lust.

'Before I forget, I have something to give you.' Caleb reached into his jacket.

'Uh-oh.' She wasn't sure what to expect, and Caleb looked serious enough that she was wary. 'Will it explode?'

'Promise no.' He handed a letter across the table with her name on it in Lyle's perfect script.

'Caleb . . .' She didn't move. The letter hung from his fingers between them.

'I told him I was going to be in Los Angeles and he asked me to deliver it. You are free not to take it. Or take it and burn it. Or take it and read it.'

'Did you read it?'

'No.'

'Any idea what it says?'

'None. Could be hope you are well, could be sorry I failed you, could be please come back to me, my life is pure crap without you.'

'Ha!' She let him know what she thought of that last possibility. 'His life would have been pure crap if he'd stayed with me.'

'I don't agree.' He gave the letter a quick shake. 'But take it. Put it away. Decide later whether you want to read it.'

Holly sighed and reached for the envelope, cursing Lyle for putting her in the position of having to decide whether or not to see his words or hear his voice again in her head. So many years trying to get past the shock of him moving on with Eliana, she was finally succeeding, and now this.

She leaned down to tuck the envelope into her purse.

'Now I've made my delivery, I want to know how you're doing.'

Over a dozen shared oysters, Holly gave him the white-washed story of her life. Cozy apartment, good friends,

309

rewarding job. He in turn talked about the satisfaction of continuing to grow Frederick Industries, of the joys and steep learning curve of being a father, the pride he took in his accomplished wife's corporate law career, though nothing else about their marriage.

Over deeply flavorful lamb couscous, they talked about the Super Bowl, the California government's financial troubles, baseball's A-Rod testing positive for steroids, whether they were for or against the switch to digital television, whether the priest played by Philip Seymour Hoffman in the movie *Doubt* was guilty or not, whether Mexican restaurants in Milwaukee could hold a candle to those in Los Angeles.

Holly hadn't been part of such a rich, easy-flowing conversation with a man – particularly such an attractive one – for way too long. Maybe because with Caleb, she was so comfortable her brain didn't trip her up more than the occasional fumble for a word, which could happen to anyone. Little wonder by the time they'd finished eating and were lingering over glasses of an incredible Côtes du Rhône, Holly was a little drunk and a little in love with Caleb – both temporary states she could enjoy now and regret later.

'So now that we've both had too much to drink and can be honest, tell me how your life really is, Holly.'

Ah. He'd seen through her whitewash. Curse those perceptive Frederick men.

'Sane. Stable. Full.' She hesitated, checking in, but found herself comfortable sharing the truth with him. 'Full of frustrating efforts to accomplish the simplest things. A pleasant enough life, but small and mundane. Lyle and I had such a large and extraordinarily beautiful life. I can't pretend this compares. But I'm content.'

Caleb pressed his lips together. 'I wish things were different.'

310

'I do best when I don't think about how I used to be. I try to live in the present, not think too much about the past or the future.'

'Very Zen, but makes your focus pretty narrow.'

Holly shrugged. 'It works.'

The waiter came to clear their plates, brush crumbs from the cloth and offer dessert, which they both refused.

'Now you, Caleb. Tell me how *your* life really is.'

'Mine?' He looked taken aback. 'Oh no no, that was for you. *I* get to stick to the perfect version.'

'Do not.'

His smile faded slowly. 'Well. My life is pleasant as well. Complicated. Maybe not all I'd hoped for.' He swirled the wine slowly in his glass, concentrating intently, but she didn't think on the wine. 'All my life I've wanted to be CEO of Frederick Industries. I used to resent Lyle because I knew that prize would go to him as eldest son and favorite. Dad was always very clear that Lyle was being groomed to take over.'

Holly couldn't help laughing. 'Yeah, that went really well.'

'No kidding.' He didn't smile. 'Once I realized the job could be mine, I worked my ass off, learning the company from the ground up. And now . . . It's the cliché, I guess, lonely at the top. I have the dream job, but there I am, still working at Frederick. I don't know what I expected.'

'A miracle transformation?' She gestured around them. 'Like stepping from a busy city street into a fairy-tale garden?'

'Something like that. Pretty childish.'

'Pretty human. How is Clarissa dealing with the change? Or doesn't it affect her?'

'She's thrilled. She wanted it as much as I did. Maybe more.' The hint of bitterness in his tone was dismaying. But then he'd never spoken of Clarissa with passion. Holly had assumed passion wasn't important to him, though she'd hoped it might grow as the relationship progressed.

'And . . . that's bad?'

'No, no. It's great. We have a solid partnership.'

A partnership. Holly couldn't imagine choosing that word to describe her marriage unless it followed a line of adjectives: passionate, intimate, uplifting, deeply satisfying . . . 'Who are you trying to convince? Me or you?'

Caleb grimaced and took a slow sip of wine. '*Touché*.'

'Sorry.' Holly put her glass down. 'That was more blunt than it should have been.'

'No, no, we're supposed to be keeping it real. You were justified.' He hesitated. Holly could almost hear the battle going on between honesty and loyalty. 'I admire Clarissa's talent and ambition, I respect her immensely. But she had a rough childhood. She's always had to look out for herself in the world. There's not as much room for me, for our marriage, as . . .'

Holly folded her arms on the table and leaned toward him. 'The only person judging you is you. It's okay to admit you want more than you have. God knows I do. Like every fifteen minutes.'

Caleb returned to swirling contemplation. 'In a strange way, I envy people with really bad marriages as much as I envy people with fantastic marriages. Because in both cases, the next step is obvious.'

Holly nodded. 'But when there are equal forces pulling you in opposite directions, there's no solution. Except getting torn in half.'

'Yes, that's exactly it, Holly.' His admiring look made her feel like Einstein. 'Thanks for listening. I have a life most people would kill for. I shouldn't complain.'

'Tonight you should.' She made a zipping motion across her

lips. 'Whatever horrors you admit to stay here.'

'It's a Pandora's Box, though.' He mimed a rush of evil into the universe. 'Once you start trying to fix some problems, you invite in many more than if you accepted what you had and stuck to it.'

'Stuck to it blindly? Accepted without paying attention? Is that what you think Lyle should have done with me?' She waited for his answer, hoping he'd see the similarities, not sure why it was so important to her that he understand.

'That's different.'

'How?'

He folded his arms in imitation of her pose, and leaned closer. 'Because you're you. And because what you and Lyle had was perfect. How could he leave that?'

'Exactly because it wasn't perfect anymore. Every day we had to face that we had a different marriage, one in which we resented each other for things neither of us could help. Is that what you wanted for him? For me? For you?'

Caleb's certainty faltered.

'It's so noble to say someone should stay in a marriage that no longer works. That Lyle should have stayed because he owed me, because I'm the one who had the mess to cope with, or worse, because I'm a woman and need taking care of. If our situations were reversed, would you want me to turn into Florence Nightingale and nurse him the rest of my life?'

'I don't know.' Caleb dropped his eyes. 'I would want you to be happy.'

'Spending the rest of his life tied down would have made Lyle miserable. *And* me. Instead, he found someone whole, someone who *could* make him happy.'

'Hey.' Caleb raised his head. 'There's nothing un-whole about you.'

313

'Thank you, you're very nice.'

'I'm very honest. As for Lyle . . .' He blew out a breath, hunching his shoulders. 'His marriage to Eliana is in trouble. Bad trouble. I don't think it will last.'

Holly could only stare, hoping to feel sympathy for the man she'd loved, afraid that instead she'd only experience neener-neener *Schadenfreude*.

To her immense relief, given that she'd already put on a sympathetic and concerned face, Holly discovered she *was* sympathetic and concerned. 'I'm sorry.'

'Really?'

'Yes. I want him to be happy.' The words came out with utmost sincerity, making her want to parade around the restaurant in triumph.

This was huge. This was epic. She wanted to call her therapist, Melinda, her parents, shout it from the rooftops. Holly was over him. Finally. News of his divorce had not brought on a longing to communicate that she was ready to try again, or hope that he would seek her out for the same.

Joy bubbled up through her. She was free. 'A toast.'

Caleb blinked. 'A . . . toast?'

'To Lyle. To his happiness, wherever he manages to find it.'

He lifted his glass, searching her face. 'Not with you?'

'No.' Her voice thickened but her smile remained undimmed. 'Not with me.'

An answering grin spread Caleb's mouth. 'I'll drink to that.'

They savored their wine, eyes holding across the table. Holly put her glass down. No more. Her head wasn't quite spinning, but her libido was, and she was old enough to know better. An uneasy glance around, away from Caleb's dark eyes, startled her into noticing they were the only table left and that waiters were already setting up for the next day. 'Oops. We've overstayed. They're closing.'

'I was having too much fun to care. But you're right, we should go.' He signaled for the check, which appeared promptly.

Holly got up and managed to find the restroom without falling on her face, though she was weaving just a tad, and giggling whenever she bumped into something.

So? She'd had such a great time. Caleb should come to LA every month.

Oh yeah, *that* would be a *great* idea. He was too tempting. And too married.

But what an evening! Holly sat, thinking she hadn't felt this free, strong and female since her accident. She ought to hang on to the feeling, close her eyes and indulge it, so she could re-create it later.

Unfortunately, since she was sitting on the toilet, the gesture lost quite a bit of its power.

More giggles.

After making sure she'd put herself back together properly, she wandered until she found Caleb waiting by the exit. 'What a shame we have to re-enter reality.'

'I know.' He held out his hand. 'We'll face it together.'

They said goodnight to the staff member standing ready to shoo them out, and stepped into the noisy dark street, where Caleb's driver waited. 'Sorry it's not a horse-drawn carriage.'

'I'm not Cinderella.' Though he made a great Prince Charming.

'All aboard.' He ushered her inside, where she laid her head back on the seat, completely blissed out.

'Tired?' Caleb shut his door; the driver pulled out into traffic.

'Not at all.' She turned her head toward him, leaving it resting against the leather. In the semi-darkness, Caleb looked

315

even more like his brother. Holly remained unmoved.

The letter. She lunged for her purse on the floor, whipped out the envelope and handed it to Caleb. 'I don't want it.'

'Are you sure?' He didn't move to take it.

'I'm sure.' She shook it insistently. 'I'm not his wife anymore. I haven't spoken to him in years. Whatever he has to say, I'm sure it's very nice, but I don't have any responsibility to deal with it.'

'Okay.' He stuffed the envelope back into his jacket. 'If you change your mind in the morning, or anytime, let me know. I won't burn it.'

'That sounds fair.' Holly watched it disappear, feeling no regret. Maybe a touch of wistfulness.

Caleb took her hand again, and the wistfulness vanished. It felt crazy good to be touched. 'This was your call, but for what it's worth, I think you did the right thing.'

'The letter? Yes.' She slid her purse on to the seat beside her. 'The alcohol, no. I'm going to feel like hell tomorrow.'

'Same here. And I have an early meeting. However . . .' He squeezed her fingers. 'Tonight was special, Holly.'

She squeezed back. 'I agree.'

'It made me realize what I need to work on at home. When Clarissa and I . . . Let me put it another way. When I talk to you, I feel like I'm getting through. You understand what I'm saying.'

Holly took back her hand to give his thigh a maternal pat. 'It might help if you taught Clarissa some English.'

Caleb threw his head back and laughed, loud and free, the way he very seldom did. 'That's *it*! I knew there had to be some reason.'

'I'm sorry, though. Not being understood can be frustrating, and isolating.' She'd lived it. Still did at times when her brain went dark.

'Exactly. You know what— Oh no.' He slumped back on the seat, hand pressed to his forehead. 'I'm becoming *that* guy. Now I'll say, "My wife doesn't understand me" and then come at you all puckered up. "C'mon, baby, help a lonely man feel better."'

'Eww.' Holly cracked up at his creepy drawl. 'I don't think you're that type.'

'I'm not.' He turned back toward her, eyes full of tenderness. As the car moved, his face went through shadow, then light, then shadow again as they slowed. 'But I do want to kiss you, Holly. I've wanted to since Lyle introduced us.'

Holly's giggles disappeared into a loud swallow as her body responded with a wave of desire. She should turn away from that open, vulnerable gaze, stare at the back of the driver's head, peer out the window at businesses crawling past.

Damn the champagne.

She wanted him to kiss her. Just tonight, just this once. Even though it was a terrible idea. Even though there would be nothing after but regret and guilt and double the loneliness.

He leaned toward her. His mouth was warm and soft; its touch sent signals zinging to parts of her that hadn't been zinged in a long time. Holly responded cautiously, letting him lead.

He was a really good leader.

The kisses heated, deepened, became more sensually charged.

She should pull away. She *would* pull away.

Soon.

No, really . . .

When they arrived at Melinda's house, neither of them had pulled away.

'We're here,' Holly whispered.

'Yeah, but . . .' Caleb rested his forehead against hers. He smelled so good, had tasted so good. 'This is a fancy car, maybe it can stop time?'

'That would be so convenient.' One last kiss . . . 'I'm not inviting you in. Just so you know.'

'No. No, this was bad enough. I'm going to feel like a massive shithead in the morning.' He tangled his fingers in her hair. 'But tonight, all I'm going to say is that I've wanted to do that for a long time, and it was really good.'

'And out of your system?'

'Has to be.'

'Yes.' She managed to move away, then unbuckled her seatbelt and retrieved her purse before she found words for what she was feeling. 'I want you to know that it's been years since I've felt that . . . desirable. Thank you, Caleb.'

'Holly.' He shook his head in disbelief. 'You haven't changed a tenth as much as you seem to think. I've always been crazy about you, but tonight I had enough to drink that it became a good idea to let you know.'

'It won't seem like a good idea tomorrow.' She gave him a playful punch on the arm. 'We'll be brother and sister again, eh?'

He made a wrinkle-nosed face. 'Yeah, I don't think that's a great image right now.'

Holly grinned. 'Good friends who got carried away.'

'Wonderfully carried away, yes.' He pushed open his door. 'Wait, I'll help you out of the car.'

They walked down Melinda's driveway, both of them tiptoeing by silent agreement so as not to tempt Melinda into coming out to chat. At the front door of her little house, Holly gave Caleb a carefully chaste hug that he returned just as chastely.

'Thank you for a really nice evening.'

'You're welcome.' He touched her cheek. 'Goodnight, Holly.'

'Goodnight.' She went inside, wondering if she'd ever see him again, hoping so and also . . . not. This would be a perfect happy-ending farewell to all things Frederick. And maybe Caleb's remorse tomorrow would give him the kick he needed to work harder on his marriage.

She turned for one more look at her so-handsome business-suited ex-brother-in-law.

He still stood there, smiling wistfully, one arm raised in a wave. Holly closed her door, blocking him out, and leaned against it, gazing dreamily at her darkened ceiling.

Since her divorce, she'd been kissed a few times on dates that had gone particularly well, though half the time she suspected the guys had been on the make for whatever they could get. Every time, Lyle had popped into her brain as if he was trying to keep her from being attracted to anyone else. It had seemed impossible that she could ever replace his image, that she could ever stop being haunted by so many days, nights, months and years of kissing him, her whole heart involved from the very first time.

But when Lyle's brother's lips had touched hers tonight . . . all she'd been thinking about was Caleb.

Chapter 18

Holly must have stared at the paper bearing what had to be Lyle's address for a full ten minutes before the immensity of her fatigue and the vastness of what the note signified became too much to bear. Very generously, her body decided to make her so sleepy she could barely manage to turn off her phone and crawl on to the welcoming bed before she was out.

In her dream she was struggling up one of the hills behind Senneck's main lodge, clambering over rocks that rose again ahead as soon as she'd put them behind her. Around her the song of cicadas bore down like the whine of a dull-toothed saw. She was crying, frustrated by memories of the athleticism that had come so easily in her youth, agility and power she'd taken for granted.

The summit taunted her, looming twice the distance above her as when she started. She was preparing to turn back, conquered, dispirited, failed, when she felt him. Lyle came up behind her and put his arms around her waist, taking her weight against his chest. The grief and fatigue left her. She turned in his embrace to find him young, they were both young, and her head was clear, thoughts moving at the speed of light as they always had. It was as if they'd never been apart but had kept living their lives together, no chance of separation until the inevitability of death. As it should have been.

As it could be now again. Holly woke with the thought spinning in her head, the longing for her husband a deep, aching pain. She lay staring up at the ceiling, confused, disoriented, still in the vise grip of her imagination.

Breathe, Holly. Breathe. It was a dream. Nothing had changed . . . apart from the fact that so much had. Lyle was alive. Holly was an heiress.

She pushed to sitting, running a hand through the strands of her hair, as if organizing them might help her regain her bearings. She didn't believe dreams were prophetic or magical; in fact she'd been on guard against their effect since junior high, when she'd dreamed about a complete dork of a kid and woken up madly in love with him, a feeling that lasted until she saw him in class and realized she had no such feelings at all.

And yet. Lyle wasn't Erik Cardeich, and this dream had tapped into a romantic reality, though a distant one, which made it harder to recover.

Needing to reconnect with current, unromantic reality, Holly grabbed her phone. Texts from Caleb, hoping she was okay; from Norman, hoping she was okay.

Holly tapped out assurances: Yes, she was okay, thank you, just tired and overwhelmed, but she'd napped and was fine.

Sort of.

Out of bed, she noticed the message light blinking on the room phone. Janet, hoping she was okay, and Eliana – wait for it – hoping she was okay. Apparently Holly's abrupt exit from the rose garden had raised some eyebrows. As much as she hated the worry her condition caused, it was warm and fuzzy to feel part of a community here.

After using the bathroom and washing her face, Holly felt more awake, though the dream followed her like a persistent cloud, ready to envelop her if she weakened. She'd dreamed about Lyle plenty over the years, but not lately, certainly not this vividly, and never when he was available and so close. Holly was one decision away from seeing him.

What would a visit put into motion, comedy, drama or tragedy? She didn't know which one she wanted. The feel of Dream Lyle's body against hers was still too vivid, the idea that they might be able to realize a happy ending after all they'd been through too powerfully enticing.

A glance at the clock showed she'd slept for a couple of badly needed hours. Ahead was the final event of the weekend, an informal outdoor barbecue. One last chance for those who knew Lyle to gather and mourn his not-death.

The idea appealed to her, a fittingly casual send-off for a man who had loved simplicity as much as elegance. But appearing once again among these people, in yet another guise – first the mystery wife, now she-who-had-scored-the-fortune – Holly would face a new round of judgments and questions. How did it feel inheriting all that money? Why do you think Lyle gave it to you? What are you going to do with it?

She couldn't answer, didn't know yet.

Maybe she'd go get naked in Florida. Maybe she'd buy a horse, or the whole stable. Maybe she'd visit Caleb in Milwaukee. She could certainly afford to do more than she ever thought possible, whether she ended up inheriting the whole Frederick enchilada or just the alimony piece Lyle had put away for her.

Right now Holly just wanted to call the concierge and change her return ticket to three days ago.

Instead, she picked up her phone again and dialed Melinda, who'd been so greedy for details of the weekend. She was going to get an earful.

'Holly! I was about to settle down and read the latest version of this bloody divorce agreement. Thanks to you, I can procrastinate a little longer. What's going on? Wasn't Lyle's service this morning? How'd that go? Tell me everything.'

'Well, gee, Melinda, there's not that much to tell. Lyle is almost definitely not dead, he left me all his money, and Caleb asked me to live with him.'

Melinda gasped. 'What? *What?* Wait, run that by me again. *You* have Lyle's money? *All* of it? Like billions?'

'I don't know the amount. But yes. However, "the dude abides", Melinda. Lyle is still alive.' She told a stunned Melinda the latest, the changes to the service, the address, and her certainty that Caleb was in on the whole thing.

'But that doesn't *prove* he's alive, just suggests.'

'I have his address. I can go see him and—'

'No no no no, Holly.' Melinda groaned. 'Not this. Not again. Not unless I get to come with you and make sure he dies this time.'

'Stop. Now.'

'Okay, okay.' Melinda sighed crossly. 'Have you googled the address?'

'Haven't had a chance.' Holly went to the night table and picked up the paper, unable to contain a thrill. Lyle still loved her. He wanted to see her.

She stopped herself mooning. Hadn't she been furious with him only a few hours earlier for what he'd put everyone through? Wasn't she still thinking he might have left her his money only to get it back?

'Give it to me. I'll look it up. And if he isn't good to you, I'll need it to send explosives.'

Holly ignored her and read out the Maine address, listening to Melinda tap-tapping at her keyboard.

'Wow, that's out there on the coast, right up against Canada. How are you going to get there? When are you going?'

Holly put a hand to her temple. 'Stop asking for logistics.'

'I know, not your strength. I wish you wouldn't go, Hol.'

'I have a billion questions to ask, not all of them friendly.'

'What if he wants you back?'

Holly opened her mouth. Nothing came out. She had nothing to say.

'Oh sweet Jesus, Holly. I'm coming with you. I can buy a gun in time, can't I? Or get Caleb to take— Wait, did you say you're moving in with my extremely rich and gorgeous future husband?'

Sigh. Holly could picture a far-off future in which Melinda, over her divorce and coupled with someone perfect for her, would be calm again. In the meantime . . . 'It was a platonic invitation, and I'm not making any long-term decisions until I can get home and sleep for about a week. Maybe two. And since it takes me hours to decide what to wear, I probably won't figure out what to do for another thirty years, by which time I'll be dead.'

'Aw, Jeez.' Melinda's voice grew husky. 'I'm sorry. You're in crazyville and I'm being manic and brittle because my husband is an asshole and I hate getting divorced, and I hate all men right now, too. This is big stuff. Huge. I just wish you wouldn't go see Lyle right now, when you're sad and vulnerable and kind of a mess.'

Holly wandered out on to her balcony and leaned against the railing. 'I feel like this weekend has built momentum toward me understanding . . . I don't know what yet, but some important truth, about me, about Lyle, about us together. What that will be, and what will happen next, I have no idea, but I have to go with it.'

'Oh Holly.' Melinda sounded mournful, but resigned. 'Okay. I'll be here to pick up the pieces . . . again. Damn the dude!

Damn both of them! I wish you'd get away from everything Frederick.'

'Everything?' Holly quirked an eyebrow. 'Even the money?'

'*No!* Keep that. You can buy us a mansion in Bel Air and we can live there until we're wrinkly spinsters.'

Holly tipped her head back, drinking in the mountain air. Los Angeles would seem loud, crowded and claustrophobic in comparison. But Melinda was right, she could live wherever she wanted now, in her own house. She could afford a cook, a driver – people who could take over where her damaged skills left off.

The thought didn't fill her with as much excitement as she expected.

She turned to go back into the room. 'I should get ready for the barbecue tonight.'

'You know you're sounding different, Holly. More like your old self.'

'I'm fried. Deep-fried. Maybe it's good for me.'

'Please, please take care of yourself. If going to see Lyle doesn't feel right, put it off. Don't let anyone else decide your life for you. Promise me. Pinky swear.'

'I promise.' She held up her pinky, even though Melinda couldn't see it. 'Bye, Melinda.'

Holly ended the call grateful to her friend, feeling stronger having shaken off the dream. It was hard to hold on to romantic notions of Lyle with Melinda's pin deflating them so efficiently.

She shuffled over to her closet to pick an outfit from the batch of clothes her mom had sent. Probably the black capris for tonight. With the yellow top.

Holly made a face. She was fifty-five years old, choosing party clothes her mother had picked out for her. When and why had she stopped caring how she looked? Admittedly in LA the majority of people she interacted with barely came up to her elbow, and she'd never been a fashion plate, but she used to care more.

Going forward, that would be different. Holly was perfectly capable of choosing her own wardrobe, even if it took longer than pre-Change, when she'd stride into a store, yank something off a rack that caught her eye, try it on in three minutes, and leave with whatever-it-was ensconced in tissue paper and a shopping bag five minutes after that.

Both capris and top behaved themselves and went on perfectly. Holly was more careful with her makeup than usual. Yes, she looked fried, but at least now her fry was more attractively framed.

Several minutes remained before she had to leave. Curiosity had been nagging at her since Melinda looked up Lyle's address, so she picked up her phone and did the same. His property was indeed across from Canada, at the mouth of the St Croix river where it poured into the Atlantic. A closer zoom showed the house, Lyle's house, the lone building at the end of a road – a lane, really – off Route 1. The closest named town was a tiny cluster of houses called Robbinston.

Holly stared in fascination, trying to picture the man she'd known, who'd made such a point of involving himself with his community and the world at large, choosing to live in such a place.

Isolated as it was, the area was not short on beauty. Close to the shoreline, his house would overlook the river to the town of St Andrews, and Passamaquoddy Bay, which fed the fantastic Bay of Fundy, whose forty-foot tides rose and fell between the provinces of New Brunswick and Nova Scotia.

Did Lyle own the house? Had he rented it? How long had he been there? How long did he intend to stay? Had he taken a new identity? Was he ever planning to resume his old one? How had he returned to the States without alerting anyone? Who were the bodies in the car? Would he ask for his money back? Would he ask for her back?

So many questions. She hoped Caleb knew at least some of the answers.

Holly slipped her phone into her travel purse, slung it over her head and headed for the door. She felt jittery, manic, positively Melinda-like, and would rather fill the extra time before the party strolling Senneck's gardens than sitting here worrying about . . . everything.

Three steps into the lobby, Megan leapt out of a chair and headed toward her, her pretty face blotchy, eyes red from crying. Apparently Holly's quest for peaceful contemplation was doomed.

'Hi.' Megan's voice was raspy and thick. 'Can I talk to you?'

Oh no. Holly had primed herself for several difficult scenarios this evening, but having to cope with Megan begging for money that might not really be Holly's wasn't one of them.

Some of her desire to do pretty much anything other than speak with Megan must have showed in her face, because Megan stepped closer. 'Please. It's not going to be what you think.'

What do you think I think? The question was too grade-school stupid to ask. 'Sure.'

'Outside?' Megan gestured toward the lobby exit. 'That okay?'

'As long as you're not planning to kill me.'

'I promise.' Her smile was so miserable it triggered Holly's maternal instincts. She needed to remind herself what this woman was capable of: husband-stealing, cheating, maybe not murder, but certainly manipulation. By her own admission,

327

when Megan wanted something, she would go to extraordinary lengths to get it.

Outside in the garden, a few others were taking in its evening beauty, including the middle-aged couple Holly had seen a few times during her stay. Still not speaking to each other. Maybe they liked it that way. Maybe they existed in a blissful state of perpetual love and non-communication. What did she really know? About anyone?

She and Megan did some silent strolling themselves. A breeze had sprung up, which made the flowers dance and brought piney scents down from the hills.

Or maybe that was Megan's hair product.

'I just have a couple of questions. I don't care what the answers are, but I want to know the truth.'

'Go ahead. I'm a terrible liar, so I don't bother.' Holly answered distractedly, aware that something wasn't right. Something was missing. She forced herself to focus on Megan, who'd also had a crappy day and deserved Holly's attention.

'Have you and Lyle been together all along? Like is that why he didn't mention you to us?'

The question shocked her. Holly wasn't that kind of person . . . but then of course, how would Megan know? 'No, no, once he married Eliana, I cut off all contact.'

'So you really didn't know he was leaving you the money?'

'No, I didn't know.' Holly turned to look Megan in the puffy eyes. A conspiracy, one Megan might have arranged for herself in Holly's place. 'It was a complete surprise. Unwelcome, actually.'

'What?' Megan looked flabbergasted. 'Why?'

'Because we've been divorced for a long time, and it makes no sense and puts me in an awkward position around everyone who knew him.'

'But the rest of your life . . .' Megan flung out her arms to show the immensity of time. 'Secure, safe.'

'I had enough. When Lyle left me the trust account you found, he upgraded me from enough to plenty. Why would I need more?'

'I will never understand you.' Megan sighed in that stuttery way that comes after a serious cry. They walked on a bit longer, while Holly wondered if that was all, and how soon she could gracefully escape. 'Bodie really gave it to me last night.'

Holly did not want to hear this. Megan's sex life had nothing to do with her. 'That's . . . great.'

Megan turned in astonishment. 'What do you mean, great?'

'Uh . . .' Holly rubbed her temple. What had she missed this time?

'He yelled at me for like an *hour*.'

'Ah.' Immense relief. 'When you said he gave it to you . . .'

Megan let out a guffaw instead of her usual nasal whinny. 'Oh man. I did not think I could even smile today. Why would I tell you about *that*?'

'I couldn't imagine.'

'Do you want to sit?' Megan pointed to a bench resting against a low wall that supported espaliered apple trees with fruits the size of plums. 'I'm beat.'

'Sure.' Holly plunked herself down next to her. 'We'll be standing later at the party.'

'I'm not going. Bodie and I are leaving.' Megan slumped down until she could rest her head against the painted wood.

'That's too bad.' Holly was surprised to find she meant it. 'I know you'd wanted to stay on at Senneck for a few more days.'

'Yeah, well, we can't afford to now.' Megan lifted her hand and let it drop on to her thigh, bared by a scarlet miniskirt. 'That's kind of what I wanted to talk to you about. Not asking for anything, but yeah, I was really bummed about the will. I know I deserved it, at least partly, but it was pretty mean of Lyle. That money was the one thing I cared about.'

Holly raised an eyebrow.

'No, no, I meant coming out of this weekend.' Megan sat up straighter, took out the elastic from her ponytail and fluffed up her hair. 'Sorry, that sounded awful. Anyway, Bodie was completely unsympathetic. I've never seen him like that. Usually he's so sweet. But he was super-angry.'

'I'm sorry.' Holly didn't know why Megan was telling her this. Or whether she was leading up to the Big Ask she'd said she wasn't going to make. 'But I can't change what—'

'No, he wasn't angry at you.'

'At Lyle?'

'No, at *me*. He said . . .' Megan's voice wavered. 'He said, "Why do you keep trying to be something you're not? I love you the way you are, why is that never enough for you?" Then he says, "I'm glad you didn't get the money. Money changes you into someone I don't know and don't always love."'

Holly gasped. Clearly Bodie Bauer-Baker had grown a pair. She knew she liked him.

'I felt so stupid.' Megan started crying. 'Like my whole life I've taken this guy for granted, and done some horrible things to him, but because I love him, it was all for us, and I thought he'd keep going along, you know? Do what I told him to because he could see it was for the right reasons. But he was ready to leave me over this.'

'Wow.' Holly probably should have clucked sympathetically, but honestly, she was impressed with Bodie.

'We're going to sell Lyle's house, the one he left me, and move to Indiana, where Bodie's from, and get married. I hope I can make him happy. I don't know, it's so different from how

I saw my life going. I hope it makes *me* happy.' Megan laughed shakily. 'I'm scared poopless. But I owe it to him to try.'

Holly was ashamed. Megan didn't want money from her. She wanted a friend to talk to about a mountainous upheaval of everything she'd always believed and lived for.

This seemed to be the weekend for that kind of thing.

'Anyway, I waited until you came downstairs because I wanted to say goodbye to you before we left. You've been really nice. I can imagine Lyle with someone like you, better than with Eliana. Definitely better than with me.'

Holly caught her breath. Considering the circumstances, that was a remarkable statement.

Megan gave her a long, warm hug, smiled into her eyes, wished her a safe trip home, then burst into fresh tears and hurried away.

Immediately Holly raised an arm to call her back, remembering. Megan deserved to know that her husband was still alive, the money was still his, that her marriage to Bodie would be illegal.

She relaxed, shaking her head. Holly couldn't do that to her. Not today. If there were legal things to work out, Caleb could take care of them, or Lyle's lawyer. The poor woman had been through enough. Frankly, so had Holly. But while Megan got to go home and begin a new life with her future husband, Holly had to go to a barbecue.

She could see the staff already at work, wisps of smoke rising from various cooking devices. A meat smoker, a grill, and a table set up by the lake with a red and white checked tablecloth denoting casual. Caleb was there, wearing jeans and a white shirt with the sleeves rolled up – did he have to look so good all the time? – conferring with one of the staff.

He and Holly would have to find time to talk after the party.

Until then, she supposed they'd continue their Dance of Avoidance.

She reached the steeper part of the hill down to the water, not far from the gazebo where she and Caleb shared champagne that first night, when Holly had been convinced this would be a mildly taxing but ultimately pleasant weekend of friendship and fond memories.

Ha ha.

Facing the sharper decline made her realize what was missing. Her cane was still back in her room.

Holly and downhill did not get along.

Sooo . . . she had a choice: stand there like a helpless dork until someone noticed her and came to her rescue.

Or go.

Deep breath. She went. Step by step, arms out for balance when the incline forced her to accelerate, reminding herself how it had felt running full tilt across the gym floor. No harness or lifeline here, but she didn't need one. Her strong muscles responded and she arrived on the gentler slope to the lakefront unbruised, triumphant . . . and relieved.

'Hi, Holly.'

Holly turned, embarrassed to have been so intent on not wiping out that she hadn't noticed Eliana's footsteps behind her. Lyle's number two looked her usual fresh, put-together self in skinny black jeans and an oversized white shirt with teal stripes.

'Hi, Eliana, thanks for your message. I took a nap and feel much better.' Holly waited until she caught up. 'Ready to go eat again?'

'I'm not staying, actually.' Eliana's face registered polite regret. 'I came to say goodbye to everyone.'

The cast was dropping like flies. 'Megan left early too. I just saw her.'

'Ah.' Eliana looked pained. 'Is she flying to Milwaukee tonight? Just my luck we end up on the same plane.'

'She didn't say.'

'I'm actually glad I bumped into you alone.' She pointed to a bench along the path. 'Do you want to sit here, just for a second?'

'Sure.' Holly sat, looking longingly toward the setup by the lake. So close, and yet . . . another bench.

'I was thinking about what Lyle did with the will.' Eliana lowered herself to sit sideways, one arm resting along the top rail. 'You looked completely gobsmacked, as my mother-in-law would say. I think I know, or have a theory anyway, about why he left you everything.'

So he could get it back easily? Holly would like that not to be the case. 'I'm all ears.'

'Besides that he obviously loved you and wanted you to have security, I think he arranged that the will should be released to all of us to validate your relationship after he denied your marriage to the rest of us for so long. I think he wanted to put that right. I see it as an apology.'

Holly's heart skipped a beat. 'That's a lovely thought.'

'There's one thing that bothers me, though.' Eliana frowned, tapping a finger to her lip.

Only one? Amateur. 'What's that?'

'For Lyle to have left money for my stepsons' college education, he would have had to know he'd die before they were old enough to go.'

Wow. Holly fought a smile. In all the plotting that had gone into this weekend's Master Plan, Lyle had missed that. Luckily Eliana wouldn't expect her to explain. 'Good point.'

'All I can think is that it means he was going abroad knowing he was going to die. Maybe the car accident was suicide, though

I can't imagine Lyle committing suicide, let alone taking someone else with him.'

'Maybe it was his male lover.'

Eliana gasped, eyes impossibly round. 'You think—'

'No, sorry. Bad joke.'

Eliana let loose with her deep, hearty laugh, pressing a hand to her chest. 'Oh my goodness. You totally shocked me. Hilarious. This weekend has been so *weird*. I feel bad leaving early, but honestly, I just can't take any more.'

Tell me about it. 'I don't blame you at all.'

'Thank you for that.' Eliana sobered back to her poised self. 'I've also been thinking about what you said at lunch. Maybe Lyle did plan to disappear. Maybe he's still alive somewhere, like you said.'

It took all Holly's skill to put on a convincing who-knows expression. 'It's a nice idea.'

'I agree. I don't like thinking of a world without Lyle in it, though I'm sad he'd turn his back on all of us who loved him.' Eliana paused to look around them, at the beauty of the gardens, the lake, and the hills wearing their vivid evening colors. 'I hope wherever he is, he found what he was looking for.'

'A beautiful world.' Holly's voice caught on the words.

'Yes.' Eliana sat quietly for another moment, breeze ruffling strands that didn't quite make it into her updo. 'Or safety.'

'From?'

'Reality. Which isn't always beautiful.' She trained her serene gaze back on Holly. 'Obviously I have particular feelings about this, given where I came from, but safety isn't about pretending the world doesn't exist. That's narrow-mindedness. Or simple cowardice.'

Her words resonated deeply. She wasn't referring to Holly, but Holly had only just begun to see that she had also chosen a small, safe life, one whose boundaries Caleb had been trying to prod her beyond. 'Sometimes it takes having that pointed out to make a person realize they're hiding.'

'True. But we won't get that chance with Lyle.' Eliana swung her body straight and stood. 'I must go, and you have a party to get to. Thanks for listening. I'll walk you over to say goodbye.'

Holly got to her feet, grateful for Eliana's wisdom. More to think over. More that could alter how she decided to go forward. Another change, but a vastly different one to the first.

The rest of the way to the lake, Eliana chatted about Jeremy and the boys, how much she missed them, and details of their plans for an August trip to North Carolina. Holly was happy for her, and a bit envious. Eliana had found her place.

'Hey, there you are.' Norman's voice barreled toward them. He and Beatrice, in bathing suits and sheer cover-ups, were standing with Janet and Caleb, whose grin faded then re-emerged when he saw Holly, like sun passing briefly behind a small cloud. She half wished everyone would clear out and let them get The Talk over with.

'I came to say goodbye.' Eliana hugged Norman and Beatrice hard and long, then Janet and Caleb.

'Bye, sweetie.' Norman enveloped Holly in a bear hug.

'I'm not leaving.' She spoke squashed against his broad chest.

'We are. Beatrice and I found a nudist site about an hour from Albany. We're taking Janet with us.'

Holly tried to cover her surprise. 'No kidding. Go, Janet.'

Janet was beaming. 'I always say if you don't keep trying something new, you stagnate.'

'They're having a dance tonight.' Beatrice did a sexy shimmy that made Holly very glad she wasn't going to be at this dance. 'Want to come?'

'Uh . . . it's not really my thing.'

'Don't know until you try!' Janet cackled and imitated Beatrice's shimmy with equally impressive if somewhat more meager results. 'I'm dying to check it out. Who knows, maybe I'll finally move out of my museum of a house and show up in Florida.'

'We'd love that,' Norman said.

There was a flurry of hugging and kissing and farewells and come-visits, and then Holly's half-wishes were answered, and she and Caleb were alone. Except now she wanted to be alone with only herself, somewhere in the Bahamas. Narrow-minded? Or cowardice?

Yes.

'I guess it's just us tonight.' Caleb looked as uneasy as she felt. 'Going to be a lot of leftovers. Would you like a beer?'

'God, yes.'

He led the way over to the tiny keg set up on a table alongside a large bowl of coleslaw, a platter of cornbread, and a crockpot of beans. Staff members were in the process of breaking down the table for eight into a twosome. Holly nearly groaned. Facing each other over an intimate table for two was not the right vibe for holding Caleb hostage at honor-point until he told her what he knew and why he'd withheld it. 'Quite a comedown from a big party.'

'It is.' He filled a glass with beer and handed it over. 'Not sure a romantic tête-à-tête is what we're in the mood for, but this is what we get.'

'Apparently.'

'Cheers.' He clinked his glass to hers. 'Hey, you don't have your cane today.'

'Forgot it.'

'And look, you're fine.' He was smug.

She hated smug.

'Well. Bottoms up.' Caleb drank half his beer in one swallow.

'Tense for some reason?' She drank a quarter of hers in two swallows.

'Yup.'

'Same here.'

'Yeah?'

He drank. She drank.

'It's good beer,' Caleb said. 'An IPA.'

'Yes. I like it. Not too hoppy. Lyle is alive, isn't he.'

Caleb raised his glass to his mouth again, expression bland. 'Yup.'

'Okay, then.' She took her next sip. 'Nice night.'

'You betcha.'

Their eyes met, slid away. They laughed uneasily.

'Come on.' Caleb swept the keg under one arm. 'Let's sit on the bench and empty this sucker while we talk.'

'It's that bad?'

He got that stony look on his face that she recognized from the rose garden the evening she'd almost been afraid of him. She wasn't now. 'Complicated. Difficult.'

Holly stopped walking. In all this time, the thought that Lyle might be unwell somehow had never occurred to her. 'Is Lyle okay? I mean health-wise and . . . emotionally? Mentally?'

'I think he's crazy, but that's me. Yes, he's fine.'

Holly relaxed a little, following Caleb to the bench – definitely her night for benches – not far from where they'd launched their kayaks. The lake glimmered in the sun's setting rays, trees lit coral-green around it.

Sitting next to Caleb, feeling the warmth from his body, sipping beer on a beautiful summer night – this wasn't how Holly had pictured this discussion.

'Lyle will tell you more. I'll—' He turned to her. 'I felt that.'

'What?' At his words, *Lyle will tell you more*, Holly hadn't been able to stop a near-convulsive jerk of her midsection. 'Don't know what you're talking about.'

Caleb's laugh was more like a groan. 'If we all live through this, it will be a miracle.'

'We'll make it.' Holly nudged him affectionately. She'd been focusing too much on her own pain and bewilderment. This had to be hell for him too. 'I'm listening. Go on.'

'I'll tell you the short version. Very short. It won't make sense until he explains more, but I'll leave that to him. After the car accident in Thailand, Lyle decided to disappear. He went on to the monastery, intending to live there permanently.' Caleb spoke calmly, but she could feel his tension. 'A few years later, he got dengue fever. While recovering, he had an epiphany and decided to come back to the US. But he needed money, so lucky me, I got the phone call from my dead brother telling me he wanted to come home but also to stay dead.'

'Stay dead?' Holly couldn't think of anything less likely. '*Why?*'

Caleb rolled his eyes. 'Don't ask me. I don't understand any of it. We argued for days. He begged me, in tears, to make this possible for him. Finally I broke down. I swore I wouldn't tell anyone he was alive and back if he swore to stay dead.'

'That is the weirdest thing I've ever heard.'

'Ya think? But you know how Lyle is, he makes sense when you're talking to him. So I promised. Keeping up this bullshit for the past five years around people who love him, having to deal with their grief . . .' He closed his eyes, exhaling. 'It's been awful. But . . . he's my brother. It's a thing.'

'Your heart is in the right place, Caleb.' She couldn't believe what Lyle had asked him to do. 'Your brain, however, is probably more broken than mine.'

He cracked up, then turned to face her, eyes catching the sun, lightening their color. 'I don't know another person who could find humor in this.'

'You're welcome.' She took another swallow of beer – nervous drinking. 'Then what?'

'Then this weekend . . .' Caleb turned back to stone. 'Even suspecting how I feel about—' He dropped his head.

'Caleb.' Holly put a hand on his arm, moved by his struggle to get the words out. 'At this point I'm so freaked you could tell me Lyle is into devil worship and human sacrifice, and I'd just say, "Hey, that's nice." Whatever it is, say it. Drink more beer and say it. As I pointed out, we will both survive.'

'Right.' He took a Dutch-courage gulp. 'This weekend, Lyle broke his promise. I realized when you told me about the Life Savers. They weren't in the plans he gave me. While the rest of the party was honestly grieving, he arranged to take you down the sweet-memory-lane of your marriage and turn his memorial service into a sneaky-fun declaration of love for you.'

Nausea roiled Holly's stomach. She felt ashamed of how she'd cherished the tokens Lyle had planted, even without knowing what they signified for Caleb. 'God, I'm sorry. I had no idea.'

'Of course you didn't.' He turned back to her. 'Of course you didn't. You got stuck in the middle of . . . this.'

This. The implications of what had happened and what was still to come, for her, for Lyle, for Caleb . . . all of it was so complex that her brain couldn't keep up. Past memories competed with possible futures, competed with what she knew of Lyle, competed with how others saw him into a stew of mass confusion.

At least she could think clearly enough for one question. 'How did Lyle buy a house if he's dead?'

'I bought the house, the one he picked out. A sixty-thousand-dollar cabin in the Maine woods. His goal is to live as completely off the grid as he can.'

Holly couldn't imagine. No restaurants? No travel? No museums and concerts, no parties and lectures? No friendships, no relationships? All of that given up, everything that had comprised the bulk of his personality and passions? 'I can't picture that at all.'

'He's changed.' Caleb refilled his glass, offered her more, which she accepted. 'The monastery changed him.'

How much could a person change? How much was just circumstance, emotion, societal expectations? Was it any wonder Lyle would be different in a Buddhist monastery in Thailand than he had been here? And how much of that change was only other people's perceptions at any given time, based on their own pasts, values and judgments? This weekend Lyle had been presented wearing many different faces by many different people.

'I need to see him.'

'Yes.' Caleb's lips shut tightly on the word. 'I'll take you up tomorrow. I'm sure he's expecting you.'

'Thank you.' Holly looked out over the shivering lake, whose blue surface was turning navy with hints of sunset peach riding the ripples. She would see Lyle tomorrow. How would she feel after so many years, after so many revelations, about him and about herself? The way she'd felt when they first met? When they married on the beach in Hawaii? When he was so frustrated with her impairment? Or that last time, at Bar Chloe, when Lyle had seemed so devoid of hope for happiness? 'I saw him, you know, a couple of months before he left the country. He flew out to LA and called me.'

340

Caleb muttered something Holly was pretty sure wasn't a compliment. 'That figures. I told him to leave you alone.'

'He said his life was about to change, but that he wanted to get back in touch. To be friends again.'

Caleb snorted. 'Right.'

'You don't believe that's what he wanted?'

'Lyle has been in love with you since the moment he saw you.' Caleb's beautiful dark eyes were full of pain. Holly closed hers against the need to comfort him mixed with the chemistry she couldn't get used to or accept. 'He's never given up hope of getting you back. Never.'

If Caleb had said that to her even yesterday, Holly would have laughed it off. *He-who-remarried-within-ten-minutes-of-our-divorce?* But she thought she was starting to understand. All that remained was her part in Lyle's plan.

'I'll get us some food.' Caleb stood up, leaving a chilly spot where his body had been, and came back with plates of the sides she'd already seen, garnished with chicken legs and pork ribs that smelled divine.

They ate together, mostly in silence, neither with much appetite, then Caleb took their plates back to the staff.

When he returned, he sat close again and put his arm around her. Holly leaned into him and they sat watching the world darken across the lake to the tops of the distant hills, until it was no longer light enough to see what lay ahead.

Chapter 19

Subject: Holly
Date: July 15, 2016
From: Caleb@FrederickIndustries.com
To: LyleFred@aol.com

Sorry I wasn't around to take your call. Now you're not around to take mine and I'm booked solid through late tonight. So I'll say this. Your idea of going to visit Holly in LA sucks. Think about it, dude. You're a mess right now. Your third marriage is collapsing. Worst time to go crawling back to any woman, let alone Holly after what you put her through. Norman might think it's a good idea, but Norman also plays naked volleyball, okay? I love the guy, but he's all happiness and light and going with your heart. This is a case for caution and respect.

Go abroad if it's what you want to do, think your life over, be spiritual, be a monk or whatever weird shit you need to get out of your system, and then figure out what you want to offer Holly. And now that I can finally talk to you about her again, yes, I was and probably always will be in love with her, so if you do anything to fuck her up, I will come after you.

Subject: re: Holly
Date: July 15, 2016

From: *LyleFred@aol.com*
To: *Caleb@FrederickIndustries.com*

Too late. I've booked my flight.

Subject: *re: Holly*
Date: *July 15, 2016*
From: *Caleb@FrederickIndustries.com*
To: *LyleFred@aol.com*

Sometimes you can be a real selfish asshole, you know that?

Holly was sitting in the living room of Melinda's little house –
fourteen years later, she still couldn't think of it as hers – wet-
haired from a shower, drinking a big glass of water, wondering
what to make for dinner, a decision that could take some doing.
She'd just finished her workout, a vigorous thirty minutes on
her stationary bike, followed by a seated weight routine, carefully choreographed to minimize her risk of unbalancing. Other
days, Melinda would drive her to the Annenberg Community
Beach House and they'd swim laps together.

She stared listlessly at the entrance to the house's tiny kitchen,
thinking maybe she'd heat up a can of soup, even though she'd
promised herself to stop eating so much canned and processed
food and try harder to keep it fresh. A salad, then?

Another salad. Yippee.

Holly was, admittedly, in a funk. Summer was hard, without
the routine of school every day to keep her occupied and feeling
productive. She still volunteered at the local animal shelter, and
had her usual gig at the Santa Monica Public Library helping
with the kids' reading program, but there were definitely still
too many hours in a day.

Earlier that summer, she'd taken another stab at dating, not expecting anything, and had met Connor. After so many dud dates, she'd gone to their first with about as much excited anticipation as a trip to the post office for tax forms. Instead of the jeans-wearing, semi-articulate guy who either expected her to do all the talking or spent the whole date doing it for her, Connor had been nicely but a bit over-dressed in a suit and tie, and excelled at the give and take of a get-to-know-you conversation. He was a lawyer, specializing in personal injury, which made her a bit queasy to hear at first, but hey, she was a kindergarten teaching assistant, she should know better than to play the assumptions game.

They'd had some fun times, a couple of dinners, a concert, a baseball game, a museum trip. She'd been pretty darned excited. It had been a long time since she'd felt hopeful about a relationship. Like thirty years.

She found herself going along with whatever Connor wanted, because frankly, it was delightful not to have to make decisions, not to have to struggle to make plans, not to be responsible for anything more than being ready at the right time.

Soon the red flags became harder to ignore. He'd urge her to order different things on the menu than what she'd initially chosen. His work stories started sounding more about lining his pockets than helping others navigate the system. His enjoyment of the arts seemed put on for her benefit, fidgeting in his seat at the symphony, roaming eyes at the museum landing more often on women than art.

Then it got worse. He told her she should practice walking with more purpose, lifting her feet for each step instead of shuffling. He told her red was not her color, and that she was being ridiculous avoiding grapes. Breaking point? When he mentioned he had some clothes of his ex-wife's that might fit and flatter her more than the ones she usually wore.

No thanks.

After that, Holly had decided to add relationships to the pile of things she'd had to give up. She was no longer strong enough to have the kind of equal partnership she'd had with Lyle, and she wouldn't settle for less.

But while Officially Giving Up had been a sensible way to save her repeated disappointments, Holly had been grieving the loss of that hope, realizing how much she had counted on another life still to come, somehow, someday, somewhere. Cue *West Side Story* and the hankies.

Maybe it was that her fiftieth birthday was coming up in February, half a year away but weighing on her already. Everyone said the fifties were the prime of a woman's life. Freed from child-rearing duties, at the top of her game at work, and in solid financial circumstances, she could finally spread her wings. For Holly, the birthday would only mark the beginning of another stunted, pinioned decade.

And with that thought, Holly could not stand her self-pity party any longer. She was hungry. Food would boost her spirits. In the kitchen, while her soup heated, she ate a carrot and a few cheese-and-cracker combos. Triscuits were practically health food, right? Cheese was an excellent source of protein.

The phone rang, making her head jerk up. Odd, because her phone rang constantly, almost always crap-calls. She hurried into the living room to peer at the display, thinking she was probably the last person in LA who still had a landline.

Caller ID showed no name or organization, but the unfamiliar number had a Milwaukee area code. Holly's heart started thumping. She stood staring at the device until the voicemail icon appeared. Then she dialed in to listen and entered her password, feeling Lyle, telling herself it wasn't possible, there would only be silence from a hang-up.

'Holly, it's Lyle.'

Ordinarily she would have recognized his voice before he got to the second syllable of her name, but he hardly sounded like himself. Not until he'd spoken a few more words was she convinced it was truly him.

'I'm here in LA. I'd like to see you, to talk to you, if you're free. Please give me a call.' He left his number and hung up.

Holly stood frozen, trembling, for half a minute, then listened to the message again, to be absolutely sure she wasn't confused or hallucinating, that she hadn't wished him into being out of her bad-mood loneliness.

'Holly, it's Lyle.'

She dropped back on to the settee, phone still in her hand, mouth open, face a shock-mask, probably looking as if she'd just had a heart attack.

Figuratively, she had.

Fourteen years since she'd last heard that voice, when Lyle had been responding to her fury over his upcoming wedding to Eliana. Seven years since that crazy night of inappropriate passion with Caleb, when Holly had refused Lyle's letter and declared herself over him.

Fourteen years, yet somehow she knew, had always known, that it wasn't really the last time, just as she assumed Caleb, too, would be back in touch one day.

When she could move again, Holly left the house, still clutching the phone, intending to knock on Melinda's door. Halfway, she turned back. There was no point talking to Melinda about this. Holly could guess exactly what she'd say, starting with *Are you kidding me? You're considering running to see that turd after he ditched you and married someone else?*

Holly needed to woman-up and make her own decision,

not only because it was her own decision to make, but also because she'd just remembered Melinda was off having her hair done.

Back inside, she tried the whole thinking-this-through approach and found she couldn't find an entrance to any logic. So she decided to listen to Lyle's message again, over the initial shock, and examine her innermost feelings. If she was giddy with butterflies and hope, she'd ignore him.

She played it again. Then again, listening carefully not only to Lyle, but to herself.

'I'm here in LA. I'd like to see you, to talk to you, if you're free.'

Remarkably – triumphantly – apart from a few forgivable flutters, Holly felt mainly a maternal concern and desire to lend a friendly shoulder or a sympathetic ear. Lyle had respected her wishes for fourteen years – except for the letter, which had left her in the driver's seat, free to choose what to do with it. For him to contact her now, there had to be a good reason. For the sake of what they'd been to each other, and because of all the years they'd been safely apart, Holly could call him without risk. From there, she'd play it by ear.

She dialed the number he'd left, guiltily hoping that if she decided to meet him for a drink, she could slip out before Melinda was back. If Melinda asked where she was going, Holly would have to tell a partial truth, which Melinda would sniff out immediately as a partial lie. The downside of having a friend who knew her that well.

'Holly.' His voice was warm and joyful, much clearer than it had been on the message.

And yes, forgivable flutters happened. 'Hello, Lyle.'

'I didn't think you'd call back. I sounded like a lunatic on the phone.'

'This is true.' She sank into a chair, spine rigid.

'I'm heading for Bar Chloe. It's not far for you. Can you meet me there? Would you like to?'

'Yes.' She kept herself from saying *of course*. Of course was what wives added, what mistresses added, what best of best friends added. Holly would not be taken for granted. 'I'll be there.'

'Thank you.' His relief was obvious. 'Thank you, Holly. I'll see you soon.'

I'll see you soon. Good Lord. What had she gotten herself into?

With uncertain fingers, Holly logged on to Uber for a car that promised to be there in fifteen minutes. It took her only seven to dress, both because she'd been wearing a decent green and white cotton shirtdress earlier that day for her hours at the library, and because she wasn't going to primp or try to look any different than she usually did. This wasn't a date.

Dress, earrings, sandals, done.

Still eight minutes.

She had time to add a simple silver necklace.

There.

Maybe a little blush.

And mascara. Just a little.

Eyeliner.

A brow cleanup with tweezers wouldn't hurt.

Enough.

Holly made it to the curb outside Melinda's house just as the Uber was pulling up, and climbed in as quickly as she could, relieved when they managed the getaway before Melinda made it home.

So. Good. Here she was. On the way to see Lyle.

Last time she'd seen him was at her parents' condo in

Torrance, when he'd come to say goodbye after seeing her safely installed, on his way home to Milwaukee. Watching him walk away had been one of the hardest things Holly ever had to do. She still remembered the pain searing in her throat as she fought to keep control, her worried parents hovering, trying to say the right things, anxious to make everything better for the daughter they loved, while Holly wanted to drop to the floor and howl like a two-year-old.

The memory made her feel suddenly vulnerable, unprepared for this encounter. What did you say to someone you'd loved so desperately and had lost for all the worst and most unfair reasons? Someone who you'd hurt, and who'd hurt you back in ways neither could be blamed for?

She gazed outside at the familiar neighborhood going by, deciding the best idea was to stay friendly and calm and listen to whatever he had to say.

The car stopped. Holly stiffened. *Already?* The ride seemed to have taken seconds. She thanked the driver and emerged on to the sidewalk, shaky with fear and excitement, then walked into the bar, surprised her legs could keep her upright, let alone move her forward.

Lyle was nursing a G&T at the long wooden counter. Holly stopped dead several feet away, shocked at the change in him. Fourteen years older, yes, as was she. Age happened: hair grayed, skin loosened, noses and ears kept growing, subtly reformulating the face . . . all that was expected. The surprise was in his lifeless eyes, too-thin frame, careless dress and hunched posture, antithesis of the charming, confident man she knew. All that she absorbed in a split second, and in that same split second he sensed her as he always had, and turned his head.

Their eyes met. He opened his arms and she walked straight

into them without thinking, because it was Lyle, and they had once belonged to each other as completely as any two people could. His embrace felt as natural and inevitable as being with him always had, and maybe always would.

When Lyle finally released her, Holly perched on the stool next to him, paradoxically both wrung out and overflowing, and accepted the tissue he handed her to wipe her eyes. Seeing him, hearing his voice against her hair, smelling and touching him again had already proved she was a fool around Lyle Frederick. No risk? Even after having successfully put their extraordinary relationship and her deep feelings for him behind her, all she wanted was to go back into his arms and stay there.

Lyle ordered her a Green Spot Irish whiskey on the rocks. They didn't bother with pleasantries, *so how have you been, you're looking well, gosh it's been forever.* Holly told him about her life since they'd last spoken, about her routines, her job, her feelings about California, about her mom and dad, Melinda and the few mutual friends she'd stayed in touch with.

Lyle told her about his job heading the Frederick Foundation, how he'd worked to change its charitable focus to bring easier access to music and art of all kinds in Milwaukee and beyond, how his marriage to Eliana had ended in divorce – which Holly didn't mention she'd already heard from Caleb – and that he'd been a fool to have been seduced by Megan, a hot young thing with more designs on his money than his heart. Turned out hers already belonged to someone she'd referred to as her ex-boyfriend, without mentioning the guy never quite made it to 'ex'.

When he got to that part, Holly barely kept herself from rolling her eyes, back on solid emotional ground. When would men ever learn? She would have thought Lyle was smarter than that.

Then he'd turned, brown-eyed and magnetic, even with worry lines deep in his forehead, and Holly's sneer faded into a desire to touch him that was so intense she'd had to sit on her hands. She wanted to follow the lean line of his cheek, trace the cowlick that made his bangs rise and swoop over his forehead, explore the new gray at his temples, the solid muscles of his shoulder and chest.

Instead, she did what she'd promised herself: stayed calm, friendly, and listened. For this she deserved some kind of medal.

'I need a life change, a big one.'

Holly couldn't help herself. 'Another wife?'

'No.' He had the sense to look mortified. 'I wanted to see you before I leave. I wanted to be able to tell you in person that I . . . failed you. More to the point, I failed us. I should have stayed with you, Holly. I should have fought harder, much harder, to keep our marriage intact. I am deeply, humbly and wretchedly sorry.'

His sincerity cut like a razor: sharp, clean and deadly accurate. Maybe he should have stayed longer. But ultimately it would not have made a difference unless he also truly understood and accepted her limitations. 'It wasn't only on you to keep the marriage going. If you had stayed, who knows if either of us would have been satisfied.'

'At least we would have been sure.' He took a sip of his drink, staring down at the counter. 'I need time, Holly. To get my humiliated, idiot self out of this marriage, and to be on my own. I need to do a lot of soul-searching before I can put myself back together.

'But I am hoping . . .' Lyle met her eyes, triggering more longing. 'Maybe it's selfish of me to ask. But I'm hoping that during that time we can be in touch. I'll let you decide how often, in what capacity, everything. But . . . I have missed you.'

'That might be . . .' Her brain went into gridlock. Might be what? Wonderful? Her worst nightmare? A true friend would be easy to say yes to. But contact with Lyle could be a slippery slope to more heartbreak. Look how she'd reacted to a simple hour sharing drinks and conversation. Holly had barely managed to sit for twenty seconds before she wanted her hands all over him.

And yet. First time after so many years, there was bound to be emotional fallout. Most of their conversation had been very pleasant, two friends eager to catch up on each other's lives. For once, Lyle wasn't asking for something she couldn't give. He wanted a friend. God knew Holly did too.

'I'm thinking of going abroad for a while. To Cambodia, Laos, Thailand, visit some temples and just . . . be away.' His face lit suddenly. 'You always said you wanted to see Thailand. You could come over for a week while I'm there. We could explore it together. Just friends.'

And there it was. Even as Holly's heart leapt at the idea of the two of them out in the world again, she'd just been handed her answer. Lyle still didn't understand her life, her limits, her new self. And until he did, even friendship wouldn't work between them.

Fourteen years after her brave decision to end their marriage, she again had to summon all her courage and make another one. Yes, she would grieve for him all over again when he left. Her apartment would seem smaller, her life unbearably dull and tame.

Heart already aching Holly thanked him for the drink and told him she hoped he would have a wonderful time abroad, and that he'd find the happiness he deserved. But she thought it would be better for both of them if they stayed apart.

Then she walked out of the bar, again cutting loose this man she'd loved from first sight, probably still loved, probably always would love, her only comfort the knowledge that once again she'd saved Lyle from having to make his big beautiful life as small and pointless as hers had become.

Chapter 20

Sunday morning, Holly stood waiting on the curb where five days earlier Charming Tom had helped her out of the car on her arrival at Senneck, then gallantly kept her from splatting on her face as she sailed off in the wrong direction. Her one suitcase had been neatly packed for her the night before, and this morning she had only to tuck in her toiletries and monkey pajamas.

She and Caleb had stayed up late, making a dent in the keg, reflecting on the weekend, making joking suggestions for how Holly could spend the inheritance Caleb felt strongly was hers to keep. After too much beer, which usually kept her up at night, and all that angst, which always kept her up at night, she'd managed to sleep, fitfully, but long enough that she felt functional and decently clear-headed now.

'Good morning.' Caleb appeared next to her folding what must be a copy of an astronomical funeral bill. Senneck's car would be arriving soon to chauffeur them to the Saratoga County Airport, where, in true Frederick style, Caleb had chartered a plane to Machias, Maine, an hour's drive from where Lyle had settled. 'How did you sleep?'

'Better than I expected.'

'Same here.' He gave a too-bright smile. 'Going to be a lovely relaxing day!'

'Why, yes.' Holly made a self-strangling gesture. 'Another one!'

'Good times.' Caleb pocketed the bill. 'I'd feel like this visit should lead to closure for both of us, but there have already been so many closures . . .'

'Boggles the mind.'

Their ride drew up, a green Lexus. Charming Tom showed up again to help stow luggage and say goodbye, urging them to come back soon, as if they were friends with whom he'd just spent the weekend of his life. Caleb and Holly climbed in and the car whisked them off to the airport, where a four-seater plane waited. A little over an hour later, they landed at Machias Valley airport, and took an Uber to Johnson's Town Line Auto, where they picked up a white Chevy Impala.

Seamless travel, minimal stress. What money could do to make life easy!

It hit Holly, as it kept hitting her, because she kept forgetting then remembering, then forgetting again: she had that much money now, if Caleb was right and Lyle wasn't scheming to get it back. She could charter her own planes. Hell, she could buy one.

The idea didn't tempt her in the least.

Caleb pulled the Impala on to Route 1, this segment of which was a commercial strip winding through the charming hill town of Machias before it ran parallel to the Downeast coast.

'Have you been to Maine before?'

'Lyle and I visited Acadia briefly on a whirlwind tour of National Parks. Lyle was taken with this coast. I'm not surprised he ended up here.'

'You're not?'

She laughed, a short, nervous burst. 'Rephrase. Had I been inside Lyle's head while he was looking for an isolated spot to live out the remainder of his death, I would not be surprised to find Maine was one of the options.'

'Got it.' Caleb answered curtly; he had become quieter and quieter the longer this journey went on. Holly wanted to offer comfort and reassurance, but she wasn't sure how or about what. They shared anxiety and tension, but Caleb's thoughts about his brother and what would happen today had to be different from Holly's. She and Lyle would be coming full circle at this meeting. But what the closing of that circle would look like . . . impossible to tell.

Since there was still almost an hour ahead of them, Holly decided she'd have the best shot at staying sane if she stowed speculation and worry and concentrated on the scenery. They drove mostly through forest or clearings of muddy-banked tidal channels through meadows of grass and reeds. Small towns interrupted now and then, showing glimpses of lives in various yards and houses. Then the road turned north and back to nature that was less and less frequently interrupted until they neared the coast again, what Holly guessed was Passamaquoddy Bay.

Caleb slowed the car when the bay view turned back into trees. 'Nearly there.'

Holly's Zen state disappeared in a burst of energy. 'Have you been here before?'

'Nope. I just filled out the paperwork.' Caleb slowed further, peering to the right. 'I think this is the turnoff.'

The road was an unmarked dirt and gravel track through the thick woods.

'*This* is his street?'

'It's sort of his driveway. House is at the end.'

Holly remembered now, from the Google map. She swallowed, feeling light-headed and strange, as if this was all happening to some other version of her while she got to hang from the ceiling and watch. 'I wish we could have let him know we were coming.'

'The only way is by mail. We didn't have time. If you're going to disappear, you have to really do it.'

'Yes.' Holly lowered her shoulders, relaxed the fingers gripping each other in her lap. The car bumped over the narrow rutted track, pebbles pinged the car's underside. A branch made a teeth-aching whistle scratching the driver's-side door.

Caleb muttered a curse. 'This is insane. I should have rented a tank.'

The driveway seemed to go on for miles, every turn bringing fresh tension as Holly kept bracing for Lyle's house to appear.

At one turn, sharper than the others, Caleb slowed to a stop.

'Wrong road?'

'Right road.' He switched off the engine. 'We can walk the rest of the way.'

'Why?'

'I don't know. Surprise attack?'

'Okay.' That was weird, but so was this entire adventure.

Caleb made no move to get out of the car, which was even weirder. 'Holly.'

Holly froze, clutching the door handle. Something about his voice . . .

'I wanted to say that whatever you decide to do has to be the very best thing for you. Or at least you have to believe it is. If there's any doubt, take more time; any tugs of resistance in your gut, take more time. I can only guess what Lyle wants from you, but I do know he has this way of convincing anyone in earshot that what he says is the truth. Most of the time that's a good thing, because he's a man of honor and integrity. But you need to know what life *you* want to live, and stick to that, no matter what.'

His words brought on an upwelling of emotion. Deep warmth over his wisdom, his concern for her, the sincerity in his eyes, his need to protect her. Mild exasperation because it had occurred to her during one of her waking bouts last night that both Frederick brothers had been playing puppet master. Caleb by pushing her to test the limits of her capabilities, Lyle by orchestrating a treasure hunt that manipulated her to this beautiful spot.

'Thanks, Caleb. You've—'

'No, don't thank me.' He unbuckled his seatbelt, staring blankly through the windshield. 'Given what Lyle has suckered me into doing over the past couple of years, I need the lecture more than you do.'

Holly's irritation vanished. She squeezed his hand. 'I appreciate it.'

'Good.' He gave her a comical look. 'So you ready for this?'

'Absolutely.' She sent him a tight smile. 'Not.'

'Let's go, then.'

They got out of the car and started through the forest, thick with ferns and undergrowth. Within a few steps, nervous as she was, Holly became enchanted. The woods smelled fresh and earthy, piney and sweet. Sun dappled the road ahead of them in gold pools set dancing when the breeze blew. Mosses of several shapes and shades of green grew in hollows, lined rocks or made spongy mattresses of the ground. Mushrooms clustered here and there, white puffs, pink parasols and bright, almost neon yellow fan-topped fingers. A tiny red squirrel darted to the end of a branch overhanging the road, glassy, neurotic eyes staring as he scolded them.

Around the bend, an open, sunny space. Holly stopped with an exclamation of delight. Raspberry and blackberry edged the clearing, fruit on its way to ripening. Goldenrod, buttercups, Queen Anne's lace, and purple, orange and white wildflowers Holly didn't recognize. Ahead, vividly blue water, adding its salty fragrance to the scents of the woods. She felt more of her tension evaporate. Imagine waking up every day to that view, that air, that tranquility. Like Senneck, but without the room service. Or the bill.

Lyle's house was a two-story building that had been added on to a few times, more for practicality than beauty. A stone foundation peeked out under weathered gray cedar shingles that climbed to the eaves. The front door had been painted dark green; the trim also wore a fresh coat, of white. Beside the house, a pair of greenhouses had been assembled from still-new lumber covered with plastic sheeting.

Caleb stopped beside her. 'Wow.'

'Isn't it amazing?' She spoke reverently. 'So beautiful.'

He gave her a look. 'I'd shrivel and die in about a month.'

The house's front door opened. Lyle appeared, wearing jeans and a gray tee with a light-blue shirt hanging open over it. He descended the steps and came toward them, mouth spread in a wide, familiar grin. Holly's heart swelled.

'You got my messages. I knew you would.' He stopped three feet away, looking back and forth with joyful, loving eyes between his ex-wife and his brother, the only two people in the country who knew he was still alive. This was Lyle as Holly had always known him. Solid, healthy, brimming with life and youthful vigor. Not the defeated old man at Bar Chloe.

Without consciously having decided to move, she dropped her cane and launched herself at him. Lyle caught her, enveloped her in his arms, repeating her name against her temple. Holly closed her eyes, cheek against his shoulder, inhaling him, feeling the strong muscles of his back under her fingers.

Lyle. Alive. Here.

Finally he released her and turned to his brother, tears on his cheeks, hand outstretched. 'Caleb.'

Caleb stood immobile, arms folded. 'Lyle.'

Lyle put his hand down. 'You're angry.'

'Dude.' Caleb tilted his head, eyes narrowed. 'You made a promise.'

'Yes.' Lyle didn't flinch, standing straight, arms hanging loose at his sides. 'I broke it. But not lightly, and just once, for Holly. After this, you won't hear from me again. If that's what you want.'

Caleb shook his head, looked around the clearing, up at the sky. 'You're a pain in my ass.'

Lyle's grin reappeared. Again he offered his hand.

Caleb took it, then dragged Lyle into a hug that had Holly rummaging in her purse for a tissue. And they'd only been there about three minutes.

When she looked up, the men were apart, Caleb's arms refolded. 'Can you give us a second, Holly?'

'Sure.'

'Don't forget this.' Lyle stooped to pick up her cane. 'The ground is uneven.'

Holly took it and moved off toward the water, relieved to have time to regroup. A curious glance back showed the brothers talking earnestly, Caleb's height advantage and darker coloring more obvious when they were together. Lyle's body language was as relaxed as Caleb's was tense.

Holly headed for the sea's careless freedom, not relying on the cane, feeling stronger than she had in a long time, and more clear-headed. She lifted her face to a cool breeze that made her grateful for her casual layers. More scents arrived on its back, tidal and moist, the air a tonic for her lungs, a balm for her nerves. She sniffed, sniffed again, like a dog testing her surroundings. Maine made the ocean smell especially good.

At the end of the mown meadow – it didn't really qualify as a lawn – there was a drop of probably ten feet to the shoreline, strewn with rocks and boulders, seaweed draping those that would be covered at high tide. She hoped to stay long enough to see the coast transform itself, a remarkable phenomenon foreign to southern California.

Nearby, a couple of Adirondack chairs painted the same green as the front door flanked a rough wooden table, a perfect spot to sit and watch sun and clouds, currents and waves, gulls and cormorants and boats cruising river-to-ocean or ocean-to-river. Holly stood doing exactly that, imagining blissful hours passing without the need for much else.

Eventually she peeked behind her to see if the fraternal conference was ongoing, and found Caleb coming toward her with his grim face on. No sign of Lyle.

'What did you do with your brother, stuff him in your trunk?'

'He's inside getting your lunch. I came to say goodbye.'

'Oh.' Holly fought dismay. Of course he wouldn't hang around. The whole point of the trip was for her and Lyle to talk.

'Lyle will take you to the airport to fly home.'

Holly was even more startled. For some reason she'd thought she and Lyle would have a nice day together and then she'd be going back with Caleb. 'When?'

Caleb's left eyebrow made a slow climb. 'That would be your call.'

'Yes. Right.' Holly felt like an idiot. Had she expected him to wait around like a chauffeur until she and Lyle had dissected the past twenty years? 'Of course.'

Caleb stood with his hands on his hips, watching her, dark eyes squinting against the wind ruffling his hair. 'I gave the big serious speech in the car. So now I'll just add that spending time with you was the only thing I truly enjoyed about the weekend. Probably the best times I've had in a while.'

'Me too.' She searched for something more substantial to add, something that would show him what he meant to her. Except she wasn't exactly sure what that was.

'I will miss you.' His face was open, vulnerable, not a typical Caleb face. 'Quite a lot.'

Again the dismay, and something like panic. 'Wait, so . . . when will I see you?'

'That's up to you. I'm flying back to Milwaukee.'

'Right.' Of course he was. He must be dying to get out of here. She hated that after such an emotional and in many ways intimate weekend, they were stuck saying goodbye in this stilted manner. 'Thank you, Caleb. For helping me, and for bringing me here. And for everything you did for Lyle.'

'You're welcome.' His grim face got grimmer. Holly rewound her words and heard herself speaking on behalf of her and Lyle as a couple, Caleb the outsider. 'As I said last night, we're brothers. It's a thing.'

Giving up on speech, she went to him. He held her close, closer than a friend would. She clung, lump forming in her throat and an absurd plea in her head: *Take me with you.*

As if he'd heard and disapproved, Caleb released her, cupping her chin. 'Take care of yourself.'

Slight emphasis on *yourself*. 'Thanks, Caleb. You too. Drive safely.'

He hesitated, then nodded and turned to go. Holly watched

him, heart aching. Drive safely? A piss-poor way of capturing what she wanted to say about the last few days. She'd have to call him from California, or write a letter, when she'd had more time to get her thoughts together.

Caleb turned back abruptly. 'The only reason I didn't kiss you just now was because it would be spectacularly bad timing. But God help me, Holly, I wanted to. You should know that.'

Worse than not finding the right words before, her reaction now was a stupidly hanging-open mouth, electricity buzzing through her system.

Caleb gave a crooked half-smile and walked away with a slight limp across the clearing, past Lyle's house and into the woods.

A few seconds later, as if he'd been waiting until his brother was out of sight, Lyle emerged from the house carrying a tray, which turned out to hold two glasses of iced tea, a beautiful salad, a gorgeously bronzed loaf of bread and a plate holding a couple of fat wedges of cheese. Another bowl held plums, and in a tiny napkin-lined basket were four thick oatmeal raisin cookies.

As always, the perfect host.

'Hungry? Or too unsettled to be?'

She was definitely unsettled. 'Both.'

'Same here.' He jerked his head toward the table and chairs. 'Are you okay eating outside?'

'Absolutely.' She tried to shake off her emotions over Caleb's departure, and walked next to Lyle, reminded of the many times they'd eaten outdoors in beautiful places. The perfect café in a charming medieval town, picnics on an idyllic beach, sandwiches around a campfire, meals in their own backyard . . .

Lyle put the tray on the table and stood drinking her in until she wanted to fidget. 'It's so good to see you, Holly. You look more beautiful and stronger than ever.'

'Thank you. You look much happier than when I saw you in LA.'

'I am much happier.' He gestured to one of the chairs. 'Have a seat.'

'Thank you.' She sat, uneasy with him, as if they were strangers on a first date. 'What a great view.'

'I never get bored of it.' Lyle handed her a glass of tea, unfurled a napkin for her lap. 'It changes all day long. The light, the shadows, the fogs, the clouds, the colors of the sea, the enormous tides – nearly thirty feet. As much as you and I enjoyed visiting the Pacific and playing in it, we didn't really see it.'

Holly nodded, not exactly sure what he was talking about. She remembered long, lazy days by its side, waves rolling, pounding, dolphins breaking the surface, a miracle she never tired of.

Lyle passed her a plate and gestured to the food. 'Help yourself. The lettuce, cucumbers and carrots are from my garden. Bread is a whole-grain sourdough, home-made. I didn't make the cheese, though I'm thinking about trying out a couple of goats, so maybe someday I'll be able to.'

'I'm impressed.' He was clearly serious about living off the grid as much as he could. While he sliced through the crackling crust of the loaf, Holly helped herself to salad, thinking how refreshing it was to have such simple, delicious food in a quiet spot. After the super-luxury of Senneck, which she'd shamelessly enjoyed, this felt much more real. 'How long have you lived here?'

'A little over a year.' He cut a few slices of each cheese and offered her the serving plate. 'Muenster and Vermont Cheddar. Can't find the fancier stuff around here.'

'Simple is fine, Lyle. You didn't know I was coming.'

He paused, fixing her with that steady, wise gaze. 'Actually, I did.'

'Today? You knew I'd be here today?'

'Yes. I felt it.' He spoke gently. 'I felt you.'

His words brought on such a rush of emotion, Holly had to refocus on her cheese, not at all prepared for that much this soon. More confusing, she couldn't precisely define what the feelings were.

They chatted while they ate, saving complicated subjects for later. Holly told him about Melinda and Matthew's divorce, how she'd need a place to live, feeling guilty for not mentioning Caleb's offer. She told him how good it had been to see Norman and meet Beatrice, and to enjoy Janet and Carol and John, as if they'd all gotten together for some other reason than to mourn his death. Lyle told her stories of his life here, the characters in town, the challenges of renovating a house that had fallen into disrepair, his plans to build an animal barn.

Slowly Holly felt herself rediscovering Lyle, how much she enjoyed talking to him, how easy it had always been, how he listened and heard, and how he now waited patiently while she searched for words or took time to get her ideas organized.

She found her appetite, ate the delicious bread, the creamy cheeses, the fresh crisp salad, all the flavors seeming sharp and pure, deeply satisfying. Or maybe she was romanticizing. It was hard to find anything unpleasant in this wild and peaceful place.

Finished eating, they sat contentedly, watching a sailboat on a Sunday ride, sipping refilled ice teas Lyle had brought from the house.

'I still can't believe you're here.' Lyle touched her arm, as if making sure. 'Actually here, beside me.'

'Given what you put us through, I think that's supposed to be my line.' Holly put her tea on the table, ready to talk about what really mattered between them. 'You had a very nice funeral, by the way.'

'Ah, Holly.' His brown gaze was open, direct; she marveled at his serenity, the new deliberateness to his speech and actions. 'I owe you that story.'

Holly looked down into her lap, feeling like a jittery mess in comparison. 'You owe a lot of us that story.'

'Just you and Caleb.'

'Not Norman? Janet? John and Carol? They were all grieving.'

'All of us die eventually, Holly. The living grieve the dead. I did what I had to do. I don't regret it.'

'Tell me what happened. Why you decided to withdraw from . . . everything.'

'Yes.' He laced his fingers around his glass, elbows propped on the wide green arms of the chair. 'After I saw you in LA six years ago, I was in despair. Megan's affair had made a joke out of working on our marriage, and when you pushed me away again, I was—'

'Again?' Holly struggled to follow. 'What do you mean?'

'I tried so many times to be with you again.'

'You . . .' Holly gaped at him, trying to come up with even one. 'You need to remind me.'

For a second, Lyle looked taken aback, then his face cleared. 'Of course. After we separated, I called you every week, hoping you'd say you made a mistake. Every call you seemed happier and stronger than the last. Out of sheer hopelessness and desperation, I married Eliana – totally unfair to her. When that obviously stupid solution didn't work and the marriage was in trouble, I sent you a letter, through Caleb. You didn't answer.

When my marriage to Megan ended, I came to see you in LA. I never stopped hoping, Holly. And every time that hope took another hit, I had to change my life again, or go completely insane.'

He waited while Holly let his words sink in, trying to sort through the timeline of their lives apart, slowly recognizing the missed opportunities, the miscommunications, the misunderstandings. And yet . . . what would have changed if she'd let him back in? They'd loved each other, but love wasn't always enough. 'Tell me how you died, and why. I need to be able to get my head around why you did all this, why you want to live this way, without anyone.'

'It's a long story; are you comfortable? Need anything?'

'I'm fine. Tell me.'

Lyle leaned back, head resting on the deep green boards, looking composed and relaxed. Did he get this inner peace from the monastery? Or from this beautiful place? Either way, Holly envied it.

'After our divorce, I felt a gradually increasing sense of uneasiness, apart from how badly I missed you, and missed us. All the things I revered and assigned deep meaning to, the arts, literature, architecture, no longer filled me with joy or satisfaction. Eventually I didn't like myself anymore.

'I'd started meditating not long after I moved back to Milwaukee as a way to escape the demons. That was the only time I found contentment or true pleasure. When I came back to LA to see you, I'd decided to travel to Southeast Asia to study Buddhism. When the visit with you didn't go as I hoped, I left with the idea in the back of my mind that if I found what I needed, I might stay. I couldn't face having tanked a third marriage, I was tormented by the fact that all my efforts and all the Frederick family money hadn't made a damn bit of difference in what was still an ugly world, grown more dangerous and more ugly by the year. I was losing hope that you and I would ever get back together.' He gave a slow grin, so like Caleb's that Holly was startled – for so many decades she'd seen Lyle in Caleb, not the other way around. 'In short, I was a basket case.

'I traveled for a few months, Cambodia, Laos, Thailand, visiting temples, soaking everything in. If the monks let me stay, I would stay, but never for long. One night I landed in a tiny town in northern Thailand, in the mountainous part of the country, the Chiang Mai province. I wanted to visit an important temple on the way to the Wat Pah Nanachat monastery.'

Holly nodded, remembering Bodie joking over the name. She was hypnotized by Lyle's story, but also by being able to watch him speak again, the way his Adam's apple rose and fell, how his lips formed words, his gestures, postures and inflections.

'I met a man at the hotel, Sunan, who said he was going in the same direction. We hit it off and he offered me a ride. I'd been taking buses mostly, and a car sounded like heaven, even his, which was probably new last century.

'We left the hotel the next morning and drove for about an hour. These were narrow, steep mountain roads. Some guy flagged us down in the middle of nowhere. He was limping badly. We picked him up, naïvely thinking he'd been injured and we could help. He pulled a gun on us.'

Holly gasped.

'Yeah, it was surreal.' Lyle gazed out at the water, speaking in an even tone so at odds with the horror he was describing. 'You see that stuff on TV but you can't imagine how bizarre and terrifying it is, and yet so ordinary. Here was a guy, here was his gun. Okay, yeah, sure.

'He grabbed Sunan's wallet and my backpack, forced me

into the backseat. Then he made Sunan take a detour on a side road. The farther we got from the highway, the more I was panicking. I had no idea what was going to happen, if we'd drop the guy off somewhere with what he stole and survive, or if it was going to be worse.

'As I was trying to work out a plan, Sunan tried to distract the guy to grab his gun. It didn't work. The guy started punching him. Sunan lost control of the car. We veered off the road, going fast. I managed to jump out, hit the ground and banged my head on a rock. The car smashed into a tree, crumpled to nearly nothing and caught fire. Or that's what I was able to figure out when I recovered enough to look. I'm sure Sunan and the other guy died on impact.'

'Oh my God.' Holly was in tears. 'That is horrible.'

'Hey.' He got up and crouched at her feet, one hand on each of her knees, smiling into her face, Lyle's smile, Lyle's warm hands. 'I didn't mean to make you cry.'

'No, it's fine.' She wiped her eyes. 'Emotional few days. What did you do?'

'I didn't know what to do, or where I was. I had a bad concussion, my shoulder was killing me. I was probably also in shock. I stood there with my brain fogged up, knowing it was my brain but not able to figure out how to get it to work again. You know what that's like.'

'Yeah, I kinda do.'

He pressed his hand to her forehead. Its weight was calming, reassuring. Holly closed her eyes, felt her muscles relax. 'Go on.'

'I walked for as long as I could, I don't know how long it was. But I knew if no one came by and I didn't find a town, I was dead, so I kept going. Miraculously, a sweet couple passing in a cart stopped. I tried to tell them about the accident, but I think they thought I was insane or raving. Anyway, they were nice enough to take me in.'

She opened her eyes. 'Thank God.'

'Yes.' He took away his hand, and sat again. 'My memories are confused after that. But I do remember at some point realizing that everyone back home would think I was dead when they stopped hearing from me. My first instinct was to find some way to call Caleb. And then . . . the other thoughts started. Crazy ones that eventually started to seem like the best, most sensible option.'

Lyle sat for a while rubbing his chin. Holly studied his face as he stared into a place she couldn't see. The years had left no mark on him; if anything, he looked younger than when she'd seen him for the drink.

'It's hard for me now to go back into who I was then and what I felt, why I thought inflicting my death on people I loved would be a good idea. It could have been depression making me think other people would be better off without me. But at the time it was more like, hey, here's an opportunity to back away from everything painful, do I take it or not? And then I would argue with myself, both sides, over and over and over. You'll be surprised to learn that when your brain is in a fog, it's hard to make a major decision.'

'No idea what you're talking about.'

His grin tugged at her heart. The more he spoke, the more she found herself able to connect with what he must have been through, and with him. Not inside his head the way she used to be, but after so many years wondering and guessing at his feelings and motivations, it was a gift and a relief to hear the truth.

'Essentially, by not making a decision, I was deciding. The longer I went without calling anyone, the easier it was to stay that way. When I recovered enough, I went on to Wat Pah Nanachat. They weren't pleased that I didn't have identification, but being spiritual men, generous men, holy men, they took me in. When I proved that I was willing to adapt to their life and serve their purpose, they let me stay.

'I was there nearly three years, feeling that I had truly found my way. They opened up the beauty of the self and the universe in a way I never understood was possible. For the first time since your accident, Holly, I was content. I'd spent so much time trying to make people and things and circumstances change from what they were. I wanted schoolkids to care about what I cared about. I wanted Eliana to be you, I wanted Megan to be you, I wanted you to be whole again, I wanted me to be different than I am. In the monastery, the world again became beautiful, because I was no longer wasting time searching and striving. I accepted and appreciated what was beautiful in all things as they are.

'I now go through life really seeing, really experiencing in a way I never did before. I was always after new sensations, more intense ones, the next one and the next. By doing that, I ignored all the new intense and beautiful sensations that were always around me, no matter where I was, always available.' He turned from gazing out at the water. 'I must sound like a zealot.'

'You do kinda, yeah.'

'I am one. Every night, I become conscious, deeply conscious, of each tooth I brush, each crevice I floss, each pore I scrub. Every morning, I am absorbed in every sacred shampoo bubble that enters my hair . . .' He finished a graceful circle with his hands, then, when she was at the peak of open-mouthed horror, gave her a sidelong smirk.

Holly burst out laughing, putting a hand to her chest. 'You *totally* had me.'

Lyle was laughing too, and she felt another burst of warmth at the familiarity of laughing with him. Her husband. The joy of her life.

'Why did you come back? Caleb said you got sick?'

'Dengue fever, a second time. First time is like a flu, second can be bad. This was bad. I refused to go to the hospital, went off by myself and let it have its way. I beat it, but it was a long haul. All I could think about during my convalescence was you, Holly. Everything about you. About us. All the mistakes I'd made, my stubbornness and my denial. For the first time I started missing the US, and having doubts that I belonged in that idyllic place for the rest of my life.

'It took another few months of soul-searching, letting myself heal completely, going over and over what I wanted, how it could work, being sure that I was absolutely sure. There were only two people I wanted to be with again, who I felt I owed to make right what I'd done, and take the lumps I was due. So I called Caleb.'

'That must have been fun.'

'He had every right to bring me home just to kill me so I'd stay dead. And yet – before he heard my crazy plan – there was so much joy and love in his voice. We're brothers.' Lyle shrugged. 'It's kind of a thing.'

Holly smiled. 'I've heard that somewhere.'

'Caleb was willing to help me get home, but we argued for weeks about my decision to stay dead. Finally he agreed, on condition that I not contact anyone else, by which he meant you. He told me you had gotten on with your life successfully, that you were happy and you didn't need me messing it up again.

'I got home by bribing the captain of a cargo ship. I had no papers, but he was glad for the money, which Caleb wired me.

The ship dropped me in St John's. I got to this place, thought it was a perfect spot, got Caleb to buy this house, and here I am, totally content with my life, for the first time since our marriage.'

Holly looked around at the living water, the land, the wild forest. *Totally content with my life.* She could imagine herself here, living simply, freed from traffic and smog and people wondering what was wrong with her, from having to battle society's expectations and demands, from the continual fight to function in society at her old level, and the continual shame at not being able to. Money wouldn't fix that for her.

'Is this why you gave away your inheritance, Lyle? To me?'

He looked surprised she'd asked. 'Of course. I admit I was vindictive enough not to want Megan to have it, and what the hell else would I do with it? That money is for you, to make your life easier. To do with whatever you'd like. Give it away, live it up, endow a chair at a university, whatever you want. I've had too much money for too much of my life. I no longer need it. Everything I want is right here.'

Totally content with my life. She was ashamed to have suspected him. Ashamed to have drifted so far from what she knew was true of him. Ashamed to have listened to too many other people's versions of who Lyle was.

'C'mon. I want to show you the house.' He stood and started stacking the dishes back on the tray. 'Don't forget your cane.'

'Thank you.' She picked it up and walked with him across the sweet-smelling grass, the feeling so familiar, it was as if they were going back to a home they shared.

Given the barn-like exterior, Lyle's house was surprisingly charming and cozy inside, everything warm and light. In the living room, a fireplace in a stone hearth, comfortable-looking furniture, and bright rugs on the plank floors. Gas lights hung on the pine walls, and a shiny black wrought-iron staircase spiraled up to the second floor. The kitchen had an old-fashioned feel, with wooden counters, a farmhouse sink, and glass-paned doors on the cabinets, but the gas appliances were new and of good quality.

Next to the kitchen, running the full length of the house, a narrow room with large screened windows facing the sea, furnished with rockers, a hammock and a chaise. In the corner, a tiny wood stove.

'You must live out here.' She certainly would.

'I laze out here. I live outside, mostly.'

'And you survived winter.'

'What winter?' Lyle puffed his chest. 'I'm from Milwaukee.'

'Practically next door to the North Pole.'

He stood naturally again. 'The house was pretty drafty that first fall. I spent a lot of time fixing that. But by the time the real cold settled in, I was set. You can't believe how beautiful these woods are in the snow. Such colors. White on dark green against a blue sky. I have snowshoes and cross-country skis. There are lakes and beaches nearby, mountains not far off to hike. Nowhere is crowded. It's heaven.'

Upstairs, he showed her the two bedrooms, one for sleeping and one he called, somewhat ironically, his library, where he meditated and read, where he learned about gardening and hunting and fishing and caring for domesticated animals.

Holly felt herself falling further for this life of his in the woods, for the pictures he painted of long summer nights, of the satisfaction he took in learning to build, learning to create, learning to get by with as little outside help as possible. Since no one was searching for him, there was hardly any danger of discovery.

'So what do you think?' He'd brought her back downstairs to the wonderful windowed room off the kitchen. Holly stood staring out at the water, wondering what a whole tide cycle would look like, how that many feet of water could go so reliably in and out twice every day.

'I think you've got a beautiful life here, Lyle.'

'Yes.' He came up behind her, took hold of her shoulders and turned her gently to face him. She had no trouble now looking into his eyes, which were open, warm and deeply serene. Again she envied him this peace he'd found, wondered what that must be like, whether it was available to anyone who chose to follow the path he'd taken, and whether she might like to find that out.

'There's time to fix the mess we made, Holly. I finally stopped listening to the panic in my head so I could understand what you need. Everything I did here, everything I built, I imagined on my sickbed in Thailand. Hour after hour, week after week, I worked out how to build a life you could share with me, in which we could be equal partners again, taking care of the house, taking care of the land, taking care of each other. Exactly the life you were trying so hard in those last months of our marriage to get me to understand that you needed.' His fingers tightened on her shoulders, but his eyes stayed peaceful, full of that shining, captivating certainty. 'Since the moment I saw you in that hot tub, I have been in love with you, Holly. Every wonderful, joyful step of my life since then, and every stupid, misguided one, has been made out of loving you, or coping with the pain of having lost you.'

'Lyle.' A rush of answering love, and tears again, helplessly sliding down her cheeks. There it was, what she'd wanted from him, begged from him all along. Everything they needed to be able to try again.

'Once a year for many, many years, you and I stood on the same beach and promised to be together until death. I'd like you to stay here as long as you'd like. Forever if that's how it works out.' His voice broke. He took her face reverently in his palms. 'I want to show you how beautiful the world can be.'

Chapter 21

July 26, 2022

Dear Caleb,

Just a quick note to thank you for bringing Holly up. Being with her is everything I knew it would be. Even in this beautiful, shining spot she brings her own special light. We move and breathe and live together as perfectly as we always have, but now with the benefit of age and wisdom from the scars life taught us to bear.

Holly has offered me use of the trust I established in her name so many years ago. That should free you from any further financial obligation to me. I still want to build a barn and invest in goats and chickens, so the money will be useful. I hope you will come visit often. It would be great to see you.

Love, Lyle

August 4, 2022

Dear Lyle,

Thanks for your note. I'm glad you have worked out some form of financial independence. It was generous of Holly to make that possible. Busy times here. I'm not sure about a visit anytime soon.

Caleb

Holly thanked the Uber driver who'd picked her up at the Milwaukee airport and, twenty clear-traffic minutes later, deposited her at Caleb's Lake Drive address.

Rolling her suitcase up his front walk through the soft, humid night air, she could see him in profile, sitting in his living room reading a newspaper. Given the time, nearly ten, Holly decided to call before she rang his doorbell.

She dialed, watched him exchange the paper for his phone, and sit bolt upright, staring for several seconds before he answered. 'Holly. Where are you?'

'Hi, Caleb. I didn't want to freak you out by ringing your doorbell so late.'

He leaned toward his window, craning to see. 'You're here? In Milwaukee? You're *here*?'

She went up to his door and rang.

'Holy sh— Hang on. Give me a sec.'

The wait was longer than she expected. She understood why when Caleb opened the door propped on crutches, wearing a T-shirt and shorts, first time she'd seen him without his prosthesis.

'I'm sorry I showed up like this, without warning. I only barely made the connection to Milwaukee.' She didn't bother mentioning that her flight back to LA had a stop in Chicago, and that visiting him had been almost literally a last-minute decision. She still wasn't entirely sure why she'd come, only that she knew she had to see him.

'I can't believe you're here.' He grinned uncertainly, glow from the outdoor lights illuminating his handsome features. Holly's heart gave a little flip. 'Come on in. Sorry I can't help with your suitcase.'

'It's not heavy.' She hefted it, trying to make it look light, and stepped past him into the foyer, enjoying the symbolism of crossing his threshold.

'Just dump it right over there.' Caleb jerked his head toward the corner, by a teak table. 'Are you hungry? Thirsty? You must be tired anyway.'

'It's been a long day. I feel good, though.' She felt great. Lucid, clear. Lyle had taught her a lot about his mindfulness and meditation practice, a remarkable by-product of which had been an improvement in her ability to withstand stress without so much confusion. A day of travel on her own had certainly put that to the test. She was happy to feel she'd passed.

Caleb closed the front door with his shoulder and limped toward her. 'Have you eaten dinner?'

'I'm fine. Lyle packed me sandwiches to take on the trip.'

His face fell. 'You just left Maine? You've been there this whole time?'

Holly put a hand to her forehead. Maybe not clear and lucid enough. 'If I'd been back in LA, I would have called you.'

'I . . . right. I thought . . . well I had no idea what to think. But I assumed if you wanted to be in touch with me you would have been.'

'I had some things to figure out. And it's complicated trying to communicate from Lyle's grave.'

'That is very true.' He turned toward the back of the house, where there was a staircase and a hallway off to the right. 'Can I get you a drink? Of anything?'

'A glass of water would be great.'

'Have a seat anywhere you want. I'll be right back.'

She watched him swing away and disappear into the hall, which must lead to his kitchen. After peeking into a few rooms, she chose a chair in the living room opposite where Caleb had been sitting. Like many older houses in Milwaukee, his was very square, very German, but beautifully designed and built, with a nice flow to the downstairs and typical touches of quality: cut-glass doorknobs on the solid wood doors, leaded glass windows and built-in corner cupboards in the dining room. The furnishings he'd added were elegant, expensive, but spare, only enough pieces to make the place functional, as if he hadn't wanted to leave a personal mark.

A few minutes later, he came in, walking more easily with his prosthesis back on, bearing two glasses of sparkling water garnished with lemon. 'Here you go.'

'Thanks, Caleb. You're very nice to take me in at this hour.'

He sat with a smile, but he looked tired, worry lines on his forehead. 'Were you afraid I'd toss you out on the street?'

'Only a little.' She drank thirstily, her swallows too loud for the silence.

'I hope you had a good time with Lyle.'

'I did, yes.' Holly wasn't sure how to go on, not certain of Caleb's mood or feelings, hoping this visit hadn't been a colossal mistake.

'Actually, I lied.' He chuckled painfully. 'I spent most of the last two weeks hoping you were having a miserable time.'

It was easier to know what to say then. 'Lyle seems very content, very sure of his decision to stay dead.'

'That's what I felt.' Caleb sat tall and composed, but his good foot moved back and forth as if it were trying to tap-dance. 'Nice to hear that confirmed.'

'He asked me to stay with him. To live there. He thought it would be the kind of life I could manage easily, without so much frustration.'

Caleb drank water. His foot danced. 'So . . . you're going back?'

'Once in a while, to visit. It's a beautiful place, and I'd like to stay in touch. But not to stay, no.'

He exhaled, body slumping, the combination making it look

as if he'd deflated. 'Thank God. I couldn't stand the thought of you hidden away in that place.'

'I was tempted at first. For one thing, life there is simple enough that I wasn't being constantly reminded of what I lack. And being able to live without constant interruptions and distractions made me realize how the days shoot by while we're all busy juggling everything demanding our attention.'

Caleb put down his water, leaned forward, arms resting on his thighs. 'And then? What changed your mind?'

'One morning I woke up and realized that though Lyle had found his beautiful life, and though I still love him in many ways . . .' her voice broke, 'I couldn't spend the rest of my life playing dead.'

'No.' Caleb got to his feet as if springs holding him down had been released, smiling his slow, sexy grin, the one that for the past two weeks had reminded Holly of him even when that grin was on Lyle's face. 'Good for you, Holly. I'm so proud of you.'

She narrowed her eyes as he started toward her. 'Coming over to pat me on the head?'

'Not a chance.' He stopped a foot in front of her chair. 'How long can you stay?'

'True confession.' Holly had to tip her head back to meet his eyes. 'I wasn't planning to come at all. But when my plane stopped in Chicago, I knew I had to see you. I've rebooked my LA flight for tomorrow afternoon, from Milwaukee.'

'Tomorrow!' He took her hands and hauled her to her feet. 'That's too soon.'

Holly snorted. 'Well I wasn't going to show up and announce I was moving in for the weekend.'

'I'd love you to move in for the weekend.' He was still holding her hands. 'Will you?'

'I can't, Caleb. I already paid one change fee to the airline, I'd have to pay anoth—' She glared up at him. 'What is so funny?'

'You make a really bad billionaire.'

She rolled her eyes, giddy inside, but worrying her spontaneous visit would put more in motion between them than it should. 'I'll have to work on that.'

'Tell you what. Spend the night. I've got plenty of room. We can talk tomorrow.' He let go of her hands. 'I've been thinking over the last couple of weeks as well.'

'Oh?' She fought off a rush of nerves. 'What about?'

'I'm going to give Frederick Industries one more year, and get the hell out before I turn into my father.' His eyes were lit; he no longer looked tired. 'I kept hearing the great lectures I was giving you, and realized I needed to listen to my own patronizing wisdom, and figure out what was most important to me.'

'That's good. That's really good. I'm proud of you, Caleb.' She reached to pat his head, but he trapped her arm.

'You were supposed to say, "Ooh, Caleb, really? What *is* most important to you?"'

'You know . . .' she gently pulled her arm away, 'it might be easier if you just give me the script.'

'*You* are most important to me.' He grinned down at her, lazy, triumphant, a bit uber-male, but also really hot. 'But right now the whole world is your oyster, Holly. What are you going to do with it?'

She fell the rest of the way in love with him then, or at least admitted to herself that she'd fallen. Who knew when the feelings had started? Possibly years ago, possibly decades. She'd come to him tonight, he'd declared himself, and the very next thing he asked was what she wanted to do, what might be best for her.

Over the weeks she'd spent with Lyle, she'd gradually come to understand that what Eliana and Megan had said about him made sense. When he and Holly had been married, they'd wanted the same things, nearly always at the same time. A remarkable coincidence, a blessing that had made their marriage blissful and strong. But that compatibility had also concealed from her that Lyle would always live the life he wanted to live, and that anyone along for the ride – granted, a wonderful ride – would have to follow his lead.

'I'll tell you exactly what I'm going to do.' This had been Holly's second major revelation, her biggest, bravest decision yet. 'I'm going home to LA, I'm going to sell pretty much everything I own, and I'm going to take Melinda traveling, for like a *year*.'

Caleb threw back his head for his wonderful laugh, then beamed at Holly as if she was the most remarkable treasure he'd ever unearthed. 'Fabulous plan. When you're back, I'll be retired, and if it seems right, you and I can go everywhere you two didn't. What do you think?'

She smiled up at him, loving that he was freely giving her all the space and time she needed. And then it was obvious what to do, and why she'd come. She stepped forward and kissed him, a kiss that traveled through her body, her head and her heart. One kiss that promised many others in the years to come. 'I think that sounds perfect.'

First thing Holly did when she got off the plane at LAX was go to the ticket counter. The second was to call Melinda.

'Holly, where the hell are you? When Caleb told me you were in Maine with that . . . with Lyle, I went frantic. Tell me you're not back together.'

'We're not back together.'

'Oh thank God. Your mom has called me about every other day asking if I'd heard from you yet. It was awful.'

'Honestly. She knew I was—' Holly broke off impatiently. 'Never mind. How fast can you pack?'

'Huh?'

She scanned the departures board again. 'There's a flight for Paris that leaves in about four hours. If you're free, I thought we might go have dinner.'

'*What?*'

Holly giggled silently. 'Why, you have something better to do?'

'Are you serious? Are you *serious*?'

'You'll have to move fast . . .'

'My God. Oh my God. Yes, I'll be there. I'll be there.' Melinda was laughing, a real belly laugh, not her brittle giggle. 'What did that guy put in your food?'

'I have things to tell you. To talk over. I have plans.'

'Do they involve Caleb?'

Holly hesitated, not quite ready for 'yes', though that was what her heart was telling her. 'Maybe eventually.'

Melinda gasped. 'Really? You really stole him from me?'

'I think I might have.' Holly was thinking a lot of things. Like if she did end up with Caleb, she could give most of her inherited money away. If she chose to stay single, she'd probably give most of it away anyway, to organizations that would do a lot more good with it than she ever could. But first, as soon as she settled her affairs and Melinda could get away for longer than a crazy Parisian day or two, Holly was going to kidnap her friend for a Voyage of Insane Spending, to repay her for propping Holly up for so many years, and to give Melinda the chance to get away from Wife and Mother and get back in touch with herself as Woman. At the same time, Melinda would have

Holly's back while she dove into the world she'd been hiding from for the past twenty years.

'Caleb is such a good guy, Holly.' Melinda sounded genuinely excited. 'I might die of jealousy, but I would be thrilled to see you happy with someone wonderful. I was so worried when you wrote that Lyle's place was idyllic. Idyllic! Stuffed away with that— What changed your mind?'

'Lyle wanted to keep me close, in his small, beautiful world, so I'd always be safe.' Holly smiled, dragging her suitcase slowly through the crowds, not letting them rush her, keeping her breathing steady and slow, the way Lyle had taught her, heart light, future brighter than it had been in a long, long time because she was finally allowing it to be.

'Caleb wants me to leap out as far as possible . . . and land anywhere I can dance.'

The
FIRST
WIFE

Bonus Material

A note from Muna . . .

My mother, Alison Shehadi, was a remarkable person. Gracious, elegant, always cheerful, and multi-talented, she was a high-school math teacher who raised three children, kept a spotless house in which she served superb meals to family and to friends in a constant parade of multi-course dinner parties, knitted, sewed her own clothes and many of mine, and found time to knit a cable sweater and make a velvet satin-lined opera cape for my Barbie doll. She and my father attended countless plays, concerts, operas and museums and traveled the world.

In retirement she became a docent for the Princeton University Art Museum, combining her passion for fine art with her gifts as a teacher and communicator. To my mother the world was an endless source of curiosity and delight. She had an encyclo-pedic knowledge of history and while I'd walk into a great cathedral or encounter a world-famous painting and think, 'whoa, cool,' if she was by my side I would learn the significance of each stone and each brush stroke in detailed historical context. My father and I would joke that we could take in an exhibit, have a long lunch and a nice nap, and Mom would still be finding new things in the very first artwork.

In 2005, a vibrant age seventy-three, she was helping my father load a stone fountain they'd bought for their newly landscaped back yard in Princeton, New Jersey, where I grew up. Dad's heart condition precluded heavy lifting and my mother was strong, so she hoisted the box into their car, hitting the side of her head on the open lid of the trunk. Ouch.

She and my father went home, had lunch and settled in for their customary nap. Mom woke complaining of a headache, which worsened until she lost consciousness. She was in a coma for over a week with brain swelling so severe the doctors had to open her skull to minimize damage.

In those early terrifying weeks, we celebrated each new sign that normal life might again be possible for her – breathing on her own, swallowing, sitting up, feeding herself – knowing how close we'd come to losing her.

For Mom, who didn't remember past having that awful headache, she went to sleep a dynamic capable woman and woke up as this other person. I remember her saying she'd become an old woman overnight.

Over the next several years she recovered remarkably. She did not lose her memories or verbal ability, but she lost half the sight in her left eye, all her organizational and planning skills and any ability with numbers. She could no longer drive, lost her remarkable culinary ability in the kitchen and many other heartbreaking changes.

What didn't change, incredibly, was her cheerfulness and delight in her family, friends, in music and the world – she continued to read the entire *New York Times* every day. Even after my father died and she moved into a retirement facility, she celebrated new friends and old, and always answered my calls with her trademark enthusiasm, 'Muna!' One of my high-school friends once said that every time she came to my house, Mom made her feel as if her arrival was the best thing that had happened all day.

In *The First Wife*, Holly's journey is different, but was obviously informed by what our family went through. The kayaking scene is real.

I will never forget the smile on Mom's face, which didn't stop or dim during the entire trip, her first time being able to move with her usual effortless grace. I had to give Holly that experience.

In 2011, my mother fell again and sustained yet another serious brain injury that landed her again in the ICU. Again she struggled back, with more lingering confusion this time, but undiminished curiosity and joy in life. Five years later, in 2016, another fall, another head injury, this one final. I can't help some bitterness, feeling my mother was cheated out of what could have continued to be a full and remarkable life. But if Mom felt that way she never let on, continuing to smile her wide, sunny smile, finding pleasure in her diminished life wherever she could.

This book is for her.